When the Night Comes

MALLORY ROBERTSON

When the Night Comes: Book one in the Dollhouse Slayer series by Mallory Robertson

Artwork by Nata Vedana

Cover by Ivy at Beautiful Book Covers

To Vanessa and Daxton, none of this would be possible without you.

-The Players-

The Royal House of Kane

Elizabeth Kane- (47- Queen of Elione- The Gilded Years)
Dominic Kane (31- The Queen's bastard son)

Marcus Rathebone (39-Duke of Berrone- Deceased- Bludgeoned to death) -- **J**uliana Rathebone (nee: Kane- 47- the Queen's sister- Duchess of Berrone)
Tate Rathebone (29)
Gabrielle Stewart (nee: Rathebone- 24) – **M**arcus Stewart (27) --- **F**rançois (4) **O**liver (2)

Barron Hadley (39-Deceased-Executed) --Eleanor Hadley (nee: Kane- 45-the Queen's Sister-Deceased-Cancer)
Owen Hadley (34) -- **C**lara Hadley (nee: Mormont-25-Deceased- blood loss) --- Charlie (0- stillborn)
Jackson Hadley (32)
Elijah Hadley (30)
Avis Hadley (27)
James Hadley (19)

-The Elite-

William Calvert (65) – **K**aterina Calvert (nee: Atwood-22)
Alexandra Calvert (nee: Roth-41-Atmoskineses-Deceased-probable suicide)
Jet Calvert (30-twin- Sensory manipulation/deprivation/Magical detection) -- Marian Calvert (nee: Atwood-20)
Esmeralda Marchand (nee: Calvert-30-twin-Telepathy/Electrokinesis) -- **F**rancois Marchand (26-deceased-scarlet fever)
Pearl Atwood (nee: Calvert-28-Seer/Airbender) -- **A**ugustus Atwood (28)
Jade Calvert (25 - Telekinesis/Firebender)
Ruby Calvert (17-Necromancer/Summoning/Mediumship)

Henry Wright (54) -- **C**laire Wright (nee: Dubois-38)
Edward Wright (27)
Benjamin Wright (24)
Meena Wright (22)

Abraham Kensington (51) – **G**ale Kensington (nee: Penrose-47)
Theodore Kensington (26)
Elizabeth Kensington (23)
Alec Kensington (22)

Joseph Cavendish (57) -- **M**ary Cavendish (45)
David Cavendish (24)

Jonathan Cavendish (22-) **V**era Cavendish (nee: Wright-19)
Peter Cavendish (23-Engaged to Diana Atwood)
Sarah Cavendish (19)

Gregory Sullivan- (58) **B**arbara Sullivan (nee: Jones-56)
Violet Hamilton (Nee: Sullivan-26)- **J**asper Hamilton (27)
Vaeden Sullivan (24)

Thomas Wellington (44-Widowed) Christine Wellington (nee: Smith-22-deceased-Blood Loss)
Crispin Wellington (25) -- **V**ictoria Wellington (nee: Sullivan-20)
Micha Wellington (26)
Sienna Wellington (24)

-COMMONERS-

Rockwell Emerich (71-Deceased- heart attack) --**E**lla Emerich (26-Deceased-blood loss)
Blake Emerich (29)
Roslyn Emerich (27)

Ferdinand Atwood (49) -- **A**gatha Atwood (nee: Adams-51)
Augustus Atwood (28) -- **P**earl Atwood (nee: Calvert-28-Seer/Airbender)
Adelaide Atwood (22)
Diana Atwood (17-Engaged to Peter Cavendish)
Grant Atwood (15)

Christopher Ashford (48) -- **R**owan Ashford (nee: Prewitt-45)
Kathrine Beckett ("Kittie"- nee: Ashford- 25) – **T**imothy Beckett (25
Olivette Ashford ("Ollie"- 24)
Theophilia Ashford ("Tellie"- 19)

George Beckett (50) – **E**lizabeth Beckett (47)
Timothy Beckett (25) -- **K**athrine Beckett ("Kittie"- nee: Ashford- 25)
Oliver Beckett (23)
Constance Beckett (17)

-Cast of Outcasts-

Cordelia Calvert (44)
Raoul Cheron (25)
Merfan (53)
Philip Preston (32)
Adam Riley (31)
Cillian O'Brien (37)
Jeffrey Feilding (43)
Gainsley (25-Hadley valet)
Duke (43-Hadley driver)
Marna (38-Jade's lady-in-waiting)
Gideon (44-Calvert Valet)

When the Night Comes

-Prologue-

Bel Deaux, Elione
1888 Years After the Fall
The Kane Era

A harsh bite lingered in the air of an expeditiously mechanical city. With precipitous slopes overwhelmed by steam-powered machinery, the opaque skyline below the steel towers was nothing to be admired. While atop the high-rise structures, where Dragon's Keep materialized through the break in the clouds, Kings Peak appeared relatively empyrean. And yet, the execution of all machines were exhaustive and filled Bel Deaux with smog, diluting the hues of the metropolis and transforming the horizon somber and gray.

An impressive railway weaved high above the buildings, shops, and flats, and as a passenger car flew by, white smoke spiraled upwards in its wake. Several airships pushed through the dense haze while carrying goods and passengers to distant villages. Below, carriages made their way up and down the cobbled road amongst cable cars trolleying through the streets. And with its many gears, the imposing clock tower nestled within the heart of the city chimed loudly, indicating nightfall.

At a time, the capital was built with significance and progressive thinking when men of goodwill set out to create an idealistic city where no class separated the rich from the poor, a wondrous dream indeed. Many scoffed at the notion, while others desperately prayed for a resolution. Yet now, when years had passed, and the grand bridge separated the glimmering streets of the Gas-light district from the sweltering passages of Trinity Row, it was evident no utopian city would ever be created.

Hedonism grew down on Fairmoore Avenue, where the lowly members of society struggled for their vitality. Structures were built haphazardly atop one another, leaving the impecunious to be crowded into a two-block radius, and the smell of waste wafted through and near the Kinnedale Harbor. Gambling halls were filled with men who thought their very own importance single-handedly changed the world, and brothels were packed to the brim with those who had not a care, as were the alleyways themselves.

Trinity Row came alive for those who sought to sin.

The east end was a cesspool of seventy thousand citizens struggling for food daily, and this struggle came hardest upon women. If one wanted to feed their children a low-quality meal or rent a room for the night, prostitution was money for old rope.

None fought this battle more than Helena Wimple, a doxy with a penchant for men who whispered words of a better life. She charged the streets in a drunken haze. The only man who ever mattered asked for the hand of another; his engagement mocked her openly. She cried over the lies that made her undress and the simple touch that allowed him to take her. But the kisses she would never get back were more damaging than the carnal act itself, a reminder of a love that would never be.

It was simply no use to dwell on these thoughts. The world spun before her, and she stumbled into a wall. Orphaned children yelled as they ran past, and music came from afar. He enjoyed music, and they had once danced as lovers do. The suffocating thought was incurably painful.

She allowed tears to fall as she walked further from the crowded streets and onto darker, quieter paths. Perhaps the silence would help her forget him.

"The night comes for me," she sang softly, "the night, the night, O goddess of light." She smiled slightly and skipped a step or two. "I am here waiting, waiting, always waiting." Her arms began to sway along with her ragged skirts, and red tendrils fell from the bun atop her head. A hiccup came every few seconds as she bellowed, "The night, the night, O goddess of light, I am here waiting, waiting, always waiting." Her voice echoed throughout the alleyway. The only other sound was her shoes clicking against the ground. "The night comes for me," she sang with the hint of a whisper.

It's not wise to sing of witchcraft, Milady," came a deep voice from behind.

A shriek sprouted from the back of her throat. The sound vibrated throughout the alley as she swiveled around, clutching her breast and panting heavily. A man stood in the clearing. His long, dark cloak touched the ground, and a gas mask covered his face entirely.

"Yew scared me, Milord!" she sputtered, all traces of hiccups gone.

"My apologies, Milady," his voice was distorted and unrecognizable.

"I'm no lady, now piss off!" she bellowed with a glare. This man couldn't possibly mistake her for high class. Not in her revealing rags, smeared lipstick, and drunken demeanor; surely one could spot the difference. She angrily turned from him, no longer in the mood for men who wished to spout lies as one would breathe.

"I meant no disrespect," he called, and she whirled back around. "Perhaps you would be interested in accompanying me for the night."

She squinted to make the doubled vision of him singular. "The whole night? I can't even see ya face!"

"My face was deformed in a terrible fire and quite terrifying to look at," he explained sadly. "Because of this, I am a very lonely man and wish for the company of a beautiful woman."

Her guard dropped a little, and she smiled. "Yew fink, I'm beau'iful?"

"Quite."

She failed miserably to hide the grin on her chapped lips and said, "It will cost yew it will!"

He pulled a coin purse from his pocket and shook it. "I can afford it."

Her grin deepened. "A'right then."

The newly accustomed lamps down by the Kinnedale Harbor were supposed to be lit, a suggestion by Captain Feilding. The thought was to diffuse crime and deter anyone from smuggling goods into the city. Yet, the lamps were extinguished on this crisp evening, and the usual police patrol had not been seen in over an hour.

Two men held down a third.

"I told you everything I know!" the man screamed at the pair restraining him; his head hung over the dock.

"I fink he's lyin!" one of the perpetrators told the other.

He nodded, and they pushed the poor soul's head under the water. The man lashed against them as he flung his feet, kicking the dock. The perpetrators laughed, pushing him in deeper.

A cab rolled up behind them. "'Bout bloody time!" the first lackey muttered as the pair pulled the poor man back to the surface. The victim was sputtering and choking on the filthy water.

When the cab door opened, a pair of polished shoes stepped out, revealing the prominent dark brow of a young man. He held a black glare and wore a mint suit that screamed of wealth and power.

He buttoned his jacket with a step forward, leering down at the victim and snapped, "Well?"

One of the thugs said, "He ain' talkin' Mr. Kensington!"

"Yes, I am!" the man wailed. "I told them everything I know!"

The other perpetrator spat, "Lies!"

"Pity," Mr. Kensington muttered with a tilt of his head. "And I thought your mother meant something to you."

"I'm not lying to you! I haven't the faintest idea how Charlie found out about the opium shipment! I swear!"

Mr. Kensington knelt over the man and forcefully grabbed his collar. "You vouched for Charlie. Therefore, he is your responsibility, and he completely fucked me over! Do you have any idea how much money you cost me?"

The other shook his head with wide eyes.

"Five hundred stacks!" Mr. Kensington snarled. "Do you have five hundred stacks to repay me?"

The other shook his head. "N-no, s-sir."

"Can you acquire five hundred stacks outside of my employment?"

The other hesitated.

"That's what I thought." His fingers tightened on the man's collar. "Now, what would you do if you were me?"

"I-I've been a loyal worker, Mr. Kensington!" the cronies behind the rich man laughed in derision. "I have!" he yelled at them. "I had no way of knowing Charlie was a bad seed! I swear I will make it up to you! Give me a chance, Mr. Kensington! Please! Leave my mother be, and I'll get you the money within the week!"

Mr. Kensington, however, was already shaking his head.

"Please! I swear I will find Charlie and set everything right!" he pleaded, and the cronies smirked at one another. "I just need a week!"

"Two days," Mr. Kensington countered.

The cronies stopped laughing, and the beaten man's eyes widened.

"I-I-"

Mr. Kensington shoved him into the ground with force and pointed a long finger. "You have two days to bring Charlie and the five hundred stacks you cost me, or I'll have your head!"

The man gazed up at him slowly. "Y-yes, s-sir."

Mr. Kensington raised his brow in false sincerity. "It's too bad you let your mother down."

The man yelled, "What did you do to her?"

Mr. Kensington smirked before stepping into his cab without a backward glance.

The man repeated, "What did you do?"

The cronies laughed and followed Mr. Kensington onto the cab before it rolled away, leaving the beaten man to scream into the cold night.

"That wasn't very nice, Teddy," came a voice from behind an unfolded newspaper.

Teddy glared at the paper, or rather, the man behind the article. "Who asked you?"

The paper dipped, revealing the blonde head of a man with a charming smile. His brown eyes blinked rapidly. "Now, the poor fool believes his mother is dead."

"Good," Teddy muttered. "Then he'll return my money."

The man rolled his eyes and raised the paper again. "I'd wager he'd be more willing if he knew she was still alive."

"I beg to differ," Teddy argued. "Now he understands his fate if he fails to bring back what's mine."

"Whatever you say," the man answered with little interest. "Oh, look, your engagement was announced!"

Teddy ripped the paper from the man's hands and tore it to shreds.

"Well, that's a completely reasonable reaction."

"Mark my words, Edward," Teddy growled. "If you keep running your mouth, I'll wring your neck!"

"Go ahead then," Edward challenged.

Teddy sat back in his seat and rubbed his temple. "I don't want to listen to your nonsense. You're nearly as bad as Eli."

Edward chuckled. "I'd hope I'm far better than him, and besides, I thought you were chomping at the bit when it came to Jade!"

"That was before," Teddy muttered and lowered his hand. "She's more trouble than she's worth!"

Edward grinned wolfishly. "Then give her to me!"

"I'll kill you both!" Teddy threatened.

Edwards eyes and tone turned flat as he said, "What claim do you even hold for her? If you dislike her, then why marry her?"

Teddy scowled and glanced out the window. "You know why."

Edward's face smoothed. Teddy was a particularly jealous man, and his ego would get the best of him. "You aren't going to let it go, are you?"

"And why should I?"

"All of this because of Dominic Kane?" Edward scoffed at the name with disdain. "Who is he to you, anyway? Besides, you were not associated at the time of their indiscretion. Therefore, you should not concern yourself!"

Teddy's pleasing features transformed in a frightening way. "She has always been mine! And I won't be crossed by anyone, no matter who their mother is!"

"What about William Calvert?" Edward drawled. "It won't be pleasant when he finds out!"

"All the more reason to move forward. We need to finish what we started!"

Edward bit his tongue as the cab slowed to a stop, and the door swiftly opened. A man wearing a bowler hat seated himself next to Teddy without a word. This man's name was Blake…not that it mattered much to either one of them. Blake was not one of significance, it was the man who followed.

A mess of black hair and fine clothing stepped awkwardly into the confined space of the cab, fixing himself next to Edward. He pushed his wet hair out of his face and barked, "What did you find?"

"Why, hello, Jet," Edward commented dryly. "It's good to see you too."

Jet glowered at him. "I didn't agree to meet so you could blather. What did you find?"

Edward tsked and looked at Teddy. "Very touchy."

Teddy smirked as his black eyes flashed in Jet's direction. "I gave him two days."

Jet's eyebrows raised. "Two days for what?"

"To bring the money," Teddy enunciated slowly.

Jet gaped at him. "You let him walk away after he robbed our entire shipment? I knew I should have dealt with him!"

"I already kidnapped his mother," Teddy snapped. "What more do you want?"

Jet glanced at Blake. "Kill her."

Teddy snorted, shaking his head in contempt.

"You surely enjoy handing out a death sentence," Edward mused. "Why is everything so final with you?"

Jet hissed, "How are we to remain on top when we tolerate thievery from our own?"

Teddy sat forward and pointed a finger. "You won't have to wait long, and the next time you question my judgment, it will be your last!"

Jet sneered and he glanced at Blake.

"Just remember this is an equal partnership here," Blake growled. "You don't get to call the shots when all of our necks are on the line!"

"Killing Pierre won't get our money back!" Teddy fumed impatiently. "I have him tailed, and he knows it. Besides, he thinks his mother is dead! We have him up against a wall with no choice but to hand over the stolen goods. I am doing this for all of us. You're just going to have to trust me."

"Then you'll have to put a little faith in us, too," Blake remarked.

Teddy flashed a doubtful look as he pulled a letter from his breast pocket and handed the parchment over. "Our next assignment."

Jet and Blake shared another look that Edward caught, making him uneasy. Yet he remained silent as he watched Jet rip open the wax seal instead.

Jet scanned the letter, his eyes bulging as he glanced back at Teddy. "Since when have the Hadleys become a concern?"

Teddy grinned wickedly. "Isn't it poetic? All their poking around has finally caught up to them!"

"But they are the Queen's kin!" Blake interjected loudly. "They are untouchable!"

Teddy grinned. "We are more powerful. It won't be long before her reign ends, and the Elite has full control of the city! I will be rid of the Hadleys once and for all!"

"Just what you've always wanted," Edward replied with a lazy shrug of his shoulders. He didn't seem to share the same enthusiasm as the others.

I
Jackson

An imposing man with a split face covered in dried blood and fresh welts rode a trolley sweeping through the effervescent city in silence. His apathy toward the current state of his appearance added to the whispers of those on the cable car eavesdropping on his conversation, though he paid them no mind.

His best mate, Raoul Cheron, rambled nervously about the unprovoked attack, unaware of prying ears. He neurotically fiddled with his thin mustache and gestured with his hands as he talked. Raoul was an average man with a round belly and a glutton for punishment, particularly vicious women.

The man had yet to say a word as he blinked back exhaustion and held a bloody rag against his nose as he listened. His black hair was messy, disheveled, and covering a long-jagged scar on his brow. Bruises formed on his pale skin, and dark circles rested under his eyes as if he had suffered many a sleepless night. His gelid eyes were incessant and endless, leaving many to recoil in some deep-rooted fear they held. He was an unusual man with no use for frilly coats, tights, or wigs. He wore black and black alone. This man's name was Jackson Hadley.

Jackson was an esteemed surgeon and alienist along with Raoul. Many sought their counsel and the pair had become some of the finest in the country. They were frequently on the road to assist in criminal cases, typically drifting in and out of varying cities in Elione. On occasion, however, they were known to travel outside of the country.

It had been five long years since Jackson and Raoul had stepped foot in Bel Deaux, and this act of violence was a prudent reminder as to why. They had long forgotten the streets of the capital and failed to comprehend how vital machines would become, yet the people they left behind were more pressing than the city itself. The two separate letters folded in Jackson's breast pocket could be ignored no longer. One was from the Queen, and the other was from the head of the Elite, William Calvert. The Queen wanted to discuss an important matter involving the future state of Elione, a subject he avoided at all costs.

William Calvert's letter, however, was far more personal. He gave one final warning that would leave no room for a mistake. If Jackson failed to keep his head down, he would be banished from the city for good. Yet, misfortune seemed to follow him everywhere.

Within a half hour of his return, five men held him in place as a sixth beat the piss out of him for not having anything of value to take—what a spectacular homecoming.

Across the aisle, a persnickety fop escorted two ladies visibly stricken with fear at the sight of these vagrants, though they had yet to bother a soul. The fussy man sat on the edge of the bench, angled toward Jackson and Raoul with a stern glare cemented on his red face. Jackson neither noticed nor would he care if he did. His head ached, his nose seared, and he wanted nothing more than to sleep for many days.

"You are incredibly offensive, sir!"

Jackson glanced at the fop with little interest. The man's lip curled, perhaps to bully him, though it didn't work. Jackson turned away, taking in the vast city with indifference. He felt nothing for the steel structures and pollution engulfing the city.

"Relax," Raoul interjected, as he often did. "We aren't bothering anyone. We'll be off before you know it."

"I said," the fop bellowed loudly over Raoul. His gaze had yet to wander from Jackson. "You are incredibly offensive, sir!"

Jackson closed his eyes briefly. Was there no reprieve to this sudden torment? Still, his voice was relatively low as he said, "Your perception of me is not my problem. It is your own."

"How dare you insult me!" The man jumped up from the bench, which forced the women at his side to tug at his ruffled jacket, pleading with him to be quiet. "Your lack of manners is more appalling than your face! Can you not look a man in the eye when spoken to?"

Raoul raised his hand. "Calm down. There is no need for this behavior!"

The fop rounded on him. "I don't believe I was talking to you!"

Jackson exhaled loudly and he said, "It would be highly advisable to contain yourself and mind your business as women are present!"

"Precisely!" the man bellowed. "It's the very reason I am addressing you, tramp! Your appearance is insulting to the womenfolk, and I must protect them!"

"My apologies," Jackson murmured as his eyes settled on the nearest of the two. He must look terrifying to someone so well put together, yet he merely felt the tiniest amount of guilt. "But as you can see, I am no bother. I am minding my own just as you should."

"I don't need lessons in good form from a blighter!"

"I'm sorry you feel that way," Jackson drawled and glanced back out the window.

"Why don't you look at me when I'm talking to you!"

He glared up at him.

"You are offensive and ill-mannered," the fop hissed.

"As you've said," he stated calmly with an inane smile. "How long do you wish to reiterate this exchange before I go mad and am compelled to break your nose?"

The fop's face turned puce as he projected spittle all over himself. Jackson bit back a laugh and turned his head away before he caught Raoul's eye and started laughing.

"You dare sit there and chastise my manner in front of women when you clearly have no regard-"

"For god's sake, fuck off already!" Jackson yelled. A laugh escaped Raoul's lips, and he quickly covered his mouth to stifle the sound. The man stepped back with explicit intimidation while the women flinched and gasped loudly, drawing the attention of other passengers and the trolley guard who stalked towards them.

"What's this guy's issue?" Raoul muttered under his breath. Jackson shrugged and raised the rag back to his nose.

With his approach, the guard barked, "Is there a problem here?"

"Not at all," Raoul stated calmly.

The fop raised a manicured finger and bellowed, "This man is offensive to my company and, quite frankly, everyone on the trolley! I demand he be thrown off at once!"

The guard jerked his head and baton and barked, "All right, the both of you get up!'

"But we haven't bothered a soul!" Raoul wailed with indignation. "We were merely sitting here when-"

The fop yelled, "He cursed in front of these women!"

Jackson clenched his teeth together to keep from shouting, or worse, swinging his fists.

"If I have to tell you again," the guard warned while placing a hand on his baton. "I'll have you arrested!"

"There is no need for that," Raoul said as Jackson grabbed his suitcase and medical bag and jumped off the trolley before either one could snatch his collar. Spending the night in the Bastille wasn't a very appealing thought.

"What the bloody hell was that?" Raoul cried loudly as he jumped off behind him.

"That will be trouble," Jackson murmured testily as he led the way toward Cordelia Calvert's manor. "I can hear Owen berating me now, 'Have you no sense, or are you really that stupid?'"

"Cut him some slack," Raoul insisted. "He had to raise three brothers and a sister by eighteen."

"I didn't need a father," Jackson argued. "I needed my brother!"

"Well, someone had to take control, or you would have ended up in the Bastille along with Elijah."

"And it didn't make a lick of difference," Jackson pointed out. "I still ended up in the Bastille, several times over!"

"Please," Raoul remarked with derision. "Don't you think his determination and discipline rubbed off on you just a little?"

"Whose side are you on?"

Raoul threw a withering look in his direction. "You know where my loyalty lies. I only meant that he deserves more credit than you tend to give. You know more than anyone how bad it was after Clara died, and he tried his best to direct you all in the right direction."

Raoul had a point, but that annoyed Jackson more than his reason. He always tended to give a rational explanation when Jackson wanted nothing more than to feel without getting judged for it.

"Perhaps his behavior has eased over the last few years," Raoul suggested. "Now that he's a detective, anyway."

"Perhaps," Jackson muttered, although he wasn't entirely sure. "But my return may not help matters. It might be best to leave before it worsens, and I ruin his reputation."

"You can lie all you want, but I know you're terrified of running into Isabella," Raoul snapped, and Jackson threw a sharp glare in his direction. "You act as if she lives on every single street corner!"

"I do not."

"Yes, you do!"

Jackson tore his gaze away and pressed his lips together.

"Did you forget how big this city is? I doubt you'll even see her while we're in town."

He hoped not.

Raoul grumbled, "It's not like we'll be invited to any social events."

Jackson laughed. This much was true.

Cordelia Calvert's Chateau loomed at the end of Sixth Street in the north end of the Gas-light district. Far surpassing every other manor with excessiveness and exclusivity, built well over one hundred years before. The estate was a gift from a brother she no longer spoke to. Copious trees shrouded the estate, along with towering iron gates where the hedges formed, casting shadows and playing tricks of the mind. Gargoyles peered down in judgment from their pillars, ready to strike intruders with the intent of ill will.

Jackson had taken a liking to Cordelia, only not in a romantic sense. She was merely a friend and, for many years, had taken care of him. She was the one person in his life who was ever consistent and had never turned her back, no matter how ill-tempered or selfish he acted.

"Imagine the life we could have on the north end," Jackson muttered as his eyes swept up toward the gas lamps, a rare commodity in Trinity Row. "The refined women we could love."

"I like the women in Trinity Row."

"That much is obvious," Jackson murmured, wiping his bloody nose. "But don't you grow tired when they swear like a sailor and ask for sixpence to toss the sheets in the same sentence? Aren't you interested in a more cultivated conversation?"

Raoul's brow puckered. "No. I like a woman who knows what she's doing if you catch my drift."

Jackson grinned despite himself. "You and Elijah were made for one another."

Raoul barked out a laugh.

The lamps were lit with the fall of light, and they stepped through the wrought iron gates of Cordelia's property. Strolling down the drive, their boots snapped against the stone walkway. Jackson gazed at the cathedral windows, where a mass of Baltic ivy leaves climbed the sandstone walls, and shadows dynamically danced across the impressive structure. A grin rose on his lips when the sweet scent of floral and earthy aroma hit his nostrils; Cordelia's rose garden was in full bloom.

When they reached the front door, he shoved the bloody rag deep in his pocket and ran a hand through his hair—flicking mud from his scalp and wiping the excess filth on his jacket.

Raoul rolled his eyes and grabbed the knocker entwined with two golden snakes, thumping it before Jackson lost his nerve. There was laughter from beyond the open windows, indicating she was entertaining.

The door abruptly opened, and his eyes widened with genuine surprise. His brother Elijah was staring right at him.

"Well, I'll be damned," Elijah bellowed loudly with a wide grin, "Jackson, you son of a bitch!" He fiercely ripped Jackson into a bear hug, who groaned under the pressure. "I didn't think you were returning until next week!"

"There was a change of plans."

He pulled back and eyed him carefully. Elijah's honey-blonde hair failed miserably to stay waxed in place, and his eyes were distinctly lighter, brighter, and full of far more amusement. His ample lips and nose were similar to Jackson's, yet his features were slightly more symmetric and aesthetically pleasing.

"Nothing has changed with you, I see."

"It was an unprovoked attack," Jackson's baritone voice carried into the foyer and echoed loudly.

"Is that right?" Elijah scoffed as if he didn't believe a word of it. Not that his brother had ever cared either way.

"Do my ears deceive me, or is Jackson Hadley at my door?" Cordelia said as she stepped into the hallway with Gainsley, the Hadley valet. She was holding a glass of wine in one hand and a cigarette in the other. She wore an unhooked white button-up, and the sleeves were folded at her elbows. He sighed at her elated grin. Perhaps coming home wasn't as much of a mistake as he anticipated.

"You're really here," she beamed and wrapped her slim arms around his frame. He enveloped her tightly and rested his cheek on her head. She smelled of cigarettes and rose water.

Miss Cordelia Calvert was thought to be a most unusual woman and tended to be massively avoided. Her rebellion against gender roles came with open disgust and harsh whispers. She was indifferent to dresses, which caused quite a commotion whenever she walked down the street in trousers and a top hat. Her once flaxen curls were cropped short precisely like every other man in Bel Deaux, another cause for gossip amongst society. She preferred the smoking parlor over the dancing hall, and her tastes could be the same as Jackson's. She had never married, and she never spoke to either of her brothers, leaving the comfort of her parent's home at nineteen. And now, twenty-five years later, she lived alone and behaved as a man would despite what society may think.

When she pulled away, her blue eyes wandered heavily over the bruises and cuts that marked his imposing face. "And as if no time has passed, I am here to clean up your wounds once again."

His smile bloomed at her words.

Elijah ruined the moment as he usually did when he bellowed, "You fucking dog, you!"

Jackson turned to see his brother and Raoul throwing their arms around one another and jumping up and down. Cordelia laughed and gave Raoul a hug once they pulled away with nonsensical grins; their reunion was loud and engaging.

Jackson's humor was short lived when he caught Gainsley's stare, which was critical. He stepped forward with an outstretched hand. "It's good to see you."

"You can't help yourself, can you?" Gainsley commented.

"It's not what you think."

Gainsley's face fell as he let go of Jackson's grip.

Elijah clasped a hand on his shoulder as they stepped through the threshold, his grin addictive as always, and Jackson smiled back. Elijah's temperament was the exact opposite of his own.

"How have you been?" Elijah asked. "Besides the face."

"Fine, and yourself?"

Elijah's eyes flashed at him, demonstrating what he had abandoned. His intention wasn't to hurt anyone, but he couldn't stay in Bel Deaux for long periods either. His disdain for the city he once called home went far beyond the heartbreak of some woman. He had never gotten along with their eldest brother, Owen, as well as he should. "It was awful not to have you around, but I'm always good. You know that."

He did.

"Are you going to enlighten us or remain elusive as always?" Elijah asked as he walked toward the whiskey decanter to pour them a drink. Cordelia hadn't followed; she no doubt fetched a rag and hot water. Raoul and Gainsley settled down to watch Jackson quietly.

He fell back against a plush chair too small for his long limbs and rubbed one of his eyes, evading the question entirely.

"Keeping with the slippery route, I see," Elijah said as he handed over glasses of whiskey and took a seat. "I suppose I shouldn't expect anything less than for you to return home covered in blood."

Jackson took a drink. His attention averted to the roaring fire, and his vision unfocused. He enjoyed the burn in his throat; it reminded him of how fleeting it was.

"I suppose it doesn't matter anymore," Elijah added before sipping his whiskey. "We're men now."

"They were merely starving," he finally said.

Both Elijah and Gainsley absently glanced over in confusion.

"I was accosted by desperate men in search for a substance to end their suffering."

"By accosting you?" Elijah repeated.

"They know not what they do," Jackson dismissed as he pulled the letter from his jacket and held it in the air. "I'm more concerned about this. Apparently, the Elite are not so enthusiastic about my return."

Disbelief fell from Elijah's face, and he shared a very sharp look with Gainsley before the valet asked, "How would they even know that you've returned?"

Jackson shrugged. The Elite had a firm grasp on the city. He doubted if there was a single interaction that slipped by them.

Cordelia shuffled back into the room and asked, "What is this about the Elite?"

He hesitated. Cordelia's brother, William Calvert, was head of the affluent organization. While he publicly ostracized her, she was still his family.

Cordelia glared. She was as stubborn as she was determined. "Come on, Hadley, don't hold out on me now."

He rolled his eyes and said, "William made it very clear that I was to keep my head down and not meddle. Why would he think I would meddle? Meddle with whom?"

The three of them shifted their stares.

"There is a clear bottle of antiseptic in my bag," he said with a point of his finger. "It will kill any bacteria that has found its way in."

Her lips jutted out with confusion.

"We've found that taking proper care of wounds, such as cleaning them, often decreases the chances of infectious diseases that have otherwise led to death," he answered quietly.

She threw Elijah a contemptuous look before picking through his bag.

"Enough scrutiny on my behalf. It may save your life one day," Jackson grumbled as she held up a glass bottle, and he nodded. "Now, what aren't you saying?"

"It's nothing," she answered slowly and doused the rag with antiseptic. "I just find it odd."

That was it? There was no further explanation as to why the whole lot of them were acting so strange.

"You know something," Raoul prodded. "We're here, so you might as well tell us."

Cordelia placed the rag on Jackson's chin, and he winced. "Elizabeth is considering William as her successor."

Jackson's eyes widened a fraction, though not entirely surprised. He hoped she would have more sense than to allow William Calvert complete reign. "What about Dominic? Does she not trust her own son?"

"Well, he's a bastard for one," Cordelia said.

"As was Julien Athos."

Cordelia's baffled stare met his. "Dominic Kane is nothing like Julien Athos!"

"Even so," he argued. "You can't use the excuse of Dominic being born out of wedlock as a strike against his right to inherit the throne when the most famous King of our country was, in fact, a bastard!"

Her brow pinched further, anger transforming her features. "He's aberrant, Jackson. Elione may be many things, but the nobles would never stand for a man of such low caliber to govern them. Dominic destroys lives. He has no moral compass!"

There was a vague touch of bitterness in her tone, which would be hard to miss had you not known her. Jackson pressed his lips together rather than argue. Through Elijah's lengthy letters, he disclosed that her niece had some debauched affair with Dominic Kane and the incident became rather public.

"She could have chosen Owen over William," Jackson murmured. She was their aunt, after all.

"She did, but he turned it down."

He took another sip of whiskey, knowing his brother had already rejected her offer. It was the very reason he was sitting in Cordelia's manor.

"He has the same view of the Elite as you do."

Where did she think he got it from? "So, they expect me to keep my head down and not disrupt the terror he's inflicted throughout the city while Elizabeth continues to throw parties and ignore her people?"

Cordelia's face twisted bitterly. "It would appear that way. William does love to send a message."

Not wanting Cordelia to dwell on painful memories, he asked, "Has he been preparing Jet for when he takes over?"

The stress from Cordelia's face eased, and the harsh lines disappeared as she said in a rush, "I doubt it, but who knows? Jet is more preoccupied with Katerina Atwood standing to inherit the Calvert estate now that she is carrying William's child."

"Hold on," Jackson said as he stilled Cordelia's hand. "One thing at a time. Katerina Atwood is carrying William's bastard?"

Cordelia pressed her lips together as the worry lines on her face returned once more.

"No, his heir," Elijah answered without any tact. "He married her the month after Alexandra died."

Ah, yes, the suspicious death of Alexandra Calvert. Owen sent the autopsy report for his opinion a month after the incident. She died from a single gunshot wound to the head, though it was set up to look like a suicide, at least from what he could tell of the report. That left one minor detail his brothers failed to disclose.

He glared at Elijah. "You neglected that bit of information."

Elijah shrugged. "I didn't think it was relevant."

"Well, he surely didn't waste any time, did he?" Raoul intervened before Jackson could make a nasty remark.

Cordelia's gaze lingered, but he refused to meet her eye, opting for a drink instead. She tended back to his wounds after some strenuous seconds and said, "As the first-born son, he believes he is entitled to the empire and not some third-class citizen."

"But he's right. Jet *is* the heir," Jackson pointed out. "And Katerina isn't of noble blood, even if their marriage was legitimized."

"We'll see about that," Cordelia muttered.

Jackson glanced at the wall ahead, eyes unfocused. There was something rather strange about William marrying Katerina Atwood, but it was none of his business.

"Enough of this," Elijah said dismissively, and Jackson blinked several times to focus before glancing over. There was a devil-may-care grin on his brother's face. "There's only one thing left to do, and you're right on time."

Jackson's face twisted skeptically, which bled out in his voice as he said, "Oh, yeah, for what?"

"We celebrate."

"What is this 'we' horseshit?" he hissed, causing Elijah to give him a perturbed glare, and eliciting a laugh from the group.

Cordelia grinned as she snatched the whiskey from his hand to polish it off. She shoved the glass back in his palm and stood to take the bloody rags to the back for the wash. "You can't run away now, Hadley. It's the least you can do to compensate for those missing years." With a wink, she stepped from the room.

"I'm not entirely to blame," he called after her. "Owen is just as culpable!"

"Yet he stayed," Elijah reminded him.

He met his stare with contempt, feeling more than a little resentful. Jackson would have to get comfortable with the finger pointed directly at him.

"Come on," Elijah grumbled. "Your return is reason enough to celebrate!"

It was too predictable. "Another excuse to get piss drunk?"

"I have never once needed an excuse to have a good time," Elijah clarified. "I'll start a party by myself if I have to!"

Jackson grinned madly. It was good to be home.

II
Jade

It was exceptionally dreary out. For the better part of three days, it had rained harshly upon the automated city. A thin flash of bright light overwhelmed the sky, followed by a thunderous uproar. The passing day proved to be as drab as any other. A baleful overcast left the streets in shadow and large rain droplets peppered the cobblestones, leaving them waterlogged and slick. A chill in the air swam throughout, pushing into one open window and dancing with the sheer white drapes fastened from above.

Inside, a young woman named Jade Calvert sat in front of the vanity with her legs pulled up into her chest as her lady-in-waiting teased her hair. Jade's lush curls were as dark and as rich as the blackest coffee, framing a porcelain face that was delicate yet formidable. Her high cheekbones rested above prolific lips and a pointed chin causing quite a stir whenever she walked into a crowded room. Yet, if her face wasn't enough of a draw, the color of her eyes differed vastly from one another. Her left eye was the hue of spring—vibrant, clear, and almost feline, while her right was soft like honey and drew you in like the warmth of the sun. A unique trait that produced whispers and ridicule whenever her back was turned, for no one would dare speak ill to a Calvert.

The name Calvert came with certain expectations, and none were desirable. She hated her father's legacy and wished to erase it from her semblance completely. She wanted more than to be limited to a dutiful, boring wife who attended tea parties and balls. To be worth more than a woman with nothing else to say than what her husband thought of the world.

She bit her lip and looked beyond the trees, rippling under the wind and inviting her to run away. A tear nearly escaped. There was no hope or happiness, nothing compelling her to move on. How did her life amount to the decisions of others? It all returned to her father and his choice to give her to Theodore Kensington, another man whose name came with specific stipulations. She heard how he spoke of her as if she were a doll with no feeling. How she dreamt of another life, even a poor one with a different face, one that Theodore did not covet.

Theodore Kensington was an entitled narcissist who enjoyed the misery of those less fortunate. Jade had lived in a sheltered prison for twenty-five years only to enter another. How was she supposed to spend her life with a man who belittled and robbed the impoverished? How was she supposed to relate to anyone, for that matter?

It had been a year since the tragedy, yet the memory tormented and paralyzed all thriving capabilities to the point of hysteria. Haunted by gruesome brutality, Jade often felt dejected, uneasy, and angry. All that was left was a deficient personality inside a once highly vivacious girl filled with an enviable amount of vitality. Some had called her outspoken mouth uncouth and offensive, while others found her wit endearing and admirable. However she came across then was far from the girl seen today.

As of late, she was withdrawn and far removed from society. Not caring to keep up with the times or marry a man she despised. If she did make it out of the house, many kept a wide berth in some subconscious barrier to distance themselves from the girl. Astounding as it was to grasp, perhaps it came about because she favored black and rarely smiled. Jade never added anything delightful to the conversation or partaking in the season's frivolities. She was perceived as an anomaly that would taint their precious reputation, and no one wanted to be considered anything other than average.

The most likely reason came from what she discovered on that fateful night. Jade found her mother's lifeless body in a pool of blood with a gun in her cold hand. The taboo of suicide added to the oddity of being the one to stumble upon the gruesome scene. How were you to treat someone who witnessed death? It was far easier to pretend nothing had happened and ignore the situation entirely, even when the event plagued the Calvert household to this very day.

With her mother's unfortunate death and her father's recent marriage to Katerina Atwood (all within the same year), she was left reeling and questioning everything she knew. How would she even confide in her siblings of late? They were all caught in their vices and rarely offered extended support.

Jet and Esmeralda were fraternal twins and the eldest, but they differed from one another in the most humanly way possible. Esmeralda was duly kind and often quiet, entirely reserved around anyone she was unsure of. She was akin to Jade in demeanor yet not as vocal. But where Jet favored money and power, Esmeralda was utterly disinterested in it all.

Pearl was next in line and fled the minute she married. She was an extraordinarily fair and docile individual who refused to waste her time and patience on someone with no regard for decency. She was even further in demeanor and often expressed her frustrations with Jade, never failing to chide her at all costs. Jade resented her arrogance, especially since Pearl had betrayed her trust, which had a cataclysmic outcome.

Jade came after and was always in trouble for being outspoken and posing questions about anything and everything. It wasn't because she wanted to be difficult; she wanted to be free.

Ruby was the youngest of the brood, and she was as despondent as she was reticent. Whether it be the death of their mother or languishing over the Cavendish boy, Jade often found it challenging to identify with her. Ruby would rather be left alone—a desire Jade could respect, but she sure did adore her.

Her eyes wandered further to the tattered book of Adrian Von Peltier on the vanity. He was a famous archaeologist who wrote of his explorations for treasures of the ancient world; she romanticized a life in which she did the same, but it would never come to be.

She glanced at her reflection. She was pretty enough on the surface, no doubt pleasing to the eye of a man who desired a prepossessing wife; the thought made her cringe with crippling suffocation alone. She was being forced into legal slavery under the guise of matrimony and mediocrity with no chance at freedom.

She turned her hand over with this thought and stared at her palm. She used to be able to manipulate objects without touching them. It was a rare gift that should be harnessed in a controlled environment because talents such as these were dangerous. Witches were believed to be wiped from civilization entirely, and any talk or signs of witchcraft led to a swift execution.

Jade knew this ability was strictly forbidden, yet she couldn't help but dance with the flame. Pearl, who shared similar potential, used to tread the waters of magic when they were young and artless. This was before their mother stumbled upon their secret, driving the utmost fear into their minds. Pearl turned her back on the possibility, and Jade supposed she did the same. The flame was muted for now. The mystic cross, however, was still etched on her palm vividly, a reminder of what might be. She sighed heavily and dropped her hand, ignoring all thoughts on the matter because it was irrelevant.

And yet, there was this anticipation of something grand on the horizon. Something monumental was going to happen, though she couldn't place it. The suspense was tingling in her palms and stirred excitement in the pit of her stomach.

Jade's stare found Marna through the mirror. The woman's heavy-lidded eyes flicked to meet her gaze for the briefest moment and returned to the task at hand.

Marna was an older woman with a weather-beaten face and wild russet curls, which flipped in every which way. There was a certain admirable carelessness to envy, though there was a hard edge to her demeanor; as if she'd seen far more than any woman should. Marna expressed the horrors of Trinity Row and how awful it was for so many women. She tried to explain how privileged a life Jade led as if she couldn't grasp it on her own.

Marna braided Jade's hair across the left side of her head and pinned it in the back. She then arranged small strands of curls around her face.

"Would yew like to wear the cream dress wit the gold trim or the blush?" Marna asked lightly. There was a motherly smile on her lips.

"Black," Jade answered curtly.

"But ya fada-"

"The one with the high collar."

Marna sighed with petulance and placed her hands on her hips. "Ya fada wants yew in light colors!"

Jade frowned. "Why?"

"He wants yew to appear virtuous and pure."

She snorted.

Marna raised her brow and asked, "Well?"

Jade brushed her off with a wave of her hand. "It doesn't matter what my father wants anymore. I want to wear the black dress with the high collar."

Marna scowled and stalked into the closet.

She brushed her lips softly; the contact was feather-light and direct. White faces were a craze Jade failed to partake in. There was no desire to plaster her skin with paint that would irritate and cause a breakout. Red lips, however, were a complete fixation she could favor. On a sudden whim, she grabbed the plant-based dye on her vanity that was strictly meant for her cheeks and began to paint her lips.

"Jade," Marna warned. "Ya fada won' like it!"

"I know," she replied and continued to color her lips the deepest red.

"Yu'll receive a lashin'," Marna hedged.

"Good, perhaps he'll kill me this time."

Marna clucked her tongue and said no more on the subject, grabbing the hoop pannier and waiting for Jade to finish.

She grinned at her reflection before standing from the vanity and raising her arms. Marna placed the skirts over her head and body. The black satin hugged her arms and chest in a restrictive way, but at least her bosom wasn't fully displayed. The collar covered her throat, ruffled down her chest, and fastened with a clear diamond.

Marna then wrapped a black corset around her waist, and her breath came in rapid spurts. She grabbed onto the four-poster bed to hold a firm footing as Marna continued to pull against the ties. Jade felt the only need for this sort of torture was to subdue her mouth so that she may be compliant in a man's world.

Marna finally stepped back and asked, "Well?"

"I can hardly breathe," she grunted and placed a hand on her pinched ribs. "Therefore, I won't be able to speak much. Theodore will love that."

Marna's mouth twitched in amusement. "Knowing yew, yu'll find a way to get ya point across…even wit ya last breath!"

Jade laughed as Ruby entered the room.

"You look agreeable, even in black," the girl said dejectedly and sat on the edge of the bed. She was wearing a pink dress. "Theodore will be pleased."

How disappointing. "The dress isn't for him."

"Of course it isn't," Ruby responded with a wry grin. "You're running late. *She* told me to retrieve you."

It was noted that Ruby had never called their stepmother by her given name, only referring to her as "That woman" or "Her" or "She."

The Calvert clan were given no time to mourn their mother's death, and with the anniversary upon them, they were reliving it all over again. So much had changed, and none for the good.

"Oh," Ruby added. "Adelaide is here for your little dinner party."

Jade grimaced. She was forced to befriend the girl despite many abhorrent objections. Adelaide was one of Katerina's unwed sisters and only pretended to be a close friend to enhance her reputation and status, which was rather brilliant. But she was highly insensitive and far too judgmental to have an ongoing conversation with. A perfect fit amongst the ladies of society, and Jade would rather she found someone else to cling to.

"Marvelous," she grumbled.

Ruby pushed a tendril behind her ear with wry amusement. Her heart-shaped face was intricate and indelible. Freckles being the most prominent feature on her cheeks and nose, dusting her pale skin divinely. Her hair was relatively softer than Jade's, and when the light hit it exactly right, hints of red shined throughout. It appeared as if she was made from fire itself and would burst into flames at any given moment.

"She also said Papa is far too ill today and won't be attending," Ruby sounded hopeful while picking at her dress. Jade knew her sister didn't honestly wish for their father to die, just the purgatory he placed on their lives.

She whirled around with a smile. "Then Katerina came at the most opportunistic time, wouldn't you agree?" Ruby matched her enthusiasm carelessly. "She marries the rich older man who is recently widowed and, not long after, ill. Leaving his fortune and child in her stomach so no one can deny her claim!"

Ruby fell into a fit of giggles.

"Stop it!" Marna squealed indignantly. "What happened to yew not bein' able to talk? It's a damn wonder a man asked for ya hand at all!"

"Oh, he didn't ask because he's in love with me," Jade answered plainly. "He's spiteful over Dominic and wants revenge because he feels we wronged him."

Marna gawked in confusion.

Jade didn't look the least bit repentant as she admitted, "I may have overheard a conversation or two."

"Yew knows what they say about eavesdroppin'!" Marna said flippantly.

"If you're going to eavesdrop," Jade answered, and her cheeks rose with amusement. "Then you better do it right!"

"A'right, get out!" the maid yelled with a critical look. "Now!"

When they stepped out into the hallway, laughter floated up the stairs. Jade would have sighed properly if a ridiculous corset wasn't squishing her lungs. How long was she expected to play along?

She exchanged a wary glance with Ruby before they descended the stairs.

Katerina was waiting tentatively in the foyer with her sister Adelaide, Theodore Kensington, and Edward Wright. A boisterous laugh hung on Katerina's breath, though Jade knew better than to believe anything she projected.

Her father always appeared highly pleased with his young wife and it was suspicious. Her stepmother faked a fair number of things in this life, and her relationship with William Calvert appeared to be one of them. How he failed to see her intentions was astonishing as William had a knack for sniffing out deceitful and untrustworthy behavior. It seemed as if his judgment was clouded when it came to beautiful young women.

They went unnoticed as they entered the foyer. Adelaide and Katerina doted on Theodore and Edward, touching them intimately and giving uncomfortable comments that would cause one to blush. And yet, the scene was idealistic. Two charismatic men and their counterparts flirting innocently enough. Adelaide stood an inch from Theodore with her hand resting on his arm, a wanton smile adorning her face.

His returning smile was one that Jade had never seen before; he was truly at ease.

After a few beats, she snapped, "Isn't this a warming sight?"

All four heads turned to her.

Theodore cleared his throat and took a step back from Adelaide, brushing her off his arm, and said, "Darling, you look…" his eyes swept over her black gown, with its long sleeves and high collar as opposed to Adelaide's and Katerina's bursting bosoms. He seemed conflicted and his brows pinched as he settled with, "Astounding."

Jade tried not to grimace while being critically observed. Katerina and Adelaide's hair was as black as the raven, and their eyes rivaled the sky. Although, there was something sinister lurking behind each of their stares. Perhaps it was a hunger for power, something they found in her family.

Katerina observed the length of Jade's gown. There was a disinclined smile on her lips. "Again, with the black?"

Katerina could always be counted on to bring up minor details that harbored ill feelings. Jade blinked, not caring if they made fun of her; she just wanted to be left alone.

Theodore flashed a fixed smile, and she pursed her lips in return. Teddy was fine enough as far as men went, she supposed. Katerina often described him as tall, dark, and handsome, although Jade objected. She didn't find anything particularly notable in his appearance. Nothing that made her feel anything other than discomfort at the thought of having to one day be intimate with him.

"You look relatively nice," Adelaide added, and there was a smugness in her voice as Theodore's attention found her again. A conservative dress couldn't compete against exposed skin.

Edward boldly lifted his hand to Jade's chin. His thumb grazed her bottom lip. "Red suits you."

She smacked his hand away when Theodore's face twisted dangerously. She didn't care for Edward and detested his advances, but there was no desire for an act of violence. If Theodore thought they were sneaking behind his back, there would be dire consequences. "I wore it to annoy my father. Yet I was told he is ill?"

Katerina lifted a knuckle to her nose and sniffed. When her hand dropped, she gave Jade a false smile. "Yes, he is far too weak for company."

"How unfortunate," Jade snapped.

"How about we move to the dining room," Theodore asked to drown out her petulance. "I'm rather hungry."

Edward held out his arm. "Yes, shall we?"

Jade wasn't given the chance to reject his advances as Theodore grabbed her elbow and steered her into the dining area. She ripped her arm from his grasp and sat down, holding her tongue.

Katerina hissed, "Your father wanted you in white!"

She raised her chin in defiance. "Yes, well, with the upcoming anniversary of my mother's death, I'm not feeling exceptionally virtuous."

Ruby groaned from behind, and Katerina looked positively scandalized, but it was Theodore who said, "There is no need to be vitriolic, dear."

Jade gaped at him. "Grieving is a vitriolic emotion to you, is it?"

Theodore glared. The lines on his face were severe and abrasive. All the malice and contentment he possessed simmered delicately on the surface, threatening to boil over. The cracks in his façade were slowly starting to show. "How long must you grieve for? She chose her fate and left you alone. Why would you waste any thoughts of her?"

Ruby's breath caught, and Jade sneered. "Because she was my mother!"

"Not anymore."

Her jaw slackened, and her stomach dropped in severe discomfort.

He gave her a smug grin. "The truth hurts, darling."

"You arrogant bastard," she whispered.

He looked unbothered as Adelaide disguised a laugh for a cough.

Her eyes narrowed, and her tone turned antagonistic, "How coincidental is it that Adelaide, who scarcely visits her sister and only uses me to appeal to her public appearance, shows up in my home on the very evening you come for dinner? Isn't that *astounding*?"

Adelaide and Katerina exchanged a mirrored glance of unsettlement. Jade ignored the growing pain in her chest and Ruby, who whispered her name urgently. She even pulled away when Theodore tried to grab her arm.

Edward, however, had the audacity to laugh.

"She has every right to visit her family," Theodore corrected, his dark gaze filled with a malign impression.

"How silly of me," Jade muttered and grabbed her fork. "There is a first for everything."

Katerina looked on the verge of slapping her, but Theodore beat her to the punch and said, "I bought us a manor in Bellemere."

Jade dropped her fork. "Bellemere? You want to live in the country?"

Theodore straightened. "Yes. Living far away from the city has always been a dream. As you know, Bel Deaux is going to the dogs quickly. I have no desire for you and our children to bear witness to the evil that continues to rise."

Jade turned away from him and closed her eyes while counting slow breaths.

"My work is here, however," he continued, "I will travel back and forth while you are protected."

"This city is as safe as any other," Katerina interrupted.

"In this manor with its many guards, it would appear that way, Kat. But the events unfolding in Trinity Row are far too foul. It will only be a matter of time before the vagrants make their way across the Grand Bridge."

Jade perked up. "Are you speaking of the recent murders?"

"Jade!" Katerina scolded.

Edward admired her boldness from across the table with a smile.

Theodore scowled. "Why would you ever bring that up?"

"How could I not? It's all over the papers," she answered, unsure what was so unsettling to him, the murders or speaking of them. "Everyone is talking about it. Elijah Hadley even wrote on them."

Theodore rolled his eyes and muttered, "Elijah Hadley," with contempt, "he and his pesky brothers will go down in flames. You mark my words. Not to mention their sister who dares to speak to men without an invitation!"

"Yes, how dare she!" Jade said sarcastically.

Theodore bared his teeth.

"I like Eli," Edward said indifferently. "He attended Brentford with us. He was in our class, a very likable fellow."

"All of the Hadleys are likable!" Theodore countered with ill-temperament. "But look at how they've chosen to conduct their lives! They are going to cross the wrong person one day. Elijah has made a lot of enemies by asking questions he needs not an answer to!"

Edward rolled his eyes and took a bite of roast.

"I think he is an excellent writer," Jade dared.

"You must not be very well read then," Adelaide provoked with a raised eyebrow.

Theodore grinned smugly and Katerina appeared to chide her by saying, "Adelaide!" but it only came off as endearing.

Jade leveled her stare. "And what profound writers do you follow? Your only concern lies with taken men!"

Katerina started to protest when Theodore held up a hand. "Your antics are fatuous, and I demand you leave your pettish behavior and lack of diplomatic conversation behind. I have no desire for a disobedient wife!"

Jade pressed her lips together and stared at his unremarkable face. His eyes were black and far too unkind; his mask of normality slipped just ever so. How was she to spend the rest of her life with a man who adamantly believed she was his property and should comply with his ever-ridiculous requests?

"See," he smiled after a few moments of silence and patted her head as if she were a small child. "I knew you would see things my way in the end."

Jade's focus clashed with Adelaide's self-satisfaction, and the sudden urge to scream emerged. She didn't, however, and when her gaze shifted to Edward, there was no laugh on his lips; his brown eyes were regretful. For the briefest moment, she thought he would reach out and touch her hand in comfort. Instead, he lifted his glass and took a drink.

"Diana and Peter will also be living in Bellemere," Katerina stated into the contention of the room.

Ruby's eyes bulged at the name and everything in her demeanor dropped within the following seconds. Her eyes, her shoulders, and any hope she held in regard to Peter Cavendish.

Jade held her tongue for the first time that evening. She knew Ruby bore a likeness for Peter that was left unreciprocated. It was an unintentional jibe, but a jibe, nonetheless.

She gripped Ruby's hand tightly in reassurance, and Ruby squeezed back, not letting go for the entirety of the meal.

Ruby was lying in bed with a book when Jade burst through the door sometime later, dressed in trousers and a shirt.

"They are a little bigger than I'd hoped," she said as she looked down at her legs. "But they'll do." When she glanced up at Ruby, there was a broad smile on her lips. "How do I look?"

Ruby closed her book and placed it beside her as she sat up. "Why? What are you doing in those?"

A devious smile bloomed on her lips. "I'm running away."

Ruby jumped from the bed and ran to her. "You mustn't! If Papa catches you again, you will be beaten severely or worse!"

Determination settled on her face. "I don't intend to be caught this time! I'm going to cut my hair short like Jet. They will never suspect it!"

"Jade, you cannot!" Ruby wailed, fear encompassing her voice. "Papa won't tolerate it!"

"I will not marry that man!" Jade screamed so loudly that Ruby took a step back. Her shoulders went slack, and when she spoke, her voice lowered to barely above a whisper, "He is the worst type of person, and I absolutely refuse to tie myself to him and bear his children! I am drowning, Ruby, and I haven't been able to get my head above the water for quite some time!"

"But we are going to live with Esmeralda!" Ruby cried as she clutched onto her shirt. "Papa promised! It shall get better!"

Jade laughed without humor. "It won't be any better with her. He still watches her every move!"

Ruby dropped her hands. "Then how do you expect to get out of the city if everything we do is watched?"

"Jet."

"Jet?" Ruby repeated.

"He understands papa's wrath more than anyone," she explained, and Ruby's face twisted with offense. "This life, Ruby... it isn't for me. I am not made for tea parties, gossip, and balls. I am made to wander, to explore."

Tears welled in Ruby's eyes. "You can't leave me!"

"Then come with me."

If she looked frightened before, it was nothing compared to how her face shriveled now. "There is no way!"

"Only a fool would say that," Jade scoffed. "Papa is dying, and Katerina hates us. Staying won't save you!"

"But I'm afraid," Ruby whispered.

"I will protect you," she promised with such conviction there was no way to doubt her words. Yet she couldn't deny the gut-wrenching feeling that either way, something menacing hovered. "I'll protect you even if it costs my freedom…My life."

"You cannot promise that!"

Jade's eyes sparked with determination once again. "Of course I can! What do you suppose big sisters are for?"

"Then who will save you?"

She gave a critical stare. The one she saved just for Ruby whenever she asked a foolish question. "I don't need anyone to save me. I am going to save myself!"

Ruby blinked. Of course she would.

"I hate the night shift!" Gregory McDonald told his companion Jasper Rogers as they walked down the gilded streets of the west end. "I never get to spend time with me wife anymore!"

Jasper threw an exasperated look in his direction.

"It's true!" Gregory wailed, and his elbows shot up to his ears. "I sleep all day and only get a few hours with her at night before she goes to bed, and I have to walk the streets!"

"You should be proud to keep this city safe!" Jasper hissed.

"I never said I wasn't proud of me job! I just hate working all night while she's home alone!"

"I don't mind the night shift, really, as much as I hate walking the alleyways of Trinity Row!" Jasper admitted. "I despise all the drunks and whores."

Gregory laughed in agreement.

"What's that?" Jasper asked and stopped in his tracks entirely.

Gregory squinted into the darkness. There was a large lump on the steps of Reignmar Abbey. He glared at Jasper and muttered, "We can't escape them. It's probably some drunk."

"All right, mate, get up and piss off!" Jasper bellowed as he skipped the steps toward the mass and gave it a slight kick without looking. He drew his foot back slowly when he noted the disarray and complete exposure of what had to be none other than a female.

"What is it?" Gregory muttered as he stood beside him and held his lantern overhead; the illumination of the deceased had them stumbling backward.

"My God! It's a woman!" Jasper yelled. "And she's dead!"

Gregory placed a whistle in his mouth and blew as Jasper's screams filled the street.

III
Jackson

Jackson's fist connected sharply with Theodore Kensington's face. His head flew to the side as spit and blood propelled across the dirt-marked floor beneath them and promptly fell on his back. Jackson dropped to his knees and directed his fist at the other's face. Faster and faster, he swung until his adversary was unrecognizable. A crowd cheered on, but Jackson didn't relent until he was ripped backward.

He was breathing heavily and saturated in sweat, ignoring the flock as he watched Teddy crumble to the floor in defeat. Rolling to his side, his opponent spat a mouthful of blood and teeth onto the ground. No one came to his aid, and Jackson refused to look away until his uncle cupped his face and yelled, "You did it again, my boy!"

He grinned as his uncle thrust his arm in the air. The man couldn't help and get a piece of the glory. The Vaults roared, and he felt a sense of pride swell within him. The notorious fighting ring consisted of youths and lost souls thrown against one another as wealthy lords bet on the players. Jackson was a crowd-pleaser, but it wasn't because he never lost; he had lost plenty of times. He was a wild card, and there was no stopping him when he was on his game.

He glanced up in time to see Abraham Kensington's angry face and grinned in satisfaction. He had just beaten his son Theodore to a bloody pulp.

However, his fulfillment was short-lived. A blaring crash vibrated throughout the room, and he nearly dropped to the ground, yet no one seemed to have noticed a thing. Just as he began questioning his sanity, his airway constricted, and it became difficult to breathe correctly. He placed a hand on his chest and felt his pounding heart. His head began to throb as an incurable thirst came from the back of his throat. Again, the calamity roared from above.

His eyes suddenly snapped open, and he inhaled loudly. His heart was beating furiously in his chest and sweat dripped down his temple. He was safe inside Cordelia's manor and not down in the Vaults. He sagged deeply against the bed with an exhale. He was fully clothed, and his boots were still on. There was an empty bottle of whiskey on the bedside table and half a bottle of laudanum. The pain pressing against his skull was sharp and unrelenting, and his throat was relatively dry; he groaned loudly.

A loud bang from below made him cringe.

"Bloody hell," he grumbled.

He stumbled out of bed and swayed on his feet; perhaps he was still a little drunk. He glanced at the watch on his arm plate. It was just after five in the morning. He exhaled loudly and trudged out of the room. His vision was slightly impaired, and the further he walked, the more strained his headache became. The pounding continued, which became more persistent with each passing second.

"All right!" He bellowed as he trudged down the stairwell.

When he reached the door, he spun both silver handles, and the wheels rapidly began to turn. The hefty bolts slid to opposing sides and, one by one, clicked as each latch unlocked. He swiftly pulled it open to see Gainsley standing on the other side.

"Are you fucking mad?" Jackson yelled. "Do you have any idea what hour it is?"

"It's about bloody time you answered!" he cried back. "Owen sent me. A woman was found!"

He sagged against the door. "I don't have the patience for an overdose. Can't it wait?"

"This ain't some overdose, Jack!" Gainsley's voice was high-pitched and fearful. "A corpse was posed on the steps of the Abbey!"

His brows drew in harshly. This had to be some dark joke because he slipped away from the pubs the night before, and the valet wasn't happy about it.

"It was a murder and a ruthless one at that!" Gainsley explained further, his voice shaking with every word.

He almost questioned if he was still dreaming because he had never seen such unraveled behavior from Gainsley before.

"Let me just grab my notebook," he murmured and turned on his heel.

"Hurry!"

Jackson glanced back over his shoulder. Gainsley was bouncing from one foot to the other and glancing wildly down the street. It must be dire. A drunken row would not leave a grown man anxious and crippled with fright.

He rubbed his temple with a moan. His headache had prominently taken over his mood, and he wished for nothing more than to fall back into bed. He hastily grabbed his notebook from the room he slept in and tore down the stairs despite the discomforting effects of drinking all night.

Gainsley's blue eyes were erratic inside the cab, and he began to fidget so loudly that it grated on Jackson's already sensitive nerves. "You need to calm down," he told him.

Gainsley shook his head as he clutched fistfuls of curly hair.

Jackson's eyes widened in concern. "Is it that bad?"

"She's all cut up," he protested with a troubled look. "I've never seen anything like it!"

Jackson frowned. "You've seen dead bodies before."

"Not like this. She was ripped from the inside out. Even her…" he paused and pressed his lips together.

"Even her, what?" Jackson demanded.

"Ah, don't make me say it," Gainsley begged. "It's bad enough that I saw it!"

Jackson's jaw snapped shut, and he glanced out of the window when the carriage came to a halt. A mob flooded Abbey Lane, which was surreal. Being summoned to a crime scene was normal enough, as he was a surgeon and examined dead bodies regularly. Yet this situation was not entirely ordinary, and the crowd was utterly disorienting. Never had he witnessed such chaos over a dead body. Even with the cast of the sun through ill-lit clouds, he could not fathom why so many were awake at this hour.

He held onto his notebook and shuffled through the mob. Many let him pass while others cursed at his back. He paid them no mind, however, and pushed forward. His brother Owen beckoned him past the barricade of police officers keeping the throng of people at bay. A close line was drawn across the steps and covered the crime scene.

Severity stretched across his brother's face as he folded his arms. Owen's mahogany hair was adequately waxed as always, and his blue eyes rested behind golden spectacles. He hadn't shaved in weeks (which was out of place), and for once, he completely disregarded the convention and appearance of a reputable suitor entirely.

"It's the worst I've seen," Owen said when he came within earshot, and Jackson felt somewhat disappointed they weren't given much chance for a reunion besides a measly handshake. Owen's eyes roamed over his battered face in judgment, though he said not a word about it. "This offender is seriously depraved, Jack. We need to catch him before he strikes again."

Jackson's irritation over Owen's lack of enthusiasm evaporated, and his face twisted in confusion as he walked around the sheet. He stopped short when the exposed body of the poor soul in question came into view. The cut-up body of a woman was exposed to the elements like some freakshow on display.

"I don't know how long we can keep them away," Constable Merfan barked as he crudely pushed between them. His enormous belly forced the pair to step away from one another. They both looked down at the fop with irritation. The Hadleys were imposing in stature, far taller than the typical man, and Jackson surpassed his brothers.

"Our main concern is this crime and the man who did this to her," Owen snapped at the portly constable. "Once Jackson finishes his examination, we can remove the body."

Jackson's frown deepened as he stared at the deceased. A gruesome sight indeed, he covered his mouth instinctively as his eyes erratically wandered over her slain form. Her intestines had been pulled from the gaping wound in her stomach and draped delicately around her body. The dress she wore had risen far enough to expose her most intimate lady parts, which were brutalized to dehumanize her very essence. Even her throat, which was so viciously slashed, was nearly severed completely. But there was one key element missing: her blood.

"God in heaven," Jackson muttered.

"What kind of man could do something as vile as this?" Merfan asked as he ripped the gray wig from his scalp and wiped his forehead.

"A very sick individual," Owen answered dismissively while heavily concentrating on Jackson, who was still gaping at the victim.

He could not contain his disconcertment at the lack of humanity bestowed upon her.

"It must be the work of the devil," Merfan grunted.

Jackson's eyes flashed to the constable, whose face twisted in fear. It was curious that Merfan always appeared insensitive and indifferent, especially to those suffering from the lower class. Now, he was anything but cruel.

Jackson pulled himself together as he drew a pair of spectacles from his breast pocket and walked around the corpse. He tried to adjust his features to resemble an impervious surgeon as he slid on his glasses. There was not an ounce of blood pooling around her body, and with gaping wounds such as these, there should be a mass of congealed fluid saturating the cobbled street. It didn't appear as if livor mortis had affected any of her exposed extremities, nor was there a single drop of blood on her skin or dress. It almost seemed as if her body had been entirely washed of all evidence. Meaning she was not murdered here on these steps. This trollop had been placed here for a purpose and posed for a thrill.

A shiver ran down his spine, and he stepped back to look at the crowd. The murderer had to be here, watching his work with pride as the masses lost their minds. Yet, there wasn't a madman smiling as he got off on the fear of others, and that's all there was: fear on every face he saw.

"I had the same thought," Owen said and followed his gaze. "He can't be far. She was placed here for a reaction. He wouldn't want to miss the reveal."

"Unless he already got what he needed," Jackson countered. His stare caught the black lilies clutched in her hand. He hadn't initially spotted them when her wounds were so extensive. "Who reported the body?"

"A couple of officers," Owen answered quietly. "They're beside themselves."

Jackson grimaced; it wasn't a question as to why. Even the seasoned officers looked incredibly queasy and kept a safe distance. He turned back to his notebook and proceeded to take notes.

"I wonder what the flowers represent."

"A motif?" Owen remarked, lost in thought. "She was last seen around ten."

"Which night," Jackson asked.

"Last night."

He stopped writing and glanced at his brother. There was a laugh on his breath as he said, "You jest?"

"I'm afraid not," Owen answered and met his stare with dour. "Half a dozen witnesses placed her in Perry's pub until about ten."

"Last night?" Jackson repeated.

"Yes."

"As in seven hours ago?"

"Yes," Owen said with an exhale of irritation.

"It's impossible," he stated, causing Owen to press his lips together. "Not only is she devoid of all the blood in her body, but she is also completely washed. Her hair is even dry!"

"Perhaps he didn't wash her hair."

"It appears to be clean."

"Look, I'm not trying to pick a fight with you," Owen growled. "I'm merely letting you know what I was told."

Jackson looked back at the deceased with an unfathomable expression. He touched her face, which was frightfully cold and stiff. He then reached for her arm out of curiosity. The muscles were changing moderately but were not in the advanced stages of rigor mortis yet and were far from breaking. There had to be some mistake. There wasn't enough time to accomplish such an atrocity in less than seven hours.

"How are we going to avoid this disaster?" Merfan barked and gave the sheet a hard stare. "If any of these people witness the macabre brutality, we'll have a riot on our hands!"

"We'll keep her hidden," Owen assured.

"I can't believe someone would place a whore here," Merfan continued. "It makes us look inadequate as a team!"

Jackson glared. The man had no tact or concern for anyone other than himself and his reputation. It was always the same, but he still growled, "So your main concern is how you'll be perceived?"

"Naturally," he said dispassionately.

Merfan was a man who favored money and catered to the rich. Most knew you could pay him to look the other way if you had enough. Jackson despised the corrupt disguised as saviors, primarily when his brother fought diligently to protect the innocent.

"What of her family?" Jackson snapped. "Surely they deserve the respect of discreet formalities!"

"What respect can they have for a whore?"

Jackson twisted the pencil between his thumb and forefinger as his eyes narrowed at Merfan's callous tone. He was surprised Merfan would even say something so vicious when Jackson knew the truth about him. "How easy would it be to go on living if you could disregard a life so easily? To not have a care at all?"

Merfan's face turned pale, and he puffed out his chest. "Listen here, laddy! I respect Owen because I think he helps the community. He locks away criminals instead of slicing up dead bodies for some sick curiosity! I keep my mouth shut when he recommends your opinion because you have been proven useful. But I will not tolerate being disrespected on my territory, do you hear me?"

"Could you perhaps hold your tongue for once?" Owen roared back at him. "A dead woman is more pressing than your preconceptions of my brother!"

Merfan glowered and repeated, "I will not tolerate disrespect!"

Jackson's face smoothed. A threat never rattled him in the way that it should because, for a time, he hardly cared if he lived or died. He was always one fight away from death. It was the only thing that made him feel truly alive. "Owen is entirely biased, of course. I will gladly leave now if you disagree with my opinion."

Merfan's voice lowered as he spat, "Just get on with it!"

Jackson focused on the victim again; his pencil scurried across the paper. "Do you know who she was?"

"Her name was Helena Wimple, and she was indeed a prostitute."

His mouth twitched, yet he said nothing.

"She was known to visit the Elite," Owen nearly whispered as he crouched beside him, but Jackson didn't look over. If Merfan heard them mention the society of wealthy men connected with the murdered woman, there would be severe consequences.

"This is a nice dress for her station," he commented after some minutes and cocked his head to stare at the fine stitching and silk fabric—an odd commodity for a harlot.

"She's been treated for a debut," Owen surmised. "In some perverse way, he's presented her murder to the city."

"He wants the notoriety," he mumbled quietly. "And he won't stop until he gets it."

Owen's eyes flashed at Jackson diligently.

"How could a man do this?" Merfan wondered loudly at their backs.

"A man who doesn't see his victims as human can commit the sort of horrors of your nightmares."

"How do you work that out?" Merfan barked.

"If one doesn't see the humanity in those around him," Jackson paused to address the constable with a fixed stare. "Then there is no sympathy, no compassion, nor understanding. When we have wronged another, the guilt we feel is lost entirely to murderers."

"Then what's to say he'll stop?"

He studied the crowd. "I can't answer that."

Still, there were no faces deriving pleasure from the scene unfolding.

"Bloody hell!" Merfan gasped. "How could this go unnoticed? This is a public area, yet no one saw a thing!"

"That's because she wasn't murdered here," Owen said.

Merfan's eyebrows knit together, and he snapped, "Moving and posing a corpse still takes a lot of effort!"

"The very reason she was placed on these steps in the middle of the night," Jackson stated, and Merfan glared at the back of his head. "It is also likely there were two perpetrators, both with a peculiar interest in defiling corpses."

Merfan suddenly dry heaved into his handkerchief and turned away altogether. A laugh escaped Jackson's lips, and he bit it back when Owen threw a grueling look in his direction.

"Where is Elijah?" he asked to subdue his brother's tempered mood.

"You tell me," Owen answered briskly. The irritation in his voice dripped heavily. "You were the one drinking with him in Trinity Row."

Jackson didn't answer. This wasn't the time for an argument over disreputable behavior. Instead, his eyes wandered over Helena's face. Her eyes were opened, and it was tragic. He said a small prayer under his breath before addressing Merfan, who was slightly more composed. "I feel it's best to conduct the rest of the examination in my lab. There is nothing else that can be uncovered here."

"You're lab?" Meran barked as his red face transformed from nausea into ridicule.

Jackson turned to him with whimsy. "I still have an office."

Merfan wisely held his tongue, though he was visibly unamused by Jackson's enthusiasm, given the current circumstances.

Owen eyed him quietly. "Are you certain?"

"Quite." The perpetrator wouldn't leave anything damaging behind.

"Very well," Merfan said, turning to address his men.

"Be careful with the body as you transport her," Owen added and rose to his feet once the constable finished dishing out orders. "And make sure she is fully covered."

Merfan appeared extremely annoyed that Owen would instruct his team, although he made no further comment to argue.

"Also," Jackson said to Merfan quietly as he removed his spectacles after tucking his notebook in his jacket. "You should keep an eye on the crowd. If the murderer strikes again, it is likely he is watching."

Merfan paled and looked toward the growing mob. "You cannot be serious."

"He's right," Owen added. "The murderer was here."

Merfan placed a whistle in his mouth, ready to blow at the first sight of conspicuous behavior.

With nothing left to be said, Jackson nodded at Owen before turning on his heel and disappearing from sight.

"Where is her uterus?" Raoul questioned with deliberate fear.

Jackson stood back and stared, perplexed at the empty crevice in her abdomen. The spectacles were back, and he was wearing a sullied apron. Helena Wimple's bladder and part of her vagina were also missing.

Raoul began to cough and heave, turning on his heel as he bent over to expel the contents of his stomach. Finnigan Devonshire, a student from the university, fainted. He knocked over the small table with his fall, spilling scalpels all over the ground.

Jackson exhaled. He didn't care to instruct young surgeons under the watchful eye of Dr. Malik, but the chief of police overruled him. He glanced at the aging mortician sitting on a stool in the corner. The man's arms were folded and wearing a putrid glare on his face.

"Have you anything to add?" Jackson snapped.

"He'll be all right," Dr. Malik grunted.

"Would you like to assess my findings?" Jackson asked. There was no mistaking the ridicule in his question.

The man shrugged. "I don't even know why I'm here."

Jackson's jaw snapped shut, and he glanced back at Raoul, who was much shorter and far rounder than his lean frame. Raoul tended to glutton his anxiety, whereas Jackson often went without.

"Are you going to make it?"

Raoul nodded as he stumbled away and continued with his heaving. Dr. Malik covered his eyes and face to hide his laugh.

Gainsley walked into the lab and glanced wildly at Raoul, to the man rousing slowly on the floor, and then questionably at Jackson. When Jackson motioned toward the body, Gainsley began to blink rapidly and put as much distance between the table and himself. He focused on anything but the dead girl, picking up the black lilies Jackson had set on the table.

"The murderer placed those in the victims hand," Jackson told him.

Gainsley instantly dropped the flowers and rubbed his hand against the flap of his jacket.

"Could you give us a moment?" Jackson asked Dr. Malik. "Or would that be breaking orders?"

The Dr. heaved off his stool. "It's fine by me. Let us get you some air, chap!" He grabbed the young man by the arm and led him out of the room.

When the door was closed, Gainsley said, "The city is in riots."

"Shocking," Jackson replied.

"Merfan's hounding the public for information," Gainsley continued, "And Owen's visited nearly every brothel in Trinity Row. He found that Miss Louise threw her out of the Dollhouse."

Jackson met his gaze briefly.

Gainsley looked queasy, and he quickly talked through his discomfort. "They got into a disagreement over money. Helena's been wasting everything earned on booze and couldn't afford rent fees."

Jackson appeared impassive, yet his voice was sympathetic as he said, "That's unfortunate."

Gainsley focused on his dirty nail bed as a distraction. "Owen has appealed to countless residents, yet no one saw a thing."

"No one ever does," he muttered.

"Not with Teddy's lot running around, they won't!" Raoul grunted and spit on the ground. "He owns the east end."

Jackson's glare solidified.

"No one will talk," Raoul went on. "Remember what happened to the Robinson brothers? There were seventeen witnesses to those murders, and not one person said a damn word!"

Jackson grimaced. That crime left Owen more frustrated than ever. How were they going to protect the citizens of Bel Deaux when criminals owned the city? Silence hung in the air, and Gainsley chewed on his bottom lip until he could no longer hold it in. "He's taken Adelaide Atwood as a lover."

Jackson raised his head in bemusement, but Gainsley refused to meet his eye. The valet stared at the ground, and it was hard to decipher his mood with his face turned just so, but his thin lips were curved downward.

"How do you know?" Jackson pressed when Gainsley denied further information.

He sighed and turned to face him with pink patches on his cheeks. "Justina runs her mouth when she's pissed."

Jackson wiped his hands and glanced back at Helena; most people did.

"She's finished with me now," he added sullenly, looking like a wounded dog.

"I hate to sound callous," Jackson answered with a wry grin. "But Adelaide Atwood isn't the girl Abraham Kensington wants his son married to."

"Why not?"

"They aren't rich enough," he stated simply. "The Atwoods are of new money and have not earned the type of privilege to consort with nobles. The Kensingtons come from an extensive line of wealth dating back centuries. The power they've acquired shall not be tainted by someone who isn't on the same level as monarchs, and the Kensingtons are kin to the crown through marriage. Rubbing elbows and flashing their money will only get them so far. It's baffling that William Calvert married into them."

"Well, if she isn't good enough for him, I sure as hell ain't good enough for her!"

Jackson wiped his hands on his apron and said, "I know you don't want to hear this, but it's for the best. You don't want to get mixed up in their war. You will never win."

Gainsley became more downhearted with each passing second. "I know that, and I know she would never choose a life with a man like me. I am not rich. I have no title, no land to account for. I have nothing to offer a woman," he admitted and ran a hand through his hair. "I just liked the way she looked at me."

"And how is that?"

Gainsley's cheek raised. "Like I mattered."

"Who is to say that you don't?" Jackson shrugged. "Titles and money do not mean a damned thing."

"You just said it yourself. In this city, they do."

"To the right woman, they won't, and Adelaide Atwood clearly isn't the woman for you," Jackson reassured. "What's wrong with Justina?"

Gainsley scoffed with a roll of his eyes.

"Too ugly?" Raoul hinted from behind with a laugh.

Jackson tried not to let his vexation show as he glanced at his friend and back to Gainsley, who suddenly tried to appear contrite. He couldn't imagine it had anything to do with her looks. His valet wasn't that shallow. At least, he didn't think he was. And while Jackson had never seen Justina for more than a passing second, he had witnessed Adelaide in all her glory. He knew it had more to do with the potency of her beauty and the charisma she exuded. She was the one to be remembered. Unfortunately, he couldn't say much about the other girl.

He snapped, "She's fine enough!"

Jackson turned back to Helena without a word. He went to great lengths to separate himself from the masses and never wanted to be compared to the likes of Teddy Kensington and the other affluent sons of the capital. He despised differentiating women from one another. It made him feel glib and far too superior for his own good.

And as he didn't care to pass any gossip along, he intended to remain silent. But seeing Gainsley looking so defeated, he felt the need to give him the tiniest bit of hope. "Teddy asked for Jade Calvert's hand over the weekend, and she's accepted. Jade is far more befitting to Kensington's lifestyle because she is far more prevalent than the royals. The Calverts hold ten times the power and riches. Anyone who marries into that family benefits from the name alone."

Gainsley frowned.

"Why do you always exclude yourself when speaking about the Queen?" Raoul interrupted with a hard stare.

It was damn well because she wanted him to take the throne. He could barely run his life, let alone an entire country. Though he would never admit it. He was going to avoid her for as long as he could.

"I just think you would be prouder of being her nephew," Raoul hedged.

Jackson glanced at him. "I never once said I was ashamed of her!"

Raoul opened his mouth to argue but, on second thought, closed it and glanced at Gainsley. He was staring at Jackson, not paying attention to the trivial comments about the Queen, and mumbled, "You'll keep this between us?"

Jackson nodded.

"I'm off then," he said and turned toward the door. "I need to meet with Owen."

Raoul stifled a laugh once they were alone and said, "A woman gets murdered, and all he can think of is the one who drove him away?"

Jackson smiled. "It's hard to argue with the heart, even if the mind knows the truth."

"Don't tell me they're all the same," Raoul grumbled. He was crestfallen, and it appeared as if a stiff drink would ease his pain. Jackson didn't offer any words of encouragement because he couldn't think of a single relationship in his past to contradict the statement.

Raoul nodded with a heavy sigh. "They're all the same."

"Perhaps they aren't," Jackson said optimistically, although it felt like a lie. Raoul's self-esteem, however, was more of a concern than his thought. "You simply haven't met the one girl to break your ideology of love."

Raoul briefly pressed his lips together as he contemplated this. He quickly overcame the simmering inner turmoil and asked, "What if she doesn't exist?"

Jackson focused on Helena once more. His attention reverted toward the wounds on her neck, and he grabbed a pair of tongs. "Now you're starting to sound like Eli." He lifted the severed pieces and uncovered something white shoved into the folds. "What in the bloody hell?"

"What is it?" Raoul asked.

Jackson ignored the question as he pulled a folded note from her throat and stared at it.

Raoul yelled, "Open it!"

Jackson placed the tongs on the table and unfolded the paper, which read,

Not my first, nor my last

"He's done it before?" Raoul cried.

"It would appear so," Jackson muttered. "And he's promised to do it again."

They eyed one another.

"I sincerely apologize," he said when he noted the time and walked toward the washbasin to clean his hands. "Owen asked if I would keep watch at the ball, and I can't very well show up covered in decay. Can you finish this alone?"

"Of course I can," Raoul answered, and his brow puckered when he observed Jackson's resentful demeanor. "Are you all right?"

He gave a halfhearted smile. "You know I don't enjoy rubbing elbows with the Elite."

Raoul chuckled. "Better you than me."

He quickly dried his hands and picked up the black lilies.

"Are you going to ask Cordelia about those?"

"Yes. I want to know where these flowers come from and if they can thrive in this city."

Raoul eyed him curiously. "What will that prove?"

"Think about it. If this is a rare flower, and I believe it is, we might be able to narrow down the suspects. If there is anyone in the city with a proclivity to herbology, we may uncover the suspect."

Raoul scoffed, "Seems like he's flat-out deranged to me."

Jackson threw a smile over his shoulder and left his colleague to finish the rest of the autopsy.

IV
Elijah

He watched Julianne gently pull her stockings up her legs as he buttoned his pants; neither one spoke a word to the other. Her blonde hair fell around her recklessly, and she gave him a wink when she caught his stare. His returning smile was strained as he sat down on the bed to slip on his shoes and lace his boots.

He stumbled toward her in a moment of weakness, which he seemed to have a lot of. He left his brother sometime after two in the morning after Julianne promised him a toss in the sheets. And as he was heavily influenced by alcohol, he didn't have the wherewithal to tell her it was an unwise decision.

Julianne stood fully once her stockings were clipped and pulled a corset over her bare chest. "Help me, would you?"

He lowered his foot to the ground and stalked towards her. He grabbed onto the loose ends of the corset and glanced at her through the mirror. "Are you ready?"

She breathed in deeply and exhaled with a nod. "Ready."

He rolled his wrists and jerked back tightly. She gasped and grabbed onto the dresser. "Did I hurt you?"

She huffed. "Just get it over with!"

He tried to tie her in quickly, but every time he thought it was taut enough, she asked him to bind her further. He complied even though she must have a fetish for pain; there was no way she could breathe.

All morning she appeared as if she had something delicious to say. Something that really made her happy. Elijah had no intention to pry, but she finally let it slip after they copulated. "Richard Beauregard has asked for my hand!"

His pause was brief and he avoided her stare through the mirror, continuing to concentrate on her back.

"Did you hear me, Elijah?"

"Yes."

She whipped around with her arms folded. "Have you nothing to say?"

What did she honestly expect? Their arrangement was neither binding nor acceptable. It hindered immorality which was frowned upon in a highly religious community.

"He will make a good husband for you."

Her grin was brief. "He will, won't he. Of course, this means we will have to part ways."

He blinked, feeling nothing. He wondered if this was how Jackson used to endure or if it ate away at him. Either way, it didn't matter. Julianne was a fine enough woman, but she deserved someone willing to fit her needs. And Elijah had no desire to meet them nor could he pretend this suited his well-being.

"I suppose we will," he said.

She didn't look happy as she grabbed her robe. Perhaps she wanted him to beg, though he never would. He quietly moved about the room to retrieve the rest of his belongings, and she watched until he was fully clothed.

He paused at the door to address her. "Goodbye, Julianne."

"Goodbye, Elijah."

He left without another word, feeling slightly guilty as he stepped onto a trolley and rode to the Bel Deaux Gazette.

Elijah stepped into the print shop and up the two flights of stairs before he slumped at his desk, rubbing his eyes slowly. It had been quite some time since he desired nothing more than a warm bed and a few hours' sleep. It was going to be a long week.

"Where in the bloody hell have you been?" Philip Preston bellowed before he could settle himself in. "Owen was looking for you!"

Elijah rubbed his eyes and grumbled, "I was indisposed."

"Do you not know?"

He peeked over his knuckles and said, "Know what?"

Philip sighed as he grabbed a chair and pulled it toward Elijah's desk. As the first Black man hired by the gazette, he opened the door for those who were overlooked and catapulted the rights for people of color. He let his work speak for him and had the entire cities respect. If one wanted information, they went to him because he wasn't afraid to go to the depths of hell to find it.

"A prostitute was found brutally slain on the steps of the Abbey."

Elijah dropped his hand and hissed, "Come again?"

"She was ripped from end to end. Posed for all to see like some macabre scene from one of Kane's unusual paintings. You know, your cousin."

"Oh, fuck off," Elijah muttered. "That slimy bloke is no family of mine!"

"I'm certain a cousin constitutes as family."

Elijah flipped him off.

Philip chuckled and said, "All right, all right. If a mere murder wasn't enough, all of the blood in her body was drained!"

Elijah's eyes widened as dread encompassed his lungs and the back of his throat. "Who was it?"

"A woman by the name of Helena Wimple."

Relief dismally struck him. It was distressing to learn a woman was subjected to such brutality. He may not have known Helena personally, but that wasn't to say she deserved it. No one did.

Roslyn's face popped into his mind. Eased with the knowledge that she wasn't the intended victim. Although, one murdered prostitute could lead to more. He would have to check in on her soon.

"Hadley!"

Elijah and Philip turned to see Henry Smith stomping toward them. "Where have you been?" When Elijah avoided his gaze, Henry continued, "A prostitute was slaughtered on the steps of the Abbey, and your off tossing in the sheets like always! Hit the streets and get me a fucking story!"

"Yes, sir," Elijah muttered while grabbing his notebook, hating how predictable he was. He suddenly wished there were better reasons to keep him at bay.

"I mean it, Elijah," Henry snapped. "I don't care what excuse you have to give Owen. I want every single detail the coppers refuse to release!"

This presented a problem. Elijah's boss expected his full cooperation, considering his brother was a detective.

"So, an easy day then."

Philip grinned as he grabbed his coat to follow.

"Hound Owen relentlessly. I want the scoop on this story before anyone else!" Henry shouted as they descended the stairs. "We are the number one paper in the city for a reason!"

They ignored their boss and stepped onto the street. "Who found her?"

"Some coppers," Philip replied while slipping on his bowler hat. "She was disemboweled and posed like a doll."

"Blimey," Elijah muttered. His itch for a story wasn't as prominent as searching for Roslyn to ensure she was safe from the vermin in Trinity Row.

"As far as I know, there are no witnesses."

That could be easily explained, the west end wasn't littered with vagrants like the east end was. "Was Owen upset?"

"He wasn't happy," Philip answered.

"I'm not talking about the murder."

"Neither was I."

Elijah exhaled. Owen disapproved of his recklessness, not that he'd ever admit to enjoying his time anymore. No one took him seriously when he was the first in the bar and drinking until he couldn't feel a thing. It was a rare occurrence if he went home alone, and he often followed squalid women to the brothels. This behavior only added to the self-loathing he felt as of late.

"We should probably go to the morgue," Philip said. "Jackson is a safer bet, wouldn't you agree?"

"Definitely," he answered, wondering how far he had gone in his night. Jackson typically kept to himself, always had. On occasion, however, he ended up in the same bar as Elijah. They played poker, smoked cigars, and hit on women. Elijah loved those moments when they were careless together. It didn't make him feel like such an outcast in his family.

Jackson wasn't the surgeon they met at the morgue. It was Raoul and he was writing an autopsy report at his desk. When he spotted them, he said, "He went home to bathe. He's helping Owen tonight."

"What is your take on the victim?"

"I've never seen such an act of brutality in a murder victim, ever. I truly thought we'd seen it all, but I can't even begin to comprehend what was done to her."

"I need something, Raoul. My boss isn't happy with me."

Raoul perched his hands on his hips and he grinned. "I'm surprised you even made it to a room. Your tongue was halfway down Julianne's throat all night and we started taking bets you were going to take her right there on the table!"

Elijah ducked his head as Philip chuckled. He wasn't feeling particularly proud of himself. "What's Helena's story? I need all the details."

Raoul's smile fell. "Two coppers found her on the steps of Reignmar Abbey just before five. Once the word spread, the city square was flooded with people, all wanting a glimpse of the dead woman. I swear Bel Deaux is filled with savages. I understand the morbid curiosity, and I think Merfan did this on purpose, though he says otherwise. He wanted her to be seen. He wanted fear in the streets."

Elijah scribbled in his notebook. "How was she killed?"

A large man hovered in the doorway, and Raoul eyed him warily. "I cannot help you, Elijah. I am sorry. I was sworn to secrecy. If Owen wants to disclose information, by all means, but I can't afford to lose my job. I've put too much work into this to give it up for a story."

"What can you tell me?"

"Nothing."

Elijah breathed out in frustration.

"Can you at least show us the body?" Philip whispered. "Just to get a sense of what we're dealing with?"

Raoul glanced at the man in the doorway, his voice dropping an octave, "Not today. I'm afraid we're being watched."

Elijah had it in mind to thump the guy on the head, though it wasn't a proper sense of etiquette in his line of work. He shared a look with Philip, wanting to get a sense of unity, but his companion looked as if he agreed with Raoul's statement. A smart move and one for appearances. Philip liked to cross the T's and dot the I's when it came to paperwork, unlike Elijah. But, his partner was willing to get some dirt under his fingernails when it came to uncovering the truth. He knew his audience and how to play the part, only this time, they were treading on thin ice.

They'd be thrown off the case if they weren't careful.

Roslyn Emerich walked over to the bed in the far corner of the room as Elijah shut the door behind him.

"I've rented it for five days this time," he told her. "Anytime Blake sends you out, just come here. I've made the proper arrangements for your supper as well."

She nervously fiddled with her hair. Blonde locks were pulled into a braid, and the shorter pieces fell around her face, which was heart-shaped and peppered with freckles. Roslyn's features were arresting, and men fell every time.

Her pale eyes rose to his. "What of you?"

"What do you mean?"

She swallowed and dropped her gaze. "I was hoping that you would choose to stay."

His face smoothed, and his voice lowered gently, "I thought I explained myself properly."

She sighed and turned to hide her embarrassment. "I was certain you'd change your mind."

He stared at her back, a sliver of shame trickling in. His fondness toward the girl was nothing more than what he felt for his sister. He sensed her affections and hoped they would fade with time, for she was young and had many years ahead to find a man who reciprocated the fondness she craved.

"Roslyn," he began.

"I don't need your pity," she hissed and turned defiantly. "I thank you for your kindness, Elijah. Surely, I don't deserve it, but I appreciate it all the same. Now leave me be, my friend has just died, and I wish to be alone."

He nodded and reached into his pocket for banknotes. "That's all I have for now. I will bring more later."

She took it reluctantly. "And what if Teddy pays another visit?"

He gave her an absurd stare and said, "Deny him."

She folded her arms and looked at him crossly. "I don't have the freedom to deny him!"

"Perhaps his engagement will keep him preoccupied."

"Perhaps it won't," she muttered.

He refrained from rolling his eyes to insult her any further. Elijah didn't care to argue about Teddy Kensington's propensity. Teddy wove a web that continuously caught those who didn't deserve it. The injustice alone would cause anyone to go mad. And Elijah had kept his end of the bargain. Roslyn was off the streets and far out of reach from odious men.

"I will check on you as soon as possible," he promised. "And, for the love of god, please do not walk these alleyways alone."

"I won't!" she snapped petulantly.

"I'm serious, Roslyn!" Elijah said. "Helena was sliced open and ripped apart. It pains me to imagine you as the victim."

She flinched, and tears began to fall.

He cupped her cheek. "You are safe here."

She placed her hand over his and nodded.

He reached for the knife in his back pocket. "Take it."

Her eyes widened when he handed it over. "I c-can't."

He grabbed her hand and placed the butt in her palm. "You can. It is a simple switchblade. Keep it under your pillow."

She eyed it warily.

"You have nothing to be afraid of. I will be back before you know it."

Her stare hardened. "Then why are you giving me a knife?"

He looked at the wall behind her as he contemplated this. "The desire for ataraxis."

Her brow pinched. "And what does that mean?"

He grinned at her apprehensiveness. "A tranquil mind. You will sleep better, trust me."

She grimaced, not knowing if Elijah Hadley was worth the trouble.

V
OLIVETTE

"Ollie!" a voice drifted up the stairs.

A unique face that was rather notable despite the illness that had disrupted her life, turned toward the sound and blinked. Graceful and refined as she was, her face twisted as she strained for the following words. The girl who held this face was naturally distinctive and curious, with an extreme passion for literature and illustration.

"Ollie!" the voice shouted once again with impatience.

The girl sighed and shut her book. It just wouldn't do; she would never finish reading now.

She took her time walking down the stairs, pausing to check her teeth in the mirror in the hallway. Her blonde hair was braided down her back, and her tawny eyes were no longer withdrawn and feeble. There was life in them once again.

It wasn't until her mother's querulous voice called her name for the third time, did she drop her finger from her mouth and entered the room.

Her mother was propped on pillows, and her hideously swollen feet rested on the coffee table. Her calves were beginning to retain dimples, and her hands, stomach, and face were swelling. Her cheeks were patchy and red, but even that couldn't hide the yellowish tinge to her skin. Ollie's sisters, Kittie and Tellie, were fanning her. Lady Ashford would be mortified if anyone had seen her this sickly.

"Will you please walk over to the market court and fetch some laudanum?"

Ollie folded her arms in contempt. "Why can't Marcus do it?"

Lady Ashford's gaze fell to the floor. "He left us. We couldn't afford to pay him anymore."

Ollie glowered as her stare stretched between them. "Where is Papa?"

"I haven't seen him since…" her mother left the sentence open, and frankly, she need not elaborate. He was last seen at the disastrous dinner where he admitted his affair with the Allen girl. She was scarcely younger than Ollie herself.

Ollie's face twisted in defiance, and she spat, "Good riddance! What a cruel man to not only have an affair but to do so while you are ill! Has he no shame?"

Lady Ashford patted her cheeks lightly as she said, "There is no use acting petulant now. What's done is done."

Ollie's eyes flicked to Kittie, who was usually very vocal about disobedience and Ollie's disregard for directives, especially regarding their mother. But the eldest Ashford daughter appeared indifferent for once, holding her tongue on Ollie's behalf. Perhaps this was because she had recently married Timothy Beckett and could think of nothing but him. Or maybe she worried about the day Timothy would admit his wrongdoings with another. How would she feel to be the victim of another woman in her husband's arms?

Tellie fanned her mother with passivity and Ollie found it annoying that she failed to act the least bit sympathetic. She threw a glare in her direction, but the girl stared back with an almost bored expression as she pushed red hair out of her face.

"I don't understand where your concern for his well-being comes from!" Ollie argued when her sisters failed to intervene. "Not only did he sin against your marriage, but he chose Charlotte Allen of all people!"

"Enough!" Lady Ashford screamed, and Ollie's jaw snapped shut. "When you marry, you will understand!"

Ollie raised her chin. "I don't intend to marry a man who spreads his love in the most hurtful way!"

Lady Ashford dropped her handkerchief and gave Ollie an incensed look. "Why must you fight me on everything? Haven't I been through enough?"

Ollie relented the splenetic demeanor she wallowed in and said, "I'm sorry."

"Go to the market court and fetch me my medicine before I strip away your privileges!" She yelled, not buying the apology. "Honestly, you're just like him! Selfish and ill-tempered!"

Ollie's face twisted in the emotional pain her mother never failed to inflict. "But there is a heinous murderer on the loose!"

"He killed a prostitute in the west end," Kittie snapped. "And as you are neither a harlot nor do you live in the Gas-light district, you have nothing to worry about!"

Ollie pressed her lips together and threw one last glare at her sisters. They'd be eating their words if something happened to her. And she was nothing like their father, even if Lady Ashford always said she was. The very reason she treated her so poorly throughout her life, and Ollie felt it was extremely cruel to be judged on his sins.

She was muttering grievances under her breath as she wrapped herself in a cloak and walked out into the misty morning; fog settled heavily on the ground. Her feet slapped against the pavement as she walked through crowded streets.

Henslowe Passage was the central heartbeat of the middle class, which hovered thinly between the rich and poor, and while they desperately craved to be a part of the former, they were often grouped with the latter. It was a distinction Lady Ashford failed to grasp because she wanted to be a part of the affluent so severely that she repeatedly ignored the children and husband who needed her. And that wasn't to say Christopher Ashford's affairs were her fault. He was entirely to blame, but had she paid better attention, the Ashford children might have been shielded from the disgrace.

Ollie pulled her shall tighter when the bitter air nipped at her cheeks. The market court was on the edge of the Gas-light district two blocks over. It wasn't wise for a girl to walk alone, but it felt safer in the middle of the day.

The noise dropped as she turned on Wayward Avenue, and the heavy crowd thinned. The street was mostly empty save for a cab grouped by four men. She hesitated and slowed, but she was frozen in their stares when they caught sight of her.

"What's a pretty little thing like you doing all alone?" one asked as the others leaned against the cab to gawk in her direction. She repressed a chill and continued despite the desperate urge to turn around.

"I can't chat," she yelled back. "My husband is waiting for me!"

The nearest of the bunch blocked her way, and his face smoothed. "You look well." She blushed and dropped her gaze. "More than well."

"Do you need a ride?" another asked thickly as he came up behind the first. "We'd be more than happy to escort you."

She shuddered when his black eyes settled over her body. "I can walk," she smiled politely. "I told you my husband is waiting."

"She isn't married," a familiar voice said, and she swirled around to see Theodore Kensington leering at her.

Her stomach sank. His father owned the flat they were living in.

"She's all alone," Theodore stated harshly as the men cornered her against the brick wall. He ripped the shall from her hands and grinned nastily. "She's Christopher Ashfords daughter."

"Is she now?" the man closest murmured. The confidence on his face was jarring, and she wanted to scream. There was something terribly off about the lot of them. She shoved against him when he pressed himself into her.

"Leave me alone!" she yelled, which only caused them to laugh and tear at her bosom. "STOP IT!"

"Do you know who I am?" he asked, and she feigned knowledge. "I am Theodore Kensington. It's interesting to have bumped into you, considering your father owes mine two months' rent!"

Her heart began to beat emphatically, and she shoved the coins for her mother's medicine in his hand. "It's all I have, I swear!"

He shook it and turned to the other man. They both laughed at her measly offering.

A small but loud voice broke from behind. "What's going on here?"

Ollie glanced over her shoulder to see a woman with long, straight brown hair and blue eyes glaring at Teddy.

"Avis!" Theodore bellowed. "What are you doing here?"

"Don't worry about me," she snapped. "What are you doing?"

"That's none of your business," he said and went to take a step in between her and Ollie, but Avis beat him to it and pulled Ollie behind her as she snarled, "Leave the girl alone!"

"You should keep your head down if you know what's good for you!" The second man barked from behind Theodore.

"You've sunk to a new low," Avis growled and shoved Teddy as hard as she could. "Women aren't toys for you to play around with!"

Theodore sneered and took a step toward her. "Yes, they are!"

"Careful," Avis murmured. "You wouldn't want my brothers after you!"

Theodore smirked at her. "Let them come!"

"I take it you haven't heard that Jackson has returned?" Avis hissed, wiping the smug smile from his mouth. "I wonder how confident you'd be if he came for you!"

Teddy glowered at her, and wisely, kept his mouth shut.

"And trust me, they will be hearing all about this!" she threatened and pulled Ollie along.

"You watch yourself! Your brothers cannot protect you every second of every day!" Theodore yelled after them.

Avis ignored him and pushed Ollie down the street.

"Are you hurt?"

"No," Ollie whispered and pulled her arm from Avis's grasp, her eyes brimming with tears. All was lost. There was absolutely no hope in the world. Not only was her mother dying but her father left them and she had nearly been attacked by a group of men. "I was supposed to get medicine for my mother!"

Avis's blue eyes swept over her face with a pause, nodding grimly when she noted Ollie's lament. "Come on. I'll help you."

"What do you mean you'll help me?" she asked meekly.

"I will buy the medicine for your mother," Avis answered without a second thought, and Ollie jumped to follow.

"But I don't have any money!"

"I do," Avis answered briskly, "But I want you to promise me that you'll never walk these streets alone again!"

"You're alone," she countered.

Avis was flippant in her answer, "Yes, but I'm a Hadley."

"Aren't you worried about what he said?" Ollie cried and continued to follow Avis in admiration. The Hadleys were well known throughout the city, and it was easy to see why she thought herself to be untouchable, but not everyone followed the rules.

"What did he say?"

"About how your brothers won't always be there to protect you."

Avis snorted. "Theodore wouldn't dare cross my brothers, especially Jackson. He would kill him if he ever laid a finger on me!"

Ollie fell silent and blinked back tears. Avis was an angel in disguise. She saved her mental state and offered help without wanting anything in return.

She smiled with encouragement when Ollie glanced over and said, "I'm Avis, by the way."

"Ollie Ashford."

"Nice to meet you, Ollie," Avis murmured and blathered about nothing and everything.

Ollie gave her a polite smile. What an odd peculiarity of character; she was trying to distract Ollie from what could have happened.

The market court was relatively crowded, and they shuffled through the mob steadily. Avis grabbed food on top of the medicine she needed. Ollie insisted she put it all back on more than one occasion. Avis brushed her off and continued fetching eggs, bread, rice, carrots, potatoes, and mutton.

She was utterly confused. Why would a stranger buy food for someone they didn't know? Avis had to want something in return.

Ollie glared petulantly and crossed her arms. "I cannot pay you back."

Avis glanced at her briefly and handed over a stack to the vendor. "I wasn't expecting you to."

"Why?" she demanded harshly. "You don't know me nor do you owe me a thing! Why would you buy all this food for nothing in return?"

She stared at her for a long time before finally saying, "I know what it's like to be taken advantage of."

Ollie's mouth parted.

"It's a terrible world to live in, where the only way a woman can survive is to give up her body to a man! You were not born for that. No woman was! I am merely lucky I have four brothers to look out for me. Who do you have?"

Her face flamed, and she glanced at her feet. Her dress was filthy, and there were rips near the bottom, not to mention the holes in her shoes. "I have two sisters and a very sick mother. My father left us for a younger woman."

"I am so very sorry for you," Avis said softly and decently looked away as Ollie collected herself.

She helped Ollie carry the baskets of food back to her flat, and there was a deep frown on her face as she looked over the building. "This street belongs to the Kensington's."

"I know," Ollie muttered as she opened the door and crept inside. Immediate discomfort surfaced when Lady Ashford's loud cry echoed throughout the first floor. Thankfully, the French doors were shut, so she could avoid explaining Avis's presence.

"This way," she said quietly, leading her toward the kitchen.

Once the door was shut behind them, she whispered, "Is that your mother?"

"Yes," Ollie replied without meeting her eye and grabbed the basket from her hands. "She is very ill and can hardly take care of herself, let alone myself and my sister. Her limbs keep swelling, but we cannot afford a doctor." She could feel Avis's stare burning into her shoulder blades. "As I said, my father left all of his debt for some girl, and I haven't a clue what to do!" She shut her eyes tightly and placed a hand over her mouth to keep a sob from escaping.

"Don't give up hope," Avis said and gently placed a hand on her shoulder. "Miracles come in a variety of ways."

She glanced at her with confusion and wiped at her cheeks. Avis was far too kind and unrealistic to be a genuine person. Never had she met such a soul in all her life. They were only a part of the fables she read about; no one offered their help freely. This had to be some trick. Yet the sense of dread never came.

"Can you read?"

Her appreciation turned to offense. "Of course I can read!"

"I wasn't trying to insult you," Avis said quickly. "I just want to give you my address if you ever need help. My brothers will take care of whatever problems Teddy and his thugs try to bring about. Teddy acts tough but he is deathly afraid of Jackson and would never move against him without cause."

Her face smoothed, and she slowly said, "I can read."

Avis pulled a short pencil and notepad from her coat pocket and scribbled on the paper. "You need to be careful. I cannot say whether Teddy will pay a visit, but you should be safe if you do not leave the flat much. Our manor is not far. It's on the main road so you won't have to worry about the distance. I'll check on you when I can, and if I can't, I'll send one of my brothers."

She blushed. "My intention wasn't to become an obligation. I can find my way if I must."

"I know," she said dismissively. "But it wouldn't feel right if I turned away and never looked back."

Ollie stared in amazement—what a peculiar woman.

Her eyes widened when she noted the time on the large clock on the wall. "I need to run. I am to meet with…" she paused with a coy grin. "I have an appointment with someone my brothers wouldn't approve of and no, it isn't Teddy or anyone in his group." There was a deviousness in her voice as she said, "Being bad can be rather fun!"

Ollie tried to smile in return.

Avis's face turned pink. "I'm sorry, how tactless of me to boast about a man when…"

Ollie shook her head. “I’m not offended. I’m sure it’s nice you found someone, even if your brothers wouldn’t approve.”

Avis grinned.

“Thank you for everything.”

“You're welcome,” she answered and slipped through the door unnoticed.

Ollie was left speechless and oddly content.

She was reading by the fireplace when a knock came. She glanced at Lady Ashford, who was sleeping soundly, Kittie had long since left, and Tellie was up in their room. Another persistent knock followed. She jumped from her chair and quietly strode from the room to keep her mother from waking.

She opened the door to a tall and statuesque man. He had slick black hair, a devastating scar on his brow, and a curiously familiar smile.

“Hello,” he said quietly. “My name is Jackson Hadley. Are you Ollie Ashford?”

Her mouth parted. Avis spoke of her brothers, but why would she send one here? “Yes, I'm Ollie.”

His smile broadened. “My sister Avis told me about your encounter today and was rather insistent that I take a look at your mother.”

Her jaw dropped as Tellie came up behind. “Who is it?”

“Hello,” he said to her. “My name is Jackson Hadley. I'm a surgeon, and my sister asked if I would take a look at your mother.”

Tellie placed her hands on her hips and demanded, “Who is your sister?”

“Avis,” he answered dismissively, his attention trained on Ollie. “You met her today, no?”

Ollie had yet to close her mouth. She blinked rapidly and remembered herself. “Yes, I did, and she was rather generous already. She bought more than enough food for the week.”

“She told me.”

“What is this about?” Tellie hissed.

Ollie shook her head and continued to stare at Jackson, waiting for him to explain himself further.

“Would you mind if I took a look at your mother?” he asked with a patient smile. “Avis mentioned something about swelling in her limbs?”

Ollie and Tellie shared a confused look.

"It's imperative for treatment. There could be a variety of causes for swollen limbs," he said quickly, "some are more serious than others."

They continued to gape at him.

His brows drew in sharply. "Or I could come back at a more appropriate time?"

"No!" Tellie screeched and brushed Ollie aside. She gripped his arm tightly and pulled him into the hallway, past the French doors to where their mother rested. "Please, if there is anything you can do to help my mother, we would greatly appreciate it!"

His face was unreadable as he looked at Lady Ashford.

Ollie tried to swallow the sudden lump in her throat. It was unbearable to watch, even when it came to a woman who never treated her like her own. She quickly grabbed onto Tellie and dragged her from the room. "We'll leave you."

She didn't wait for his response and closed the door behind them.

"What happened today?" Tellie demanded.

Ollie sighed heavily and unloaded the story. It wasn't intentional, and she didn't want to be a burden to anyone, but she was incredibly grateful to Avis. She would never be able to give back what was given. Tellie wrapped her arms around her frame and cried about what had happened and what was to come.

They sat on the bottom step for nearly an hour before Tellie gave up and went back to their room. The grandfather clock chimed loudly, and Ollie picked at the ends of her hair before abandoning the fair strands for the dirt under her nails. When Jackson finally stepped from the room, he hesitated in the hallway, and the seconds ticked by. The silence was grueling, and she finally met his eye. His face was bleak.

"Oh!" she gasped and placed her head in her hands. The tears fell quickly.

Through her sobs, she could hear him take a step toward her. He didn't touch her or say a word until she lowered her hands.

He crouched in front of her. "She has dropsy, which is causing the bloating and swelling of her limbs and stomach. The underlying issue can either be heart disease, kidney failure, or liver disease."

"And which one does she have?"

"I can't say for certain."

"Mr. Hadley, please!"

"It's hard to determine, but I would guess it's kidney failure because her breath is starting to smell like urine. Although, if she has had anything hard to drink recently, that could explain the scent," he answered quietly. "Alcoholism and malnutrition can be other factors to dropsy."

"She is a drinker," Tellie said, and his eyes flicked to her. "And as you can see, we aren't on a rich diet."

"Is it treatable?" Ollie asked with little hope.

"If it was caught sooner, perhaps, but I can't repair a failing organ."

There was a sharp intake of breath from Tellie. "How much time do we have?"

He blinked at her.

"Be honest," Ollie pleaded. "We need the truth."

His eyes hardened. "A month at best, and that's being generous."

Tellie began to weep loudly as Ollie held his stare. Her mother was on the verge of death, and then what? They wouldn't be able to afford the flat. There were no jobs available to women that would cover rent fees. She had barely escaped the day with Avis's help, and it was entirely unrealistic to think she would do so again, even if she offered. The dread finally washed through her body. She would end up on the streets, and Theodore would come for her.

"I'll be back in the morning to check on her," Jackson stated as he stood. It was here that she noticed he was dressed in his best.

Ollie nodded. "Thank you."

He nearly reached the door before saying, "I almost forgot." He reached into his bag to pull out a small note. Her eyes widened in complete surprise as he handed it over.

His cheek lifted when she ripped it from his grasp and read.

Don't give up hope.

Avis

"I don't know how I can ever repay you," she admitted. "The both of you."

He gave her one last smile. "Payment isn't required. We're happy to help."

She gaped at him. Was meeting the Hadley's coincidence or fate?

VI
Jade

"Have we decided on a fashionably late entrance?" Jet bellowed as he entered her room with Blake Emerich trailing behind. Marna was tying her into an elaborate lace ball gown for Queen Elizabeth's masquerade, a distraction from the ghastly murder.

She met her brother's stare morosely. There was no desire to attend, and yet, as in all aspects of her life, she was overruled. Not feeling particularly inclined to participate or act friendly toward a single soul, she nearly begged her father to let her stay.

"You could try and smile for once," he snapped when she refused to play along. "You have such a pleasing face. *Use* it."

She tore her gaze away in irritation. Jet was as sybaritic as they came: from his black velvet jacket and vest, ochre silk shirt and tie, to his cane and top hat. His mask was as metal as hers, sans the clear diamonds.

Ruby was fanning herself near the window, wearing a gold gown and mask.

Jet paused to assess her. "Never let the world see you fall to pieces, ever. No matter how hard it is to breathe. And I'm not talking about your corsets!"

Ruby's head tilted toward him, though she said nothing. She was the least verbose of them all.

Jade couldn't find the words to argue. He knew everything about pain, worse when you considered the severe degree he had been treated by their father.

"I would never give anyone the satisfaction," she growled.

Jet grinned while wrapping an arm around her waist and pulling her from the room when Marna stood back. "Come, dear sister, the citizens of Bel Deaux await our arrival!"

Jade allowed him to escort her out of the manor, forcing both her and Ruby into the cab.

"I don't think I have to tell you to play nice with Teddy," he said once they were seated safely inside. She glanced at him, suspicious of his motives. "Father doesn't want a scene. He was strict in his orders."

"Is he attending?"

"Yes," Jet drawled with a roll of his eyes. "They left over an hour ago. Katerina will make quite the statement in her yellow wig."

Blake chuckled, and the pair began to gossip about the nobles for the entirety of the journey. Jade tore her eyes away and stared out of the window, focusing on the tiny droplets of rain that fell. There was something comforting in a storm that made her feel at home.

A foot nudged her after a few minutes, and she glanced over to Ruby, who had a slight smile on her lips. Jade gave a fake smile in return. The one everyone fell for. Somehow though, it felt as if Ruby saw through her. She was intuitive enough to know when one was being artificial.

Dragon's Keep sat above the city on King's Peak in the heart of Bel Deaux, exceeding the skyscrapers and flats as a beacon of hope in what felt like hell. Often revered for its beauty in a rapidly nondescript world, Jade saw it as another prison. The Queen was known for her lavish balls, wasting the crown's gold on parties rather than her people.

As they rolled around the curve of the expansive drive, Jade exited last and brought up the party's rear. Jet and Blake left them behind to consort with nobles, giving false compliments to anyone who would listen. It wasn't long before Ruby was stopped by her friends, lingering in the foyer to hear their gossip.

Jade ducked out of sight and stepped into the lavish ballroom. The palace was far too crowded and spilled well beyond the French doors that led into the garden. The room was grand and circular and very well-lit. A string quartet entertained red-cheeked and boisterous dancers while laughing dispersed throughout the room.

"I almost gave up hope that you would show," Vaeden Sullivan drawled as she sidled up with a glass of champagne in her hand. She wore a white powdered wig that stood a foot tall with pink feathers poking out of its top. Her gown was also white and ruffled, as was her mask.

Jade grinned as she said, "I was dragged here kicking and screaming."

"Of course you were," Vaeden chuckled and sipped on her bubbly.

"How spectacular is this?" Adelaide Atwood gushed while knocking into Jade and grabbing onto her arm. Vaeden's eyes narrowed at the intrusion.

Many of the Highborn's hadn't taken a liking to the Atwoods and still considered them as paupers, although marrying into the Calvert family forced the court to pay attention. This masquerade was the first of many, as they were now regarded worthy enough to attend. It must be exhilarating to finally step into a world that was always out of reach, but if they honestly saw the nobles for what they were, perhaps the Atwoods would've held onto the life they once had.

"Oh my gosh!" Adelaide yelled with a point of her finger. "There is Dominic Kane!"

Several females surrounded Mr. Kane as he undoubtedly boasted about something irrelevant. He was too much of a vagrant and a deviant to hold any sort of affection for—a real cad. Jade grimaced in resentment at the thought. It was a distressing thought to have given in to him, and she wished she could take it all back. He didn't value a damn thing in life, nor did he deserve to know her in such an intimate way. His sexual depravity was widely known throughout the city, yet it didn't matter. He was the bastard son of the Queen, the only reason his behavior was even tolerated.

"I cannot believe he's here!"

"As the Queen's son," Vaeden retorted with little interest. "Why wouldn't he attend her ball?"

Adelaide gave her a nasty look and pulled on Jade's arm. "Let's go talk to him!"

Jade sighed in disgust; that sounded like her worst idea yet. "I would rather watch the grass grow!"

Vaeden burst out laughing, while Adelaide instantly dropped her hand with a fold of her arms. "You know very well, as a newcomer, I can't waltz up to royalty and address them without an introduction. Why can't you do that for me?"

"He's not someone you want to associate with!" Vaeden stated, trying to deflect any attention off Jade, but the damage was already done.

When Jade caught Theodore's eye, he seemed satisfied with her current company and followed Edward Wright into the smoking parlor.

She could see Adelaide's head tilt out of the corner of her eye, perhaps for more judgment, an action of the masses that was hard to avoid. She circumvented their intrusive stares and took a sip of her champagne instead. Everyone knew about her fall from grace, but it wasn't much of a concern, not anymore. The months after her mother's death were immobilizing, and she needed an escape to feel alive. Falling into Dominic's bed wasn't out of love. It drowned out the heavy burden of grief and the sting of submerging loneliness. When her life spun rapidly out of control, and she needed something tangible to hold onto.

Dominic kept his braggart mouth shut for once, but Pearl and her husband Augustus, hadn't. The family was supposed to be in the country for the weekend, and as Jade blamed the female anatomy for getting out of the excursion, she was left alone. Yet, for whatever reason, Pearl stopped to check in on her and proceeded to run straight to their father after finding them in bed. Augustus didn't help matters. He held no loyalty for either herself or Dominic, running his mouth to all the affluent sons of the Elite.

The city knew of her carnal sin, painting another black mark on the family, but her father ensured it would never happen again. This was the first ball she was allowed to attend since the misconduct, all due to Theodore. He became obsessively violent over the matter though he couldn't touch Dominic and she feared the moment he would turn his wrath in her direction.

"You don't want to be one of his victims," Jade interjected when she caught Dominic's stare. "Your fall from grace will be public and irreversible."

"It didn't affect you," Adelaide hissed.

Jade tore her eyes away from the one face she used to find appealing and peered at her. "Is that what you think?"

Adelaide flashed a look of dubiety, almost as if she would rather find out for herself. However, she didn't press on Kane, even though she continued to stare at him until Jonathan Roberts asked to dance; she accepted with little eagerness. Jade presumed Jonathan wasn't the man she wanted, though there wasn't enough leverage to turn anyone away just yet.

"How long is this going to last?" Vaeden demanded with petulance.

"Until she's married to Theodore, I suppose."

"You're not going to give up on that outcome, are you?" Vaeden said with another chuckle.

"Hardly," Jade scoffed. "They already feed the dumb glutton. With any luck, she'll end up pregnant."

Vaeden blinked at her. "Your mouth never ceases to amaze me."

She tried to hold back a grin.

"Ah, Miss Calvert!" A ruddy voice rumbled in her ear.

A chill of disgust swept through her limbs as both she and Vaeden turned to the red-faced Mr. Landsberry. He was a weedy older man with oily hair and yellowing teeth, and much to Jade's displeasure, he seemed to have a soft spot for her.

He licked at his rotten teeth. "I was hoping for a dance."

She swallowed the bile that began to rise. "I need to find Theodore!"

"I want a dance!" he demanded and clutched onto her arm.

She ripped her arm away. "I'm not sure he will allow it! He's a very jealous man, you know."

"He doesn't give a damn!"

"Well, I do!" She snapped. "I said no!"

He took another step forward. "I won't take no for an answer!"

Jade grabbed Vaeden's hand and blurted the first thing that came to mind. "I need to relieve myself!"

He blinked at her brash words, clearly taken aback, and they bolted from his presence.

"I want a dance before the night is through!" He yelled at her back, but it only caused them to laugh harder.

It continued that way for the better part of an hour. She was starting to lose hope that anything memorable was going to happen. Every time she tried to flee the ballroom, her friends pulled her back, wanting to gossip about Theodore. All she desired was to go home, alone, where she wouldn't be bothered.

It wasn't until Mr. Landsberry was nearing a second time that she slipped away and hid behind some plants between the ballroom and parlor. He quickly lost track of her and headed in the opposite direction.

She turned from behind the plant and walked straight into a broad chest as he tried to step into the ballroom. The contact pulsed throughout her chest and shocked her to her very core. Her eyes raised to a pale man who was entirely too tall. There was a faint bruise under his right eye and a cut across his nose, but his square jaw and prominent Adam's apple were more distracting than his injuries. She gaped at him with a mix of fear and admiration.

He wasn't wearing a mask, and his sharp gaze watched her openly without a sense of propriety. His eyes quickly moved between hers, the way everyone's had when they spotted the difference. Yet, it didn't feel as harassing as it usually would. It was exhilarating that he didn't have the decency to look away. She had never been so agreeably devoured by one look alone. His black hair was slicked back with pomade, uncovering a jagged scar that ran down the length of his left brow, and disappeared into his hairline. She didn't find it repulsive, however, it enhanced his face somehow.

"Excuse me," she said after finding her voice.

His eyes flicked to the plant and back to her. "What are you doing behind there?" his timbre of voice was low and demanding, sending goosebumps down her arms. She felt heat creep up her neck and face, and his eyes dipped to her flushed cheeks. His stare made her feel extremely nervous, an emotion she was fairly unfamiliar with.

"I'm hiding from Mr. Landsberry," she admitted quietly.

He blinked in surprise before laughing loudly, and her eyes widened at the sound. His laugh was rich and inviting, making her want to join in. She frowned when she caught herself inching toward him, which was a most surprising gesture. She had no intention of being friendly with anyone.

"Well," he said after regaining composure. "He is quite frightening."

"You laugh," she growled, wiping the grin from his face. "But the old fool isn't trying to dance with you!"

His eyes lit with amusement. "Could you imagine the scandal if he was?"

She grinned despite herself.

"What is your name?" he asked softly, and his piercing gaze had yet to look away, causing her to feel naked, exposed. The tenebrosity of his eyes differed from anyone she had ever met. It was as if he was made from something ethereal, unattainable, and out of reach.

She tore her gaze away and focused on the dancers in the center of the room. She briefly contemplated on giving a false name because she didn't want to be Jade Calvert anymore. Yet, for the oddest reason, she wanted him to know.

She glanced back up and said, "Jade Calvert."

"It is a pleasure to meet you, Miss Calvert. My name is Jackson Hadley." When he reached for her hand, the contact pulsed between them and heat shot up her arm. She yelped loudly, but it was more out of surprise than actual pain. He instantly let go.

She took a step back in embarrassment. "I'm sorry."

He gaped at her, and she stared right back. She continued to flush and wished it would stop; it was embarrassing enough. He didn't need to know how much he had affected her. The sudden urge to flee came to mind because it was evident his touch and presence had a pertinent effect on every fiber of her being.

Still, she couldn't find it within her to look away just yet.

"What was that?" he asked with a touch of uncertainty and bewilderment. And yet, there was a trace of understanding in his eyes, almost as if he already knew the answer to his question.

She ignored her suspicions and whispered, "I don't know."

His brows knit in further concentration while rubbing his hand.

She ignored the warning in her mind and eagerly skimmed over every inch of his staggering face. He was easily the most striking man she had ever laid eyes upon, but not in the traditional sense. It went far beyond being visually attractive; she could feel it profoundly within his stare. It beat loudly in her chest and caused a pull in her stomach, which was magnetic, and she had to resist the urge to take a step toward him.

He searched her face for an answer.

She licked her lips and his eyes followed. "I apologize. I suppose you caught me off guard."

His stare raised to meet her gaze without a response, leaving her uneasy. She prayed he would never figure her out.

"There you are!" A man around the same height as Jackson announced loudly. He also wasn't wearing a mask and had a rather annoyed expression written upon his winsome face. "I've been looking for you every-" he stopped short by the mere sight of her, and his eyes doubled in size as he finished his sentence, "where."

Jackson exhaled loudly with a roll of his eyes and gestured to the other. His tone flattened as he said, "Miss Calvert, this is my brother Elijah. Elijah, meet Jade Calvert."

For some peculiar reason, Elijah gave his brother a suspicious stare.

"Hello," she said quietly as her eyes flicked between the two.

Elijah nodded at her curtly and said, "Miss Calvert," before turning to his brother. "I don't know how much longer I can take this party! Every unwed girl in the city is hunting for a husband, and for whatever reason, they seem to think I'm up for the job! Mary Bishop just pinched my ass, and Sarah Cavendish will not give up on a dance!"

Jackson's head fell back with a deep belly laugh, and Jade's lips rose in wonder once again.

Elijah's gaze turned murderous, and he clenched his jaw. "Not everyone wants to marry!" It was evident he didn't find the situation amusing, looking thoroughly annoyed and undeniably uncomfortable.

"Oh, I quite agree," she concurred, causing his face to relax slightly. "If I had my way, I wouldn't marry at all, but my father is most insistent and thinks he can dictate my life!" She quickly shut her mouth, her gaze turning fearful. What possessed her to admit her most genuine feelings to complete strangers?

"My apologies," she said hastily. "I have trouble holding my tongue. It has more often than not gotten me into trouble."

"It's how I like them!" Elijah grinned with his admission.

Jackson threw a sharp glare in his direction.

"You deserve better than Teddy anyway," Elijah elaborated, and her face smoothed. He knew exactly who she was…even with a silly mask. Did Jackson know and only pretended out of courtesy?

"Eli," Jackson warned.

He glanced at him with wide eyes. "You can't deny it!"

"Elijah!" Jackson yelled harshly.

He threw up his hands in surrender.

Her eyes narrowed at Jackson, but he refused to meet her gaze.

"I cannot believe Owen ditched us for this."

Her eyes widened suddenly, and she whispered, "Hadley." They both looked at her. "You are Owen Hadleys kin?" She had been so caught up in the draw of Jackson himself that she completely dismissed his name and felt rather idiotic for doing so.

"We are," Elijah answered when Jackson didn't.

"You're the surgeon?" she exclaimed loudly.

A sly smile formed on Jackson's mouth. "The very one."

Excitement filled her, and she clutched his arm. The touch vibrated through her palm and tingled down to her fingertips. "You examined the slain woman found at the Abbey?"

He frowned at her hand, or perhaps it was the sudden enthusiasm for murder, and muttered, "I did."

She glanced down at her hand; the veins on the surface were slowly beginning to glow a faint orange, like the embers of a flame. She instantly pulled back in fear. "I'm sorry."

Elijah and Jackson shared a look, but their faces were very controlled. She couldn't be sure what they were thinking, though she hoped neither had noticed the spark in her touch. She was unable to control how she felt at any given time; every emotion was written plainly across her face and body.

She closed her mouth and observed Elijah. She'd heard all the stories, of course. His reputation had far preceded him, and if what had been said was true, he was a real skirt chaser and boozehound.

She was unsure of Jackson. She didn't know much of who he was, except that he fought in the Vaults as a youth and now worked as a surgeon who generally overlooked the dead. Their eldest brother Owen was a detective and had spoken to her a few times before that, but she couldn't recall much of what he asked, given the circumstances. They also had a sister named Avis, who was seeing Micha Wellington, though Jade was sure none of her brothers knew about the affair as he swore her to secrecy. The youngest was James, he was around Ruby's age, but she didn't know anything about him other than his name. They also happened to be Dominic Kane's cousins, a disappointing fact.

Their mother was the sister of the Queen, but they certainly didn't act like royalty. Her father was amazed how none of them wanted her privileges, allowing the Elite to uphold what Queen Elizabeth refused to do. This was something Jade could understand; she didn't want an ounce of her father's legacy either.

"You don't care to dance?" Elijah asked lightly.

"I like dancing just fine," she said. "I only wanted to avoid Mr. Landsberry."

Jackson smiled then, and it was the kind that reached his eyes. It transformed his face, which was unmistakably elysian. He had a dimple just below his lips, a distinguishing mark that only appeared when he smiled. She resisted the temptation to reach up and touch it.

"I read your piece in the paper," she told Elijah, even though her attention was still on his brother. "It was compelling."

Jackson's eyebrows raised, and she let out an uneasy breath. A warmth spread into her chest uncomfortably, and her heart began to beat wildly in its cage. What an unsettling feeling. What was this?

"Oh?" Elijah said. "How so?"

She ignored him. Her fixation with Jackson was too distracting. He held her attention effortlessly, and it was almost embarrassing. *Almost.* She'd never been so drawn to a single person in her life, and if she had known Jackson Hadley existed, she would have gone in search of him long ago.

She instantly craved to see his smile again, but her mind was blank. It was evident he was an intense person and this was an interesting facet. Did he smile often, or was it a rare trait she briefly brought out in him?

Elijah coughed loudly.

Her gaze snapped to him, "Um... what- what did you say?"

Elijah's eyes widened, and he glanced at his brother.

Jackson blinked and continued to observe her with zeal. It was utterly inviting and beginning to feel far too suffocating. She needed to get away from them. Nerves twisted in the pit of her stomach, causing frissons of static to erupt in her palms.

She tore her eyes from his face and muttered, "Excuse me, I have to…" before practically running away from the Hadley brothers.

Of all the times she teased Pearl and Ruby, and here she was acting the same! How infuriating to forget yourself over one foolish face!

She ran through the French doors and into the courtyard, withdrawing as far from the crowd as possible. When the darkness enveloped her, and she was out of sight, she sagged against a pillar and ripped the mask off her face. She placed a hand on her chest and breathed out heavily. The cold air was refreshing and cooled her overheated cheeks. Each collective breath slowly began to quiet the thrum in her chest. Her hands tingled sharply and the emotions flowing through her body were immense and nauseating. A panic attack hovered.

"Calm down," she whispered. "And breathe."

She slowly opened her eyes and stared up at the moon, which was large and bright. A thousand stars littered the sky, giving hope to all the perils of life. As she stared up in wonderment, she knew it was him. Even with her attraction to Dominic Kane and his easy words coercing her into explicit actions, those feelings paled compared to what was thriving inside of her now.

Half of her wanted to keep him at a great distance, while the other half wanted to inch a little closer, but it could never be. If her father ever found out, Jackson's very life would be at risk. Not to mention what Theodore would do.

It was a dangerous attraction, and his touch sparked the hidden magic within her. Which only meant, if she wanted to avoid detection, she needed to steer clear of Jackson Hadley completely.

VII
Ruby

Ruby stood beside Diana Atwood as she gloated about her recent engagement to Peter Cavendish. A gaggle of women surrounded with peaked ears and bellies full of champagne; the chits giggled as she gave them every sordid and juicy detail of the pairing. Ruby held onto her glass of champagne with dainty fingers and a strong urge to throw the contents in Diana's face. The animosity boiling in her belly was a surprise when she thought too much of it, for Ruby had always been a docile and proprietress young lady. She was never one for rebellion and unruly behavior. Those characteristics were saved for Jade, who never had trouble speaking her mind or ignoring orders entirely.

Whatever thoughts were brewing in her mind, however, she never showed. Her lips curved upward with fake warmth and admiration. She raised her glass as a toast and brought the chute to her lips, the bubbles hit her tongue, and she sucked them down in haste.

While wallowing in her own misery, she had nearly forgotten the evil that stalked her soul. One guest went unnoticed by the entire crowd, a woman who had tragically been murdered that very morning. Ruby glanced slowly to her right, and Helena Wimple stared right back at her.

"It isn't over, Ruby," Helena said between Diana's obnoxious story. Ruby's cup paused in midair. No one surrounding her noticed a dead woman in their presence, they were far too absorbed in Diana's story. "Blood only satiates his hunger for brief periods. Precious hours are wasting!" A tremor of fear swept through Ruby's body. What had she done to be stalked by death?

And aside from knowing her killer wanted her blood, a blood drinker as she called him, Helena knew nothing else. Nothing Ruby could go to the police about.

Diana grabbed Ruby's delicate wrist and pulled her attention away from Helena, laughing as she whispered of Mr. Cavendish's soft kisses and improper touch when no one was watching. Ruby closed her eyes and clenched her jaw to hold back tears. It was all too much, both the dead woman and Diana. It wasn't fair that something so unnatural happened to her, nor the rejection of the man she thought to marry. And while the mask was a nice distraction, it didn't take long for her to be reminded of the truth.

Mr. Cavendish had been something of an infatuation for Ruby. He was someone she had secretly longed for in her mind but had never spoken of her desires aloud to anyone. She was hopeful, of course, that he may find the same passion in her that she had seen in him. That he desperately craved for her touch as much as she did for his. It became apparent, however, that Ruby was the victim of unrequited love when he asked for Diana's hand in marriage and not her own. She felt sick to her stomach, knowing that he would find himself naked on top of Diana in a few weeks.

So here she stood with a fixed smile next to her friend, who gave away the secrets of Peter's intimate nature. Ruby's wide eyes shifted to Jet. He stood in the far corner of the room with Blake Emerich, whispering rapidly as his friend silently watched on with intent. She wished to be a part of her brother's conversation more than the one she was currently listening to.

She glanced further around the room and spotted Pearl, a sister who went to great lengths to separate herself from the family and attached herself to her husband's kin instead. Pearl stood beside Augustus and their sister Esmeralda. They were laughing and looked rather beautiful while doing so. Ruby suddenly felt inadequate while looking at her siblings.

Jet and Esmeralda's hair was nearly as dark as Jade's, but their eyes were entirely different shades from one another. Esmeralda's irises were so indistinct that they appeared black, while Jet's were a striking shade of blue, a trait he received from their father. Pearl's hair was dramatically lighter than the other three. Where they favored inky hues, her hair and eyes were the color of chestnuts, although she had the same pale complexion as the rest.

Freckles sprinkled Esmeralda's nose and cheeks, but it was nothing compared to Ruby herself and even further from Jet, Pearl, and Jade. Their faces were entirely spot-free. Pearl and Esmeralda were tall and spindly, both appearing undernourished and somewhat frail, but they were far from unfed. Jet was the tallest, Jade was the shortest, and Ruby fell somewhere in between, but where Jade was shapely and feminine, Ruby was firm and angular.

There was an instant rebuttal in Esmeralda's attitude toward Augustus while Pearl watched him with adulation. And yet, it was almost too picturesque. It was as if Pearl was projecting a perfect life instead of living one. And while it was hard to miss, her chin turned indifferently when he tried to kiss her, a rather strange reaction. Shouldn't she crave her husband's kisses?

Now that Ruby noticed, Pearl's concealment was quite evident. She angled herself away from Augustus, standing close enough to appear as if she were entirely enthralled though far enough away to imply disdain. There was nothing captivated by her demeanor, and Ruby suddenly felt sorry for her.

Jade was nowhere to be seen. She must have snuck away as she always had. If Ruby were more intelligent, she would have followed Jade instead of her friends. They did nothing to distract her heartbreak, and Helena still hovered.

She sighed loudly before finishing her bubbly and shook her empty glass for another. Everything about Diana was starting to grate on Ruby's nerves for no reason other than pure jealousy. Diana's sultry voice was thick with lust and jabs of heartbreak. It made Ruby want to scream at the top of her lungs so she could never hear the words again. It was bad enough that Diana's eldest sister, Katerina, had recently married her father, and Marian claimed Jet. Now Diana was taking away the only man that filled her life with any hint of joy, regardless of whether he knew it.

Ruby glanced at her friend, trying not to let any of her bitterness show with all her concentration. She knew her rising hatred was unjustified. She couldn't even find herself annoyed with Mr. Cavendish for finding Diana lovely. Diana recently came into her life, and it didn't take long to become envious of her looks.

Diana's porcelain face held a uniqueness that men found desirable. Her mouth was small and slightly crooked, causing a certain deviousness when she smiled. She had a sharp upturned nose and oval-shaped eyes that were the desired blue men hungered for. She was often outspoken and witty, something Ruby had trouble with when a man was near, particularly one Peter Cavendish.

Diana sighed with eagerness, her cheeks flushed, and a smile bloomed on her lips when she found her fiancée from across the room. "What is the most interesting insight into our courtship? I had never actually thought much of him until the night of Ivanhoe."

Ruby ripped a glass of champagne from the butler's tray and tossed back a mouthful.

"He was talking to my dear Ruby here when I approached," Diana continued, oblivious to her friend's discomfort. "And as our eyes met, I knew in an instant that I would marry him."

Ruby watched Diana laugh with her sister Marian. She quickly lost her smile as the depression began to hover. It was an ugly feeling that made everything Ruby deem as useless. There was no connection with anyone, just a cloud of despair sitting in the pit of her belly and chest, never allowing her to feel any joy or interest.

She wished she could run free with nothing but the wind on her cheeks. Without any of the entrapments that held her in these moments. It was that alone that made her demons fall silent. She sipped her champagne and smiled at the women beside her, never once admitting the pain she harbored inside.

Ruby could hardly walk in a straight line when the party was nearing its end, stumbling over her skirts and slurring her words. She was less the vision of a Calvert daughter and more of an ill-reformed girl who couldn't hold her liquor.

"How much have you had to drink?" Esmeralda hissed in her ear.

Ruby's head was spinning so terribly that the contents of her belly threatened to unleash onto the floor. "Mmm..not...Schuur."

Esmeralda sighed loudly, but she did not scold her younger sister as expected. "Come with me. You can stay the night."

Ruby leaned into Esmeralda as she led her out of Dragon's Keep.

A deep voice she wished to forget, demanded, "What's wrong with Ruby?"

"Nothing," Esmeralda answered hastily. "It was a lovely party, was it not?"

Ruby could not open her eyes as she allowed Esmeralda to steer her toward a carriage. The gravel crunched under their feet, causing Ruby to wobble in her shoes.

"Here, allow me to help," Peter offered and ignored Esmeralda's niceties.

He placed a strong arm around her waist and pulled her toward him.

"Really!" Esmeralda squealed. "I appreciate your concern, but I don't need an audience! I am trying to get her out of here without her reputation in shambles!"

"Her reputation is intact," he grunted. "No one noticed her with Diana around."

"What is going on?" Jade demanded as she came around the bend. Her face hardened at the sight of Peter, and she yelled, "What is he doing with Ruby?"

"How dare you!" Esmeralda snarled, ignoring Jade. She grabbed onto her skirt and nearly ran to keep up with his long strides. "First, you mock her devotion by asking for her best friend's hand, and now you mock her beauty. I suppose she is better off without you!"

Peter placed Ruby into a cab and rounded on Esmeralda. "I had no choice in the matter!"

Esmeralda blinked impartially and crossed her arms.

Jade stopped beside her and said, "Of course you had a choice. You're a man!"

Peter's face fell as he stared out into the night. He placed his hands in his pockets and said, "I had no choice in this."

"You can spew your lies elsewhere," Jade objected with a sneer. "And I'm only telling you this once, never seek out Ruby again, or there will be severe consequences your father won't be able to save you from. Do you understand?"

Peter merely stared at Jade. It was as if he had a threat hanging on the tip of his tongue, but he must have forgotten to whom he was speaking because Esmeralda growled, "Do you understand what my sister is saying to you, Mr. Cavendish?"

Peter's glare dropped, and he nodded once. "I understand."

"Good," Jade said and stepped into the cab without a backward glance.

"Thank you for the assistance," Esmeralda told him coolly. "Good evening, Mr. Cavendish."

He didn't respond as she slammed the door shut behind them, and when the carriage rolled forward, Ruby fell over. Jade and Esmeralda pulled her onto the bench.

"Here, lay your head on my lap," she offered and helped her adjust.

The cab was silent before Ruby's sobs began to interrupt the space. Jade stared out of the window, providing nothing for once.

"Shhh..." Esmeralda soothed while stroking her hair.

"How am I to ever get over this?" Ruby wailed.

Esmeralda bit her cheek and glanced at Jade, who continued to gaze out of the window without a word. Unable to give a satisfying answer, she remained silent.

Love and heartache were useless feelings that Ruby could not explain or make sense of. She continued to cry as Esmeralda stroked her hair. If nothing else, it was a nice gesture of comfort from a sister she rarely connected with.

"Ruby," came a whisper from the darkness. Her eyes flung open with a wince. The excess champagne from the ball tore her head in two, and she groaned, settling deeper into the bed.

"Ruby," someone called again. She opened her eyes, unsure if she heard an actual voice or not. She blinked the exhaustion away, staring out of the French doors Esmeralda left open. It was raining and the sound quickly began to lull her to sleep.

"Come to me, Ruby," came another whisper. This time, she jumped up. "Free me from this eternal punishment."

She glanced around the room, ignoring the pounding in her head. Helena was nowhere in sight, an instant relief to her mental capacity.

She nearly fell back against the pillows when movement caught her eye. Her ill-considered wishful thinking gave her a false sense of comfort, and she expected the slain prostitute to appear. Yet, Helena was not the one to emerge from the shadows; a statuesque man approached the bed. The complex left her limbs confined as she stared wide-eyed. A strangled cry nearly escaped when fear seized hold of her vocal cords, rendering her silent.

He had black hair, red eyes, and a provocative grin. "Free me, Ruby, and you'll never be alone again."

She pulled the covers over her chest, clenching her shaking hands into fists. Her stomach dropped, the hairs on her neck rising with fear.

His grin deepened. "You can trust me."

This was an obvious lie. His eyes were incredibly portentous, something that disrupted the calmness in her soul. When he took another step toward her, the flesh on his cheek slowly began to rot and disintegrate. His teeth clearly visible through the gaping cavity on the side of his face. This time, her scream tore into the stillness of the night…

Her eyes opened with a shake of her shoulders. Jade and Esmeralda were standing over her, rousing her from sleep. Had she been dreaming? She couldn't have been, his presence felt all too real. The pneumatophany left her heart beating emphatically as fear settled deep within the pit of her stomach. She was left tongue-tied, drenched in sweat, and unadulterated fear.

She was unable to find her voice while Esmeralda relentlessly demanded for answers. The only function she could manage was a trembling finger toward the balcony.

Jade's personal guard, Adam, charged through the doors at once, causing her to flinch at his overbearing presence.

"It was just a bad dream," Esmeralda assured as she sat down on the bed, wiping at her heavily saturated brow.

Although it wasn't, her palms were full of static electricity. The same current that erupted whenever Helena or any other dead being found her.

The man was real. He was here, standing over her and peering into her very soul. But even if he was a figment of her imagination, the demon would ever be imprinted into her mind.

"There isn't anyone on the balcony, Miss Calvert," Adam said as he stepped back into the room. There was no solace in his words. Tears immediately fell down her cheeks, and she could barely breathe. Some devil wanted her to release him. She could sense it as she had with all things that were dead, another rotting mass to torment the very existence she held onto. Her eyes swept the room but Helena was still absent.

"You better check the property, just in case."

Esmeralda's words barely registered. Where had the deceased woman gone? Adam left without another word, but it didn't matter. Ruby couldn't shake the baleful feeling, threatening to pull her under.

VIII
Jet

"I think it's time we discuss Ruby," came the supercilious voice of Jet Calvert. He sat across from his father in the study on the ground floor, notepad, and quill in hand. With the previous months ailing his health, William was given the grave news everyone feared: consumption. With his worst trepidations confirmed, he begrudgingly began to instruct his ungrateful heir.

"What about her?" Mr. Calvert's muffled voice carried over. Brass telescope binoculars covered his eyes so that he may see as he wrote. His attention stayed on his ledger.

"Well, as you know, Charles Southerland is coming for a visit at the end of the month," Jet stated as if it were only so obvious.

"You have spoken of nothing else. How could I forget?" Mr. Calvert muttered. "And what does that have to do with Ruby?"

Jet blanched with his father's dismissive refusal to meet his gaze. "I don't want her to mope around and affect Charles negatively. He is a well-respected gentleman who shall not be left with an ill taste in his mouth of our family!"

Mr. Calvert's gaze flicked up to his son briefly in annoyance. "And you fear Ruby would be the one to leave that taste, do you?"

"Given her lack of social grace," Jet drawled. "And lack of proposals that support my statement."

"She is seventeen. There is plenty of time for marriage."

Jet snorted. "Not anyone from Bel Deaux, I can promise you that!"

Mr. Calvert pushed his binoculars onto his forehead to reveal a widened blue gaze. He set his quill down. "Oh?"

"Come, father," Jet said with a roll of his eyes. "She isn't the comeliest girl in town. You cannot deny her paucity of appeal compared to Jade, Esmeralda, or even Pearl!"

"Ruby's features are adequate enough. A pretty face does not bargain a good marriage. They are secured with money, and she will make a fine wife indeed," he said dismissively and grabbed his quill.

"One would hope she'd fare better than Esmeralda, and we all know Jade is a lost cause entirely!"

Mr. Calvert slammed his fist against the desk and yelled, "Enough!"

His jaw snapped shut, eyes narrowing.

"You are incredibly judgmental for someone with your *interests*."

Jet's jaw dropped, his heart picking up speed. There was no way he knew about Blake. They were careful.

"It matters not; I will be gone soon enough, and I won't be here to protect them from you," Mr. Calvert dropped his quill and rubbed his temple. Jet frowned at the accusation. "Ruby will leave by the end of the month to live with Esmeralda."

Jet's face went blank. "You intend to send Ruby to live with Esmeralda, who is barely widowed?"

Mr. Calvert leveled Jet's gaze. "Yes, I do. As will Jade until she's married."

"Esmeralda is in no condition to look after Ruby!" Jet cried in derision. "Let alone Jade, who flouts all authority! Running that mouth of hers as if she is some common, uneducated girl!"

"I disagree. I think Esmeralda needs her sisters now more than ever."

Jet sat back in his seat and shook his head in anger.

"What are you so upset about?" Mr. Calvert snapped. "They won't be in your way, and I will rest easy knowing they will be in good care and not a nunnery or asylum as you've so callously mentioned."

Jet pressed his lips together.

"And while we're on the subject, I refuse death, knowing my line will end with you! I have spent my entire life building an empire and high-class status that you've heedlessly taken advantage of. You *flout* the law and trash my name and reputation by acting like a petty thief and criminal! You've scammed far too many poor and innocent people by taking the little money they have to feed their own families!"

Jet sat up. His face was flushed as he said, "Now, father-"

"I'm speaking, goddammit, you will listen!" William yelled, and Jet shrank into his seat. "You will stop acting like a low-class piece of trash and help the community you've stolen from by giving your time and allowance back to them! You will cease all contact with Blake Emerich, or so help me, I will send you to Vendekk to live the rest of your days. You will stop insulting your wife and consummate your marriage once and for all!" Jet began shaking his head, but Mr. Calvert ignored him and gruffly continued, "And you will fuck her every night until she is carrying your child!"

Jet's eyes widened. "But father-"

"But nothing!" He growled. "If you don't comply with my wishes, I will assign Esmeralda to head of estate, and you will no longer receive a dime of your inheritance! Then you can live out on the streets since you have never once acted like the noble you are! I have yet to ink your name in my will, Jet; don't give me any more reason never to do so!"

"You wouldn't dare!"

Untouched by his son's discomfort, he smirked. "I don't make idle threats."

Jet swallowed.

"And lastly, you will stop speaking ill of your sisters. If I ever hear you speak so poorly about our family again, you will be cut off entirely, even when I am gone. You will leave them be, or you will not see an ounce of your inheritance!"

Jet nodded slowly with a wry smile.

"Don't smirk at me as if once I'm gone, it won't matter. You have a lot to prove before anything is given to you, and that is in writing!"

"I can prove anything you ask of me!" Jet countered, undeterred.

Mr. Calvert appeared unconvinced. "You seem to forget that Katerina is with child."

Jet's nostrils flared.

"If she gives me the son I've always longed for," Calvert growled harshly, "Then he will be head of my estate."

Words failed him.

"Now get out!"

Jet coughed uneasily and shut his notepad. He stood awkwardly and slowly walked toward the door, hoping his father would call him back and apologize. It never came, however, and he stumbled into the hallway.

Jet stared incredulously back at the study door once shut. He had wildly lost control of everything within minutes.

There was no way in hell he was going to allow Esmeralda the estate over himself or some bastard child he impregnated the eldest Atwood girl with. He'd been so careful all these years, yet his father had missed nothing. He'd have to be more discreet and lay low until his father's demise.

Jet's gaze flicked up to the stairwell when he got the prickling sensation of being watched; it was Jade. He snapped his teeth together to keep from shouting at her. The hatred reflected on her face matched his own. It was good to know the feeling was mutual. He turned quickly and slammed the door as he left the Calvert manor behind.

"I thought you didn't like Jade," Blake said.

Jet glanced up from his glass of whiskey. "I don't.

"Then what's the hesitation?"

He settled in his chair and glanced around the room. "Because she's my blood, and I don't know what Teddy intends to do."

"Do you honestly believe he would hurt her?"

"Yes, especially once my father is gone."

Blake leaned in closer, and Jet's eyes dropped to his lips. "But wouldn't she be able to stop him?"

"That's what frightens me," he hissed, "What if she ends up being more powerful than the whole lot of us put together? I tell you, there is something positively terrifying about that girl!"

"Even more so than Esmeralda?" Blake questioned with a raise of his brow. "You don't even know what Jade is fully capable of!"

"That's my whole point!" Jet growled.

Blake pursed his lips, clearly unsatisfied. It was hard to explain how he could delve into their minds and ferret out their secrets, even those never meant to be heard. And while Esmeralda could destroy them all with a flick of her wrist by bringing the sky down upon them, there was just as much possibility with Jade. He feared she had complete power over the mind, which was a terrifying prospect. Thank God she was so downtrodden.

Blake focused on someone in the center of the room, his scowl evident. "What is Augustus Atwood up to?"

"Who cares?" He drawled with a sip of his whiskey.

"Roslyn said he's been stalking some of the girls from the Dollhouse."

Jet lowered his glass. "In what context?"

"Is there a difference when it comes to being a creep?"

Jet's eyes slid to Augustus's back. "Yes."

Blake sighed and ran a hand through his hair. "Well, I don't know how deep his perversion lies, but Roslyn swore he's followed her home. Even Elizabeth has said he peers through her window time and again."

Jet gazed back at Augustus sharply. He never liked the bloke. His father forced the marriage between his sister and Augustus, and he was surprised she was so compliant. Pearl may have been proper, but she was not demure as Ruby was. She never failed to speak her mind, though people usually blamed Jade for being direct. They just didn't pay attention because Pearl used her words well.

"She wouldn't allow a killer to walk free just to save her reputation," Jet said.

Blake gave him a doubtful look.

"I'm more despicable than she is, and even I wouldn't do that!"

"She's far more ambitious than you!"

Jet rolled his eyes. "That's not true. If she were ambitious, she wouldn't have married Augustus Atwood and would've chosen someone far more prevalent. Then again, she wasn't given the option to choose her suitor, just like I never was."

Blake gave him a sly smile; his green eyes crinkled at the sides. It occurred to Jet that he should speak of his affections aloud, but he was interrupted by Teddy and Edward, who loudly entered the bar with a pair of doxies on their arms. One of them happened to be Blake's younger sister, Roslyn. Blake's smile fell, and Jet grimaced as they plopped down at their table.

"Good evening, gentlemen!" Edward bellowed. His eyes were bloodshot, and his cheeks were red. He had been drinking quite heavily, by the looks of it.

Neither Jet nor Blake said a word.

"A little birdy told me you are going to be a big brother and that your father is going to sign the estate over to the child if it's a boy," Teddy said, placing a stogie in his mouth and striking a match. Slowly, Jet's face fell as Teddy's black eyes raised to meet his; there was a smug smile on his lips. "Tell me, how does it feel to have fucked up so poorly as a son that your father would rather give his money to a baby?"

The bile in his stomach turned and soared upwards; he instantly swallowed the vile substance and clenched his hand into a fist. Katerina thought she would take over the Calvert assets, did she? Well, not if he could help it. And to hell with Teddy. He wouldn't even bother with the son-of-a-bitch if he wasn't an affluent son. Jet was merely biding his time until his father died, and when he took over the estate, things would change, but it wouldn't go according to plan now. Teddy was here to blackmail him for something, and he could take a wild guess and say it had to do with Jade, a maddening obsession.

"Am I wrong?" Teddy inquired as Edward laughed like the idiot he was.

Jet's lips curled. These mother fucking dregs of society were testing his patience. He suddenly yearned to use his power to put them in their places once and for all. "I can make your life a living hell if you don't watch yourself."

Teddy grinned. "What could you possibly do?"

Blake squeezed his leg from under the table, knowing where his mind had wandered.

"Cat got your tongue?" Teddy pressed with a raise of his eyebrow.

"What do you want, Teddy?"

He chuckled and glanced at Edward, who said, "You're far too sensitive Jet. You need to try and calm down for once. Or maybe you're continuously upset because Blake is not holding up his end of the bargain!"

The table erupted with laughter as Blake retrieved his knife from his pocket and jerked Edward out of his seat, placing the tip of his blade into the base of his neck. The good humor evaporated quickly.

Edward's eyes bulged as he held up his hands. "It was a joke!"

Blake pressed into his neck a little harder, enough for Edward to still. "Am I laughing?"

Jet grinned. Teddy and Edward seemed to think they ran the operation; how very wrong they were. Neither one respected Jet nor Blake because of their relationship, which was considered indecent, but with Blake's blade pressed into the hollow of Edward's neck, he didn't appear so confident. He looked as if he were about to piss himself.

Blake growled. "How dainty do I seem to you now?"

"I never said that!" Edward wailed.

"You've said a lot worse," Blake hissed. "Now, tell Jet what you want, or I'll slip this knife into your windpipe!"

Edward whimpered and glanced at Teddy. "Help me!"

"You wouldn't dare," Teddy challenged. "There are too many witnesses. Everyone here in this pub would rat you out, and you wouldn't last a day in prison!"

"I wouldn't?" Blake said and sliced superficially into Edward's skin.

Edward shut his eyes tightly, with a sharp intake of breath. His face twisted as a drop of blood quickly ran down his neck.

"You've made your point," Teddy grumbled while biting onto his stogie through clenched teeth. "You can let him go!"

"I don't think so," Jet said, and Blake tightened his hold. "Tell me what you want, then I'll decide if he can go."

Edward closed his eyes. "Tell him, Teddy!"

"I want to move the wedding with Jade as soon as possible," Teddy barked quickly. "I cannot wait until next spring!"

His eyes narrowed. "Why?"

"Because I…" he stammered, his eyes shifting to Edward and back. "I love her."

"Horseshit!" Jet snarled. "If you loved her, you would have given her a choice!"

"You aren't in charge here!"

"Oh, but my father is," he prodded. "And once he's gone, the reign will go to me and not some bastard like the lot of you believe! Katerina will be long gone before my father is. I will see to that! So, you better think twice about whatever deal you have made with her; it will get you nothing in the end! And just know that I can sway my father away from your favor! I can make him see that you are the worst choice for his daughter and intend to inflict pain on her for consorting with Dominic Kane! A man more liked than you, despite his reprehensible behavior. I know what you're after, Teddy; remember that. It would be good of you to keep in mind that the name Calvert holds more esteem than Kensington ever will!"

Teddy puffed on his stogie for some minutes in contemplation. When he exhaled, he grabbed Roslyn by the waist. "No one can take your sister away. She belongs to me and you should remember that she holds more respect than you!"

Jet's brows drew in. "Are you sure about that?"

Teddy hesitated.

"Here's the thing, I don't trust you, nor do I like you." It was good to finally say it, even when Teddy's face creased with harsh lines of anger. "I don't think you could run a business at all. You are better off partying with your friend here and leaving the work to us men!"

"You've got some nerve." Teddy roared. "What kind of men are you? Don't think I don't know about your wickedness!"

"Oh, we know what you've said," Blake snarled darkly and gripped the back of Edward's neck tightly. "Do I look like a molly boy to you?"

"No," Edward grunted with his eyes pressed tightly together.

"I will tell your father if you don't let him go!"

"He knows," Jet answered flatly. "Why do you think he threatened to give his money to Katerina's child? Or should I say, the one she's *pretending* to carry?"

Teddy's face smoothed as he sat back in his seat, and Edward's eyes opened. If they knew something, they weren't saying, but their lack of rebuttal confirmed he was hinting at the correct supposition.

"You can lie to yourself all you want, but it won't change the outcome," Teddy muttered after regaining some composure.

"Only time will tell, won't it?"

Teddy's face darkened. He was just as determined and carried the same burden Jet had, living in the shadow of a father who didn't seem to think he was good enough. There was a time when Jet thought they belonged to one another, though he never mentioned it. Teddy was interested in women, particularly women he could take advantage of. And while Jet may be many things, he never forced his will upon anyone.

"I could ruin your name and reputation to the entire city," Theodore threatened. "How far will your money go when no one wants to associate with some-"

"You aren't selling your case to save your friend," Blake interjected, causing Edward to whimper loudly.

"Let's forget I even brought it up," Teddy said hastily. "My intention wasn't to insult you. I just want to marry Jade sooner rather than later."

"Why? What does it matter when you marry her?"

"I'll give my seat up at the council if you make it happen," Teddy pressed.

Jet gaped at him. Never would he have thought Teddy would ever give up his place in the Elite for a woman. He almost questioned if Teddy actually loved his sister when Blake's eyes flicked to him for the briefest moment; there was a touch of concern on his face. He had more compassion for the girl than Jet ever had, and the distress forced him to realize that Teddy had ulterior motives.

"Blake can have it, or you can take over. Just make it happen."

He tapped his fingers on the table. Without magic in his veins, he might feel threatened, frightened even. If he could release just a sliver right now, Teddy would never provoke him again. Blake cleared his throat. It wasn't the time, not when there was so much at stake.

The barman was watching them closely, as were many others. Worried that he may have sent someone for a copper, Jet glanced listlessly at Blake. "He isn't worth going to jail over."

"I know. I just wanted to frighten him a little."

Jet met Teddy's stare once again. He was sitting on the edge of his seat, waiting for Jet to give him the word. "I'm not making any promises," he sneered, leaving Teddy in smug satisfaction. "But I can make a suggestion."

"Oh, I believe you can do more than that."

Jet pressed his lips together. He didn't want to give Teddy a damned thing. In fact, he wanted to watch him squirm. He wanted to rip the rug right out from under him and take everything he valued while watching as it destroyed him.

Jet stood abruptly. "We'll keep in touch."

Teddy glared but didn't say a word on the contrary.

Blake didn't initially release Edward until Jet ordered him to do so. The man had the gall to shove Blake in his seat. "Are you mad?"

Blake grinned frenetically as he stood. "I thought you figured that out by now."

Edward glared as Jet and Blake left without repentance.

IX
OWEN

"No one in Trinity Row is willing to talk," Owen said as he leaned against the far wall in Captain Feilding's office. He held onto a cup of coffee and a heap of resentment, though he tried not to let it show. He spent the majority of the previous evening patrolling the streets of Trinity row with no outcome.

"That's easily explained," Cillian said with boredom peppering his voice. His foot was propped on his knee and he picked at the dirt on the bottom of his boots with a switchblade. "No one holds any faith in the law when The Elite hover like a dark shadow. Why would anyone open their mouth?"

Feilding rubbed his temples from his desk, and he muttered, "This doesn't look good for the city. The Queen is demanding answers at once!"

"Why don't you direct her to Jackson?" Merfan barked from the other side of the captain's desk where he held onto his own cup of coffee and a nasty glare.

Owen returned the gesture. "And why would she need to speak with him?"

"You've seen him!" Merfan cried. "His face is all busted up!"

"What does that have to do with anything?" Feilding asked dismissively and lowered his hands. "His face is always busted up!"

Merfan sat forward. "A woman was murdered on the very night he returns to the city! Don't you find that odd? It was also reported that he caused a ruckus on a trolley car hours before the massacre! He is a menace to society and should be locked away for good!"

"The Queen is the one who specifically asked Jackson to return to the city, so if you have a problem with him, take it up with her!" Feilding remarked. "And besides, he has been accounted for. Several witnesses placed him at l'Arche Nobel along with Elijah, Cordelia Calvert, and Raoul Cheron until three in the morning."

Owen's brows pinched. He knew they had to explore all options, but he felt a little betrayed that Jackson was their first suspect. He had made great strides in his branch of work. Why would he come home only to defile it?

"And was he accounted for from three to five?"

"Please, this couldn't have been done in two hours," Owen snapped at him. "It's astounding that it was done in seven!"

Cillian shrugged. "Perhaps Henry got his timeline wrong."

"Well, if he got her timeline wrong, then Jackson's eyewitnesses could be off as well!"

"Would you drop it?" Owen barked. "Jackson didn't kill Helena, and you know it! Their paths didn't even cross! You can't lock up an innocent man because you detest him!"

"He isn't innocent," Merfan growled. "I told you the problem he created on the trolley!"

"Getting into an argument with someone isn't a crime," Cillian stated.

"Arguments anger people, and anger leads to murder!"

"Enough!" Feilding yelled. "I'm not going to listen to predisposed nonsense when there is a murderer on the loose! Forget about Jackson as a suspect, or I will remove you from the case! There wasn't enough time for him to commit such a crime!"

Merfan's jaw snapped shut, and he glowered at Owen. The constable had never liked Jackson and for a good reason. His brother wasn't the easiest person to get along with because of the rage and flippant attitude he displayed as a youth. Time and again, Merfan had detained him for fighting and disruption in the city.

"Jackson has been ordered to testify in court about the murder of a baker," Feilding told Owen. "I would like for you to be present."

"What about Helena?" Owen asked.

"The city doesn't stop for one dead prostitute. If people aren't willing to talk, then there isn't much we can do at the moment. With that being said, the murder of a baker takes precedence. I am ordering you to attend court and take Elijah with you. People like him, perhaps they would be more willing to speak after he gets a few drinks in them."

Owen placed a hand on his chest. "Are you telling me I'm not a likable guy?"

The men laughed.

"Sure, you are," Feilding said. "But you represent the law, and none of those people care for it unless it's directly affecting them."

He gave him a tight-lipped smile and strode toward the door with Cillian in tow. It was true they weren't necessarily welcome in Trinity Row, but he was vigilant when it came to protecting the impoverished, and that should be accounted for.

He nearly made it to the door when Feilding added, "I will only tell you this once, Owen. Stay away from the Elite. They are off limits to questioning and implications."

Owen paused and slowly turned to look over his shoulder, gauging their reactions. "But what if one of them committed this murder?"

Feilding grimaced. "It doesn't matter. We can't touch them."

Owen shook his head angrily as he left the room. The primary reason he was never allowed to do his job correctly was due to the hierarchy in this city. The Elite had too much money and could encourage anyone to look the other way. Including the police.

He sat in the corner of Greenwell's courthouse with Elijah. They were waiting for the police to bring in Christopher Culpepper, a young man accused of the murder of Peter Delmont, a baker in the Gas-light district. Peter had been found with his throat slashed in the back of his shop four days before Helena's murder. There were no witnesses, nor any evidence left behind. The only reason Christopher was being held responsible for his death was due to the fact that he had Peter's watch in his possession. Or so Merfan claimed.

Owen had his doubts. Merfan had an uncanny ability to find a culprit, even in the most unlikely of subjects. The citizens praised the constable, but it was somewhat suspicious that a man who never once failed in his entire career.

Laughter brought Owen out of his thoughts. Sitting four rows below, two young women deliberately glanced over their shoulders and giggled amongst themselves. Elijah didn't help matters. He leaned on the row ahead and flashed a wolfish grin in their direction. Owen despised being gawked at, unlike Elijah, who relished in female attention and usually deflected any attention from him.

Owen and Elijah stood out in the most renowned way. Both refused to wear the ridiculous wig in trend and were unfashionably tan. It was almost as if they willingly spent their time in the sun, unlike many of Bel Deaux's upper-class patrons. Their faces were remarkably eye-catching despite their blatant rebellion against cultural norms. And if separating themselves from societal customs wasn't enough to stand out, they were closely watched because of their ties to the Queen and the fields they chose to work in.

Elijah had just as much pressure on his shoulders as the police department. As a prominent reporter for the Bel Deaux gazette, the public demanded answers over the slain prostitute. Although, Owen felt it was more out of morbid curiosity than concern for the departed.

He tore his gaze from the chits and pushed his spectacles up his nose, nervously chewing on his bottom lip and glancing at the watch on his arm plate.

Cillian O'Brien entered the courtroom some minutes later with Jackson trailing behind. O'Brien was a head shorter than Jack, but it didn't diminish his authority. Cillian carried himself in a way that demanded respect.

When he spotted them, Jackson pointed toward the top corner, and Cillian led the way.

"Jack looks upset," Eli commented.

He did appear irritated as he followed O'Brien up the stands. This made Owen feel instantly defeated. Whatever bothered Jackson tended to have weighted consequences.

"Is there a problem?" Owen inquired when Cillian and Jackson sat down beside them.

"I found Christopher unconscious in his cell," Cillian explained, and Owen's jaw slackened. "I sent for Jackson immediately."

"Is he seriously injured?" Owen asked, his attention settling on his brother.

"He'll live," Jackson muttered. "And even though I recommended the trial be postponed until tomorrow, Merfan demanded to continue onward. His fate has already been decided and your department could care less for a conscious defendant in court."

Elijah groaned, but Owen wasn't offended by the statement because it was true. "Merfan was trying to coerce a confession."

"Undoubtedly," Cillian remarked. "And he nearly had Jackson thrown out of the courthouse until Tobias overruled him."

Owen turned to his brother. "How often do I have to warn you about that man?"

Jackson's eyes flicked to his. "Remaining silent while one commits heinous acts is no different from committing such atrocities!"

"That may be so," Owen argued. "But you can't change the world if you're dead!"

Jackson flashed a look of incense and ran a hand through his unruly hair. His knees bobbed up and down impatiently as he glanced over the crowd. The women ogling Owen and Elijah, now had their eyes on Jackson. Women always loved a mystery, and Jack was the epitome of eccentricity and ungovernable behavior.

"I can't take over the force with Feilding in Abraham Kensington's pocket," Cillian admitted and reverted Owen's attention. "Especially when he has Henry Wright and Joseph Cavendish to back him up."

"I've spoken to the Queen on the matter," Owen divulged. "She assumes it's false accusations when they are breaking no law."

"That's because they will never do anything to sully their name," Jackson interjected. "They plant seeds in the minds of others and keep their hands clean of the dirty work."

Cillian shrugged and rubbed his chin. "Well, the Elite aren't stupid, are they?"

Owen murmured his agreement.

"I'll need that when Tobias calls for my testimony," Jackson nodded toward Elijah's short pencil and pad.

Elijah's face twisted in confusion, and he said, "sure," as he glanced at Owen questionably.

Owen shrugged his shoulders in response and glanced back at Jackson. "I apologize for my absence at the morgue, but I read your report. Is there anything you failed to disclose?"

Jackson eyed him steadily for a few measured seconds, only choosing to speak when he gave him a pointed look. "Maybe if you hadn't snubbed us at the mask, you would know."

Owen rolled his eyes. "Come off it. I was ordered to patrol Trinity Row all night with no result. I am running on two hours sleep and a captain up my ass if it makes you feel any better."

Elijah scoffed. "Hardly! You weren't the one getting accosted by desperate women in search of a husband!"

"Oh, don't act picked on," Owen snapped at him. "Getting accosted by women is your favorite pastime."

"Not those women!" Elijah argued.

Owen ignored him. "C'mon Jackson, what is your take on Helena?"

"There was a lot of unnecessary mutilation. I would guess your culprit has a hatred directed toward women, but his attention to detail after her death is quite interesting."

"That much was obvious," Owen said flatly. "Is there anything her body gave away that couldn't be seen from one glance alone?"

Jack sighed. "I didn't leave anything out."

"You have before."

"Yes, well, that was concerning Alexandra Calvert's apparent suicide. This was clearly a murder."

"I didn't see her," Elijah butted in before Owen could argue. "What happened?"

Jackson rolled his eyes and opened the notebook he was never seen without.

"Did you burn your hand?" Owen asked abruptly when he noticed a long red streak across his palm.

Jackson instantly closed his hand into a fist and shook his head. Owen glanced at Elijah in question, but his brother merely shrugged. What was Jackson hiding?

He flipped to Helena Wimple's page and read, "She was choked from the front until she fainted. He then slit her throat to near decapitation. There were two knife wounds. The initial cut was four inches long, while the second was seven. Bruising surrounded either side of each cut, much like the indentation of a thumb and forefinger. It's unclear how he extracted all the blood from her body in such a short period of time and it makes me wonder if some sort of apparatus was used to drain her. The mutilation was postmortem. Her uterus, bladder, and upper part of her vagina were removed." He slowly glanced up at Owen. "The body was also bathed."

"What is that?" Elijah snapped, and when they glanced at him, he clarified, "A uterus?"

"It's the organ she conceives and carries children," Owen answered briskly.

"That is revolting!" Elijah bellowed. "Why would he want that?"

"I've known patients at Bellevue to eat their victims," Jackson answered, and Elijah's face twisted in disgust. "Maybe he was saving it for dinner." He then gave him a sly smile. "Or perhaps, in this case, breakfast."

"You are sick in the head!" Elijah muttered, and Jack chuckled.

"Was he skilled?" Cillian inquired. "Do you believe him to be a doctor?"

"It's always a possibility," Jackson replied. "But just because he removed an organ doesn't necessarily suggest it. He could be a butcher if you want to broaden your search, and he had the time to poke around in her abdominal cavity. However, with his precision, I would bet my entire career that your killer is a mortician. Helena was eviscerated, which is the disembowelment of the patient. This is why I could extend the possibility of a butcher, however slight. They have anatomic knowledge, though the species are different."

"What makes you think he is a mortician?" Owen asked.

"We deliberately make an incision around the belly button so as to not split the navel in half, and this is how Helena was cut. It would be ingrained in his mind, and he would divert the cut accordingly. He also happened to leave a note in her throat."

Cillian's ears perked up. "What did it say?"

Jackson extracted the note from his pocket and held it out for Owen, who eyed it carefully. "I figured it was better in your hands than Merfan's."

Owen snatched it and read, "Not my first, nor my last." He then scratched at his chin. "I was hoping this was a one-time offense, perhaps a scorned lover, but this only confirms my suspicions."

"Which are?" Elijah asked.

"He's only just begun."

"Well, that narrows your priorities," Jackson grumbled.

Owen eyed him steadily.

"All rise!" Merfan yelled out as Judge Tobias entered the room.

They stood until the judge was seated. Merfan's men carried a bloodied and shackled young man into the courtroom, and there was a collective gasp in the crowd.

Owen exchanged a glance with O'Brien.

"Christopher Culpepper, you are accused of the murder of Peter Delmont. How do you plead?"

The man hung his head and swayed slightly on his feet.

"He isn't lucid enough to testify," O'Brien whispered harshly under his breath.

Tobias repeated, "Mr. Culpepper, how do you plead?"

Christopher glanced up at Merfan with hesitation.

Tobias sighed heavily and turned to Christopher's lawyer.

Jerome Smith jumped up from his seat. "Christopher pleads his innocence, your honor."

"Does he?" Tobias barked and glared at Merfan. "He won't even talk!"

The constable had the gall to appear unaffected.

"Your honor, with all due respect," Jerome said. "My client was beaten into silence."

"Lies!" Merfan cried. "Your client killed the baker over a watch!"

"You can't prove that!" Jerome argued. "Nothing was left behind, and the watch wasn't even reported as missing until you kicked down Christopher's door and dragged him into the station! Which begs the question, why did you kick down Culpeper's door in the first place?"

"What are you suggesting?" Merfan growled.

Jerome glared. "I think that's quite obvious."

"SILENCE!" Tobias yelled. "We aren't here to listen to the two of you squabble! I want this settled today!" He then glanced up into the stands. "What say you, Hadley?"

The three looked at one another.

"Which one of us, your honor?" Owen asked.

Tobias rolled his eyes. "As Jackson saw the body, I would like his opinion."

Jack glanced at Elijah, and he handed over his short pencil and pad.

"Peter's throat was slashed from behind," Jackson stated as he walked down the stairs to where Christopher was shackled. Several women gasped in his wake. "I believe the knife to be six inches long with a pointed top and about an inch in width." He then stopped in front of Christopher. "Do you know how to write?"

Christopher watched him apprehensively.

Merfan barked, "This is pointless!"

"I have an essential point," Jackson stated loudly without turning around.

Tobias waved his hand at Merfan. "I'll throw you out if you cannot control your tongue!"

Merfan's jaw snapped shut with a glare.

Jackson watched the shackled man and asked, "Do you?"

"Yes," Christopher replied.

"Will you write your name and the street you live on this notepad for me?"

The man frowned and glanced at the judge.

"Do as he says," Tobias grunted.

As Jackson handed over the pencil and pad, Christopher hesitantly reached for the contents with his right hand. He eyed Jackson suspiciously and leaned over to write down what was asked of him.

Jackson stepped out of the way so the judge could see. "Peter's throat was slashed from right to left, your honor."

Owen exchanged a rather smug glance with Elijah and Cillian.

Tobias shrugged. "Your point?"

"Elijah, would you please?"

Eli grinned as he stood. Everyone watched as he skipped down to the floor.

Jackson stepped in front of the judge. "If one were to attack from behind, they would use their dominant hand to control the knife."

Elijah stopped behind Jackson and placed his left hand on the back of his head while moving his right hand around Jack's neck. He used his thumb in place of a knife and trailed a line across.

"Left to right," Tobias whispered.

"Peter's killer is left-handed, and as you can see, Christopher is not."

Christopher stopped writing and stared at Jackson with wide eyes.

"Nonsense!" Merfan cried. "You could easily use your non-dominant hand in a murder!"

"And why would one do that?" Jackson questioned and he threw Merfan a dirty look. "The non-dominant hand is far weaker and harder to control. It makes no sense for a perpetrator to attack in such a nonsensical manner! The only thing Christopher is guilty of is naivety. He unwittingly bought a dead man's watch, assuming he was getting a good deal on an antique item!"

"That's quite impressive, Hadley," Tobias said.

"Or rubbish!" Merfan hissed and stood in front of the judge. "How would he acquire the items if he wasn't present at the murder?"

"You know how Trinity Row works, Merfan," Jackson argued. "Thieves come at first sight of a crime."

"You cannot prove a murder based on the dominant hand!"

Jackson's eyes narrowed. "I just did."

"This is madness, your honor!" Merfan swirled around to the judge. "You cannot seriously believe the shit spouting from his mouth!"

Another gasp came from the stands.

Jackson took a step forward and snapped, "If you send Christopher Culpepper to the gallows, you're condemning an innocent man to death!"

Owen flushed with pride as he watched his brother. He was confident that Christopher would be sentenced to death, but with Jackson's statement, the man would walk free.

"He isn't entirely innocent!" Merfan pointed out. "You claim he bought the items, but you can't prove it! Swindlers in Trinity Row do not leave paper trails! What if he was the one who broke into Peter's shop and stole the watch? That seems a more likely scenario, and we all know the penalty for thievery."

"You can't prove he stole the watch!" Jack said.

"I didn't do it!" Christopher cried. "I didn't steal anything! I bought it off a bloke with red hair and a mustache!"

The crowd began to murmur loudly.

Tobias grabbed his gavel and smacked it several times. "Quiet!" The crowd continued to talk and disrupt the room. "QUIET!" Tobias yelled, and spit flew from his mouth.

The room fell silent as they watched the judge anxiously.

He sat forward in his seat. "The court recognizes Mr. Jackson Hadleys statements and shall dismiss Christopher Culpepper of the chargers for murder. However, as the watch was in Mr. Culpepper's possession around the time of death, we can assume that he stole the watch and will pay for his thievery with his left hand." And he slammed his gavel down. "This case is dismissed."

"I DIDN'T DO IT!" Christopher cried.

"Your honor, please!" Jackson yelled, but he had already left the stand. He turned around and threw up his arms. Owen grimaced in return.

"What an absolute joke," Jackson snarled as they stood on the corner outside the courthouse. His eyes flicked upwards when a passenger car flew by.

"At least he's alive!" Elijah wailed. "He would have been hanged had you not intervened, and what a fucking testimony! I thought Merfan was going to keel over. Did you see his face?"

"He was rather red!" Cillian laughed.

Owen watched Jackson, who hadn't found humor in the situation, and said, "You saved a man's life, Jack. Take that as a win."

"He's going to lose his hand and a lot of blood," Jackson snapped while glancing down the street. "If that doesn't kill him, the infection will!"

Owen watched him steadily and with confidence. "Somehow, I doubt you would let that happen."

Jackson didn't remark and shoved his hands in his pockets instead.

"Merfan wasn't going to let Christopher get off, was he?" Cillian observed lightly and took a puff of his pipe.

"Why would he break into Culpepper's flat in the first place?" Elijah questioned.

"James Newton saw him with a fancy watch," Cillian answered. "Said it was suspicious."

"That's awfully convenient," Jackson commented and walked to the edge of the sidewalk. "James Newton has red hair and a mustache."

Owen's eyes widened in surprise, and he muttered, "So he does."

Cillian grinned devilishly. "Perhaps we should pay him a visit."

"Perhaps we should," Owen said with a smile. "Where does he work?"

"He's a bodyguard for William Calvert," Cillian answered airily. "And predominantly watches over his daughter."

Jackson swiveled on his feet and stared at Cillian with a touch of curiosity and enthusiasm.

Owen's face twisted in confusion. A sudden palpable eagerness radiated from his brother, which was out of character. He glanced at Elijah for an answer, but as the other's eyes slid over to Jack, there was a touch of bitterness, however brief; Owen caught the searing reflex. When he glanced back at Jackson, the harsh creases lining his face were nowhere to be seen. His face was smooth and receptive to whatever trigger Cillian had just pulled.

Even Cillian frowned at his sudden attentiveness. "What is it?"

Jackson quickly blinked several times over, seemingly remembering his present company. "It's nothing. What were you saying?"

Cillian's eyebrows knit even further in bewilderment as he answered, "He acts as a bodyguard for Esmeralda Calvert." Jackson's shoulders sagged in disappointment and he turned back to the road. "I mean Marchand. She did marry that bloke before he died."

Owen's eyes narrowed suspiciously between his brothers. Something about the name Calvert had Jackson on the edge of exuberance, a trait Owen had rarely seen in him, and left Elijah with a touch of enmity toward the other.

"Not that her name matters," Cillian continued to mutter as he rubbed his head, oblivious to the sudden shift in the Hadleys. "William's gone to great lengths to protect all of his children."

"Why would they need protection?" Elijah snapped. His wayward tone was sharp and perplexing.

"Do you not recall the amount of wealth they hold?" Jackson drawled.

"Who cares if they're rich?" Elijah prodded despite his sour demeanor. "And besides, William publicly ostracized her just as he did with Cordelia, so why would he care what they do?"

"They're his blood," Owen remarked. "He won't let any of his children out of his clutches."

Jackson eyed him hesitantly.

"What is with you?" Owen demanded harshly. "What is it about Calvert that has your… undivided attention?"

Jackson's face was smooth as he peered back at Owen. "There is absolutely nothing about Calvert that has my attention."

Owen's gaze slid to Eli, who refused to meet his eye and said, "I feel like you're lying."

Was the sudden shift in his brothers over one of the Calvert girls? If so, they were dead men. But which girl was it? It certainly wasn't Esmeralda. Jackson completely lost interest the second her name was mentioned, and Owen was rather doubtful he would suddenly take a liking to Pearl. She was married to Augustus Atwood and far too haughty to be agreeable, even if she wasn't…which left Jade and Ruby. The only viable option would be Ruby, but she was too young. With the abuse Jackson suffered as a child, he would never cross a line of perversion.

He felt the blood drain from his face as he realized that Jackson was more than likely infatuated with Jade Calvert. He wanted to yell at him for even thinking about the girl.

Jackson ignored Owen's accusation and said, "So, what now?"

"I can track down James on my own," Cillian answered hastily, "I need you to pay Adam a visit at Bellevue. There is a patient that I want you to interrogate named Leonard Holloway. He killed his mother and sister and three other women in Jendoux. Merfan has him fixed as Helena Wimple's murderer."

"And why is that?" Owen asked flatly.

"Because he mutilated their corpses," Cillian said wearily. "Fifteen years in the field, and we suddenly have a country full of sadists." He dropped his hand and gave Owen a rueful smile. "Anyway, he's itching to close the case, and in typical fashion, he's wanting to point the finger without doing any investigative work."

Owen laughed dryly and shared a look with his brothers.

"I'd greatly appreciate some discretion on the matter," Cillian added. "Merfan won't take kindly to us standing in his way a second time."

"Of course," Owen promised as Cillian tipped his hat.

"Well, I'm off," Jackson said with a glance at his watch. "I'll make an appointment with Adam."

Owen's jaw snapped shut when Jackson shuffled into the crowd. A nauseating feeling of discontentment returned. It was the same unrest from all those years ago when he wasn't on speaking terms with his brother. He thought he had finally escaped hell and there was some balance in his life, but he wouldn't be that lucky. Hardship was a constant battle in Owen's routine, and all he could do was hold back a yell of frustration and panic, for he was the solid one, reliable and sure. The one who held his family together.

But no matter how unstable he felt on the inside, he couldn't allow the mania threatening to rip him apart to break free as he watched Jackson's receding form disappear like a ghost. Of all the losses he suffered in this wretched life, he couldn't lose Jackson too.

He would never recover. There would simply be nothing left.

He stepped onto a trolley and rode to the cemetery after buying a bouquet of red roses; they were Clara's favorite. He hadn't missed a week since she had passed on, and he usually visited on the Sabbath, but he felt as if he needed to make it up to her; she wouldn't be pleased with his actions of late.

Owen and Clara had been married for six years by her death, and it took nearly that long to conceive a baby. They'd almost given up hope of a child when she became pregnant, a blessing in disguise. He grew increasingly apprehensive as the due date drew near, and he knew it then. He just didn't want to admit it.

He wasn't speaking with Jackson at the time, and their lack of communication was incredibly detrimental to Owen's life. He never told Clara how he'd thought of Jackson every day and prayed for him to come home. It was supposed to be the happiest moment in his life, but it was only the beginning of his constant melancholy.

They had gotten into a row, but it wasn't a simple shouting match. They raised their fists against one another as Clara, Avis, and James screamed for them to stop. Elijah was no help. He'd been on a bender with Teddy and didn't check in until days later when everything was already fragmented. Windows were broken, furniture was broken, and so was their relationship.

The problem was Jackson's fighting and he couldn't control his anger. It was like another being enslaved his body and made him cruel and untouched by reality.

Two years had passed before Owen would see Jackson again, though he still looked for him everywhere. He could deny it all he wanted, but he desperately missed his brother for the duration of that lost time, needing that relationship back. Jackson grounded Owen in ways others could not, especially when he felt his sanity was slipping entirely. Elijah was wildly out of control, and James was starting to show paralleled signs of debauchery. Avis and Clara didn't help. They stressed him to an anxiety-ridden breaking point.

There was no relief whatsoever, which was mainly due to his child that would soon be born. Owen was deathly afraid of becoming a father. How could he care for a child when he couldn't even steer his brothers in the right direction?

He had nearly given up hope of ever talking to Jackson again when Clara died giving birth to Charlie, and his son failed to take one breath of life. Owen turned into nothing more than a shell of a man. He became so numb that he tried to kill himself several times, regardless of what it would do to his brothers and sister. That's when Jackson came home. The moment he learned of Clara and Charlie's death; he was at Owen's side. Their fight was entirely forgotten. He ripped the gun from Owen's hand and forced life back into him when he overdosed on drugs to numb the pain.

He had illogically blamed Jackson for every sour moment in his life, yet he could never repay him for saving it. Even if Jackson had never once complained, he didn't deserve the torture of having to revive his brother back to life.

Owen trudged in between the tombstones and settled on the end of the line where Clara and Charlie lay. The sky was black, and it began to drizzle as he set the fresh roses against the older ones. He stood back with his hands in his pockets and stared at the tombstone for quite some time. He replayed all the moments he treasured the most, her smile, her laugh, and her voice. It was tragic that he was here, and they were not. He held back a sob when he felt himself suffering the loss all over again.

"Owen?"

He glanced over to see Esmeralda Calvert peering hesitantly at him. When he turned to her fully however, her indecisive face bloomed. Freckles delicately peppered her nose, cheeks, forehead, and chin. His gaze was drawn to her wide mouth and teeth. "I thought that was you."

He felt himself smiling despite it all. "Esmeralda! It has been too long!"

"Yes, it has!" The grin never slipped from her mouth, and her eyes were committed to his face, almost as if she was retaining every inch to memory. It was only then that he realized his heart had started to pound a little faster.

"I didn't mean to interrupt you," she admitted, and her eyes slid to the tombstones in question. "I know grief is better left alone. I just didn't want to frighten you as I walked past."

"You aren't interrupting," he stated while letting his chilled limbs catch up to him. "It isn't wise of me to stand in the rain and freeze."

"I forget myself too when I'm here," she said and glanced out to the rows of headstones and monuments.

He watched with intrigue as her eyes searched the grounds and was pleased to find that he was at ease in her presence. Her charm was illecebrous, captivating him in all respects and giving a spark to a long-forgotten emotion. He wondered then if she was visiting her mother or husband…perhaps it was both.

When she glanced back at him, the smile returned. "I'll leave you to your thoughts. I have family to visit as well."

It was a brief repose, but he wasn't ready to let go of her company just yet. "Can I walk with you?"

She swiveled around with a wide smile. "Of course you can!"

He felt his cheeks rise and fell into step beside her.

"How is Bel Deaux's finest cop these days?"

"I don't know about the finest," he grumbled and shoved his hands in his pockets.

She gave him an appraising look. "Ever modest, you Hadleys."

He chuckled, navigating his way behind her to avoid stepping on the headstones deeply embedded in the mossy floor. "Bad habit."

She chuckled.

"How have you been?"

Her lips protruded with thought. "It depends on the day, I suppose."

Though he could relate, he wasn't fond of her pain.

She blurted, "Can I ask you an honest question?"

"Yes."

"Does it ever get easier?" When he glanced down at her, the humor had slipped from her face. "The grief?"

He swallowed and looked away. They say it did, but he found the statement to be complete horseshit. It became more difficult to breathe with each passing day and he struggled to find the correct coping mechanism to suppress the pain.

He glanced back at her with what he hoped was a convincing smile to match his lie. “One day.”

Her face relaxed with a ragged breath. She understood how he felt completely, but he didn’t want to give her more reason to cry. He prayed time would bring her solace in this life, unlike its refusal to release its unrelenting grip on his soul.

Time only seemed to make his heartache amplify.

X
Jackson

"He killed his sister at least a week before," Adam Riley explained. "His mother was thought to be killed two days after Helena's murder."

Jackson was barely paying attention as he read through the case file. He was sitting in Adam's office at Bellevue with Owen.

"I believe the three other women were substitutes for his mother and sister," Adam continued.

"He was disinclined at first," Owen mused. "Working up the courage to kill them."

"Yes," Adam agreed. "And from what I've been told, Lady Holloway was terribly cold toward Leonard. She blamed him for all of her misfortunes in life, including the regrettable departure of his father."

"Ah," Owen smiled grimly and glanced over Jackson's shoulder at the drawing of the deceased.

"She unwittingly groomed him to kill," Adam said with disgust, whether at his mother or Leonard, it was unclear.

Jackson glanced at him. "You believe had he grown up in a loving home, he would not have committed murder?"

Adam's stare twisted in perplexity. "You don't?"

Jackson gave him a wry grin as he answered, "It's a debate we have had. After conducting tireless interviews with these men, we deduced that while many have remarkably similar backgrounds, some simply don't. It's far too complex to pinpoint, although I do believe there are several contributing factors to push one over the edge, such as the environment of youth. A one parent household has been a common element, but this cannot be said for all. Violent physical and sexual abuse is another factor, yet even that varies. Some started their perversions by killing small animals until they dared to strike something much bigger, and some even suffered from head trauma as a child, but..." he paused and flipped over the drawing of Lady Holloway's mutilated corpse. "This is rooted deep within. I don't know if it really mattered what happened in his childhood."

Adam frowned. "I don't understand."

"Take Brandon Adams, for example," Owen interjected. "He grew up in a very normal home, and he still managed to kill half a dozen men for no apparent reason. While bewildered and horribly disgraced, his parents still talk lovingly about their son. They say what a good boy he was and how gentle he came across. Jack simply suggests that while there are definite connections, they do not necessarily pertain to every individual. Perhaps Leonard would not have killed his mother and sister had they treated him differently. We cannot say for certain, although," he shifted to address Jackson. "I do find it odd that the five victims were all highborn."

"Why?" Adam demanded.

"Highborn women get noticed when they disappear," Jackson answered briskly. "One wouldn't start with a highborn and then switch to a prostitute unless he was absolutely desperate for a kill."

"What are you talking about?" Adam griped. "Helena is all over the papers. Everyone is talking about her!"

"Only because she was posed on the steps of the abbey," Jackson explained. "If she were kidnapped and dumped in Trinity Row, no one in the Gas-light district would know or care."

"Precisely," Owen agreed. "Leonard has chosen well-associated women for the thrill. They also resemble his sister. Helena does not."

There was a brief pause to which Adam said, "But you've connected three points to Leonard. His father left when he was three and his mother never remarried. She raised the two on her own and distinctly treated the pair differently. While his sister was doted on and given the world, Lady Holloway was mentally and physically abusive toward Leonard. He was known to mutilate animals, and that is confirmed by his uncle. Which I find confounding. Leonard is unassuming and comparatively soft despite his size. His demeanor is quite gentle and entirely humble. I have never met a murderer like him. I would have defended him in court had I not known that several witnesses saw him walking about with severed heads." Adam's face twisted in disgust. "He isn't arrogant when he speaks of his kills. He is very calm, almost as if he was talking about the weather."

Jackson steepled his fingers and glanced at Owen.

"Every man who is a repeat offender suffers from a lack of remorse," Owen stated.

Adam nodded his head and dropped his eyes. "Does it make me a terrible person to say that I want to help the lost boy in Leonard?"

Jackson shared a disarmed glance with Owen.

"I know," Adam admitted. "I can't help but wonder how he would have turned out under different circumstances."

"Maybe he would have been better at cloaking his darkness," Owen surmised. "Although it would have come out eventually."

"I want to help him, but I can't because he killed five women!" Adam admitted and rubbed his temples. "It goes against everything I believe in! Perhaps if you wrote a letter to the Queen and asked to take his execution off the table."

There was silence as they stared at one another.

After some time, Jackson asked, "Did he violate the corpses?"

Adam pressed his lips together and averted his eyes.

Jackson threw a manic look. "He is severely ill, Adam! I don't know what you expect me to tell her majesty!"

"But Leonard is rather intelligent and especially talented!"

"They all are!" Owen cried. "That doesn't change the fact that he is a sadist and a necrophiliac! The people of Bel Deaux would be outraged knowing you want to keep this mutilator alive because he's unassuming! He charmed you just like he charmed those women before they died!"

Adam glared. "That is unfair!"

"It's the truth!" Owen snapped. "He may appear decent and respectable, but he isn't! Every murderer knows how to fake emotions and tell people what they want to hear! It is how he gained their trust! If Leonard were turned loose today, he would continue to kill. He has a need that no one can control, not even himself!"

Adam folded his arms as a petulant child would.

"It's tragic that anyone would have to grow up in such a hateful way," Jackson murmured. "It's especially heartbreaking, it truly is. But do you want to know what the difference is?"

Adam continued to glare.

"Choice, Mr. Riley. There is a clear distinction between what is right and what is wrong and the morals we all abide by. Yes, he grew up in a dreadful house, but he could have walked away and *chosen* to make a better life for himself. Many people are faced with a difficult path, yet they don't turn to punishing innocent people because of it! Not to mention the psychological issues associated with defiling and sexually abusing a dead body! It's a disorder, and I believe Leonard would have been killing regardless. It was only a matter of time because it's not some habit you pick up through the years. It's a need that can't be reasoned with!"

"Then what is the point of talking to him?" Adam snapped. "It seems you're already convinced he didn't kill the prostitute."

"Helena was mutilated postmortem, and her organs were removed. It sounds like Leonard's specialty," Owen answered.

"You lot are rather ambiguous," Adam griped.

"All the same," Jackson drawled with a shrug of his shoulders. "We were asked to interview him."

Speaking with criminals was not one of Jackson's favorite pastimes. Owen was more engrossed in the matter, and he seemed to get more out of it. They'd spent a fair number of months conducting interviews with these men to further their understanding of the criminal mind.

"Very well," Adam replied curtly.

"You know," Jackson told him while disdainfully eyeing the wet specimens of rodents on his desk. "Seeing the humanity in someone doesn't make you an awful person. Rather, the opposite."

Adam gazed at him curiously. "I must admit, I've heard many rumors, but you're nothing like I was expecting."

His blue eyes landed on Adam without a word. Jackson didn't give a damn about small talk or one's preconceived notions about him.

Adam seemed to realize this quickly, and he stammered, "Yes, well, I'll show you to Leonard's cell."

Jackson held onto his coveted notebook and medical bag as he followed him out. The hallways were a stark white, and with the light illuminating overhead, it only seemed to amplify the banality. The silence was so deafening that the hairs on Jackson's neck rose with discontentment. It was as if there wasn't a single soul inside the building. There weren't any patients lingering in the hallway, none pacing back and forth while muttering to themselves, nor were there various screams or irrational laughter floating up and down the hallway. Most asylums were predictable, but Bellevue was as quiet as an opera house.

"Where are the patients?"

Adam gazed over with a hint of smugness. "In their rooms, I've perfected how to treat the insane."

He tore his gaze away from Adam in distress. Most asylums were informal, and their practices were relatively standard, so Adam's methods didn't initially stand out. Patients weren't given much of a voice after they were locked away, and the belief came from Richard Bradley, a priest in the fifth century who claimed that mental illness stemmed from demonic possession.

"You'd be surprised at how receptive one is when we offer freedom from their inner torment."

They passed several armed guards, and Jackson found this excessive. The receptiveness Adam described no doubt came from fear rather than the therapeutic methods he used.

Jackson held his tongue as Adam stopped in front of the last door on the left. Owen peered in first, and he tried to gauge their reactions, but neither his brother nor the doctor gave anything away. When Jackson glanced into the cell, he was taken aback by Leonard's sheer size. He had to have been pushing three hundred pounds and was nearly seven feet tall. He was sitting cross-legged on the ground and playing with a deck of cards. His shoulder-length hair was greasy and fell around his broad face.

"Hello, Leonard," Adam greeted.

The man glanced up, his pale eyes flicking to Adam and Owen before sparking at the sight of Jackson. "Hello, Dr. Hadley."

Jackson glanced at Adam with uncertainty.

"Yes, I know who you are," Leonard continued calmly, his eyes dropping back down to his deck of cards. "I must say, it's quite a pleasure to meet you. I have seen you before, of course, working on various cases throughout the city. Did you read about my mother and sister, along with the other women I killed? If so, what did you think of my work? "

Jackson blinked; Leonard was wildly manic. He did speak serenely, but it was a very clever act he saw through. The mask he wore was easily transparent. He was pretending to be sympathetic, yet there was no remorse in his eyes.

"I'm not impressed if that's what you're implying," Jackson clarified flatly.

Leonard lowered his hand, which was as dirty as his shirt, and he smiled. "Oh, I doubt that."

Jackson remained unbothered. Leonard was trying to assert his dominance, but it wasn't working.

"You and I aren't so different," Leonard continued, his eyes darkening. "We both cut up the dead."

Owen and Adam glanced at Jackson, but he refused to drop Leonard's stare.

"We are the outcasts of society, discriminated against because of our calling. But society is wrong, Jackson, not us. It isn't our fault that we were abused as children. That kind of oppression cripples the brain and changes it entirely," Leonard said in a far-off voice. "You, of course, were more fortunate than I. You had a father who rectified the injustice inflicted upon you. My father never loved me, nor did my mother. I looked too much like him. I was a constant reminder of the man who abandoned her. She never let me forget, and I hated her for it!" He said through clenched teeth. "As I hated my sister. She asked me to kill those women for her. Gretta was a bitch like that. She had to be the prettiest girl in town, but she wasn't," he finished with a disturbing laugh. He slowly heaved himself off the ground and walked closer, pressing his face up against the bars for a better look. "Can't you feel it?"

Silence followed as Jackson continued to observe the burly man behind bars critically. It was distressing that someone could fixate on your character and manipulate it to fit their agenda.

"You are wrong," Jackson disagreed. "We are very different from one another. Your purpose is to torture and humiliate women because it's the only superiority you can gain over them. You didn't kill those women for your sister. You killed those women *because* of your sister! You didn't dare to kill her at first because you were frightened of her. So, you took your rage out on women who looked like her!"

Leonard merely grinned. "Think you have me figured out, do you?"

"You are easily transparent," Jackson answered. "You may have fooled Adam, but I can see you for exactly what you are."

Adam threw a reproachful stare.

"And what are you?" Leonard asked with curiosity.

Jackson shrugged. "An average man, nothing special at all."

Leonard laughed and walked back to his cards on the ground and said, "An average man who cuts up dead bodies."

"I examine bodies for answers," Jackson addressed. "My intent isn't to hurt others. It's to help."

Leonard's smile sank.

"Tell us about Helena, Leonard." Owen snapped, clearly over the man's antics.

He glanced at Owen and grunted, "What about her?"

"Did you know Helena?" Owen asked.

"Merfan says I did."

"What do you say?" Jackson inquired.

Leonard's eyes strayed back. "I don't have much regard for whores. And by that, I don't mean to say I want them dead. I just don't see the point in paying for sex. They also said she had red hair. I don't favor that color at all, fair hair is what stimulates me."

"That won't mean a thing to Merfan," Owen told him. "He will simply say that you lost control."

Leonard shrugged.

Owen continued, "It will be hard to sway the department when you don't have an alibi. Unless, of course, someone can account for you the evening Helena was murdered?"

"Yes, in fact," he answered lazily as he placed more cards onto the ground.

"Who?" Owen demanded.

Leonard looked up with a mad smile. "My mother."

The cab was silent between Jackson and Owen on the ride home. He was convinced Leonard wasn't their man. While entirely psychopathic and deranged, he wasn't a man capable of draining a prostitute and posing her in such a meticulous manner. He was dirty, compulsive, and thoroughly frenetic though he appeared to be the opposite. It would take some convincing on O'Brien's part to get Merfan to back down, but they were confident that Leonard Holloway had nothing to do with Helena Wimple's death.

Of course, the only troubling thing now was the worried glances Owen kept throwing in his direction.

"I really wish you would stop doing that," Jackson stated flatly.

"Do what?"

"Scrutinize me," Jackson answered with a cold stare.

"My only concern lies with your well-being, not to press your patience," Owen admitted. "I don't want you to begin to think you are anything like that man."

"I don't."

"Are you sure?" Owen pressed.

Jackson glowered.

"If you ever need to speak of it-"

"I won't."

"If you do."

"Owen please," Jackson muttered and rubbed his eyes. "The Vaults were all the therapy I needed."

Owen exhaled in frustration.

"Why would I listen to what Leonard Holloway thinks of me?" Jackson snapped and lowered his hand. "Honestly, Owen, do you truly believe I would allow some murderer to break my will?"

Owen's brow smoothed. "Well, no, but you've never once spoken of the past. I want to make sure your head is in the right space."

"Do I need to go over the differences in choice with you?"

Owen glared. "No."

"Then drop it," Jackson growled.

Owen shook his head and gazed out the window. It was touching of course, but he didn't need to relive the horror he had spent nearly a lifetime forgetting.

Once they stepped inside the intricate archway of their home, they parted ways. Owen headed for the library as Jackson walked past the staircase leading up to their rooms and down the stone steps to his lab.

He shrugged off his jacket and placed it on the rack. There was a note with elegant handwriting sitting on his desk. It was from Cordelia.

'Come for dinner tomorrow, would you? Raoul will join us. How does six sound?'

He smiled briefly and tossed the paper aside. He grabbed onto the crucifix hanging from his neck and raised his other hand to inspect his palm for the hundredth time. A red welt shaped like lightning embedded into his skin like a tattoo, starting just below his middle finger, and fading onto his wrist. His stomach turned every time he glanced at the blemish. Jade had marked him, but he wasn't entirely sure what that meant. They were connected on some level now, yet he'd never see her again, so he planned to take her secret to the grave.

He spent the next few hours poring over his notes, and when his eyes were starting to blur, a headache formed. He decided to go to bed, thinking perhaps he was missing something in plain sight.

It shouldn't be this difficult to find a killer, but then again, maybe it was.

Jackson walked through Saint Julien's Park with James. As his youngest brother, he missed some of the most important years of James's life, and he felt rather guilty for it. Owen, Elijah, and Avis raised James in the best manner they knew, yet it was apparent they had failed him. Each one had been so wrapped up in their own lives that they weren't giving him the attention and guidance he needed, and his following statements proved how true they were neglecting their baby brother.

"I don't want to go to Brentford," James admitted.

Jackson stopped walking altogether. "And why not?"

James shrugged and continued, "I don't have to go to school to be successful."

It was one thing to hang around Alec Kensington in his spare time, but it was highly problematic to decline his schooling altogether. James's split lip gave him away as if Jackson wouldn't notice; he'd been fighting in the Vaults. And while Jackson should have discouraged him from doing so, he felt a sense of pride over the matter, though he shouldn't. James would rather entangle himself in crime than receive a proper education, and that was alarming.

James paused and turned to look at him when he realized Jackson was no longer walking beside him. His shoulders went slack, and he rolled his eyes. "C'mon, Jack, it will be hard enough as it is with Owen and Elijah, not to mention Avis. I don't need it from you as well!"

His words stemmed from the fact that Jackson was the only one who didn't try to push his opinions. Unlike the other three, who wanted to mold James into a better version of themselves.

Jackson placed his hands in his pockets. "Does this have something to do with Teddy Kensington?"

James shrugged and kicked at the ground.

"You'd rather be a criminal than have an education?"

"I can be rich without a degree. It has got nothing to do with being a criminal! I want to," he paused, and his cheeks turned a little pink.

Jackson's gaze narrowed. "You want to what?"

But James wasn't paying attention to Jackson anymore, he was distracted by someone in the distance, and he muttered, "Ruby?" under his breath.

Jackson frowned, and he turned to see a girl in a green gown standing on the bridge and peering over the railing. She was yelling at someone below.

James gazed back with a broad smile. "I know her."

Jackson's face twisted even further in bewilderment as he slowly followed his brother. He glanced around wildly, but to his immense surprise, no sentinels were watching. How was William Calvert's daughter alone, unnoticed by her family?

"Fancy meeting you here," James said.

Ruby did a double-take and wailed, "James!"

"Are you all alone?" he asked, placing a voice to Jackson's thoughts.

"Oh, no, I'm just here with my..." she hesitated when her eyes found Jackson, failing to finish the rest of her sentence.

"RUBY!" someone yelled from below.

Ruby's face twisted in embarrassment, and she gave them an awkward smile.

"Who is that?" James asked.

"My sister," she grumbled.

Jackson glanced over the railing. Jade was standing in the pond with her skirts in a ball around her stomach; the water came to the top of her bare thighs. He laughed loudly. All the tension with meeting Leonard and James's recklessness had vanished instantly. He placed his hands on the rails and asked, "What have you gotten yourself into?"

Her eyes widened at him. "Jackson!" and she stumbled forward into the water on all fours.

He bit his lip and walked around the other two.

"What is she doing in the pond?" James asked from behind.

"I dropped my fan, and she insisted on getting it," Ruby admitted and began to follow Jackson. "What're you doing?"

"I thought I'd assist her out of the water," Jackson answered and climbed down to the edge of the embankment. Her heels and stockings were casually discarded on the ground. He grinned over at her and began to remove his shoes.

She was still on all fours. "I'm stuck in the mud!" she explained, but there was a wide grin on her face and a laugh on her breath.

He chuckled and began to roll up his pants.

"I don't like this," Ruby whispered loud enough for him to hear as she wrung her hands together.

"Why?" James asked.

It was damn well because of Teddy and whatever rumors she'd heard of Jackson, but it didn't make him mad. He liked that Ruby was an excellent sister to Jade. She needed that.

"If father finds out," she hedged.

"He won't find out!" Jade argued from the middle of the pond. "I got you away from prying eyes, did I not?"

Jackson stepped into the water and flinched at the mud that snaked in between his toes.

"It won't be for long," Ruby grumbled.

"You don't know how to relax, do you?" James asked.

Jackson ignored the rest of their words and focused on the girl trapped in the water. What a wild creature. He had never met a woman who would willingly get dirty or wet for a simple fan. Weren't the daughters of society supposed to be dainty and tame? They loved playing coy and helpless and craved for a man to save them from their tawdry lives, yet it seemed as if Jade was anything but.

Her muddy hand raised out of the water when he came within reach, and he braced himself for the pulse to shift between them as she placed her palm in his. The contact surged up his arm once again, unable to contain the strangled groan that escaped the back of his throat. Her touch was sharp and unrelenting, and he resisted the urge to break the connection because it was so overwhelming. His hand vibrated against her palm, which traveled down toward his navel. He swiftly pulled her into a standing position, and she swayed into him. Black spots clouded his vision as his face flooded with heat; the notion of fainting came to mind. He quickly let go of her hand and grabbed onto her shoulders before he fell into the water. Her lips parted, yet she didn't say a thing as he blinked several times to make sure he was lucid enough to be of use.

He glanced down at her. Was she even human? Her touch was far more potent today than the first time he grabbed her hand. It was rather strange and incredibly frightening, but it didn't really matter. With the sun illuminating her face as it did now, flecks of gold blended within her eyes and gleamed back. He couldn't tell which complimented her face better, the green one or the brown. But what he did know for sure was that they were delightfully expressive and unsettlingly deep all at once.

She couldn't be real. Someone couldn't possess this much pulchritude.

She gave him a small smile and said, "We cannot continue to collide with one another."

He blinked rapidly. Is that what was happening between them, a collision? Whatever it was, he hoped it would never fade.

Ruby interrupted the moment by yelling, "Jade! Are you two stuck?"

"You better let me go before she has a fit."

"What if I don't want to?" The words were out of his mouth before he could take it back.

She swallowed, and her eyes widened larger than they already were.

"I'm only teasing," he smirked with his lie.

She dropped her gaze, and he wanted to lift her chin back up to peer into those telling eyes again. Instead, he turned and crouched down. "Grab on."

He would've carried her in his arms, but he didn't think she would like that much, nor would her sister. She placed one arm around his neck while the other held her skirts, and she half jumped onto his back. Her dress weighed them down as he quickly grabbed onto her legs and swayed in the water. They almost toppled over, but he somehow kept his footing. They both laughed for a few measured seconds, but the tingling in his palms brought him back to reality. He loosened his grip on her bare legs, trying to touch her exposed skin as little as possible. Because it not only caused a physical reaction within him, but if anyone saw them, it would be troublesome for her. His thoughts rang clear when he took in Ruby's face.

Jade didn't notice their predicament and wrapped both of her arms around his neck, her breath tickling his ears. "What are you doing here?"

"You're the one who's stuck in the mud, and you're asking what I'm doing?"

She chuckled and said, "Yes, you don't seem the type."

"The type for what?"

But she didn't answer as they reached the embankment; James lent a hand to help him out of the water. He reluctantly set her on the ground and turned to look at the mess she was in.

"How are you going to explain yourself out of this one?"

She grinned. "My father will never notice. He's never around."

"Jade," Ruby warned, and she looked at her with a hint of annoyance. It was rather amusing; Owen was always doing the same to Elijah. "I think we should leave before this gets back to Theodore."

Jackson folded his arms. "Why? What would he do?"

James grinned, loving every moment of Jackson's assertive nature when it came to the Elite. Ruby blushed and bit her lip. She was a very hesitant person, but Jackson sensed it was because she was trying to protect her sister.

"Nothing," Jade answered quickly while grabbing her stockings and shoes. "Ruby is right. We should get going."

"I wish you could stay. I've only just found you," Jackson admitted, and the three glanced at him. He wanted to smack himself for falling all over this girl.

Both James and Ruby stared as if he'd lost his mind.

Jade blushed, and the color did extraordinary things to her face. "You're too late."

"There is still time," he countered. "You aren't married yet."

James groaned as a guttural noise escaped Ruby's lips.

She glanced at Ruby and then at James. There was something else she wanted to say, but not in front of them.

"We'll leave you, of course," Jackson blurted before one of them could jump down his throat. "You've bought yourself some time, but I fear it won't be long before your father's guards sniff you out."

A shadow passed from above, and Jade's eyes raised upwards as an airship traveled slowly across the sky; there was longing in her eyes. What appeared to be a simple gaze was really a means to an end, he knew the look of desperation and flight. He was suddenly stricken with an affliction of the heart as she gave him a curt smile and pulled Ruby along. "Thank you for the assistance, Mr. Hadley. I greatly appreciate it."

He placed his hand on his chest and watched until they disappeared before glancing over at his brother.

James shook his head and grumbled with frustration, "I hope you know what you're doing, Jack."

He grimaced. It was clear he didn't know what he was doing, though he knew it was a foolish decision to pursue Jade Calvert. But the more he thought about it, he realized it didn't matter because there was no turning back now. Her touch was indissoluble, and he would drift toward her like a moth to a flame, even if it meant his demise.

XI
OWEN

Owen found Esmeralda standing in front of her mother's grave, dressed in black, like some gothic caricature. "Well, this is certainly an unexpected surprise."

She glanced up at him, the corners of her mouth curved upwards. "So, it is."

His excitement vanished when he noticed that she had been crying.

"I wish she would have said something. I could have helped her."

He held his tongue, wanting to tell her that her mother didn't die of her own hand, but now didn't seem like the appropriate time. "I'm sorry."

"Me too," she said.

He didn't want to intrude on her time. "I will leave you."

"I actually don't want to be alone," she admitted and peered up at him. "Are you working this afternoon?"

"I have to patrol Trinity row, but that's not until nightfall."

Her eyebrow raised. "Would you like to get a drink somewhere?"

His returning smile transformed his entire face. "How about we get something to eat?"

"I'd like that."

They fell into step with one another. A silent walk through the cemetery, but it was comfortable.

When they reached the street, she asked, "How are your brothers?"

"They are pleased with themselves."

She chuckled and said, "And Avis?"

"She is well, thank you. How are your sisters?"

She opened her mouth, but nothing came out.

He gave her a puzzled look. "Is something wrong?"

She shook her head and smiled. "They are in good health, thank you for asking."

He gave her a polite nod, curious about what she wasn't saying.

He treated her to coffee and a croissant at a small café on Abbey Lane. He wasn't afraid of conversating and held most of the exchange as she listened quietly. He spoke about his brothers and brushed over his parents with finesse. She didn't broach the subject, and he soon began discussing his job and the sort of people he met daily.

"L'amoureux."

Both he and Esmeralda glanced up to an untidy woman leering down at them. She had short spiky hair and green eyes. She wore beads and chains around her neck and had rings on every finger; even one of her teeth was gold.

Owen tsked and said, "Mahala."

Her eyes gleamed with amusement, but they never strayed from Esmeralda's face. She glanced at Owen in question, but he only sniggered and quickly told the gypsy to leave her alone in the language of Bensch.

She ignored him and repeated, "L'amoureux," to Esmeralda.

Her eyebrows pinched as she admitted, "I'm sorry, I don't know what that means."

Mahala placed a card in front of her. Depicted was a naked man and woman locked in one another's embrace as their lips met. Owen grumbled some more under his breath as she grabbed the card to inspect it closely. It was a card of the occult that could tell fortunes and was linked to witchcraft. Fear and curiosity rose in his chest, worried about what she would think.

"The lovers," Mahala stated with a thick accent, and this time, Esmeralda glanced up at her. "This card flipped out of my deck the moment you entered the café with my dear Owen here."

Her eyes drifted to him, and his cheeks warmed. He averted his gaze and shifted in his seat.

Esmeralda handed the card back to Mahala.

Mahala grabbed it carefully and flipped over another card labeled Le Bateleur. A man in a floppy hat with fair hair held an arm high in the air. He stood in front of a table with a cup, a coin, a wand, and a sword.

"The magician," Mahala explained. "All of the elements are there, earth, water, fire, and air. There's no need to fear, dearest Esmeralda. It is within all of you."

Esmeralda frowned, looking uneasy. Owen's heart started to pound; Mahala was going to scare her off before he had a chance to make his move. He started muttering in Bensch once again, but she merely flipped one last card, La Maison Dieu. Lightning struck a tower, and two people fell from it.

Discontent settled in the pit of Owen's stomach when Esmeralda gaped up at Mahala, who stared right back. People feared the gypsy's because they didn't understand their beliefs. Yet it was a culture Owen had been raised in, for his father was a gypsy.

He exhaled loudly and said, "Mahala," impatiently.

Mahala laughed and it was full of gravel and rath. She then grabbed his chin and said in Bensch, "She is your match."

He grinned and squeezed her hand when she dropped it from his face.

Esmeralda watched Mahala drift from their table and join a group of migrants in the far corner.

"I'm sorry," he said hastily, and she glanced firmly back at him. "Mahala has silly superstitions, and she likes to make up stories with her cards, but gypsies are completely harmless."

She stared at him for a long moment, and he worried she would excuse herself, but instead, she said, "I'm glad I ran into you today."

He smiled in relief. She had no idea. "As am I."

On the city's lower east side, five prevalent establishments tempted those who lacked any sense of self-control. It was in these halls that one could learn things. Things that weren't spoken freely in conversation, whether for the sake of propriety or justly skepticism amongst the destitute.

Owen read from a letter in Perry's pub while gripping a glass of amber liquid. Elijah was focused on a charming brunette across the way, there was an impish smile on his lips, and he gave her a wink. She stared openly with a blush.

"How can you read at this hour?" Elijah drawled when he glanced over at Owen in restlessness. "Do the common people bore you so?"

"No," he answered swiftly. "But you do."

"Ha!" Elijah bellowed, "There's no need to lie. Not only am I the most intriguing person you know, but I'm also, the best looking!"

Owen's eyes flashed to him briefly and down to the paper again without a word.

"Stephen rather enjoys making us wait, doesn't he?" Elijah said and took a quick shot of whiskey. "I don't know why you even bother. Everything that spews from his mouth is a complete invention of that insane mind of his."

"He hears things we don't," Owen muttered, his eyes trained on the paper still.

"We can hear anything he can," Elijah argued, "If speaking to the right person."

"That's not entirely true," Owen countered and nodded toward a table to the right. "If you haven't noticed."

"I saw them," Elijah grumbled and lifted another glass.

Bodyguards were easily identifiable, and many ignored their presence. While in the capital, the Queen's guards were seen daily. These men, however, were not on the Queen's guard, even though they would be dismissed as such. Only Owen and Elijah seemed to spot the subtle differences in their attire. The Queen's guard wore maroon and navy blue with golden faceplates. The gas masks these men wore covered their entire heads, while their suited armor was black and red.

"Why do you suppose Calvert wants our attention now?" Elijah asked as he looked over his shoulder at the sentinels.

"He's making a statement."

Elijah's glare deepened. "Which is?"

"He wants us to be aware of his power," Owen conceded. "And that he's watching."

"Watching us?" Elijah exclaimed while looking back at Owen. "Why?"

Owen stared for a few moments longer than necessary before glancing back down at the letter and answering in a clipped tone, "I'd wager it would have something to do with your piece in the paper."

"I never pointed any fingers," Elijah muttered.

"You made heavy implications."

Elijah pursed his lips.

"And with the upcoming anniversary of Alexandra's death, I'd be disappointed if he didn't come after me when I've recently asked a few questions."

"Such as and to whom?"

"I was assessing Feilding's loyalty."

Elijah gave him an absurd stare.

"Her death left more questions and doubt than a simple suicide. I know he had something to do with it, and of course," Owen gave him a rather crafty grin. "I let him know it."

"So, you've mentioned."

"Must you always ignore whose city this is? And until we keep our noses out, we will be followed or possibly worse."

"You have one wild imagination," Elijah said. "No one gives a damn about the life we live, and what of Elizabeth? This is her city and not the Elites!"

Owen's eyes and tone turned flat as he said, "they have far more influence than she ever will."

"But Elizabeth is a monarch," Elijah argued. "Therefore, she makes the rules!"

"And when have they ever followed them? Calvert controls the money; therefore, he makes the rules!"

Elijah sighed with indignation and glanced back at the brunette. She kept sneaking glances over her shoulder despite the disapproval of the drunk next to her. "I'm onto something, Owen and the Elite are the key players."

"I am quite aware, brother."

"Calvert must not understand how I operate," Elijah mused and gazed at the bodyguards.

"I'm sure he's dug up every sordid detail of your life."

Elijah grimaced.

"I do find it curious, however," Owen added. His earlier sullenness vanished and was replaced with cogitation as he stared ahead.

Elijah glanced at him, waiting.

"With three of the Atwood's marrying into the Calvert household, how many do you suppose will be subjected to death?" Owens' intrepid gaze shifted to his brother. "Do you think they dare take down the entire house without arousing suspicion?"

Elijah snorted. "Jet would burn the entire city to the ground before he would let that happen."

"Perhaps…" Owen agreed while not entirely convinced. "And as for Stephen," Elijah turned away with a roll of his eyes. "Even though he's gone slightly mad, doesn't mean he cannot be trusted. He helped uncover Georgina Pecks' murderer."

Elijah failed to respond; his face twisted with aggravation.

"As ungrateful and unimpressed as you like to appear," Owen stated flatly to the back of Elijah's head. "It doesn't change the fact that you boasted about him to anyone who would listen."

Elijah's face whipped back with a scowl. "Not only was I completely pissed, but I had just gotten paid more money than I knew what to do with!"

Owen finally dropped the paper on the countertop. "And yet you've spent nearly all of it."

"Oh, piss off! I never interfere in your affairs," Elijah lied.

Owen pressed his profuse lips into a hard line. His eyes challenged the statement entirely.

"Well," Elijah smiled and scooped up the letter he discarded on the bar. "Not if I can help it."

Owen paused to watch him studiously. Elijah was holding the letter relatively close to his face, squinting as he tried to read what it said. It was always the same with him.

"You know," Owen muttered. "It would be far easier to read if you wore your glasses."

"There is nothing wrong with my eyesight," he snapped. "I don't know how often I've told you I don't need glasses!"

"Perhaps not in the general sense," Owen argued. "But you need them to read."

"Do not," he disagreed and threw the letter on the bar.

They were all born with poor vision, and unfortunately for Owen, he had it the worst out of them all. He needed spectacles for all-day wear, whereas the rest of the brood simply needed them for reading or close work, but Elijah was the most stubborn about the situation. He would never admit that there was anything wrong with himself. He was rather vain in that matter, and it bugged Owen tremendously.

He glanced at his watch. "I will agree with you on one thing."

Elijah smirked. "And what is that?"

"Stephen is rather late, more so than usual."

The pair looked toward the door with no luck.

"Stephen's on a bender," A woman's sharp voice intruded loudly. They turned to see a doxy with dark hair and a hard stare. "I'll talk to ya if yew has some questions, but yew gotta buy me a drink first."

Owen glanced at Elijah; it was better than nothing. They escorted the bangtail to a room on the second floor, far from prying eyes and ears, behind the smoke and clatter. Yet, as she introduced herself, Anne wasn't as vocal as she originally made herself appear. Owen figured she just wanted free drinks and cigarettes.

"You need to give me something, Anne," Owen muttered with frustration after ordering another round of ale, growing tired of her drunken antics.

She pressed her lips together and glanced at Elijah. He lit a cigarette and shook out the match when Owen glared at him.

He exhaled. "What?"

Owen hissed, "A little help, if you will?"

He nodded once and held out the box of cigarettes to her. "Annie darling."

"I don' want to hear it, Elijah!" She yelled. "My best friend was just murdered!"

"Why do you think we are here? We want to find the murderer!"

"Ha!" She bellowed, "Why, so yew can let him walk free and place an innocent man behind bars?"

"I'm not that kind of cop," Owen stated, and she glanced at him indifferently. "I need to know whom she was seeing and when, so I can stop another murder before it happens!"

Anne's lips quivered. "Yew fink, he will kill again?"

"Jackson certainly believes so," Elijah murmured, and her eyes widened.

"The only way for us to stop it is for you to talk," Owen encouraged.

She stared at him for a long moment before turning back to Elijah. "Let me have one of those, yeah?"

He held out the box of cigarettes once more. She hastily took one from the box and held it to her lips while he lit a match.

She took a long drag, and when she exhaled, she said, "I didn't want to mention anyfing, but I 'spose I can't keep it hidden for long, though I don't like talking about him."

"Who?" Owen demanded.

She took another inhale of her cigarette. "Dominic Kane comes about once a week. He picks out a girl and takes them back to his flat to make these stag films." Elijah's head turned in his direction. Their cousin's stag films certainly had many people talking. If the rumors were true, the films were illegal, and he could be arrested for lude and lascivious acts. "They go 'cause he's so handsome, and he's filthy rich. He filmed Helena a few times, even me." She sniffed.

"What did he film you doing?" Owen asked, even though he didn't want to know.

"Sexual fings, and he paid us plenty," she muttered. "Boy, we was happy to see him at first, but the more we went, the more he wanted."

"Such as?"

"Whip each other, stuff like that."

"And did that bother you?" he prodded. Consent was the line that defined sadomasochism from abuse.

She scratched her chin. "As I said, it was enjoyable at first. Fun even."

Elijah asked, "So, when was it no longer fun for you?"

"When he got involved," she said above a whisper. She wiped her eyes quickly. "I could never remember what happened, only that I'd wake up hours later in a gutter with a headache."

Owen watched as she shrank against her chair. Dominic violated her unconscious body, which was perverse and entirely inexcusable. She may have made a living on sexual favors, but this went beyond finding one's desires and expanding on them.

"His eyes ain't right," she said a little louder. "They're as black as the devil, and so is his soul. Yew knows when someone says somefing sexual or shows it? It's supposed to make yew hot and bothered? Only the fings he says and does are perverted and leave yew feeling disgusting in ya skin. I may not be an ideal woman, Mr. Hadley, but I still have feelings! I has the right to say no if I don't want it, and no man can tell me otherwise!"

"You are absolutely right," Owen agreed, and her face smoothed, though she didn't look any less suspicious. "No man should force their will nor their body upon you, but that's why my brother and I are here. To make it right."

"Where were yew before I got into this mess?" She inquired with a small smile. "Don' ever change, yew hear me?"

Owen glanced at Elijah, who smirked.

"There is another man who still visits nearly every night," she sniffed again after another inhale of her smoke. "But he just likes to watch the girls get naked wiv one another. I've never heard any of them say he actually stuck it to 'em."

"And who is that?"

"Augustus Atwood," she whispered.

He shared a look with Elijah. The Atwood's were just one of the many names connected with this predicament.

"He doesn't participate in any sexual activity?" Elijah reiterated.

"No, he just likes to watch," she murmured, paleing as if she suddenly realized something vital. "If they finds out I was talkin to yew…"

Owen breathed out of his nose in frustration as he grabbed a clipped stack from his back pocket and tossed her a few fives. "For your trouble."

She failed to suppress the grin that bloomed on her chapped lips.

Owen looked at his arm plate. "I'm running out of time and have another appointment."

Elijah grinned widely as he leaned casually against the table, one leg slung over the other. He seemed jovial that Owen was taking care of his needs, even if he wouldn't speak of them openly. "I cannot fathom how you enjoy the company of one woman over several."

Owen glanced at his brother; his anxiety was nearly forgotten as a new sense of amusement rose. The woman Elijah was hinting toward was no one of significance. She was simply a woman who helped him in a dire time of need. Still, he played along. "Sarah has enough… personality to keep every part of me stimulated."

Elijah laughed heartily; his head fell back with his howl. "Yes, I always thought she had an impressive mouth."

Owen's sharp gaze narrowed, which only caused Elijah to laugh harder. Anne smirked as her stare wandered between them.

He briefly debated on telling Elijah that the girl was no real source of interest to him. But the longer he contemplated it, the more he realized that it was none of his brother's business and kept his thoughts to himself.

"Go on then," Elijah said once the laughter subsided. "I'll finish up here."

Owen suddenly appeared uneasy, as if it were his worst idea yet.

"Don't you trust me?" Elijah asked.

"Implicitly," Owen answered the question as if it were absurd to think otherwise, yet his eyes appeared to convey something far different, especially when his focus landed on Anne.

Elijah's tone flattened, "Then what is it?"

Owen opened his mouth and shut it several times before spouting, "All right then! But please try and behave yourself for once!"

Elijah took another drag of his cigarette. "I always do."

"A diversion, if you will," Owen reminded him. "So, I can slip away unnoticed."

Elijah downed the rest of his whiskey and glared at his brother with a snarl, "You owe me."

Elijah left the room without another word. Owen followed, pausing at the door. "Thank you for your cooperation," he told Anne. "If you think of anything else, don't hesitate to reach out."

She gave him a bitter smile. "Oh, I don't fink I'll risk another conversation."

He ground his teeth together and scanned the crowd for Elijah, who was taunting Thomas Grady, a man who was always down to brawl. The entire room was watching, including the sentinels.

Thomas shoved Elijah backward. "Watch where you're walking before I beat the ever-living piss out of you!"

Elijah chuckled as he grabbed Thomas's cuff and threw him into the table of sentinels. Chaos broke, and fists started swinging; Owen ducked away quickly.

Their driver Duke was standing beside their cab.

Owen nodded to the pub. "Go fetch Eli. He's gotten himself into a fight."

Duke took off without a word, and Owen slipped into the night, walking briskly through Trinity Row. Several prostitutes called after him, and after a moment of thought, he stopped, turned around, and pulled out a fat stack.

"Hello, handsome," one of them said. "Yew can have me for a note."

"Get inside," he said as he placed the entire stack in her hand. "And don't leave until morning. There is a murderer on the loose, and he's promised to do it again."

The woman gaped at him.

"Are yew for real?" her friend asked while gawking at the money.

"What are you waiting for?" He yelled gruffly, causing them to jump. "Get out of here!"

They fled with the harsh tone of his voice. He would have felt guilty for yelling at women if he didn't think it would save their lives. He watched until they ducked into the nearest lodging house, despite being late.

He ran through the near pitch-black streets. The worry that Gregory Taylor would not wait on his precise timing and disappear into the night bothered him. Gainsley mentioned that the fooz wouldn't linger long, not wanting to draw much attention to himself if Kensington's sentinels sent word of his absconding from home. The man was hiding in Melody Andrews' rented room at a flat above the drugstore, which was located on York Avenue.

Once there, he walked around the side of the building to a stairwell leading to Miss Andrews's room. He knocked three times, once at the top.

A female voice called, "Who is it?"

"Owen Hadley."

The door cracked open, spilling a sliver of light into the night. "Yew alone?"

"Yes."

The door opened wide. She was standing in her undergarments and had a large smile on her lips, revealing three missing teeth. Her red hair fell carelessly around her exposed body. "Owen," she purred.

He nodded at her curtly. "Miss Andrews."

She turned to look over her shoulder. "He even treats me like a lady!" she glanced back at Owen and beckoned him inside. "We 'avn't got all night, Milord. Yew best gets in before anyone hears."

He stepped into the small flat. A large bed sat in the center of the room with a ruffled-looking man upon it; his stare was strained, and his hands were anxious.

"Mr. Taylor," Owen said and stepped forward to introduce himself.

Gregory held up a hand. "That'll do."

Owen halted.

Melody walked around him and brushed her body against his. A smile still lingered on her lips. "Would yew like some tea?" her arm snaked around his waist, and her chin rested just below his shoulder. Her large green eyes stared up at him with ardor.

Owen didn't want tea or Melody touching him, but out of politeness, he answered, "That would be great, thank you."

Her stare lingered uncomfortably before turning to the small stove with a teapot sitting atop.

Owen glanced back at Gregory. "I'll get straight to the point, Mr. Taylor. I was told you have information that I desperately crave."

Gregory flinched at the tone of his voice. "There is nothing to crave about that damned family. Nothing but horror and death awaits anyone who wishes to seek their hidden facets."

Owen's frown deepened. "What do you mean exactly?"

Gregory wrung his hands together. "There's no use pretending, I suppose, even though he would have my head if he knew I was spilling his secrets."

"None of the information you share will be traced back to you," Owen encouraged.

"Very well," Gregory said, at last, there was simply no fight left. "Abraham Kensington was having an affair with Alexandra Calvert in the months leading up to her death."

Owen grabbed a chair from Melody's table and dragged it toward the bed. Once he was settled, he rested his elbows on his knees and asked, "are you absolutely certain?"

Gregory nodded grimly. "I used to cover for them, take her to and from the flat."

Owen dropped his head. There was the motive for murder.

"I know it wasn't moral, and I could be seen just as guilty," Gregory admitted. "But I had no choice in the matter, he was my employer."

Owen glanced back up at him. "And did William find out about this affair?"

Gregory pinched the bridge of his nose. "No, not that I know of, but I've heard of his suspicions. Abraham suspects it's why he foils their plans constantly."

Owen sat back with a frown and folded his arms. The public tension between the two houses was becoming problematic. "Her death was set up to look like a suicide."

Gregory glanced at Melody with pursed lips as she handed Owen a cup of tea.

"Thank you, Miss Andrews."

"Yew know yew can call me Melody if yew wants," she told him and placed her hands on her hips.

He nodded at her and said, "Of course I do, but it isn't polite."

She smiled after a moment. "Yew Hadley's are rare birds. Yew knows that?"

His lips raised, and he glanced back at Gregory. "Please, continue."

Gregory exhaled and ignored Owen's statement about a likely murder. "If that isn't enough, Theodore has dipped his hands into a rather scandalous business, and I hate to say it's extremely lucrative."

"Which is?"

"Slave trade and drug dealing."

Owen stared at Gregory critically.

"He's made quite a name for himself in the underworld, and his business is unlikely to founder in the foreseeable future."

Owen lowered his hands and set the cup back on the saucer. "Slaves have been around since the dawn of time. What makes his enterprise more profitable?"

"It started when his father ordered him to get rid of all the babies born in the brothels, but instead of killing them like he was instructed, he started selling them. These babies are being ripped away from their mothers and sold to God knows who."

Owen pinched the bridge of his nose.

"And the more money he made from it, the more he got a taste for it," Gregory answered darkly. "It didn't take long for the emperor of Efinek to catch wind of him."

Owen lowered his hand. "Meaning?"

"He sends opium by boat, and Teddy ships off people in turn."

Owen sighed heavily. Disappearances were quite common, and often, bodies scarcely turned up. The task force appeared inept, and families would end up wondering over a lifetime what happened to their child. If enslaved children were being carted out to foreign countries and opium dens were prosperous, it made the police look even more foolish. Human and drug trafficking had been right under their nose, and they never saw it coming. They never had control; it was just an illusion that fed their arrogant minds.

"All of the sons are a part of it," Gregory said. "Edward, Benjamin, Peter, David, Jet, and they don't give a damn how many lives they ruin or how it affects the victims as long as they get paid."

Owen shook his head in anger. "I assume their fathers know about their little ventures?"

"Oh, yes. They are the ones who passed their perversions down and look at what has become of them!" he hesitated and squinted at the wall behind Owen. "Well, not Jet so much. He strictly deals with the opium trade and has relations with Blake Emerich. I believe that is the only reason why the Emerich boy is involved at all."

"So, Elijah was right," Owen whispered.

"I don't know if you've got any suspects in mind for Helena's death," Gregory grumbled. "But you might want to consider Theodore Kensington. He was her most loyal client."

Owen's face twisted in disgust.

"She told the girls he was gonna marry her," Melody interjected. "He said he was gonna get her out of Trinity Row and make her a lady."

"He did?"

"Why does that surprise you?" Gregory asked.

"Because I don't think it was a lie. I mean, what would be the point? He didn't need a rouse to get her into bed; she was willing and able."

"Yew fink he loved her?" Melody asked.

"It's hard to say," Owen shrugged. "He was Elijah's friend, not mine. I only know what I've read in the papers about him."

"I hate that man!" Melody snarled. "He ruined Helena!"

"I'm sorry for your loss," he told her, and her lip started to quiver.

Jade Calvert came to mind with all this talk of Teddy. He interviewed the girl after her mother's death, which was one of the most gut-wrenching experiences. The only other person he'd ever encountered that was as vanquished in life was Jackson.

There was no denying William Calvert and Teddy Kensington were dangerous. Jade deserved a far better life than being ignored and ridiculed, spending a lifetime of attachment to someone who held no empathy. And that's when he realized Jackson would be a good man for her. It made complete sense now, and he wanted to laugh at his inept ability to overlook this conclusion at once. They had both been subjected to cruelty and abuse and deserved a life of happiness in the end.

"There is something else," Gregory said, and Owen glanced at him. "Abraham has ordered his son to…" he bit his lip, watching hesitantly.

"Ordered him to what?"

Gregory sighed loudly, his voice lowering an octave, "He ordered the sons to kill your family."

Owen stilled, shock and anger coursing through him.

"I'd tread carefully if I were you."

Jackson attained more rumors for his anger, but they had yet to see what Owen was capable of. If they tried to come for his family, he would tear them apart one by one.

XII
ELIJAH

He lit a cigarette.

A delicate hand took it from his lips and placed it on her own. He gave the brunette named Agnes a polite smile and took a sip of whiskey. He introduced himself at the pub and followed her home shortly after. He wanted to keep his mind from swaying to thoughts of the ball at Dragon's Keep. And while the masquerade was rather stultifying and exhausting, one minor detail stood out. Yet, he tried not to think about it because he wasn't the only one who noticed.

She asked, "How do you feel?"

He blinked, not as well as he should.

"I feel wonderful," she said with a stretch. "That was just what I needed."

He frowned. Was it what he needed? It didn't feel that way, even when she pulled him into the room. He knew he should've turned around and gone home instead, but he didn't, as always, and allowed her to direct the whole episode, which was subpar at best.

"You're awfully quiet," she commented and rolled to her side. "Are you always this way after?"

He shrugged.

"You're unhappy," she surmised.

He tossed back the rest of the whiskey and set it on the bedside table. Was he?

She traced a finger on his bare chest before turning the burning end of the cigarette. It hovered inches from his skin. "This man I knew used to ask me to burn him with cigarettes and whip him with a belt."

He grabbed her wrist and snapped, "I'm not touched in the head!"

"So, he does speak," she giggled. "I thought I lost you."

He caught his mouth from slipping because she had. He let go of her hand and rubbed his eyes. He desperately wanted to leave; it was time to come up with an excuse.

"Does your brother have any suspects in that prostitute's murder?"

He dropped his hand and blinked at her, a surprising turn in the conversation. "A few," he lied. She didn't need to know of their suspicions surrounding the Elite.

"Do you know who the prostitute was?"

He snatched the cigarette from her fingers and took a drag before saying, "Sure, Helena Wimple."

"I don't mean her name. I meant who she was."

He inhaled the cigarette once more, his blue eyes swept over her face, and as he exhaled, he said, "How would I know her?

"You fancy whores," she answered as apathetically as possible, yet the jealousy in her voice was deafening. A curious revelation as he hadn't met her until the night before. "Has no one told you?"

"Stop with the games, Agnes," he snapped and sat up. He needed to flee before she kept him around for more useless sex.

She sat up and placed her chin on his shoulder. "Helena Wimple was seeing Teddy Kensington right up until the day of her murder, and before that, she was William Calvert's mistress."

He gazed at her with incredulity.

She grinned, knowing that she had his unwavering attention for the first time that evening. "When he married that twit Katerina, the affair ended, and she began seeing Theodore. She had a thing for wealthy men."

"If you're lying…" he warned.

"I wouldn't lie to you, darling," she said and fell back on the bed.

"No one mentioned that bit of information," he muttered, and a smile broke. He had Teddy once and for all.

"Aren't you glad you came over?"

He turned back to look at her. "I-"

"Agnes!" came a deep voice from below.

"Who is that?" He whispered harshly.

She jumped from the bed. "My husband!"

"You're married?"

She laughed sheepishly while wrapping herself in a robe. "You better get out of here before he sees you, or your brother will be trying to solve your murder as well."

He jumped from the bed and began to pull on his pants faster than he ever had before.

"I'll stall him," she said from the door.

"And how the fuck am I to get out of here?" He hissed while shoving his feet in his boots.

She giggled again. "There is a window."

He grabbed his shirt. "You expect me to jump from the second floor?"

A large man burst through the door, and he pushed past his wife, eyes flashing between them. "What's all this?"

"Darling, it's not what it looks like," Agnes cooed.

"I had no idea she was married, mate," Elijah admitted and held up his hands.

The man's face twisted in anger, and he barged straight for him. Elijah jumped onto the bed and ran across it. His knees smacked into his chest from the buoyancy, and he nearly fell over. The man dove headfirst, allowing Elijah the time to throw open the window and climb onto the ledge. He barely made it out when the man came for him. He landed on the ground with a loud crack and screamed in pain. The burly man's face was looking down at him from the window and pointing a fat finger. "You're fucking dead!" and disappeared.

"Fuck me," Elijah muttered and rolled onto his side.

"It's a good thing Owen had me tail you, or that man might finish you once and for all!"

Elijah looked up to see Gainsley and his driver Duke.

"Just get me out of here!" He hissed.

Gainsley and Duke grabbed Elijah from under his shoulders and dragged him to the cab before tossing him in. Gainsley stepped in behind as the driver climbed to his pedestal and took off swiftly.

The valet began laughing at once.

"I'm glad my near-death experience amuses you," Elijah hissed.

"You've done it now!" Gainsley bellowed. "I know it's hard for you to keep your hands to yourself, but a married woman?"

"I didn't know the little scamp was married!" Elijah grumbled and rolled onto his side.

"Agnes Johansson? Everyone knows she is married to that Arcaen bloke! Owen will be in fits when he finds out."

"He doesn't need to know anything about it."

Gainsley gave him a hard stare. "Owen's incredibly astute and not entirely blind. Your misfortune won't be lost on him."

Elijah grumbled, "He doesn't need any details."

Gainsley pressed his lips together.

"Ah, fuck!" Elijah groaned.

"Do you need a doctor?"

"Just give me a minute," Elijah howled as he grabbed his foot and gasped. "Never mind, get me to Jack!"

Gainsley began to laugh once more and knocked on the wall behind him. "Take us to Jack's lab."

"I do know one thing for certain," Elijah said through clenched teeth.

"And what is that?"

A shadow crossed Elijah's already pinched face. "We need to pay Teddy a visit."

"It isn't broken," Jackson muttered as he delicately twisted Elijah's foot. "But your heel is badly bruised."

Elijah's head fell back onto the table in pain.

"Luck is definitely on your side," Gainsley muttered with a laugh.

"Luck isn't what I would call it!" Avis griped as she walked into the lab with four glasses and a bottle of whiskey. She was blue-eyed, long-limbed, and lithe like the rest of them. Her hair was deep brown and fell to the middle of her waist. Her face was just as aligned as Elijah's, but she didn't rest on her looks in the way he did; Avis didn't care for beauty. She craved to be respected, and though Owen wouldn't allow it, she wanted to be a surgeon like Jackson.

Jackson walked to the counter to grab some cloth to wrap his foot. "You'll need to keep off of it for a few days."

"I can't afford to lay around. I have a murderer to catch!"

"If you weren't out having affairs with married women," Jackson said sternly. "Then you wouldn't be in this mess!"

"As I said before, I didn't know she was married," Elijah grumbled and rubbed his eyes. Of all the mistakes he made, this had to be one of his worst. He'd never fallen into bed with a taken woman before, and while Agnes was entirely to blame for her lack of honesty, he never would have followed her home if he were happier with himself.

Jackson shared a look of doubt with Avis and said, "I really find that hard to believe, and besides, Owen was the detective the last time I checked."

Elijah scoffed. "The citizens of Bel Deaux deserve the truth!"

"Meaning?"

He grabbed the bridge of his nose. "He can't be trusted to get all of the facts!"

"If you don't trust him," Jackson murmured and began to wrap his heel. "Then why do you even bother?"

Elijah leaned up on his elbows and frowned at him. "You know I trust Owen with my life!"

Jackson's shoulders went slack with an exhale. "Then what is the problem?"

"The problem is we both have jobs to do, and I can't do mine while lying around!"

"Fair enough," Jack stated and set down his foot. "But walking around on your heel will only aggravate the injury. You need rest."

"I'm fine," he muttered without conviction. He could hear the deception in his voice.

"You need to take care of yourself!" Avis wailed as she shoved a glass of whiskey in his hand.

Elijah barely caught the glass before it spilled all over his chest and said, "You're even more vexing than Owen. I don't need your mothering!"

"Someone's got to take care of you!" She snapped and turned to pour another glass. "No woman will have you!"

"Who said I wanted one?"

"Oh, right," she scowled at him. "You'd rather entertain another man's wife instead!"

"That's enough!" Jackson yelled, and the pair fell silent. She pressed her lips together and looked away in aggravation.

Elijah sat up fully and peered at her. It must be hard to live in a house of all men, especially men who thought too much of themselves. Avis was the pure one. Though she tried to act otherwise, she cared for them and never asked for anything in return.

"I'm sorry," Elijah told her.

She didn't look at him. Instead, she nodded and said, "Me too."

Jackson sank into a chair beside Elijah. He looked pale, more so than usual, and overly exhausted. There were purple bags under his eyes and stubble on his chin.

"You look awful," Elijah blurted. "When was the last time you slept?"

Jackson ran a hand through his already unkempt hair. "Since the night before last, I examined four other bodies besides your prostitute."

Elijah glowered. "There have been four other deaths?"

Jackson nodded and accepted a glass from Avis.

"And the cause?"

"Opium overdose." He tossed his notes on the table next to his brother. "Three men and one woman."

"The Elite back at it, eh?" Elijah grunted as he grabbed the discarded notebook.

Jackson ground his teeth together. "Oh, they've been leaving their mark all over the city and have enlisted the affluent sons as partners. Opium dens are thriving, but the men who don't want to be seen in these establishments are getting their fix directly from children…fucking children! They are forcing the youth of our city to deliver the drugs. Five men were beaten to death, and one was Pierre Dubois. His mother was also murdered the same night as Helena. It is said to be over drugs, but no one is willing to speak about it. Two brothels opened in Trinity Row and one in the Gas-light district, and Merfan won't do a damned thing!" He rubbed his temple and then released his head when he remembered, "Oh, and Teddy's taken Adelaide Atwood as a lover."

Elijah glanced up from the notes in confusion over Jackson's unruly demeanor and caustic tone. "Why would that bother you?"

Gainsley panicked slightly and shouted, "Owen asked me to visit Miss Louise's Dollhouse!"

Elijah peered at him in perplexity and Jackson with wry amusement.

"I've only just remembered," he stammered and walked backward. "I will, uh, see you later!"

Elijah turned to Jackson. "What was that about?"

"An infatuation gone to his head," Jackson answered.

"The Atwood's certainly snaked their way into society, didn't they?" Avis grumbled before tossing back a mouthful of whiskey. "We assumed we were much smarter because we lived with our hearts and chose to follow our dreams. We lived by example to the people we grew up with. Ran up and down the streets with and shared the same dreams with. We had the very same life as the Atwoods and they surpassed us by leaps and bounds. They married into money and are above royalty, while we're just working-class stiffs like the rest of the filth in this city."

"I'd rather be a working stiff than be a part of the Elite," Jackson growled.

"You seem to be the only one," Avis muttered, and they eyed one another steadily.

Owen's booming voice erupted from the hallway, stopping to chat with Gainsley on his way out. Elijah hastily grabbed his boot and pulled it on, wincing while at it.

Jackson rolled his eyes.

Owen stepped into the room and threw a thumb over his shoulder. "Am I missing something? Why is Gainsley all keyed up?"

"Too much whiskey," Elijah lied with a laugh.

Owen nodded once and glanced at Avis. "What are you doing here?"

"I live here," she snapped.

"What have I told you about coming into the lab?"

"I enjoy medical science," she answered with a fold of her arms.

"It's not a woman's work," Owen said.

"Says who?"

"I say, Avis!" he growled.

"How dare you put a limitation on me because of my sex!"

"Owen," Jackson interrupted, but he simply held up his hand. The tension was thick between them, and Elijah had to bite his lip to avoid worsening it.

"I wouldn't dare put a limitation on you because I know what you're capable of, but there has to be another outlet in science. Our family gets talked about enough. Your reputation doesn't need to be ruined for dissecting dead bodies."

Elijah glanced at Jackson, who merely shook his head in disgust while taking a drink.

"I don't care about my reputation!"

"You will," Owen promised. "When a man comes along-"

"How typical," she wailed. "That's all a woman's life should amount to, right? Serving a man!"

"I didn't say that, but you might think differently when you fall in love."

"No, I won't."

"Quit fighting me, you will," he stated calmly. "Where is James?"

"How the bloody hell should I know?" She hissed and stalked past them. "I'm not his mother!"

Jackson's jaw clenched when the door slammed. Elijah braced himself for another fight to break out, and when Owen whipped back around, his anger was palpable. He ran a hand over his face, evidently holding back what he truly wanted to say. Elijah knew it was hard for him to stand by when he felt responsible for each of their lives since their parents passed on. He hadn't been the same since. But the moment he looked back at Jackson, he was all business. "There is something about the note that's been bothering me."

Jackson blinked at him. "The fact that he's killed before?"

"That's just it," Owen shrugged. "What other murders could be considered by the same hand? I've never seen anything like Helena's slain form before."

Jack scratched at his blue chin. "Two prostitutes were brutalized the week before Raoul and I left for Jendoux. Both raped and severely beaten, died some days later."

Owen folded his arms, and his eyes narrowed. "That was five years ago."

"Perhaps their murders pacified him until now."

"Yes, but I don't remember this," Owen said incredulously. "Why weren't the murders reported?"

Jack shrugged. "Merfan hushed it all up. I'm only aware because Raoul examined the bodies and wanted my input." He turned to sift through notebooks dated by year in his cabinet, grabbing one in particular and flipping through the pages. "Let's see… Isabella Stoatshead and Thiana Grady were mutilated with a knife similar to Helena. The only difference is that they were alive when it happened."

Owen's brows pinched. "And no one was caught?"

"There were two, actually."

"Who?" Elijah demanded. It was out of place for Jackson to conceal information. Out of the three, he was the most sympathetic to those subject to ridicule and Merfan's injustice.

Jackson glanced back at his notes. "Thomas Whitefield and Jones Parker."

Elijah clenched his teeth. They were executed by firing squad on Merfan's orders, leaving the Elite in an uproar. They were in Teddy's pocket, and that alone should have been enough to save their lives.

"Ah," Owen murmured with clarity. "Merfan wouldn't disclose their crimes to O'Brien, and Feilding kept tight-lipped on the matter."

Jackson watched Owen with deliberate concentration. He pressed his lips together, clearly debating on disclosing something vital.

Realization dawned on Owen's face. "You know, don't you?"

Jackson smiled grimly and dropped his gaze.

"Jackson," Owen warned.

He glanced back flatly. "Isabella was Merfan's bastard daughter."

Elijah blinked at him. It simply couldn't be. Merfan stood firmly against the impoverished on the east end and went to great lengths to separate his character from them.

"How do you know about this?" Owen asked with an air of irritation.

Jackson exhaled loudly, looking as if he didn't want to discuss it.

"You can't bring it up and not explain why!" Elijah bellowed. "If his daughter was murdered and he sought revenge without waiting for a proper trial, then he has some explaining to do!"

"He barged into the examination room like a madman," Jackson answered gruffly. "He was screaming at the top of his lungs and throwing things about. Feilding had to threaten to have him sedated to stop the destruction. He then cried and admitted everything, begging us to keep our mouths shut, and as it wasn't my secret, I didn't mention it."

"I am your brother, Jackson!" Owen yelled at him, and there was a hint of betrayal in his voice. "I want you to fucking tell me when something like this happens!"

Jackson eyed him carefully. His voice was far too low as he said, "It was early spring. I didn't want to bother you."

Elijah glanced at Owen carefully. It would be the anniversary of Clara and Charlie's death's that Jackson was referring to. Owen was never himself when it came about.

"This is something I want you to bother me with!" Owen yelled. "No matter what time of year it is!"

"Whatever you say," Jackson answered quietly.

Owen turned around in anger.

Elijah watched Jackson steadily, and when he noticed his attention, he gave him a pointed look. "What?"

There was something off with him, and it had to do with Teddy. "What aren't you saying?"

Owen frowned between the two of them.

Jack arranged his expression to appear confused. "What are you talking about?"

"Don't play the fool. You know exactly what I am talking about!" Elijah challenged. "You were speaking of Teddy's wrongdoings and ended with him taking Adelaide Atwood as a lover as if it bothered you. Why?"

He shrugged. "It doesn't."

Hope sprang into Elijah's chest. "Do you fancy Adelaide?"

Jack's face twisted in disbelief. "You can't be serious!"

"What's not to like?" Elijah pressured. "She's ravishing."

"No, she's hypercritical and vexing," Jack corrected with nonchalance.

"Aren't they all?" Elijah drawled, yet there wasn't as much interest as before.

"She is also unchaste and untrustworthy," Jack countered. "And while you don't care for anything other than a body, I'd rather not waste my time on a woman who fucks her way into society!"

"And you suppose I do?" Elijah shrieked.

"Considering how you've never had an honest relationship in your entire life, I'd say yes!"

Elijah's mouth opened to argue, but Owen intervened, "Whatever spat the two of you are having, I want it to end now! There are far more pressing matters than your disagreements on women."

"Don't tell me how to live my life, Owen," Jackson snapped. "You may think you can bully Avis, but you won't boss me about!"

Elijah shielded his gaze when Owen started to dispute his claims. The resentment rising within him was wholly unjustified, and he felt sick to his stomach for having any ill will toward his brother. Elijah would never admit that he was slowly feeling envious over a woman. He also didn't want to give Jackson and Owen a reason to fight. It was catastrophic whenever they did.

"Shut it, will you?" Elijah yelled, and they both looked at him. "We need to focus. Catching this murderer is the priority here! We cannot do that if we are at odds with one another!"

"You're right," Owen answered and glanced back at Jackson after a moment. "I'm sorry."

Jackson took another sip of his whiskey.

Owen walked over to the bottle and empty glass Avis had left behind. "While scouring Trinity Row, I've found that William Calvert was connected to Helena Wimple. This is the second woman to turn up dead with direct ties to him."

"So was Teddy," Eli said. "She began to see him when old Calvert kicked her to the curb when he married Katerina."

"I heard," Owen murmured. "Did Stephen tell you this?"

"He never showed," Elijah said with a shrug of his shoulders and turned his gaze elsewhere not to give away the lie. "Philip found out from the girls at the Dollhouse."

"But he was accounted for the night of her murder," Owen said dismissively. "And so was William."

"They are also very influential," Jackson muttered darkly. "Employing a wide variety of men, many capable of crimes such as this."

"All of them are criminals," Owen barked back. "I can't imagine any of them would be so precise in murder."

"You never know what a man is capable of."

Owen eyed him steadily. "Have you found anything on the flowers?"

Jackson shook his head. "I haven't spoken to Cordelia yet."

Owen pressed his lips together. There was an argument on the tip of his tongue. Elijah could see it clearly, but he was tired of his brothers fighting with one another and he said, "How do you suppose we track down Calvert?" He barely sees the children he lives with, let alone outsiders."

"The police are hard to avoid," Owen drawled.

"Ha!" Elijah mocked. "You lot are easily avoidable!"

"Would it be of interest to either of you that Calvert has requested an audience with me tomorrow?" Jackson asked.

The two appeared confused and bewildered.

"You?" Elijah scoffed.

"Yes, me!"

Elijah instantly began to voice his disapproval. Owen, however, plucked at his beard and watched Jack with curiosity. "He wants to know what you've uncovered."

"Obviously," Jackson answered flippantly and began looking over his notebook.

Owen continued to stare until Jack stopped rifling through the pages and lifted his gaze. "What is it?"

"Would you be willing to help us?"

Jack flashed another maddening look. "You expect me to interrogate him? I will end up with a bullet in my head for hinting at any sort of involvement on his part!"

Elijah eyed him. "If we are going to nail Calvert for the murder-"

"Murders," Owen corrected. "He likely killed his wife, remember?"

"Murders then," Elijah repeated disdainfully with a roll of his eyes. He didn't find this bit of information as interesting as his brothers. He wanted to nail this on Teddy more than anything. "We need to catch him off guard, and he'll never expect anything from you. You have the meeting we need."

Jack's mouth twitched, yet he said nothing.

Owen glanced at him and repeated, "Would you be willing to help us?"

"Do I have a choice?" He snapped and strode past them without a straight answer.

"You still need to visit Elizabeth before the week is through!" Owen yelled after him, and the door slammed in response. He rounded on Elijah. "All right then, out with it!"

Elijah dismissed the question with a gulp of whiskey.

"You can't fool me. Why are you acting so petulant toward Jackson?"

He wasn't going to play Owen's games. His brothers didn't need to know every little thing. "I'm not."

"You are, though, and it has to do with a female. What does Jackson care how you spend your time and with whom?"

"He doesn't, and I would never fight with Jackson over a woman!" Elijah growled and jumped off the table. His leg nearly gave out, but he caught himself and limped toward the exit.

There was mirth in Owen's voice as he bellowed, "Now, what have you gotten yourself into?"

"I'd rather not talk about it," Elijah grumbled and Owen's laughter followed him out of the room.

XIII
Jackson

Calvert Steel was located on the west side of the extensive city and loomed as the number one supplier in the nine kingdoms. The monumental factory hedged the Kinnedale Harbor beside Lewell Lumber and Kensington Air, run by the adept and shrewd William Calvert the second, just as his father before him. William was one of the most influential and affluent men in the capital. His time was sparse, as was his patience. Many found it more challenging to gain an audience with him than with Queen Elizabeth. And unfortunately for Jackson, Calvert sought him out. But rather than meet at his factory in the middle of a working day, William invited Jackson to his home instead.

Jackson took the trolley and acquired a lot of unnecessary attention. He avoided nosey stares by intently looking at the paper, reading his brother's recent article instead of letting intrusive behavior spike his anger.

Once he stepped off the train car and strolled down the road, he walked through a nefariously wrought iron gate, caging a manor with massive double red doors and countless turrets disappearing into the sky. The structure was as impressive as Dragon's Keep. William Calvert clearly didn't hold back when displaying his wealth.

Jackson ignored the nervous stir in his stomach, his heart beating louder and wilder with each step. The restriction in his chest was sudden, and he had to focus on each breath to calm his rising anxiety. The sudden tension was not over William Calvert himself. He was more nervous about the possibility of catching a glimpse of Jade. He closed his fist with the thought as he knocked on the door swiftly.

The Calvert butler whipped open the door and sneered down from a large, aquiline nose.

He cleared his throat. "I have an appointment with William Calvert."

The butler wasn't given the chance to answer as Jet stepped in front of the man with an alarming matter of self-importance.

"What do you want?" He barked with contempt, and Jackson's face twisted in bewilderment; the bursting animosity was confusing. While he wasn't necessarily that fond of Jet, he didn't know much about the guy to be on the brunt end of distinctly insolent behavior. Jet used to run around with Elijah and Teddy Kensington years ago, and as Jackson was not only older, but he was far too lost in his vices to extend any sort of friendship. However, that didn't mean they were adversaries.

Jet's eyes continued to burn with hatred. "We don't accept handouts nor solicitors, now fuck off!" He went to reach for the door and slam it in his face when Jackson placed his large boot in the doorway to keep it from shutting. Jet continued to push against the door with all the force he could muster, but Jackson's foot was inflexible and he pushed back.

"I have an appointment with your father!"

The door went slack. "What do you want with him?"

Jackson released his foot and stood at full height. "My business is with him alone."

"For god's sake, Jet," William Calvert yelled from the hallway of his office. "Stop berating my guest and let him in!"

Jet took a step backward. "But father-"

"Don't you have a community to give back to?" Mr. Calvert snapped; his daunting stare swept over his son.

The butler allowed Jackson inside, and he stalked past Jet, who was trying to regain his composure. "Yes, father."

Mr. Calvert's face twitched. "Then get to it."

Jackson stepped into Calvert's office and closed the door behind them.

"You'll have to excuse my son," William amended after shaking his hand and pointing to the chair in front of his desk.

Jackson waved him off and murmured, "It's no bother."

The pair stared at one another for several tense seconds.

"I suppose you know why I sent for you?" Calvert was abrupt and imposing.

Jackson shifted in the chair, which was too small for his long limbs. "I gather it has something to do with Helena Wimple."

The smile on Calvert's lips didn't touch his eyes. "I was most... unsettled when I heard of her demise."

Jackson's eyebrows shot up and down quickly with a shrug. "It was more than unsettling. It was downright revolting and horrifying."

Calvert continued to stare without a word, and it began to unnerve Jackson. The hairs on his arms and neck rose with each passing second.

He shifted again. "Look-"

"I'll get right to the point, Mr. Hadley," William interrupted. "I know you and your brothers are aware that she was a woman I saw occasionally." He stood and walked over to the whiskey decanter by the window. "And when Alexandra took her life last year, your brother seemed to think there was more to it." He poured two glasses and handed one over.

Jackson eyed it for a few reluctant seconds, not wanting to share a drink with such a nefarious man, but he reached for it out of courtesy instead of insulting him further.

"I don't see what that has to do with me," Jackson responded and placed the glass on his knee. Calvert watched as he refused to take a drink and settled his palm over the top. "I'm not a detective."

Calvert's cold eyes raised to Jackson meticulously as he sat on the corner of his desk. "I know exactly what you are, Jackson Hadley. You slice up dead bodies for what purpose exactly? Pleasure? Or is it some idiosyncrasy embedded in your character?"

He glared. Was he trying to paint a narrative that Jackson himself could have a hand in Helena's death? It would be a way to get back at Owen and perhaps even Jackson himself for consorting with Cordelia. It must have angered him to know the pair were close.

Calvert's eyes were relentless and penetrating, and he was still waiting for an answer. But Jackson wasn't going to give the satisfaction and bow down. "Science, actually. A great deal of good can be collected by dissecting a body and uncovering one's cause of death. Especially in cases such as criminal matters or even if the death is sudden. Wouldn't you want to know how to avoid it if you could?"

"Did you look over the autopsy of my late wife?" Calvert asked, and a shadow crossed his face.

Jackson bit back a curse. "I did."

"And do you corroborate with your brother's… theory?"

Jackson gazed impassively. Who did Calvert think produced the notion? "What theory?"

Calvert's eyes narrowed. He knew Jackson was lying. "He never mentioned that he thought Alexandra was murdered?"

What could he say? He looked at the report and knew Owen would ask what he thought.

"He may have mentioned it," Jackson answered vaguely and finally took a drink.

One of Calvert's eyebrows raised. "And?"

Jackson swallowed the liquid slowly, deciding then to lie. "He is wrong. She died of her own hand."

Calvert's cheek lifted, but Jackson got the sense he wasn't buying this fabrication. Still, he didn't argue and said, "Well, at least one of you has some sense."

Jackson changed the topic quickly. As much as he wanted to punch William, the bastille was a dreadful place to spend the night. "Helena was slain most viciously. Her body parts were exposed, and some even removed."

Calvert's eyes widened with this statement. "Which parts?"

Jackson frowned with confusion. "Organs."

Calvert rubbed his temple warily and muttered, "My God," under his breath.

This was news to him, which meant he had more than likely not committed the crime itself, leaving Jackson to believe he made the official order if he was indeed involved at all. But what would be his motive?

"The person capable of something as vile as this will strike again."

Calvert's face was inscrutable now as he dropped his hand.

"Helena didn't deserve it," Jackson hedged. "Even if she chose to live her life as a prostitute. No one deserves a fate so revolting."

"I cared for her. I truly did, but when I married Katerina, she ensured the affair ended once and for all. Although, I should have taken better care of Helena, paid for an apartment, and given her an allowance."

Jackson frowned, unsure of why he was even pretending to deceive him. "When was the last time you saw her?"

"Why don't you leave the inquisitions to your brother?" Mr. Calvert laughed.

"Fair enough," Jackson answered and held up his hand.

"There was nothing left behind then?" Calvert asked with finality, and Jackson knew the meeting was closing.

"Absolutely nothing."

For the first time since entering his office, Calvert appeared relieved, elated even, as he asked, "You're certain?"

Jackson glowered with a nod.

"Well, I won't keep you then," he said abruptly and stood. "I know how busy a surgeon can be, and I have other business to deal with."

Jackson downed the rest of his whiskey and handed Calvert the glass. "It was… interesting, to say the least."

Calvert laughed heartily; his mood had significantly improved from their conversation. It unnerved Jackson to the core, and he almost made it to the door when Calvert said, "Oh, and Jackson?"

He turned.

"You tell your brothers to tread carefully."

Jackson glared, and his voice lowered an octave, "Are you threatening my family?"

"Me?" Calvert said with a raise of his brow. "Oh, no. I'm just giving a friendly reminder of who's watching."

Jackson pressed his lips together and exited the room without a word.

Jackson found Cordelia Calvert standing in the glasshouse of her manor. She was admiring her latest painting. It was a nude of Juliet, one that wouldn't be well received in any gallery.

"Finally finished?"

She turned with a smile and said, "Spent all night on it."

"Subtle," he muttered as he peered over her shoulder.

It was as elegant as a nude could be. Juliet was stretched to show off the angles of her feminine form, yet she wasn't spread in a vulgar way. It was a shame that such a talented piece would never be praised.

"I thought you'd like it," she admitted with a broadened smile.

He winked and held up the black lilies.

Her eyes widened, and her jaw went slack.

"The murderer placed these in Helena Wimple's hand."

Her brows pinched as her eyes slid up to his. "He did?"

"Do you know what kind of lilies they are?" Jackson asked as she reached for them. "The exact breed and where they come from?"

"They are Landini Asiatic lilies," she muttered as she looked them over. "They can thrive here, but they aren't native."

Jackson's face fell.

"Why do you ask?"

"I was hoping to narrow down the region they came from."

Her eyes flashed to him in perplexity and down to the flowers again. "They primarily come from the west in Noic, but Vendekk grows them in spades as well." His eyes flashed at her diligently. "I'd wager not many people have these planted in their gardens in Bel Deaux, but maybe they do. They are perennials. Everlasting."

"Do you suppose that's how he sees her?" Jackson mused. "In eternal death?"

Cordelia's eyes widened as she stared at the flowers, utterly mesmerized.

He turned to pour them a glass of wine. "Where's Raoul?"

"Sleeping it off, I suppose," she murmured and gazed back at her work. "He got rather pissed last night, something about Antoinette."

Jackson clucked his tongue and handed Cordelia a glass.

She grinned up at him. "Thank you."

"I met with your brother."

Her smile fell. "You did what?"

"Just now," he looked down at her. "He wanted information on the prostitute that was murdered."

Cordelia dropped her gaze and took a drink.

"She was his mistress," he continued with her silence. "But Katerina ended the affair sometime after they wed."

Cordelia gazed back up at him. "She would never have made you happy, you know."

"I know that."

Katerina was anything but kind and loving, yet it was not her overwhelming personality that kept him calling. She differed as far from Isabella Dubois in every way possible, the very reason he sought her out. She was ruthless and seriously depraved, which meant she could give him exactly what he needed without the risk of falling in love. It was an emotion he didn't want or need because Isabella tore the fantasy away just as quickly as she gave it, leaving him bitter and cynical.

"I wasn't talking about Katerina," Cordelia corrected, and he dropped his gaze to the flowers in her hand. "You would have lost interest in Isabella when you came to your senses and realized the pair of you didn't value the same qualities in a partner or have a single thing in common. Well, other than sex."

He hated to admit she was right, so he refused to answer.

Cordelia pursed her lips, and her gaze lingered far longer than was necessary. He was starting to feel uncomfortable when she finally tore her eyes away, peering back at her work and she drawled, "What did William have to say?"

He took a drink as he contemplated. Should he discuss his suspicions? She knew what kind of man her brother was, so there was no use lying about his character. But was it wise to tell her that he killed Alexandra? Cordelia was quite fond of her sister-in-law and was most distraught by her death. He kept his thoughts to himself and said, "He wanted to know if there was any evidence left behind."

Her brow quirked. "And was there?"

"No, nothing that could lead to a culprit."

She nodded and glanced back at the painting.

He eyed her thoughtfully, and a strange impulse emerged. The odd encounters with her niece Jade were interactions he continually thought about. She'd been in his mind for the last week. But how to bring her up without arousing suspicion? He licked his lips and blurted, "Jade is a captivating girl, is she not?"

He closed his eyes briefly. Subtle.

She smiled widely, but it vanished just as quickly. "Indeed. I fear she is unhappy. I doubt William has taken care of her mental stability."

"While my conversation with her was brief," he muttered and sat down in the plush chair Juliet posed in. "She seemed fine enough, although she wasn't partaking in the party's enthusiasm, hiding more like."

Cordelia snorted. "That is because she isn't one to relish in such frivolities."

"Meaning?"

"She's uninhibited and curious and unbound," Cordelia stated with so much enthusiasm that her eyes even lit up, and she quickly became very animated with every word she spoke, causing Jackson to grin. "She has this unstoppable spirit and brilliant mind. She isn't the type of girl to be obedient to any man nor settle down and have a brood of children." She set her glass down and picked up a pack of cigarettes, offering him one, but he waved her off. She placed a cig on her lips and continued, "But I don't mean to imply she isn't susceptible to the opposite sex. As I'm sure you know, she was caught with your cousin, and I also believe Edward Wright is deeply smitten, or so they say, but I could not tell you if those feelings are reciprocated. I do know, however, that she despises Teddy."

"That doesn't bode well for their engagement," he answered briskly and ignored the rising annoyance that was Edward Wright himself. How odd.

"Indeed," she concurred and cocked her head to the side as she thought more of it. "I wonder why. He is one of the most affluent sons."

Jackson refrained from stating his opinion and rolled his eyes instead. Teddy was one of the most useless human beings he had ever met. His corruption and ill nature insulted everything Jackson stood for as a man. It was offensive that Teddy was praised because he had money. Why was his life valued more when the Hadley's actually helped people instead of cutting them down?

His dream came back to mind with this thought, and he nearly laughed aloud. Jackson had never actually fought Teddy, and it was strange to have dreamt of it at all, but it was a satisfying concept and one he wished to relive.

Cordelia watched him curiously; a small smile tugged at her lips.

"I hate when you give me that look," he divulged with a glare. "It makes me feel like you have some secret I'll never be privy to."

She tapped the fingers on her right hand against the ones on her left. The smile never diminished. "You brought her up for a reason. Why?"

He took another drink instead of answering the question. He didn't know why he wanted to speak about Jade, it was a bizarre compulsion, and he'd rather not dissect the reason as to why.

Her grin widened. "Would you like to see her again?"

He shook his head and shifted in his seat. "I don't want to talk about this."

She rolled her eyes. "Yes, I forgot, you can't discuss your fucking feelings to save your life!"

He grinned. "There's the charm."

"You are infuriating," she answered with a cheeky smile in return.

They moved to the parlor, and her butler placed a tray of cheeses, meats, and olives in front of them. They drank more wine and picked at the food for quite some time before Raoul made his way into the room. His hair was sticking up at all ends, and he was still in his robe and undergarments.

"I wish I had the luxury of sleeping until two in the afternoon," Jackson commented dryly.

"I didn't go to bed until dawn," he grunted and sat beside him.

Cordelia flashed a knowing look and raised her hands as if to say, I told you so.

"What kept you up all night?" Jackson inquired with a smile.

"Booze," Raoul muttered and lit up a cigarette. He took a toke and then scratched his brow with his thumb. "It started with one drink, and before I knew it, the bottle was gone. Then I opened another."

Jackson smiled. How many nights had he been there?

Raoul tugged at his mustache, and his dark eyes flicked to Cordelia. "Pour me a glass, would you?"

"And the drinking continues," she muttered with a touch of judgment but poured him a glass anyway.

"We had an awful week," he snapped. "I don't know if I can get the image of Helena out of my head."

Jackson glanced at him. It was unnerving. The woman was unnecessarily cut up, and with the discovery of the note, she was a victim of chance. Easily preyed upon because of her profession, and more would follow. It would get a hell of a lot worse if they didn't catch the perpetrator quickly.

Cordelia's eyes narrowed, but she didn't answer, opting for a bite of cheese instead.

"I saw Antoinette yesterday," Raoul continued. "She's marrying that bloke, the one from Teddy's gang. She's meddling in a dangerous game, and I don't see how she'll ever get out."

"That's not your problem," Cordelia muttered.

"But I love her," Raoul reminded them. "Even after all these years. How could it not be my problem?"

"Yet she doesn't love you," Cordelia answered bluntly.

"That's rather harsh," he said and puffed on his cigarette again.

"The closer you come to accepting it," she replied as she stood to grab another bottle. "The better you'll be."

Raoul sat back in his seat and stared unseeingly at the table before him. Jackson gazed at her critically. He would never throw one's emotions in their face, and even if Cordelia's heart were in the right place, Raoul needed to sort through his feelings on his terms, not hers.

"Enough with this," Cordelia said after she sat back down and poured more wine into their glasses. "What was the scene like?"

Jackson leaned his head back against the chair and stared at the ceiling. "It was shambolic, and yet, it was completely meticulous."

"How do you figure?" Cordelia asked. She was always helpful in uncovering tidbits of a crime scene he may have overlooked.

"His passion for the crime was disorganized and erratic, but the precision itself was diligent and very thorough," Jackson answered.

"He has to know the female anatomy," Raoul bellowed. "He specifically cut out her uterus with precision."

"You believe him to be a doctor?" Cordelia asked as she looked rapidly between the two.

"It's always a possibility and one that shan't be overlooked," Jackson answered dismissively, though he was certain it was a surgeon. "But we've got to keep our options open and not fixate on one detail alone. The organ trade has also grown in popularity over the years. What if all he is after is money?"

Raoul paled and muttered, "Are you serious? If a man is willing to kill for money, what is to say that any of us are safe?"

Cordelia snapped, "Would you rather he only attacked women?"

"Of course not!" He cried and held up his hands. "I don't want no one to die, Cordelia. The thought of killing for money goes well beyond my thought process!"

She took a drink, clearly not impressed by his explanation.

"I was just making an observation," Jackson declared to break the tension. "It is another possibility that should be considered, especially if the next victim strays from a prostitute, but I doubt it will. He is most likely a predator with a particular type."

"What does Feilding intend to do?" Cordelia asked.

"He ordered to double the police presence throughout the city," Jackson answered with a rub of his eyes. "He's hoping to stop another murder before it happens."

"And how likely is that?"

He dropped his hand. "Very unlikely. This is especially true when prostitutes willingly follow strange men down dark alleyways or step into their cabs without a second thought. We can't end prostitution in a day, and even if we could, he'd still find a victim."

"That doesn't make me feel any better," Cordelia muttered. "Those poor women."

Raoul held up a glass. "To Helena."

Jackson's cheek lifted as both he and Cordelia raised their glasses of wine. "To Helena."

XIV
JADE

"Are you out of your bloody mind?" Jet cried loudly. "Father would have my head if he found out I helped you out of the city!"

Jade rolled her eyes and sat in the chair next to his desk. She came to his house without an invitation and interrupted a liaison with Blake Emerich, but this isn't what concerned her, far from it; what he did behind closed doors was his own business. She was bothered by his wife Marian who was lingering in the hallway to eavesdrop. Whenever Jade saw her, she ignored Jet (just as he did with her), a perfect relationship of mutual hatred, as he said. But it was suspicious for her to loiter, and Jade became overly paranoid that she would run to Theodore about the visit.

"I don't understand why you even care," she whispered, and his jaw snapped shut. "And as it's my life, shouldn't I be the one to choose with whom I spend it with?"

He barked, "Why are you whispering?"

She mouthed, 'Marian.'

"She won't say anything."

She gaped at him as if he were a complete idiot. She was an Atwood for God's sake. "You don't know that."

Jet pinched the bridge of his nose. The two were constantly at odds with one another. She couldn't remember when their conversation hadn't ended in an argument.

"You simply refuse to agree with me because you know I'm right! Besides, I thought you'd be jumping at the chance to get rid of me! You don't even have to share any money! I just want to get out of the city unbeknownst to Theodore and Papa and anyone who wants to control my choices! I want to live my life how I please!"

Blake watched her from the window; there was a smirk on his lips. Unlike Jet, he was fond of Jade and seemed to enjoy her antics.

Jet dropped his hand and leveled her stare. "Will you shut the door?" Blake pushed off from the window and shuffled through the room silently. Marian huffed loudly as she stalked off, her shoes smacking against the ground in the opposite direction.

Once they were alone, he said, "If I get you out of the house, I need you to do something for me in return."

Her stomach dropped. She knew exactly what he was suggesting, and she shook her head. "If it has to do with Theodore, I won't agree!"

He sighed loudly and said, "I need you to play nice and distract him until I get you out of the city."

"Why?" she demanded and glanced at Blake. "Distract him from what?"

Jet followed her stare.

"Perhaps you should tell her," Blake said.

"Are you mad? What if she runs to Teddy?"

"Considering how she wants to run away from her entire life to get out of marriage with him, I highly doubt it," Blake answered with a wry grin. "This could be the insurance you need, her silence in exchange for freedom."

Jet glanced at her. His eyes wandered over her face in search of something. She waited patiently. To get anywhere with Jet, you had to play by his rules.

"I plan to hand him over to the Queen," he admitted after some time. "We've been ordered to kill the Hadley's, but I don't want any part of it. The city will riot."

Jade stood abruptly and hissed, "I beg your pardon?"

Jet gazed up at her in bewilderment. "What?"

"What have the Hadley's done to warrant a death sentence?" Her hands began to shake, and it was hard to decipher which was more pressing, the static erupting in her palms or her thunderous heart. She didn't have the nerve to calm down, and if she knew what would happen next, she would've walked away instead.

Jet's face smoothed quickly, and he muttered, "I see. What has Elijah done?"

"What do you mean?"

"What has Elijah Hadley promised to make you want to walk away from Teddy?"

"Please, I don't even know him," she hissed.

"It must be Jackson then," Blake said. "We saw you talking to them at the mask. Is this why Abraham and Teddy want them dead?"

"You never know," Jet snarled, glaring at her. "How long have you been seeing him?"

"I'm not! I only just met him!"

Jet snorted. "That seems unlikely. You like to whore around just as mother did!"

Anger swelled within her chest, which glowed like an ember of a flame, soaring down her arms such as the ebb and flow of a river throughout her veins. Her hands flexed at his smug face, and the rage emphatically projected outwards; the tea set atop Jet's desk shattered. The brew, cream, and sugar exploded across the room with a loud boom that had Jet and Blake covering their ears.

Jade's eyes widened briefly in astonishment, and she glanced at her hands, which were glowing. She looked back at Jet. For a fleeting second, she saw the fear in his eyes. Even Blake appeared unsettled and he took a step backward. Jet quickly recollected himself when Marian stormed into the room and demanded an explanation for the noise. His face twisted with malice and resentment though he didn't immediately answer.

"There's no need to break the china," Marian scolded and ran to Jade's shaking form. The glow in her veins, fingertips and chest dimmed with the overwhelming sense of horror emerged. The silence that followed was deafening, and the distress had her hyperventilating. Marian thought Jet smashed the set-in anger, and though she hadn't caught her slip, Jet and Blake had. It was nearly impossible to handle ever since Jackson Hadley permeated her crumbling existence.

"You look in dire need of a bed," he snapped at Marian, and she glared at him. "I want my son to be robust and healthy, and he won't if you're stressing over my sister!"

"Please," she argued. "I've been lying in bed for days. We don't even know if I'm carrying your child!"

"Now!" He barked and slammed his fist against the desk. Both of them jumped, and Marian sighed in defeat before leaving the room.

Jade clenched her teeth and glowered at him. She wasn't afraid of Jet or Blake, fully capable of handling whatever vitriol they spewed. The static expelled from her palms once again, and his desk began to shake so violently that all the papers sitting atop flew off one by one.

He placed his palms on the desk and yelled, "Stop it, Jade!"

Her stare narrowed, and the desk only began to convulse with more ferocity. Jet stumbled backward over his chair, and Blake reached out to grab him.

Within seconds, all her senses vanished, and there was nothing but vast darkness. She screamed, but nothing came out; fear had quickly taken over. Her will crumbled, and she buckled on her knees; the desk stopped shaking immediately, and her sight returned. Had she blacked out?

Jet strode toward her with a devilish grin, causing her to fall back on her palms. She didn't like his smug face. It was far too superior for comfort. He wouldn't be the one laughing if she knew how to harness her emotions better.

His pale eyes met her with loathing. "Do you have a death wish?"

"Of course not!" She retorted anxiously. "I don't know what you think you saw-"

"Please," he interrupted with a roll of his eyes. "We all shared the same womb!"

She gaped at him. He had stopped her?

"You are so blind! Did you honestly believe that you were the only one? Where do you think you got it from?"

"I don't know what you mean," she answered evasively with a shake of her head.

"Enough!" Jet yelled and knelt to grab her; his fingers pressed violently into her skin. "Once I realized that I could bend the energy of the lives of everyone around me, I looked into our heritage. Father comes from a long line of Dukes and lords. He was entirely ordinary and against all signs of witchcraft; still, I looked. I couldn't feel an ounce of magic in him, but I thought perhaps it was buried deep within his blood. I poured through books in the library, and after months of searching, I finally found his lineage and discovered there isn't a single witch in his ancestry." His grip tightened, and a dark shadow passed through his eyes.

"You're hurting me," she wailed and tried to pull away.

He ignored her and carried on with his story. "I knew I wouldn't find our mother's parentage amongst father's books, so I went to Vendekk."

She stopped struggling and leveled his stare.

"I found her there," he stated with clarity, but his eyes were unfocused. "She is a direct descendent of Sorcha Llewelyn." His eyes slid back to her, and his teeth clenched as he said, "*We* are direct descendants of her!"

He was mad. All witches were burned at the stake and a wide variety of innocents. "She never had any children!" Jade's voice snapped with ire.

"That's what she wanted everyone to think," he said, giving her another pitying smile. "But why would she give up her children when she would be crucified?"

"You can paint any narrative you want, but it doesn't make it true!"

"I can feel it pouring out of each of you!" He snarled and shook her harshly. "All five of us have it flowing in our veins. You cannot call that a coincidence!"

Perhaps there was some truth, but only in Pearl. Esmeralda never admitted to anything, and Ruby would never associate herself with such rubbish.

"Let me go," she finally whispered harshly.

He gripped her tighter for an instant and only released her when Blake said, "Let her go, Jet!"

She watched him rise, the glare never left his face, and when he spoke, his voice was more threatening than she had ever heard before, "When you're ready to have an actual conversation about what we are, you know where to find me."

She pressed her lips together and slowly got to her own feet, ignoring Blake's offering hand.

"And if you want my help out of the city," Jet called. "Then you'll play nice with Theodore."

She didn't respond and fled the manor as panic led her mind to run rampant with the worst type of scenario. Jet was a terrifying individual and had to be stopped before he destroyed the lives of others.

She couldn't very well go home now. Her emotions were too close to the cusp for exposure. But where to? Esmeralda wasn't returning from Bellmere until nightfall, and Pearl would only question her relentlessly. The only place she supposed was Cordelia's, where she would remain uninterrupted, and perhaps in retrospect, she should have gone to her instead of Jet.

"Take me to Cordelia's, please," she told her driver as he helped her into the cab.

"You aren't allowed there."

"And why not?"

"Your father has forbidden it."

She rolled her eyes. "Yes, well, I don't fucking care what he says. Please take me to Cordelia's!"

He stared at her in frustration. She had convinced him to break her father's rules on more than one occasion.

"Please, Adam."

He exhaled and shut the door, scrambling to his stoop.

She sighed and rubbed her temple. Could Jet be believed? Were they indeed descendants of Sorcha? She couldn't see why he would make up such a ridiculous story: it only implicated them in witchcraft. And, if there was one thing about her brother, he would never put his life in peril.

Adam's annoyance was written on his face when he assisted her from the cab, and it was only after she made it to the door that she realized she should apologize to him. She wasn't merely risking her freedom, but his as well.

She hesitated in Cordelia's doorway. It had been quite some time since she had been here, and she was unsure of how she'd be received.

The door swiftly opened, startling her. She screamed loudly at the sudden emergence of Jackson Hadley.

He jumped and said, "Jade?"

"You scared me!" She yelped and placed a hand on her chest.

"I'm sorry," he answered, his lips curving upwards. He was wearing spectacles, and his hair was unkempt.

The static returned. It couldn't be helped. "What are you doing here?"

"I was about to ask you the same!" He grinned widely, exposing an impressive set of teeth. The dimple below his mouth was even back.

"Jade!" Cordelia bellowed as she stepped around Jackson with open arms. She smiled warmly in return as her aunt embraced her tightly. "I've missed you terribly!" Cordelia abruptly released her and began to fuss over her at once. "What's happened?"

Jade shook her head through a short laugh. "Nothing, I'm fine. I just didn't know where to go."

She carefully avoided glancing up at Jackson. It was odd to feel particularly shy now. Perhaps it was because she could feel him watching her intently and was afraid of what she would find in his stare. The interaction with Jet still had her shaken.

"You're always welcome here," Cordelia encouraged.

A cab rolled around the drive, slicing into their interaction.

"I'm sorry I have to run now," Jackson stated, and it sounded like he genuinely meant it. She peered up at him and let a smile settle on her face. He was even more charming with untidy hair and glasses. His eyes fixed on her, and a hunger ripped through her with intensity. His stare did wondrous things to her body. How would it feel to be wrapped in his arms as he whispered her name? Or better yet if he leaned down to kiss her lips…

Cordelia cleared her throat loudly.

He grinned and placed one hand in his pocket while holding onto a black notebook with the other. When his eyes slid back to Jade, his smile faded. His voice was husky when he finally said, "Good day, ladies."

She watched him walk to his cab, not caring what Cordelia would think, and she could see that her aunt was watching through her peripheral vision.

He turned to look at her again, and his eyes widened in surprise when he spotted her staring. He shook it off with a wide grin and placed his hand over his heart. He didn't jump into his cab until a sandy-haired man stuck his head out of the window and yelled, "Jackson, we need to go!" with urgency.

She chuckled as the cab rolled away and glanced back at Cordelia with a smile that stretched from one ear to the other.

Her eyes narrowed. "And how long has this been going on?"

"Nothing's happened, and nothing ever will," Jade grumbled. "I'm engaged, remember?"

"So what?" Cordelia bellowed. "If you don't want to marry Theodore, you don't have to!"

"My father hasn't given me much choice!" Jade argued and chewed on her bottom lip.

"I'm honestly surprised at you. Have they broken your will that badly?"

Jade blinked. Had they? It had been quite a while since she felt like herself, although something was shifting within her, and she didn't know where to place it. The only solution was to run away.

"I know this year has been rough," Cordelia said more subtly and placed a hand on either side of Jade's shoulders. "It will get better."

Jade tried to smile.

"I promise it will," Cordelia assured. "And so what if your father doesn't like your decision? He'll only disown you."

She laughed.

"Come on," Cordelia said and steered her through the door. "Let's have some tea."

"I hate tea."

Cordelia grinned. "So do I."

Jade found herself in the glasshouse with a siphon of champagne and staring at a nude painting. Her head was cocked to the side as her eyes shifted over the vibrant colors radiating across the canvas.

"Do you think it's too much?" Cordelia asked from behind.

Jade pondered this, and she supposed it was, but it was also much more. "I find it quite freeing," she answered quietly, her eyes never straying from the picture.

"What do you find freeing about it?"

"I'm envious of her confidence and how liberating it must have felt. There is no shame in her eyes," she paused to admire the courage of the subject. "She's her own woman. That's all I want."

"Then be her."

She finally glanced over. Cordelia was sitting in a plush chair and sipping on her own bubbly. Her voice stuck with confidence as she stated, "I intend to be," with clarity.

Cordelia grinned slyly. "And do you intend to take Jackson as your lover?"

Jade looked out beyond the walls of the glasshouse to the Elm trees in the yard. She couldn't make a reason for her attraction to him. It was sudden and demanding. A myriad of emotions she had never felt surfaced. She hardly knew him at all, but would she like to? That much was obvious. Of course, she would. Would it then be too inconceivable and irrational to dive headfirst into someone she truly wanted? "I think I'd like him to be."

"I love the idea of you two together," Cordelia said brightly. "I think you would complement each other in the most delicious way. Jackson has always been an enigma, and I've never understood him until now."

Jade flashed a doubtful look.

"I've watched him become distinctly grounded, dependable, and vastly sure of himself. I forget that he used to be aggressive and flippant with his love. Many didn't find him very likable, especially his brother, Owen. But you would never know. He has calmed down quite a bit. It's almost as if he is an entirely different person."

"What made him so angry?" The question was out before she even thought about it.

The heavy burden of knowledge settled over Cordelia's features, and it appeared as if she was contemplating revealing a secret. Jade was about to tell her she didn't have to betray his confidence when she said, "He was severely abused as a young boy, and when his father Barron found out, he lost his mind and hunted the man down."

Jade placed a hand over her mouth. What an absolute tragedy.

"Jackson has since made peace with the past," Cordelia said with a small smile to ease her anxiety. "I wouldn't imagine he would ever bring it up. He doesn't like to talk about his childhood or his emotions. It makes him feel vulnerable like he once had. I only mentioned it so you understand how far he's come."

This revelation sparked pain in her chest, and she sympathized with him deeply. The scars on her back were evidence of a terrible childhood, and she understood what it was like to be violated. She realized the abuse Cordelia alluded to was entirely different from her own, but it didn't make it any less tragic. They both were subjected to the horrors of man.

"He has always treated me better than my brothers," Cordelia admitted sadly, and Jade grimaced. Her father had never been kind, and her uncle was just as vicious. "He's never questioned or judged me. He has never even asked if I would change my ways to fit in with the common woman. It's why I adore him. He'll never ask you to be anything other than what you are."

Jade glanced back, and her stomach sank with trepidation. "I don't think he wants me."

Cordelia's face twisted with absurdity as she chuckled, "Oh, I think he already does."

Jade bit her lip.

Cordelia's eyes narrowed as she lit a cigarette. With her exhale, she said, "You have to know. It's quite obvious by the way he looks at you."

She bit back a smile. His stare was unlike anyone she had ever met. It was as if she was the only woman in the city, and it made her feel worth something more than being William Calvert's daughter.

"I suppose I've noticed," Jade confessed. "But it doesn't matter. I intend to run away and never return."

Cordelia gave her a brief look of disbelief, but her confusion quickly faded with a laugh and a point of her finger. "I forgot how funny you are!"

"It's not a joke," Jade said, and she felt slightly annoyed with her aunt for laughing. It brought forth static in her palms, leaving her heart in her throat. An overwhelming sense of Deja vu emerged.

"And how do you intend to get out of the city unbeknownst to your father?"

"Jet will help me," she whispered and rubbed her head. "If I play along for a little while longer."

"But where will you go?" Cordelia demanded.

"Vendekk," she answered as if she had already planned it. She needed answers, and if what Jet said was true, she needed to understand the past.

Cordelia's face twisted even further. "You know what they say about that village."

"Theodore will never look for me there."

"You aren't afraid?" Cordelia asked with a touch of incredulity.

Jade evened her stare. "I'm more afraid of wasting my life."

Cordelia watched steadily, and there was no telling what she was thinking. It would be miraculous to pull it off, but she had to try. She couldn't wither away in this city at Theodore's side. Not that he'd give her much, to begin with, the marriage appeared to be a plot for revenge, and she didn't intend to stick around for the outcome.

XV
Ruby

"Jade doesn't appear to be very happy," Meena Wright commented as she sidled up next to her in the hall. The occasion was for Elizabeth Kensington's debut, just one of the many balls in the upcoming days. Ruby's attention snapped to the center of the room, where Jade stared miserably at the ground as Teddy wrapped a possessive arm around her waist. Ruby's stomach twisted in disgust. Was she finally giving in to him?

"I've never seen a more depressed-looking bride before!" Meena continued.

"That's because she hates Theodore," Ruby exclaimed as she found Diana giggling with Peter in the corner of the room. She didn't care to have a forced conversation with Meena, but she didn't want to stand awkwardly alone, especially when Helena Wimple followed her everywhere.

"Then why marry him?"

Ruby tore her eyes from Peter and glanced at Meena. "It's a forced decision."

Meena's eyes widened briefly, her lips forming an O before she said, "At least he's rich."

Ruby shook her head, her voice low, "Please, Jade doesn't care about money."

"Then what does she care about?"

"I'm not entirely certain," Ruby frowned as she looked back at her sister, who wasn't even pretending to play the blissful bride. "Being Mrs. Kensington isn't the desired thought... Being any man's wife doesn't seem to appeal to her." This was a lie, though she'd never admit it. Jackson Hadley completely enthralled Jade, but he was dangerous.

Meena's bright eyes flash in astonishment. "Are you saying she doesn't fancy men? How can that be? She was sneaking around with Dom-"

"That's not what I'm implying!" Ruby interrupted loudly. "I think it's more that she doesn't want to be defined by a man and pave her own way."

Meena laughed as if that were the most absurd notion, and for some reason, it irked Ruby. There was this common opinion of Jade because of how she presented herself in social situations. Most people didn't know how to take blunt honesty because it forced them to face truths they buried deep or refused to come to terms with. Ruby always found it refreshing that Jade dared to say how she felt. You never had to question yourself when it came to her.

"My brother has a deep fondness for her," Meena blurted, causing Ruby's mouth to part. "He was complaining about it over dinner. He said that Teddy had no idea how to handle such a passionate woman and that he would crush her spirit. Her spirit that Edward loves so much."

"That is quite the confession," Ruby said with a raised brow. It seemed as if there were men out there who didn't care about her scandal.

"That is Edward," Meena's grin deepened. "He falls in love so often it's hard to say where his heart truly lies."

Ruby grimaced. Did all men have a wandering eye?

"Speak of the devil," Meena nodded.

Ruby looked over her shoulder to where Meena was suggesting and saw a rather strapping man surrounded by a gaggle of women. It was Dominic Kane. He had thick blonde hair and a devil-may-care smile on his lips. When his eyes landed on her, she shivered.

"The scandal didn't seem to affect him," Meena sneered as she watched him bewitch those around him.

"So?" Ruby exclaimed and peeled her eyes away.

"What do you mean, so?" Meena snapped.

A soft voice interrupted their conversation. "Nothing ever changes, does it?"

The girls turned to see Esmeralda holding a chute of wine with a wry smile on her hollow yet distinctly absorbing face.

Ruby asked, "What doesn't?"

Esmeralda smiled, an almost motherly affection settling on her features. "Jade."

"I wish she would watch herself," Ruby complained. "Has she no regard for self-preservation? She will receive another lashing if she doesn't cooperate!"

The wry grin on Esmeralda's face never diminished. "Have you known her to be any other way?"

Ruby thought for a moment before saying, "No."

"She has mother's spirit," Esmeralda stated, a sense of sadness sweeping over her features. "Wild and free, nothing can cage her."

Ruby felt a stab of bitterness. If there was one thing she hated, it was when anyone other than herself was compared to their mother. Mainly because out of all the children, Ruby resembled her the most. She was never given compliments on her appearance like her sisters, but when she was addressed with the exact likeness of her mother, it made up for being overlooked. It also irked deep within that Jade was described as free and untamable, especially when Ruby craved that for herself. But how? She would never dare to let herself go and run freely as she always wished to.

"I cannot believe Elijah Hadley showed up here!" Meena suddenly cried.

"And why is that?" Esmeralda asked with a sharp glare.

Meena rolled her eyes with a scoff. "Are you serious?"

Esmeralda gave her a pointed look as if to question the girl further.

Ruby was starting to feel anxious with the sudden approach of her eldest sister. She hated to admit that there was any friction between them. But to be perfectly honest, the pair had never had the opportunity to bond, which was likely due to the thirteen-year age gap. Esmeralda had run away with Francois Marchand when Ruby was only four years old, an action considered severely immoral according to society. Ruby had grown to know that Esmeralda was a sinner and should be punished severely for it. However, whatever her father had in mind was further from the cards she had been dealt, and Ruby felt she had paid for it severely. Esmeralda was barren, and with the sudden death of Francois, she was left behind to face the world alone.

"Not only did he have a huge fallout with Teddy Kensington!" Meena snickered. "But he was also having an affair with Katerina right before she married your father!"

Esmeralda watched her coolly while Ruby couldn't suppress her curiosity. She loved to gossip. "You lie!"

"My father says the babe she carries is Elijah's and not your father's!"

"What a scoundrel!" Ruby gasped. Katerina was merely pretending so that she could attain their wealth.

"I find that rather unlikely, Elijah never courted her. It was Jackson, and as he hasn't been in Bel Deaux in years, the rumor doesn't hold up," Esmeralda explained, and Meena's face smoothed. "If there is one thing about the Hadley's that no one can dispute, it's their loyalty to one another. Elijah wouldn't cross that line and besides, Katerina was sneaking around with my father well before my mother died, and she isn't even showing yet. She cannot be more than three months pregnant! If the child she carries isn't my fathers, I still wouldn't look in Elijah Hadley's direction!"

Meena gaped at her with absurdity written all over her face. "Are you calling my father a liar?"

Esmeralda cocked her head to the side. "It sounds like slander because none of them are interested in being a part of the Elite. The Hadley's could run the entire city if they wanted, but they don't, so Katerina set her sights on a man who does."

"What makes you think that?"

"Because of who their family is," Esmeralda drawled. "On both sides!"

"Yes, well, that's just your opinion," Meena said flippantly. "It runs in the family. Avis is a harlot, and James runs around with women all over town just like Elijah! I wouldn't be surprised if one of them slept with the murdered prostitute!"

"Now that's a lie!" Helena snapped from behind Ruby. "I've never once been with one of the Hadleys. I was seeing Theodore Kensington!"

Ruby's stomach twisted. She'd almost forgotten about the deceased woman stalking her.

"My father thinks he asked his valet to kill her so nobody would find out!" Meena answered smugly.

Esmeralda watched her for a measured second, her eyes narrowing with displeasure. "You're kind of a bitch, aren't you?"

Ruby gasped, and Meena backpedaled as if Esmeralda slapped her. How dare she say something so degrading to a girl she knew nothing about.

"You gossip far too much!" She continued unrepentant. "This sounds more like a plot from one of those gothic novels your mother warns you about!"

"It's the truth!" Meena snarled though she didn't sound as confident as before. "My father was most insistent!"

"Because he listens to lies! It's entirely unfair to judge someone you know nothing about. Their characters shan't be solely based on rumors. Wouldn't you agree?"

Ruby felt contrite as she watched Esmeralda. People were so quick to judge the actions of another, and she hated to place herself amongst the critics. To overlook one's flaws was not a trait she had, so she simply muttered, "I suppose you're right." Quietly.

Meena glared petulantly. She obviously had no issue condemning those she felt were unworthy.

"You see," she continued as if Ruby hadn't spoken. "You don't know why they choose to live their lives in the way they do or if they act upon their basic urges, as you say. People whisper, much like your father, because they are bored and unhappy."

Meena's jaw dropped. This unexpected turn of conversation startled her into silence.

"Esmeralda," Ruby whispered as fear began to rise upwards. It was common knowledge never to speak ill of the Elite.

"If there is one thing I've learned," Esmeralda's dark eyes landed on Meena, her self-preservation long forgotten. "The only way to discover who a person truly is, is to speak with them directly and not make an assumption."

"What are you implying?" Meena questioned with obvious contempt spewing from her words.

"But I have to admit," Esmeralda said with a slight grin, disregarding Meena's question. "They are rather handsome, those Hadleys!"

Ruby looked at Meena, who was mouthing wordlessly in protest.

"I can tell we won't see eye to eye on the matter," Esmeralda said when the silence stretched on, and there was humor in her voice. Her eyes were bright, another mesmerizing sight. "I'd be careful spreading gossip. You might be destroying someone's life!"

Ruby's face heated, yet she nor Meena discouraged the statement.

Esmeralda's eyes slid to Ruby. "I suggest you find new friends."

Ruby flushed as she walked away. Her sisters never failed to embarrass her.

"How dare she call me names!" Meena screeched when Esmeralda was gone from earshot.

Ruby cornered her. "You'll keep your mouth shut, will you?"

Meena's face twisted as she took a step back. "Not only did she insult me, but she was also slandering my father's judgment!"

"Meena, please!"

"What are you two bickering about?" Diana interrupted. There was a devious smile on her lips.

"Nothing!" Ruby nearly yelled and turned to the open room. Several people had entered the dance floor.

Meena was seething as she continued to stare at Ruby, her refusal to comment left Diana with wide eyes and a slack jaw.

"How is Peter?" Ruby blurted to defuse the tension. She would rather listen to Diana's lovestruck version of Peter than goad Meena over Esmeralda's cheeky comments. Because if there was one thing Diana Atwood was good at, it was lighting the match to start the fire.

Diana's eyes softened with lust, and her grin widened, unbothered by the hostility boiling between them. "He can hardly contain himself around me. His hands yearn for the moment he touches my naked flesh again!"

Ruby heaved a breath and looked away. Jade had finally broken from Theodore and was speaking with his sister. Katerina and her father were close by, conversing with those around, including Jet, Esmeralda, and Pearl. If Ruby didn't know any better, she would say they looked like the perfect family, and this caused her chest to constrict. How she truly wished for that. Her mother should be here celebrating with them, and Jade should be with a man she truly wanted. But the most distinctive of all was how her father should be. He should be doting and caring without the money and power to pollute his mind.

She stumbled around the garden after having far too much champagne again. She disappeared from the party to avoid Diana and any other person who would witness her humiliation and drunken stupor. She hated hiding, but how could she not? Diana provoked her to the point of incessant tears, and Helena turned out to be treacherous to her well-being. She wrapped her arms around herself as the wind came, the rain had stopped, but it was still quite chilly.

"Sneaking off?"

She whipped around to see James Hadley leaning against a pillar and smoking a cigarette. His dark hair was slicked back like his brothers, and her lips rose with amusement. It must be a Hadley thing.

His eyes narrowed at her slightly when he took a drag.

"It's rather crowded in there," she mumbled and tried to stand straight.

His pale eyes continued to watch her intently as he exhaled smoke. His lip was split, and there was a very faint bruise under his eye. He'd been fighting, perhaps in the Vaults.

"I needed a minute to myself," she rambled, feeling more obtuse by the second, and she couldn't explain why, as James Hadley was no one of importance. She instantly cringed at the callous thought. She had been spending far too much time around vapid women.

His cheek lifted at her confession, and he asked, "Not your crowd?"

"They are fine enough, people," she answered demurely.

He chuckled and took another drag. After he inhaled, he flipped his hand and held the cigarette to her.

She glanced down at it in hesitation.

"Have you ever tried it?"

Her eyes flashed to him. "Yes."

His dark brows raised as a mocking smile formed.

"I have!" She said defensively. "Meena snuck a box into Vanessa Prewitt's debut. We smoked them in the coat closet."

He laughed and stepped away from the pillar. He towered over her and held out the cig. "Then take a toke."

Her eyes flashed diligently as she brazenly grabbed the cigarette. She stared at him directly and placed the butt to her lips. However, instant regret came when her throat rejected the invasion of smoke and she immediately began to cough when inhaled.

His brow smoothed with a smirk, and he said, "easy there. I don't need you throwing up in the bushes."

She took a step back and placed a hand on her throat as she coughed still. His eyes widened, and he put a hand on her shoulder. "Are you all right?"

She nodded, embarrassment heightening with each passing second.

"I'm sorry," he said with a wry grin. "I didn't mean to cause a fit."

"I'm not having a fit," she sputtered and slapped his hand away.

"Of course not," he said and briefly rubbed his lips together before saying, "I like your dress."

She ignored the ache in her throat and smiled up at him. He was grinning softly at her. There was a warmness surrounding his soul. "Thank you."

"It's good to see you again in so many days. It has been a long time before that, hasn't it?"

She nodded. There wasn't much to remember about James other than that he was rather weedy as a young boy. He only came around a handful of times, and when he did, they argued about anything and everything. He was no longer slight, and she realized how handsome he had become the longer she stared. She wasn't paying much attention at the park, not when she was preoccupied with his brother and Jade.

He frowned when she swayed into him and gripped her arms softly. "Are you drunk?"

"Perhaps a little," she admitted and grabbed onto his arm. He allowed her to lean into his chest, and she peered up at him with big eyes as she whispered, "I don't want to be here."

His gaze wandered over her face, and maybe it was the champagne, but he didn't appear repelled by her freckles. He seemed intrigued by them. "Then let's leave."

She smiled dejectedly. "I can't. I'm heavily guarded."

He glanced around. "I don't see anyone watching."

"It won't be long before someone notices my absence," she said quietly, and her eyes fell to his lips. "I wouldn't be able to forgive myself if you went missing because of it."

"That's unfair."

Her eyes raised back to him. "Fairness isn't a quality of my life."

"What would you do with freedom?"

Her face fell. No one could ever know her secret. The only sort of freedom she wanted was the happiness that seemed to evade her, but she couldn't say that aloud because that would be admitting there was something wrong with her.

Someone shouted, "JAMES!" in the distance, and they both turned to see Alec Kensington and Grant Atwood standing in the drive.

He nodded at them before turning back to her. "We're going down to the docks. Do you want to join?"

"I already told you I can't."

"So sneak out," he prodded.

She gave him a risible stare. "You don't know my father, do you? I have no desire to be whipped. I have seen the scars on Jade's back, which doesn't appeal to the mind."

"He whips your sister?" He growled. The disgust in his voice and on his face was evident.

She blinked. While it wasn't in her character to disclose family secrets, it was odd for a male to be repelled at the thought of punishment for one's child.

"He hasn't done it much in the last year," she replied slowly. "Not since he married that woman."

He gazed at her quietly, and she wondered what he was thinking. He clenched his jaw when he finally tore his gaze away and looked out into the vast city.

She pushed away from him and stumbled back to her feet. He grabbed her shoulder to steady her, and she giggled as she said, "I'll leave you to your friends."

"Just come with us," he begged. "Anyone can get lost in a sea of faces."

She peered at him with uncertainty.

"I'm good for it," he answered with a grin. "No one will ever know. Your father already left, and if the Atwood's are your guardians, you could disappear for days before they even notice."

She didn't know what possessed her to grab onto his hand, but she clasped it tightly and didn't let go until they were far from the property. Alec and Grant seemed slightly bothered by her presence until James's genial attitude smoothed the whole thing over, and they quickly got over whatever objection surfaced. They rode to the docks, where she watched them skip rocks across the harbor as they passed a bottle of whiskey around. She found her inhibitions lowering with each ounce she drank. It was as if every trouble she ever faced diminished completely.

"Is this what you would define as a good time?"

The three boys gazed at her, Alec and Grant were suddenly defensive, but James merely smirked with amusement.

"I meant no offense," she said casually with a shrug of her shoulders. "But we are standing in the dark and drinking terrible whisky as you throw rocks into a smelly harbor! This is a terrible way to pass the time!"

"Well, what would you rather do, princess?" Alec snapped, and Grant sniggered.

Usually, she would blush and feel stupid for offending someone, but as she was drunk, she hardly cared. "If I am to get in trouble, I would rather be doing something worthwhile."

"We can be anyone we want when nobody's watching," James stated and threw another rock across the water. "There are no rules in the dark." He gazed back at her and smiled. "No one to tell us how to behave."

A shiver ran down her spine, and she instantly regretted following these boys down to the docks where no one would hear her screams. "Being a morally decent human is repelling to you, is it?"

"That's not what I meant," James replied with a shake of his head. "We aren't inclined to hurt anyone or break the law, just the strings of which the masters of the city pull. Don't you find it exhausting living in a gilded cage, Ruby? You should know better than anyone." The three of them waited for her answer, and when she refused to respond, James continued, "Freedom is an illusion created by men of power such as your father. It allows us to believe we are unchained birds fully capable of flying, even though our wings have been clipped since birth. Money permits corrupt men to do whatever pleases them, and I hate to say it, but the Elite are nefarious assholes who take advantage of those less fortunate, and no law will ever touch them! You'd lose your mind if you knew how vile they are as men, if you can even call him that! Your sister is in for a rude awakening!"

Alec made a noise under his breath about the implication, and she stared at him with no response sitting on the tip of her tongue. He painted the world far bleaker than she'd ever accepted. Life wasn't that cruel. Yet when she glanced over her shoulder to look at Helena, she could see that perhaps it was.

And as for Jade, if anyone could take care of themself, it would be her. The marriage was a strategic move for the Kensington's and nothing more. They valued a long line of noble blood, and the only family to uphold this tradition was her own. Although, her father's declining health was beginning to be a problem. Jade was starting to suspect Katerina was handling all of his affairs. If that woman had her say when her father was too sick to uphold his word, Jade would not be the one to walk down the aisle to meet Theodore at the altar. It would be Adelaide.

"That's why we come here," he finished and threw one last rock. "There is no one hovering to ensure our cage is locked."

If they felt this way on the outside, how could she find any sort of balance for gaiety? If tonight were all she had, then she wouldn't waste it.

"Help me out of my cage," she insisted, pulling up her skirts.

"What are you doing?" James yelled and tugged her dress back down. "I wasn't implying that you should get naked!"

"I'm not trying to undress!" She wailed, pushing him away. "I want out of this hoop pannier and corset! I can hardly breathe, and my hips are wider than the harbor! I don't want a chain to hold me back if I am to fly!"

His mouth slowly curved upwards. The action made her stomach flutter…or perhaps it was the booze. Still, she couldn't believe she had never noticed how handsome James Hadley truly was and for once, she was glad he saw something in her when no one else did. She also chose to ignore the implication Meena made about him running around town with women because it was heartbreaking in a sense, though she could fully understand why anyone would follow him.

"The city is ours, James Hadley!" she said, and his lips fully bloomed into the most incredible smile.

It was relatively bright out when her eyes fluttered open. She quickly rolled onto her side with a loud gasp, the sun was far too impairing, and her eyes instantly burned. The pounding in her head became more prevalent with each passing second, and all she wanted was to fall back into the mindless abyss of sleep. Her memory was extraordinarily hazy, and she couldn't even remember going to bed, let alone the events leading up to it. The last thing she could recall was James Hadley helping her out of a hoop pannier. She jumped up quickly and cringed. She was in an enormous room with marbled floors and a red tapestry. She was also in her undergarments.

She covered her mouth and flushed with embarrassment. Her gown was in the middle of the room, with her stockings strewn about. She fell back against the covers and pressed her fingers into her eyes.

"Oh my god," she grumbled. Her father was going to kill her. The amount of trouble she would be in wouldn't compare to James's problem.

"Yew see, this is where the trouble starts, love," Helena thundered, forcing Ruby to bury herself deeper into the bed. "A good-looking man smiles at yew, and all logic goes out the window!"

A knock came at the door to save her from answering. "Hey, are you awake yet?"

She placed her arm over her eyes. "No."

His laugh followed him into the room. "I made you breakfast."

She lowered her arm with surprise. He was holding out a plate of food and he held up a mug. "I even brewed you a cup of coffee."

She sat up and pulled the blanket to cover her chest. Her hair had fallen out of its pins and flowed around her shoulders. A man had never seen her with her hair down before. She blushed as he appraised her appearance.

"Are you hungry?"

"I'm embarrassed," she admitted and lowered her gaze. "I don't remember what happened last night."

He walked to the bedside table and placed the plate and cup on the surface. "You were pretty drunk."

"Did I do anything embarrassing?"

He grinned. "Depends on who you ask."

She flushed further and covered her eyes once again. "I think I'm going to be sick."

The bed dipped, and she peeked through her fingers. "I'm only teasing. You are a fun drunk."

She grimaced. The only discomfort was a headache, so she knew they hadn't done anything sexual, but it still didn't explain her state of undress.

"Is there a reason I am in my undergarments?"

He averted his gaze. "You insisted on getting undressed."

"And did you assist me?"

"I loosened the ties, but I left before you were out of your dress," he said, and he glanced back with sincerity. "I didn't lay a finger on you, I promise."

She lowered her hand and watched him steadily. That wasn't entirely true; a memory of a kiss resurfaced.

"You better eat before your food gets cold," he said as he stood from the bed. "I'll give you some privacy and meet you downstairs when you're ready."

She sat silently for a few beats as the door closed behind him. It was hard to process the decisions she had made. Sneaking off with a boy while drinking all night only to end up nearly naked in his bed, which would cause a lashing from her father, was not something she would ever think of doing in all her life. She couldn't explain what came over her, and now she didn't want to return home to face the consequences, but she couldn't put James at risk either. She would have to bear it alone.

"What, no snarky comment?" Ruby asked Helena.

The dead woman merely grinned smugly with a shake of her head.

Ruby quickly ate the eggs he had made and downed some coffee before she sprang from the bed and pulled on her stockings and dress. She brushed her fingers through her hair and wiped her face. It would have to do. There was no getting around a hangover. If she were lucky, she'd be able to sneak in through the kitchen and remain unnoticed by her stepmother.

She opened the door and stuck her head out. There were endless doors and more marbled floors. She quietly shut the door and tiptoed down the hall and the stairs.

"Why did you sleep in the blue room?" came a loud voice from the room to the left of the foyer, and she followed the noise. James was sitting in the library with his brother, the blonde one. He stood abruptly when she entered the room and smiled.

"Ah," his brother said when he spotted her.

She glanced at the grandfather clock. It was after seven in the morning. She might be lucky enough to sneak into her house without waking her father.

"What is going on?" Jackson asked from the other side of the room. The savage scar on his brow was unnerving, and she averted her eyes, focusing on the agile woman at his side. Ruby knew her to be Avis, which immediately brought memories of the conversation with Esmeralda and Meena from the night before.

"Nothing," James muttered and started toward her, but Jackson grabbed him by the collar and hauled him backward. "What is William Calvert's daughter doing in our house?"

"She stopped to say hello."

"From your bedroom in an unfastened dress?"

James wailed, "I didn't touch her!"

Jackson flashed a strained smile in her direction. "Would you excuse us please?" He didn't wait for her answer as he shoved James through the far door.

She blushed as the blonde one laughed.

"You Calvert girls are quite interesting," he mused and pointed to a chair. "Have a seat. They may be awhile."

She took his advice and sat as he stepped into the other room, where there was shouting. Avis gave her a long stare before following her brothers through the door, and she suddenly felt ashamed. Her aim wasn't to get him into trouble.

"What's her problem?" Helena shrieked. "The snob!"

Ruby didn't answer. Guilt hit her again when the door opened several minutes later, and more shouts followed. It was Avis. Ruby's stomach knotted up. She didn't look pleased.

She barked, "Up you get."

"Pardon?"

"You can't very well go home looking like that!" Avis snapped. "We have to return you better than how we found you!"

Helena folded her arms and spat, "She could say please!"

"I didn't mean to cause any trouble," Ruby said meekly.

"Of course, you didn't, but men are stupid when it comes to the attention of a pretty girl," Avis rattled, and Ruby blushed.

Avis fastened the ties of her dress and offered a clean rag and a bowl of water to wash her face. She was very curt, which made Ruby incredibly uncomfortable.

"I don't want this to sound like a threat," Avis said while braiding her hair. "But I don't want you to see James ever again."

Ruby's stomach dropped as Helena snorted, "It sure sounded like one!"

"It's nothing personal. I'm sure you are fine enough, but I can't lose my brothers, and your father is far too possessive and cruel for a happy ending."

Several emotions floated to the surface, but none of them was good. She blinked back several tears. The only person who truly saw her was out of reach.

"I need acknowledgment from you," Avis whispered harshly. "I need to hear you say that you understand!"

"You know what's funny," Ruby said in a shaking voice. "It sounds like you're threatening me!"

"Atta girl!" Helena cheered.

Oblivious to the dead woman, Avis walked through her to grab a cloak from the hall. When she returned, there was no remorse on her face as she handed the garment over and said, "Well, I suppose I am, but I won't apologize. My brothers are all I have, and I won't ignore this recklessness."

Ruby wished she had the confidence to tell her off.

"Put this on," Avis demanded. "And pull the hood over your head so no one recognizes you."

She was shoving her arms through the sleeves when James finally burst into the room, looking grave. He was followed by his brothers and neither looked pleased.

James didn't say a word as he grabbed her hand, pulling her away from Avis.

"Take her to Cordelia's," Jackson murmured, and they paused to look at him. "You spent the night there and didn't see James at all. You got that?"

She nodded as James nudged her out of the room. He stuck his head out the front door to ensure no one was around and pulled her along quickly. He helped her into the cab, but he didn't follow. "I'm sorry about that, but it's best if I don't go with you. Jackson is right. It won't do us any good if anyone sees."

"I understand."

"I'll see you again," he promised.

She gave him a small smile; tears were hovering. She waited until he closed the door, and the cab rolled away before she let them fall.

He was right. A gilded cage was still a cage, and she would never be set free.

XVI
Jet

"What are we going to do about the bang tail who was all cut up?" Henry Wright asked the men seated at the round table. The Elite met once a month in the underground chambers of the abbey. "It's been over a week now, and no one's come forward."

William Calvert eyed him disdainfully and sat back in his chair. He glanced over at Jet expectantly but didn't care to meet his gaze. Jet didn't even want to be here. His whole life had been planned before he was born, and the expectation was too much weight to carry for one child. How he was raised was cold, detached, and abusive. All he knew was power and money, the only thing he cared about until Blake came into his life. There was no sympathy from a ruthless father waiting for him to buckle under the pressure and prove how unworthy he truly was. His mother was a disgrace, running around with married men before her death. She fooled them all, but she got what she deserved.

Pearl was slightly agreeable, but she was married to an idiot. Jade was feral, which he admired, though he would never admit it. It annoyed him even to be jealous of her. That left Ruby, who was comparatively meek. He didn't really know his youngest sister, nor did he care to learn anything about her. Esmeralda was the one he should hold any affection for, yet there was nothing but indifference. She was a sympathetic fool, an emotion he was greatly opposed to.

"That's because none of us killed her," Jonathan Cavendish grumbled with a glare.

"I wasn't implying that it was anyone in this room," Henry growled. "But of everyone the police have interviewed, it seems they are none the wiser, and neither are we."

Jonathan snorted and glanced at his father and brother. "And this bothers you. Why?"

"Because of what it means," Edward interjected, and they turned to look at him. "When a murder happens in Trinity Row, we know the men who commit them. We have a firm grip on the city, even the impoverished, but there is no telling what will come about in this situation. It makes us look weak."

Jonathan sat back in his seat with a snap of his teeth.

"Well, she isn't the first prostitute to be killed, and she won't be the last," Benjamin Wright said dismissively. "I'm more interested in the Hadleys."

"What about them?" Teddy grunted.

"How are you going to proceed?"

"The instruction was simple," Abraham said as he puffed on his stogie. "Kill them."

There was a collective intake of breath.

"The Hadleys are more significant than you'd like to believe," Micha Wellington argued from the other side of the table. "How do you presume to get away with eliminating them?"

Abraham's lip curled, and Teddy bellowed, "Rubbish," disdainfully under his breath.

"Whose idea was this?" Gregory Sullivan inquired and leaned on the table to better look at the group of men.

Everyone turned to William, but he threw up his hands and said, "Don't look at me. Abraham was the one who felt the need to make such a bold decision concerning them."

"And why is that?" Joseph Cavendish asked.

"Because I'm sick of them," he growled.

"Yes, well, be that as it may, you can't put a hit on someone for annoying you," Joseph answered, and Gregory murmured his acknowledgments. Jet agreed, and when his stare connected with Blake, he knew the lines were being drawn.

"I'm with Abraham on this one," Henry Wright said and glanced at his son. "It goes beyond disliking a family. They simply stand in our way. We'll never have full control of the city when they strive to bring down our outfit."

"It's a terrible idea," Gregory said. "We can't go against the Queen, and the Hadleys are well-liked."

"By whom?" Teddy barked. "The whores in Trinity Row?"

Abraham and the Wright's laughed.

Jet finally glanced at his father. He looked well today. The blonde hue of his graying hair stood out, and the bags under his eyes had vanished with some rest. When he met Jet's eye, a hard stare followed. He was being excruciatingly quiet for his piece of mind.

"We could frame Jackson for the murders," Edward proposed. "Bel Deaux wouldn't be above a public execution if they thought he was killing women for pleasure."

Augustus Atwood stopped his pacing and smiled wickedly at him.

"With what proof?" Jet asked.

"Merfan doesn't need proof," Abraham barked. "He just needs a suggestion and it's well known how much he hates Jackson."

"So, are we in agreement?" Henry asked.

"No," William intervened, and Jet exhaled in relief. There was a brief instant where he thought his father would agree with the men at the table, but William had the final say. Henry and Abraham went out of their way to orchestrate the Hadleys deaths under William's nose, and he wouldn't have noticed had his illness taken over. Luckily, it hadn't. Jet was grateful that his father had enough spite carrying him on until the bitter end.

Abraham's jaw dropped along with the hand he was holding his cigar in.

Henry demanded, "And why not?"

"We can't wage a war with the Queen," William barked. "Bel Deaux won't choose us over her, and if we don't have full control, what is the point?"

"But if we framed him for the murder, his death will be by public opinion."

"The Queen would never allow it," William said.

"Why wouldn't she?" Teddy growled. "It won't be that hard to frame him. Everyone knows how deranged he is."

"It's not the time," William answered dismissively. "The Queen will protect him. You don't even know who the killer is, so how could you frame him to begin with?"

Theodore didn't have a snappy retort, bringing a grin to Jet's lips. He shared a look with Blake and glanced back at his father.

"Don't concern yourself with them," William continued. "I'm having them followed. I know what they're doing."

"It's not enough," Abraham barked. "Elijah has too much influence over the public with his column in the paper!"

"But you've said it yourselves, no one in this room committed the murder," Jet reminded him. "So, what does it matter?"

"I'm not going to explain it again," Edward snapped.

"Teddy has been in charge of everything thus far and look how it's played out!" Jet seethed. "We've lost an entire opium shipment because of his obsession over my sister and Dominic Kane! He even let Pierre go, so it is safe to say he is not ready to lead an empire!"

Abraham hurled a multitude of insults as William chuckled under his breath.

"His jealousy will be our downfall! It's a weak emotion, and he blatantly lets it show like some fool. If everyone only knew how Teddy begged for Jade and paid my father instead of the other way around, they would think quite differently of the Elite!"

"My son never begged for that harlot!" Abraham snarled.

"Is that what you think?" William asked, his voice full of ire.

Abraham glanced at his son questionably.

"She is mine," he said through clenched teeth, and Micha flashed an aggravated look in his direction.

"You keep telling yourself that, Teddy," William muttered as he sat up in his chair and grabbed the gavel. He was done bickering with the Kensingtons and the Wrights. "My decision is final. There will be no strike against the Hadley's for now." And he slammed the gavel down.

Theodore directed a disdainful look at William as he left the room, and when his stare found Jet's own, he realized then that Teddy would stop at nothing to get what he wanted, even if it meant taking down his entire household.

It wasn't enough that he had to break Katerina's hold on his father. Now he had to take on the Elite as well. But it didn't matter what Teddy planned. Jet was already a step ahead of him, and he would be the one laughing in the end.

He despised the thought of asking Dominic Kane for help. In fact, he disliked the idea of asking anyone for help. But if he was going to get ahead of his father before he was cut out of his will, he needed to have powerful allies at his back, and Dominic Kane was a powerful ally to have.

The sound of the rain heightened as the trolleys flew past them in the Gas-light district. The storm hadn't deterred any haze and kept the cities vantage obscure. He sighed heavily when the carriage crossed the Grand bridge, a vast divider between the magnificent streets of the west end, which were immaculately paved and filled with reputable citizens, to the lower east end, where the roads were covered in trash, piss, and shit, piling in the gutters which festered in the tempered weather. Trinity Row was rife with prostitution, drugs, and crime. One had to look over their shoulder wherever they went as pickpockets ran rampant or avert their eyes if they didn't want to witness a salacious encounter.

Needless to say, it was a group Jet couldn't care less for.

He tried to shake off his anxiety as they rolled into Trinity Row. It was a nervous thing to be in such a crime-ridden area, but the Queen's only son relished in the far reaches of society. Deep in the slums where he could partake in any unsavory act, where no one would judge or speak an ill word on his behalf.

Yes, he had a handsome face, but that was the only pleasant thing about him. His sexual degradation and drug use were known far and wide. He kept the company of beggars, users, and sinners. If Jet thought Teddy tested the limits, Dominic was far worse, and it was utterly inconceivable to think Jade had an affair with him.

"Are you sure about this?" Blake asked for the hundredth time.

Jet eyed him in aggravation. "Yes."

Blake shook his head and glanced back out the window.

"What is it?"

Blake opened his mouth, but nothing came out, his green eyes darting across every inch of the east end. Jet wasn't a very patient person, even with Blake, and he wanted to scream at him for holding back. "Well?" he said as calmly as he could muster.

Blake rolled his eyes at the insolent tone, and his stare was vacant when he turned to look at him. "It feels as if we are making a deal with the devil."

He swallowed the thick lump of distress. There wasn't anything comforting to say that would pacify Blake when he felt the same. The risk sat heavy in his head and sank into the pit of his stomach, leaving him nauseous.

"You mustn't forget who he is and what he's done to get there," Blake continued when Jet bit his lip. "Don't be fooled by his coquettish grin; the very one, your sister, fell for! He may make things sound far better than they are, but you must remember, he is only out for himself, and he will only be loyal to the highest bidder."

"I have more money than Teddy."

"For now," Blake reminded him.

Jet pressed his lips together. Why did everyone underestimate the man he had become? He may have acted impetuously in the past, but it wouldn't be long before they choked on their words, for he was in complete control of his power. A power no one would be able to compete with when he unleashed his full fury on every single person who had wronged him.

The carriage stopped outside a dilapidated brick building, and the street was pitch black. There weren't any gas lamps in Trinity Row, but some people had placed a lantern with a single candle on their stoops to indicate that someone was home.

"We should have come in the middle of the day," Jet muttered.

Blake threw a withering look and exited the cab testily; Jet clenched his teeth as he followed. Blake was already up the stoop and knocking on the door before he was out of the cab.

A burly fellow ripped the door open. He had a pinched face and a stogie hanging from his mouth. The glare that perpetrated his wrinkled face would certainly make any man shrivel in fear, but Blake merely gazed up in boredom.

"What do you want?"

"We're here to see Dominic Kane," Blake answered, although the man already seemed to have made up his mind because he jerked his thumb in the opposite direction.

"He isn't taking any visitors, now fuck off!"

"You will let us see Dominic Kane, or you'll end up in the harbor before the night is through!" Jet barked from the bottom of the stoop.

The man let go of the door with his right hand and grabbed his stogie with his left. "And who the fuck are you to say whether or not you can see him?"

"Jet Calvert."

The man's face instantly paled. Whether from the Calvert name or the four sentinels jumping off the back of the cab and holding onto rifles, it didn't matter. His demeanor changed into a shrinking, blubbering fool.

"Do we have a problem?"

The man shook his head vigorously. "No, sir. Right this way, Mr. Calvert," he muttered, his tone less disgruntled than before.

Jet threw Blake a rather smug expression, but he didn't hold the same gusto. He looked peaky.

"Wait here," the man growled and disappeared through the far door. Jet halted in the hallway and Blake stood right behind him.

The room before them was derelict, comprehensive, and relatively dark; a phonograph repeatedly played the same two piano keys. There was a mass of vagrants squatting throughout the flat, taking hits of opium or passing out in some corner. Several naked people writhed atop one another as voyeurs watched while sipping on absinthe.

Jet turned his head to meet Blake's eye. The amount of revulsion rising was severe.

The man with the stogie emerged from the door some minutes later. "He's making one of his films, but they're wrapping it up now."

Dominic's stag films were more popular than any righteous man would like to believe. William threatened Jet's very life if he didn't burn Dominic's entire work in fear that Jade would be featured on one of the reels. He was adamant she wasn't, but Jet got rid of every last one in case he wasn't telling the truth. It appeared as if he was starting a new collection.

He stepped into a room that was illuminated by dozens of candles, covering nearly every inch of the space, and surrounded a chaise lounge in the middle of the room. A naked woman was sprawled atop; she wasn't moving. Dominic was pulling a robe over his stark form, and the man behind the 16-lens movie camera was rolling up the reel and leching over the naked woman obsessively. Jet didn't care for it, and his hand twitched. Dominic would change his ways if he could only unleash a snippet of power. But Pearl begged him not to reveal himself unless it was dire. She said it was unwise to expose themselves so soon. Blake would get hurt if he weren't careful.

"Ah, Jet Calvert in the flesh," Dominic bellowed with a self-possessed smile.

Jet repressed a shudder.

Dominic's chin was tilted toward his chest, and his blue eyes bored into his soul. "To what do I owe the pleasure?"

Jet glanced at Blake, but his attention lingered on the woman. She still hadn't roused. She didn't even look like she was breathing.

"She'll be fine," Dominic assured, but Jet didn't like the dismissive way he spoke of her, as if she was a bucket of waste ready to be thrown away.

Blake growled, "Are you sure about that?"

"What do you want? I am a very busy man and don't have much time to waste on some false concern for a woman," Dominic drawled as he poured himself a glass of wine.

"We need to have a little chat," Jet snapped.

"I'm all ears," he said and took a sip.

"In private."

Dominic rolled his eyes. "Of course."

Blake hesitated over the woman and reached out to feel her pulse.

Dominic slammed the wine bottle down on the table before him and roared, "LEAVE HER!"

Blake's eyes narrowed in his direction.

"If you don't get on with it," he snarled viciously, "I'll make sure you never leave this premises again!"

Blake moved his hand around to the revolver in the waistband of his trousers. He watched him tirelessly as Jet questioned his commitment when something putrid hit his nostrils. They both covered their mouths. "What is that smell?"

But Dominic wasn't interested in his question. Instead, he held open his study door and said, "You have five minutes."

They shared another measured look, and there was a sudden urgency to flee, but they still followed Dominic into the room. Jet suddenly regretted his desire to ask for Dominic's allegiance because Blake was right. They were making a deal with the devil himself.

"How is that ravishing sister of yours?" he asked casually while sitting at his desk and lighting a cigarette.

"That's not why I'm here," Jet snarled. "So don't ask about her again. What I need is a favor from you."

One of Dominic's blonde brows popped upwards. "You do?"

"It is no question to anyone that Katerina married my father for his money, and now that she carries his child, or so she says, she stands to inherit my father's entire fortune."

"Does she now?"

"She does," Jet confirmed and relaxed in his chair. "This is where you come in."

A grin tugged at Dominic's chapped lips. "What would you have me do?"

"I want you to ruin her reputation by making her the object of one of your films."

A shadow crossed Dominic's face, there was something rather perilous about him. Jet repressed the shiver that threatened to ripple through his entire body.

"I need you to make my father see her for what she truly is."

"Oh, yeah?" Dominic drawled. "And what's that?"

"An opportunist."

Dominic's eyes narrowed. "How am I going to propose this? Your father would shoot me dead if I knocked on his door!"

"Send a letter to her sister Adelaide. They'll be so excited by the invitation that Katerina will insist on escorting her."

"What makes you think she'll even agree to film with me?"

"You once convinced Jade to get in your bed," Jet reminded him. "If you can convince her, you can convince anyone."

"I didn't-" Dominic began and closed his eyes briefly. "She wasn't some woman I… forget it. What are you hoping to achieve from this?"

"You can't prove the date in which the film was made, and not only will he be repulsed by her actions, but he'll also question if the child she carries is his."

Dominic snorted. "And they say I'm egregious."

"I'm not looking to compare dastardly deeds," Jet said dismissively. "I'm here to ask if you'll help me take down Katerina's hold on my father."

"What's in it for me?"

"How much do you want?"

Dominic's eyes narrowed. "Seven hundred stacks."

"How about eight?" Jet countered.

Dominic's eyes widened slightly, and he whispered, "You're serious?"

"Do I look like a man who would waste my own time?" Jet barked, and Blake bit his lip. Dominic's frown deepened as his eyes moved between them. "The Atwood's have strategically placed themselves into my family, and they stand to inherit my father's entire empire if anything should happen to him or myself. Katerina thinks she can take what is mine by batting her eyes, but she knows nothing about me. She doesn't know the lengths I would take to keep what belongs to me!"

"I must admit you are far different than I envisioned," Dominic stated as he leaned back in his seat and appraised Jet. "If I agree to this, I want you to do something for me."

"That's not how this works. I have agreed to pay you, and quite generously, I might add."

"I don't want your money," Dominic interrupted. "I want your sister."

Blake stiffened next to him, and Jet's face slowly twisted into sheer undeniable hatred. "Over my dead body."

Dominic chuckled, hardly bothered. "Those are my terms. Take it or leave it."

"Jade would never agree-"

"I'm not talking about Jade," Dominic barked. That damned smile returned. "I'm talking about Ruby."

Jet was stunned into silence. Blake didn't even have a thing to say as Dominic's mouth curved devilishly.

He had them right where he wanted them.

XVII
OLIVETTE

"Mum needs you to run to the market court again," Tellie stated from their bedroom doorway.

She glanced up from her book. Her heart thrummed out of rhythm, as it often did when she was nervous. "What do you mean?"

"She needs more laudanum."

Ollie shrank against the chair. The magnitude of the situation threatened to pull her under. Tellie didn't wait for a response and left the room before she could think of an excuse to say no. What if she ran into Theodore again? She knew it was too good to be true. Jackson hadn't returned, and neither had Avis. They were on their own once again.

When she stepped through the French doors on the first floor, Kittie was at her mother's side. "You need me to run to the market?"

Lady Ashford glanced up at her with glossy eyes. "Please hurry back, would you? I'm in pain and wish to sleep."

"Yes, Milady," Ollie answered and slowly grabbed the coins from Kittie's outstretched hand. She was wrapped in a shawl and nearly out the front door when her mother said, "No loitering around the city Ollie, do you hear me?"

She hesitated in the doorway. She didn't even want to go to begin with and nearly begged to stay. But this was different. It almost sounded like a warning.

"Ollie?" Lady Ashford repeated.

"Yes, I understand," she answered and slipped through the door. She strolled down the street quickly and proceeded to the main road. Her gait slowed when the unease genuinely sunk in. Was there something amiss, or did Lady Ashford merely want to exert all control over Ollie in her last days? It was a callous thought, and she realized her focus shouldn't be on questioning her.

"Well, look who it is."

She cringed at the terrible voice and slowly turned around to see Theodore Kensington glaring at her. Fear tore through her, and she tried to run when he gripped her hair and pulled her back. "Not so fast. You're going to pay your father's debt."

"But I don't have any money!"

"You won't be repaying your father's debt with money," he sneered.

She screamed to no avail as he dragged her across the street and threw her into a cab.

It was dark when a hansom cab stopped in front of 2374 Willem Avenue. The cab door opened, and bare feet stepped out onto the pavement. Olivette Ashford's legs gave out when she bore her full weight and stumbled onto her hands and knees. Laughter followed her onto the street, and something hard hit her back. Tears rolled down her cheeks as nearly every muscle in her body throbbed and ached. Her arms were shaking and threatening to buckle as she glanced over at the discarded bottle just as she was.

"I'll see you next month, Olivette," Theodore promised as he shut the door and, soon after, rolled away.

She let the tears fall as she grabbed the bottle and crawled up the stoop. Thunder clashed loudly from above. She held onto the doorknob and pulled herself to a standing position. She sagged against the door and wept. Every inch of her body had been debased and penetrated by not only Theodore, but a man named Edward as well.

There wasn't a thing she could have done to stop it, and it was entirely her fault. Had she only taken another route and not been so distracted by her selfishness; she could have retrieved the medicine with ease and would have been settled in bed with a book instead. Shame infiltrated down to her core as she attempted to ignore her throbbing extremities, which were bruised and raw. She staggered through the front door when the rain truly pelted down upon her, and she turned to lock every bolt. The French doors were open, but the room was dark. Lady Ashford must be sleeping.

"Ollie!" Tellie whispered harshly. "Where have you been? Lucky for you, Jackson Hadley showed up and brought some medicine!"

Ollie shoved the laudanum in her hand. "Father's debt to Abraham Kensington has been taken care of for the month. Theodore saw to that."

Tellie gasped at her disheveled appearance when she truly saw her and demanded answers at once. She knew a bruise had formed on her cheek, which was chafed with her tears. She ignored her questions and walked toward the kitchen to where the tin bathtub resided. Tellie rushed to her side and assisted her. She continued to cry in silence as Tellie helped her undress, and it was only with her sister's sharp intake of breath that Ollie knew the bruises on her back were the worst of all. She instantly cringed and turned away with humiliation, covering her tainted body in a shawl and sitting at the kitchen table in disbelief.

It couldn't be real. It must have been some terrible nightmare she was having trouble waking up from. She had been violated to the severest degree and wanted nothing more than to scrub their infringement upon her skin with scalding water and a coarse brush.

Tellie filled the tin tub with scalding water per Ollie's request and continuously threw anxious looks over her shoulder, though Ollie hardly noticed. Her eyes were unfocused as she stared at the floor. She could still feel their hands all over her body, leaving her sickened. The bile was slowly beginning to rise, and it wasn't long before she upheaved all over the floor. Tellie sprinted to her side and pulled her hair out of her face. She wiped all the sweat and vomit away once Ollie had nothing left in her stomach and whispered, "It's ready."

Ollie grabbed onto her hands for support as she stepped in. The water was scalding, and she cried out, but it wasn't because of the heat itself. She preferred her bathwater hotter than usual—the rope burns across her ankles stung with the contact.

"We can wait for it to cool," Tellie offered and tried to pull her back.

"No," Ollie insisted. She needed to burn away their touch. "I can take it."

She settled into the tub and groaned in pain as each bruise became exposed to the water. After she was comfortable, Tellie began to pour water down her back to wash her hair. Ollie blinked back exhaustion as she said, "I've never been with a man before."

Tellie's hand paused in midair.

"I never expected it to be like that," she finished with a whisper, "I've always heard the act of sex was pleasurable but this experience was quite painful."

"I'll kill him," Tellie grunted and continued to wash her hair.

Little did she know it wasn't just Theodore, but Ollie couldn't form the words.

Instead, she wrapped her arms around her legs and wept.

She spent most of the next few days in bed, and her mother didn't bother her for once. She didn't know what excuse Tellie gave, but she was grateful, especially since she made her sister promise not to tell. The door opened often, but not a word was said. She lay on her stomach with her head turned towards the opened window. It stormed the whole time, and she listened as the attack replayed in her mind over and over. Just when she thought she could overcome the tragedy, grief would hit her like a wave, and she would crumble again and again. She didn't want to be inside her skin anymore, it was infected with disgrace, and she knew she would never be the girl she once was. Olivette Ashford no longer existed. What was left was a damaged wretch incapable of the delectations of life.

The hollowness settled in firmly, and no more tears fell in the following days. Ollie began to resent all men, and it started with her father. She wouldn't have been subjected to rape as a flat payment if he had not abandoned them. He was despicable, and he left Lady Ashford for the sex of another. The thought made her angry. She wanted to scream for her mother, her sisters, and herself. Not that it mattered, no one would hear, nor would they care. No one would notice if they suddenly disappeared.

It was also becoming apparent that she needed to comply with Theodore to endure this strenuous existence. He was expecting to see her next month, perhaps if she were cooperative, she could get more out of the bargain, and it wouldn't be as painful. What would a few minutes of defilement mean in the end if it led to a roof over their heads and food in their bellies? She was already dead inside anyway.

"I'm going to go to the police," Tellie told her once she found her sitting in a chair and staring out the window.

"No, you won't," Ollie stated flatly.

"And why not? Theodore Kensington violated you!"

"He's our only chance at survival," Ollie said. As dirty as she felt, it was the truth.

"You can't be serious!" Tellie yelled. "I refuse to accept the handout of a man who… who-" a sob escaped her lips, and she covered her mouth.

"Papa is gone, and mum is dying," Ollie said. "We'll be out in the streets, and then what? He'll allow us to stay if I cooperate; perhaps he'll even give money for food."

"That's prostitution!" Tellie wailed. "How could you even consider after what he did to you?"

"I'm not saying I would enjoy it," Ollie answered and turned to look back out the window. "Only that we would be taken care of."

"No," Tellie barked. "If you even think about returning to him, I will tell mum!"

"Don't ruin the last days of her life with this! We live in hell, and the devil wants our souls as payment. It is either kill or be killed; if we want to survive, we need to do what is necessary, and Theodore Kensington is the answer. Papa left without a care. If you want to blame someone, then blame him!"

"I just think there has to be another way," Tellie whispered.

"If you ever figure that out," Ollie hissed as she strode past her. "Then you let me know."

XVIII
Jade

Ruby had climbed into bed with her for the past two nights. She used to do this when nightmares claimed her dreams as a child, but not since they were grown. Though Jade didn't ask questions as to why. She barely opened her eyes when Ruby entered, rolling over as she tucked herself in.

"Can we keep the candles lit?"

"Sure," Jade murmured.

She had vivid dreams that night. Ones of open doors and a strong urge to close them, leaving her uneasy and restless. She had awoken several times before falling back under relatively quickly. Yet, when the candles were nearly spent, she had awoken once again after dreaming of a man resembling Jackson, although she couldn't be sure it was him. When her eyes focused on the room, she jumped when she noted Ruby was sitting up in the bed.

"What is it?"

Her sister didn't answer.

She glanced around, but there was no one in the room with them as far as she could see. Perhaps there was someone on the balcony. "Ruby?"

Again, nothing.

"Ruby, what are you looking at?"

Silence.

Jade sat up, touching her arm. "Ruby?"

The girl's eyes were glazed over as she stared at the wall ahead.

Fear swallowed her whole and she whispered, "Ruby!"

The girl didn't stir as she continued to stare at the wall. Her breathing was shallow and labored.

"Ruby you're scaring me!"

Her sister sat suspended in time, unmoving and unblinking.

"Ruby!"

Nothing.

She shook her roughly. "RUBY!"

The girl finally blinked and snapped, "What?"

"What are you doing?"

Ruby glared. "I'm trying to sleep," before lying back down with her back facing Jade, leaving her to gape at what transpired.

"I daresay that Mr. Wellington is the most eligible," Lady Calvert's sharp voice cut throughout the parlor room. Marian squealed in delight and grabbed Adelaide's hand.

Jade sat across from the three, watching the conversation unfold with a flat stare. Pearl came for tea and was adamant that Jade should not make a scene, practically forcing her to interact with these women she had absolutely nothing in common with. Pearl laughed with false sincerity, and Jade glanced at Ruby, but the girl merely took a sip of her tea.

Unrest surfaced whenever she looked at her. The girl had no memory of her unusual behavior in the dead of night. Jade prompted a conversation once they had awoken and asked if Ruby was having nightmares again. Her sister merely gave her a confused look and demanded to know what she was talking about. She shrugged it off, maybe it was better not knowing.

Jade gazed back at her stepmother politely, trying with all honesty not to grimace. She was all alone in her feelings, which were nearly impossible to hide, as were her nerves.

Her hands were constantly full of static, and her limbs persistently convulsed. Magic was beginning to erupt without command at the slightest rise of emotion ever since she had met Jackson. He was invading every crevice in her mind, which was maddening.

"You will just die when you see his face, dear," she said to her sisters, ignoring her stepdaughters entirely. "He has grown into the most handsome man you have ever laid eyes upon!"

Adelaide's nose twitched. She didn't want to entertain anyone other than Theodore, and everyone knew it. Still, Jade wasn't upset over the fact. She hoped by some miracle that he would come to his senses and choose Adelaide instead.

"What about Dominic Kane?" Adelaide said, but her eyes were trained on Jade.

Pearl went rigid beside her, and Ruby flushed, but Jade wasn't bothered. If she wanted to upset her, she would have to try harder than that.

"He isn't looking for a wife," Katerina said with a glance at Jade. "Micha Wellington is a safer bet."

Adelaide sneered. "What if I don't want Micha Wellington?"

"Dominic Kane is a worse option," Jade interjected, and Pearl flashed a warning look in her direction.

"And why not?" she challenged.

"If you knew what he did," Jade said evasively, and Adelaide's stare hardened. "You wouldn't even entertain a thought of him."

Neither Katerina nor Adelaide had a snappy retort.

"Everyone is speaking of him, Katerina," Marian agreed. "I've heard more than half the girls whisper about Mr. Kane in church."

Adelaide's eyebrows rose as she lifted her teacup. "Why would you ever worry about what anyone else says of him?"

Marian frowned. "How could I not?"

"Because I am the prettiest," Adelaide answered smugly, and Jade stared at her flatly. A pretty face didn't mean a thing when her behavior was repugnant. She was just as callous as Marian and Katerina and far more judgmental.

She snorted when Adelaide explained further about how no one could match her looks, and Pearl kicked her foot. She had no patience to sit and discuss Micha Wellington with Katerina and her vapid sisters.

"Do you have something to say?" Katerina asked curtly.

"All this talk of men," she answered fiercely. "Have you nothing better to do with your time than gossip about them?"

All three of them threw scandalized looks in her direction, and while the antagonism grew, she wondered how long it would take for Katerina to burst at the seams.

"Do you remember how Micha chased you through the gardens?" Ruby blurted to defuse the tension, although it only made it worse. Jade's face smoothed, and Pearl's eyes widened at her.

"I beg your pardon?" Katerina asked, her voice acidic and full of a challenge to continue.

Ruby missed their stepmother's tone and frowned at her sister's reactions as she said, "Mr. Wellington used to chase Jade around the yard, and they played in the mud. They were particularly close."

Jade closed her eyes, and Pearl laughed without humor. "Ruby, you are too much!"

Ruby's face flamed, and she shriveled under Adelaide's stare.

Adelaide rounded on Jade. "What do you mean they were close?"

"We grew up alongside them," Pearl explained hastily, "they would come for dinner once a week, sometimes more. Micha would chase Jade around because she would play with him like a boy. Jet and Esmeralda were too old, and Ruby was too young. I refused to get dirty…He called me boorish."

This made them laugh again, and Ruby's eyes dropped to her tea. She stirred it unnecessarily and peeked over after a strained pause, but Jade didn't acknowledge her. Katerina was a very vain and a very jealous woman. It would be a dangerous notion to let her assume something had happened between her and Micha. He was nothing more than a friend, a friend who was more like a brother, but they wouldn't understand. Pearl's comments weren't even meant to hurt her though it would seem that way. She was merely trying to deflect the attention of a situation that could be misconstrued.

"Well, that is funny," Marian said.

"How embarrassing it is to be compared to a boy," Adelaide teased, and Katerina choked on her tea.

"Who said it was an embarrassment?" Jade hissed.

Adelaide glared at her. "I just said it!"

Jade opened her mouth to argue, but Pearl interrupted her, "Why don't you go upstairs and lie down?"

Jade glared at her. Sleeping was the last thing she wanted to do, but she didn't want to be in the company of the Atwoods either. Slowly she stood with an impassive look and hissed, "Of course, how awful a life it is to get exhausted by conversation!"

Katerina's eyes narrowed. "I was going to persuade your father to lift your punishment, but if you're going to act like a petulant child, then maybe you aren't ready and should return to the nursery!"

Adelaide and Marian giggled under their breath.

"You have no authority over me!"

"Jade!" Pearl snapped before Katerina could dish out another punishment.

She glanced at her, and her nostrils were flaring. Even with the contention between them, she didn't have the desire to upset the sister she used to be the closest with. Instead, Jade gave the Atwoods a sugary smile and strode from the room.

Without missing a beat, they began talking of Micha Wellington again. What a shallow life, speaking of men like a finely bred horse to buy. As if it truly mattered.

"Would yew quit slouchin?" Marna barked as she kneaded a big ball of dough against one of the counters in the kitchen. The head chef Felipe was already preparing dinner and placed a plate of olives and cheese in front of Jade that went untouched. "Ya fada would have a damn right fit if he saw ya elbows on the table!"

Jade placed her head in her hands and blinked over at her. "It's hard to notice things when you're never around. I haven't seen him in days."

Marna pursed her lips.

"Katerina probably killed him," she added as an afterthought and Felipe chuckled until Marna glared at him and he stifled his merriment.

Marna grabbed a handful of flour and tossed it on the dough as she muttered under her breath, "Ya driving me crazy!"

"I'm bored," Jade complained. "I was kicked out of Katerina's tea party."

"Ha!" Felipe scoffed. He was chopping onions and carrots on the adjacent table. "You aren't fooling anyone! We all know you ran your mouth on purpose!"

Jade picked at the table with a scowl. "She provoked me."

The chopping stopped, but she didn't need to raise her eyes to know he was staring at her with a level of condescension. He had a list of warnings and advice for Jade that she rarely listened to. "You need to learn to control your emotions around the Atwoods. They're a dangerous lot they are…and quit picking at my counter!"

She dropped her hand with a sigh.

"Why don't yew go for a walk," Marna suggested.

"Around the yard while my father's guards leer at me? No, thank you!"

"Go read a book," Felipe added.

Jade huffed. "I'm not in the mood."

"Go play the violin in the greenhouse."

Her hands twitched, but she wasn't in the mood for that either. "Why are you trying to get rid of me?"

"Because I have fings to do, and yew is distracting me!"

When she looked at Felipe, he grinned.

She pushed away from the counter. "Fine."

Marna clucked her tongue. "It's not my fault yew disobey direct orders. If yew just listened to what yew was told, yew wouldn't be confined to the house!"

"Why do I have to be told what to do? I am not a child anymore!"

Felipe snorted in mirth and Jade threw a handful of olives at him.

"Oh!" Marna wailed and threw up her flour dusted hands. "Then quit actin' like it!"

"Wanting to live my life as I please isn't childish. It is a desire for freedom!"

"No one is free," Marna muttered.

She thought of Jackson. He was free. He lived his life with reckless abandon despite what society thought. She wanted nothing more than the possibility of being free with him.

"I'm never going to get what I want, will I?"

Marna stopped kneading and gawked at her. Felipe's chopping paused briefly before picking up speed again.

"I'm going to end up just like my mother."

Felipe dropped his knife when he took note of the extra staff hanging on Jade's every word. "All right, show's over!" and herded them out of the kitchen.

"Don' say that," Marna whispered and walked around the table. "Yew won't end up like her. Once yew has ya own home and children, it will get better!"

"Not while I'm married to Theodore."

Marna gripped her arms, and tears welled in her eyes. "Whatever yew is planning to do, please don't. I don't think yew understand how much yew is loved!"

Jade smiled at her. "I'm not going to hurt myself, Marna. I'm going to run away."

Marna's face fell. "Oh, lord, ya gonna give me a heart attack!"

"Calm down," Jade said. "I have to get away from my father and Theodore to where they can't touch me. I am not their puppet to twist and pull in any direction. My purpose isn't to make them happy. My purpose is to make *myself* happy. If there is a chance I can achieve that, I will take it no matter the consequence!"

Marna's grip loosened, and her face smoothed.

"I don't have another choice. He'll never leave me alone in this city."

Marna pressed her lips together.

"I wish I could be free with a man like Jackson Hadley."

Marna's face twisted as she repeated, "Jackson Hadley?"

She nodded.

"Jade-"

"I know, I know," she blurted and turned away, but Marna was at her heels.

"Yew mustn't get involved wit him!" Marna shrieked and grabbed her arm. "Listen to me! There is no telling what ya fada or even Theodore will do if yew sneaks around wit Jackson Hadley!"

"I'm not going to!"

"This is serious, Jade!" Marna was practically on the verge of a panic attack.

"I know it is. I cannot be with him."

"Ya fada will kill yew!"

"Would that be so bad?" Jade said carelessly.

Marna frowned. "Do yew has a death wish?"

She glanced at the wall behind her as she contemplated this. "I don't think so. But as for Jackson, he makes me feel better than I have in years. To have someone see you for who you are… to know your mistakes, and they still look at you with wonder." He made her want to be a better person. She didn't want to hold on to so much anger anymore, it was exhausting. It was time to let the past go and live. "He is the one exception in this city and should not be taken for granted. If I can't be with him romantically, simply being his friend would be nice."

"My, my, my," Marna said with a grin.

Jade's brows pinched. "What?"

Marna gave her a knowing look and returned to the dough she had abandoned. "I haven't seen yew smile since ya mutha died," she answered, and Jade staggered backward. "Jackson Hadley must be something if he can make yew forget about the pain."

Jade stared at the wall in front of her, confined by the truth of Marna's words.

XIX
Elijah

There was a fat envelope on his desk when he arrived. He gave it a questionable look and turned to Philip. "What's this?"

Philip raised his head from his typewriter and shrugged. "I haven't a clue. It came in around eleven, although, I think someone is messing with you. It smells like pig shit and something leaked through the package. I've wanted to throw it out all morning."

Elijah ran a hand through his hair and sat at his desk without another word. The folder had a pungent smell, and the bottom was starting to soak through. He was hesitant to open it, and when he looked back at Philip, his colleague had already gone back to typing.

He picked up the envelope, which was heavier than expected. There was more than just a letter inside. He unwound the string quickly and looked. There was something wrapped in a dirty rag beside a letter with red ink. He pulled out the letter, the words on the page were fuzzy, and he sighed impatiently. He glanced around, rummaged in his desk for his glasses and placed them on his face, and read,

Dear Mr. Hadley,

I am writing to you because I found your article rather alarming as opposed to the others. You mentioned nothing of me and everything about the whore. It was almost sympathetic, and I don't quite understand the reasoning. Why would you want anyone to feel anything other than relief at the death of a prostitute? And they say I'm strange.

I don't find anything unusual about my practices. In fact, I am saving the city of its filth and sin. But don't worry, Mr. Hadley, I'll give you another chance to get it right tomorrow.

Yours truly,
The Dollhouse Slayer

P.s. I do hope you enjoy the gift I have given you.

Elijah reread the letter several times before reaching for the rag and what was folded inside, although he had a hunch. He shoved the rag and the letter back in the envelope when he confirmed his suspicion.

"What was it?" Philip asked when he stood.

"A joke, as you said," he called over his shoulder and didn't turn back with any follow-up questions. Jackson and Owen needed to be the first to look at the contents of the package.

He could barely contain himself on the trolley; it simply wasn't moving fast enough. He would have run if he thought he could get there sooner.

By the time he reached the morgue, it was nearly quitting time, and he found Jackson inside his office along with Raoul and Gainsley.

"You won't believe what was delivered to the Gazette today," he muttered as he shut the door behind him. He thrust the envelope into Jackson's hands. "It's from the killer."

Jackson's confusion was brief as he ripped open the package and pulled out the bloody rag and letter. His hand hovered over the bundle, a pregnant pause as he shared a wary glance with Raoul.

A bloody mass emerged as he unfolded the rag. Raoul immediately began to dry heave, and Gainsley cleared his throat. Jackson pulled his spectacles from his breast pocket and picked up the letter.

Elijah watched him patiently, his heart in his throat.

"The Dollhouse Slayer?" Jackson remarked with derision. "Does he believe himself to be clever?"

"Seems like," Elijah muttered. "And I knew he was watching us, but not this closely."

Raoul leaned over the table for a better look, blinking back tears and covering his mouth and nose with a handkerchief. Elijah couldn't help the grin transforming his mouth. It was comical that he was a surgeon when his work made him ill.

"It's the smell," he explained as he laid out the mass.

"Who else did you show this to?" Jackson asked before Elijah could respond to Raoul.

"Just you."

Jackson's eyes flicked up to him. "You aren't going to release this, are you?"

"And give him the satisfaction?" Elijah answered with a shake of his head. "I don't think so."

"You wrote about Helena because she is what matters. Whoever wrote this letter didn't like that."

"You don't believe this is from the killer?"

"I'm not saying either way," Jackson murmured. "It could be from him, or it could be from someone trying to sell papers."

"What are you suggesting?"

He rolled his eyes. "I wasn't implying that it was you! It's not even your handwriting, although it does look familiar."

"Whose?"

Jackson shrugged.

"If it is the killer, do you believe he has his next victim?"

"Helena was abducted seven hours before she was discovered. If he hasn't found his next victim, it won't be long before he does." He tossed the letter on the table and glanced closely at the organ.

"Considering how we never released any information about a missing uterus, this should be Helena's, correct?" There was confidence in his question, not to mention a sense of intrigue.

"I would guess, but this is only a partial," Jackson muttered and walked over to the cabinet on the right side of the room. He opened drawers loudly as he began to rifle through them.

"What's missing?" Elijah asked.

"It's cut vertically in half," Raoul answered.

Elijah's face twisted, and his stomach was starting to curl. He glanced at Gainsley, who had yet to say a word, and swallowed.

Jackson returned to the desk with a pair of tongs, calipers, and brass binoculars. Elijah watched as he handed the binoculars to Raoul, and they began muttering, hovering mere inches above the organ.

"It's seven centimeters in length, an inch in thickness," Jackson stated as Raoul twisted one of the lenses until it lengthened and clicked into place. "The isthmus, left fallopian tube, and ovary are all intact."

"The shape is still distinct," Raoul said. "I wouldn't even question it."

"There is no mistaking it," Jackson agreed and placed the organ on the scale. "Twenty-five grams, a little less than half."

"The precision is astounding," Raoul commented. "The cut is clean and straight, with no jagged edges. The weapon could be a Catlin knife or a butcher's blade."

"A scalpel is more than likely."

"He's got to be a doctor."

Jackson's face smoothed as he sat back in his chair. "This could be hers, but I can't give a definite answer other than it's human."

"But how would anyone know when the information wasn't released?"

"I wouldn't trust anyone other than Owen and Cillian in Fielding's office. Everyone else is in the Elite's pocket, and I am not entirely convinced they aren't involved. It's also unwise to walk into the station with the contents of the package. I can send for Owen if you'd like."

Elijah glanced at Gainsley. "Get him here."

Within half an hour and several cigarettes with Raoul later, Owen walked into the room with a peeved expression. "What couldn't wait until morning?"

"Oh, I don't know, perhaps the partial uterus that was mailed to the Gazette!" Elijah snapped, and Owen's face smoothed as his eyes slid to Jackson in question.

"You'll have your work cut out for you," Jackson said. He was leaning against the wall with his arms folded.

Owen's stare dropped to the table where the uterus and letter lay. "You can't be serious."

"If only," Elijah muttered. "No one told anyone about a missing uterus, did they?"

Owen's forehead creased as he picked up the letter and read, ignoring him.

"It's more than likely hers," Jackson confirmed, and Elijah breathed. Whether out of relief or aversion, he wasn't sure. "I was just keeping an open mind. We can't get distracted by one lead because it looks good. We need to explore every option."

"But who knows about the uterus?"

Jackson glanced at Owen, and Elijah followed his gaze.

"We've got a real comedian on our hands," Owen murmured and scratched his chin. "The Dollhouse Slayer, eh?" He glanced at Elijah. "Don't release this just yet."

"I wasn't going to release it," Elijah answered with a frown. "Why would I give him what he wants?"

"Because it may help us catch him. He may get so upset that if you ignore him, he'll slip up."

"But what if he gets more violent?"

Owen met his stare. "I'm counting on that. We need to patrol Trinity Row!"

"What difference will that make?" Jackson barked. "It's not like the next victim will be killed in the open, and not only do you have no clue what he looks like, he won't abduct her against her will. She will willingly walk away with him. So, unless you plan to watch these interactions individually, you're wasting time."

"Are you suggesting I do nothing?"

"If you want to patrol, by all means, go ahead," Jackson shrugged. "I just think it's useless… but I'm not a detective."

"You're also not an imbecile," Owen fumed. "You have to see the benefit of patrolling the streets. If there is an exchange that looks off or unsavory-"

"That's my whole point, Owen! Women won't walk away with a threatening man. He will come across as disarming and even a little timid. Get women off the streets if you want to make a difference!"

"Then let's do it," Owen challenged.

"You can't end prostitution before nightfall. Women will continue to risk their lives because they are trying to survive, and this is the easiest solution!"

"We have to try," Elijah interjected. "We may not find him, but no one else will die in the possibility that we do."

Jackson pressed his lips together. He didn't seem to agree, but he nodded anyway, and they were filing out of his office within minutes.

It was dusk by the time they entered Trinity Row, and much to Jackson's dismay, Owen showed the entire force the letter. The streets were heavily patrolled in time, forcing many to shut themselves in. Not that they were utterly barren, but with coppers on nearly every street, many ran in the opposite direction.

"It would be wise to put gas lights on every block," Jackson muttered as he and Raoul walked in step beside him, each carrying lanterns.

"Why would they waste the money?" Raoul asked.

"If they were placed at the harbor, they could be placed here," Jackson answered. "We should have a little chat with Elizabeth about it."

"She won't spend any of the crown's money in Trinity Row," Elijah said. It was a shame that the affluent didn't feel any concern for the well-being of those on the east end. Just because they didn't have money didn't mean they were a waste of life.

They patrolled the streets all night, and when the sun began to rise, Jackson wanted to call it. Nothing strange happened, and no one was reported missing, but Elijah didn't feel it was a complete waste of an evening. He also didn't want to admit that the letter was probably from someone at the Gazette whose objective was to sell more papers.

"Just because we didn't see anything strange doesn't mean he didn't strike," Jackson said. "Women follow these men of their own accord. That's why it's so hard to pinpoint a nefarious transaction when they're so common."

Elijah shoved his hands in his pockets and thought this over. He had a point, but he would rather believe they stopped something before it happened, that they made a difference tonight.

He halted when he spotted Teddy and Edward around the corner. They were standing beside a truck outside of a gambling hall. Several men were unloading boxes from the back and carrying them into the building. He held out his arm before Jackson and Raoul exposed them.

"I don't care what William says," Teddy snapped. "I want them dead!"

"Don't we all?" Edward drawled. "But we must be careful about arousing suspicion, although it would be satisfying to see them bleed out on the streets. They think they are untouchable in this city; it is preposterous! Look how Avis strolls around and runs her mouth! A woman!"

Jackson pushed past Elijah and stormed straight for Edward. He grabbed him by the lapels of his jacket and slammed him against the wall. "The day you utter my sister's name again will be your last!"

Edward's eyes widened as he tried to shove Jackson away.

"You want me dead, do you?" Jackson growled.

"I didn't-"

"You stay away from my fucking family if you know what's good for you! I know where you sleep and what you do. I know what you value and the people you love. Do you think you've seen what madness looks like? Wait until I come for you!"

Elijah couldn't even think to react.

"I'd like to see you try!" Teddy snarled from behind.

Jackson released Edward and punched Teddy in the nose within the next second. He fell on his back motionless, having been knocked out with one hit. Jackson stepped over him without a backward glance, and Raoul scrambled to follow.

Edward dropped to his side and smacked his cheek to no avail. He glared over his shoulder. "You're all mad, and you'll get what's coming to you!"

"As will you," Elijah threatened. "You aren't the only one watching. Have a good day."

He could feel Edward glaring at his back, but it didn't matter. It was a nice feeling to have the upper hand for once.

He had been sitting at l'Arche Noble since sundown, observing Teddy Kensington gamble with Edward Wright from the upper floor of the gambling hall with James perched to his right. He wanted to believe the letter was from the killer and was hell-bent on catching Teddy in the act, spending the last two nights in Trinity Row with his youngest brother.

"How long are yew gonna stare at Mista Kensington?"

Elijah and James looked up to see Elizabeth DeWitt grinning down at them, and he rolled his eyes. He didn't want the unnecessary attention or the distraction. He'd already drunk several glasses of whiskey, and if he had anymore, he might as well call it a wasted evening. He'd be far too drunk to remember anything of importance.

"Not now, Elizabeth," Elijah mumbled and glanced back at Teddy. "We're busy."

"What's it got to do wit him?" she asked loudly, practically sitting in his lap, and glanced at his brother. "Hello, James!"

"Elizabeth." He nodded and took a drink of his ale.

"I'll give yew boys a two-for-one special if yew does that thing with your tongue I like!"

James choked into his cup, and a laugh escaped from Elijah as he clapped him on the back. "Not today. We're on the job."

"Ah, come on," she pouted and placed her arms around his neck. "Are yew really gonna treat me like that?"

"Please," he grumbled and pulled her arms off him. "I need to stay focused!"

Her cheeks raised, and her eyes crinkled at the sides. "I can help yew focus on a thing or two."

"Not now."

She relented and stood up, winking at James as she went. "Yew boys come find me when ya ready!"

Elijah rolled his eyes, and as he looked down at Teddy's table again, a petite blonde caught his attention. Anger sparked like a flame. "Elizabeth?"

She turned around and bellowed, "That was quick!"

"Not that," he said dismissively and pointed down to the table. "Is Roslyn still streetwalking?"

"He hasn't given her much of a choice!"

"Who? Blake or Teddy?" Elijah asked as James leaned in closer.

"Teddy," she said, and Elijah clenched his teeth together, glancing at James. His brother's gaze was a mirror of his feelings. "He said she needed to make up for all the trouble she caused the royal house."

"That son of a bitch," Elijah snarled.

Elizabeth frowned. "What yew mean?"

Elijah merely shook his head and glanced back at Roslyn.

"Anyway, yew knows Teddy," Elizabeth continued. "He loves whores just like yew do."

"I am nothing like that man!" Elijah fumed.

"Oh, I know," she said with a coy grin. "Yew are generous and sensual."

She went to reach for his groin, but he quickly grabbed her hand and flung it away. "I said no!"

She took a step back as if he'd slapped her and yelled, "Don' bother comin to me anymore!"

As she stomped off, several tables looked over. Great, this was the last thing he needed. When he glanced back at Teddy, the whole table was looking up at them. He cursed under his breath when they were waved down.

"You follow my lead, no matter what happens," he muttered to James. "And if it turns nasty, I want you to run."

"I'm not leaving you," James said at once.

"If it turns for the worse, you will."

"No. I won't."

"I'm not asking you."

"I don't need your permission," James said. "I'm not a kid anymore!"

This much was true. He looked increasingly like a man every day, and his loyalty was something to be accounted for. Perhaps James could be his right-hand man just as Jackson was to Owen. Even though they disagreed and fought savagely, their bond was evident and irreplaceable. A relationship Elijah envied.

"You think I'd leave you to fend for yourself?" James blurted with incredulity. "You must give credit where it's due. Look who raised me."

Elijah nodded toward the stairs grimly, leading the way and limping down one by one. He counted the sentinels, men employed by Teddy, and the innocent patrons that would get in the way if there was a fight.

He grabbed the empty chair and dragged it against the ground with James beside him. Teddy puffed on his stogie when he sat, his dark eyes glaring as he withdrew his hand and tapped the cigar in an ashtray.

Elijah couldn't help but grin at the black eye.

"What are you doing here, Eli?" Teddy rasped.

Elijah's eyes flicked to Roslyn, then to Edward and the doxy to his right, and back to Teddy himself. "Well, as this is a gambling hall, wouldn't you think I am here to bet?"

"And yet, you haven't touched any cards," Edward contradicted. "You've been leering all night as if we wouldn't notice!"

Elijah glanced at him. Was he going to pretend as if Jackson hadn't bested him?

"I'll ask you this one more time, Eli," Teddy said. "And I expect an honest answer. What are you doing here?"

"Or what, Teddy, you'll have me beaten? Killed? I wasn't aware it was a crime to sit and drink in a gambling hall."

"It's always nonsense with you," Teddy said and stuck the stogie back in his mouth. "That was always your problem. You never knew when to shut your mouth."

Elijah let out a humorless laugh. His eyes swept toward the sentinels who were waiting for the word to take him out. "I've never had a problem, Teddy. That was you."

Teddy's hand went slack with a glare.

Elijah leaned forward. "You were the one who never knew when to quit."

Teddy grinned at him. "I broke from my father's shadow and created my own legacy. If you only knew what I have managed to accomplish, you wouldn't be insulting me. You'd be begging for an opportunity to become rich beyond your wildest dreams!"

"I like my job."

Teddy laughed boisterously, and the men at the table joined in. Elijah smiled as his eyes moved from one face to the other.

"You're a journalist!" Edward cried in derision. "How much can you make at that?"

"Considering how you still live with your fucking brothers," Teddy added and glared at James. "I'd say not much at all!"

The table roared again, and Teddy nudged Roslyn, prompting her to join along. Her shoulders jilted forward, and she looked on the verge of tears. Her eyes landed on Elijah in complete devastation. He connected her stare briefly before glancing back at Teddy. "Owen, I can see why. Since losing Clara, he hasn't been the same, and Jack has always been unbalanced, but you." Teddy shook his head. "You had a real gift, Eli. It's rather disappointing to see you waste it."

"I feel my talents are better used on paper," Elijah said.

"That's why you're here, isn't it? You think we had something to do with that whore's murder?" He laughed, and Roslyn closed her eyes tightly in grief. Elijah ground his teeth together. He could kill Teddy before he was subdued and save Bel Deaux from this savage that once held the face of his childhood friend. There was a hint of the youth he knew, but perhaps with every crime he committed and the excessive drinking and smoking, there was a grayish tinge to his skin. As if his humanity was slipping entirely.

"You knew her," Elijah said calmly.

"So did you!" Edward bellowed.

Elijah shook his head. "I never bedded her."

"So that makes you a saint?" Teddy growled.

Elijah pressed his lips together, and his eyes landed on Roslyn again. Her pale eyes stared at him in a pleading sort of way. His eyebrows drew in as he further gazed without the knowledge of Teddy, who continued to ridicule him along with Edward.

He didn't understand what she was trying to convey. So instead, he said, "What about Jade?"

All humor fell from Teddy's face as he whipped back with a growl, "What about her?"

"Will she allow you to continue on this way?"

"That stupid chit will never tell me what to do! And how dare she even think she can make a fool out of me!"

"Oh, yeah," Elijah chuckled and glanced at James. "Dominic Kane sure made a cuckold out of you, didn't he?"

Teddy seethed and shoved Roslyn from his lap. James jumped to her aid as Teddy ripped Elijah from his seat by the collar. "Your days are coming to an end, old friend."

"Is that right?" Elijah murmured and shoved back.

"If you think you can insult me, you have another thing coming!"

"I'm shaking in my boots," Elijah mocked as Duke came bursting through the crowd. "Sir!"

Teddy chuckled. "You don't have it in you, Eli."

Duke pulled on Elijah's arm and hollered, "There's been another murder!"

The pub went silent, all attention switching over to the driver.

"It's madness, sir! You must come quick!"

Elijah shoved Teddy back, and he fell over a chair and onto the floor. Elijah followed Duke out of the gambling hall, passed the stunned pikers, and into the streets.

"She was found on Chaney Avenue," Duke explained.

"Do Owen and Jack know?"

"They're at the scene now," Duke huffed as he tried to keep up with Elijah's hobble.

"We need-" Elijah stopped abruptly when he saw Roslyn trailing alongside James. He pulled a stack from his pocket and slapped it in his brother's hand.

"The same room?" he asked as she wrapped her arms around herself. Elijah shrugged out of his coat and placed it on her shoulders.

"Yes, and quickly, before Teddy or Blake notices," he instructed and glanced at her. "I'm sorry I failed you."

"I know."

"It won't happen again," he promised. "You hear me? I will kill Teddy before he lays another hand on you."

She gave him a small smile before James steered her away. He turned back to Duke. "Do you know who found the body?"

"Some blokes walking through the park," Duke grunted. "Gainsley was found at the scene out cold."

Elijah stopped walking. "He was?"

"Merfan has him in chains."

Elijah took off without another word.

XX
Owen

He tore through the streets, wondering what Gainsley would even be doing at the park at this hour. It had to be a case of mistaken identity. Gainsley was with the Hadleys the night of Helena's murder, and not only that, but he also lived with them. Where would he commit such an act without arousing suspicion? Draining someone's blood was not only messy but time-consuming. He didn't have the means or capability to execute such a crime.

The victim was displayed on a bench, and Gainsley was nowhere to be seen. This caused him to panic, had Gainsley uncovered the killer and been attacked? If so, he needed to speak with him immediately, as precious time was being wasted.

Jack was already there, taking turns scribbling into his notebook and leaning over the corpse with a lantern in his hand to see her wounds better. Cillian and Merfan spoke with an older gentleman whom Owen had never seen before.

Owen placed his hands in his pockets and headed toward Jack. He tried to ignore his rising annoyance as he asked, "How bad is it?"

"More mutilation and lack of blood," Jack murmured as Owen's face twisted at the corpse. There were two x's slashed deeply over her eyes. Her arms were stretched across the back of the bench as if she was casually relaxing in the park. Her bare legs were exposed, one leg resting over the other, and black suede boots with a ruffled bow were tied on each foot. He could see the gaping slash across her lower abdomen as her skirts were pulled up above her waist.

"This one fought back. There are defensive wounds on her hands."

Owen walked over to her left hand, and Jackson handed over the lantern, which was indeed covered with knife marks and more lilies.

"Again, with the flowers?"

"I wish I knew what it meant."

"Perhaps there is no meaning," Owen stated. "It's feasible to deduce insanity when he's ripping women apart."

Jackson's face twisted in skepticism.

"Although I'm sure you're right, and there is a reason. One that's rather simple; we just can't see it."

Silence settled between them briefly as Owen's eyes strayed to the unknown man standing next to Merfan and Cillian.

"I'm going to throttle Merfan," Jackson said after some minutes. "How could he even think Gainsley had something to do with this?"

"Don't worry," Owen said. It was starting to look very grim on their end. "I'll get him out."

"She is far beyond help, and the crowd is growing," Jack snapped as his eyes locked on the people hovering on the edge of the street. "She needs to be taken to my lab."

"That is all?" Owen croaked and held out the light.

Jack's face hardened as he took back the lantern. "That is all."

Owen wanted to protest but refrained when Cillian began to yell obscenities as Merfan jauntily strode toward them.

The constable spat, "There is no need for either of your assistance!"

"And why is that?" Owen snapped.

"Because your valet was found at the scene of the crime! You had the killer under your roof and failed to catch him! I believe that forfeits your involvement!"

"How do you know it was Gainsley?" Owen badgered.

"He was covered in blood and holding a knife!"

"The killer could have easily knocked him out and planted the knife on him!" Owen scoffed. "And if you've failed to notice, this woman also lacks blood to have been killed here!"

"He could have killed her at your house and then brought her here!" Merfan roared. "Just like he did with Helena! Which is being searched as we speak!"

Owen rolled his eyes. "Have my home searched if you wish, but why would he stay at the crime scene?"

Merfan narrowed his eyes. "Maybe he became overwrought with grief and fainted!"

"Whoever committed these crimes," Jackson interrupted, "would not have a sudden guilty conscience. The man capable of murders such as these is very ill."

"And what makes you so certain?" a nasal voice asked. The man who approached had a thick beard and a rather large nose. Thick spectacles covered his eyes as his front teeth hung past his lips. He wore a tweed suit, and his flaming hair was gelled against his head.

"Who are you?" Jackson demanded.

The man's lips twisted pompously. "The name is Georges Dupont, Chief Deputy Inspector of Berrone."

Owen glanced at Jackson, who raised a hand to check his watch in response. His voice was low as he said, "Good of you to come all this way." Jackson's attention then reverted to Merfan. "You can have her sent to my lab now."

"Have you not listened to a word I said?" Merfan choked out.

"Sure, I have," Jackson acknowledged before turning away and calling over his shoulder. "I'll be waiting for your arrival!"

"Yes, I see what you were saying. The overconfidence." Georges' lips turned downwards as he rested a hand on his side and watched Jackson walk away. Elijah was the one who usually downplayed Merfan's authority; and Owen found it rather amusing that it was Jack this time.

Merfan's puce face rounded on him. "You and your brothers are no longer welcome!"

"You don't have the authority to make that call!" Cillian snapped.

Merfan grinned nastily at him. "Yes, I knew you'd be a problem. Your love for the Hadleys is disgusting!" He withdrew a letter from his pocket and waved it in Cillian's face. "I had you overruled!"

Cillian ripped the letter from his hand and read quickly.

Owen sighed heavily. Merfan was irksome. He always tried to cast Owen and Cillian away because they were honest and thorough. It hindered Merfan when all he wanted was an open and shut case.

"If you honestly think Anne will be taken to Jackson's lab, you're outright mad!"

"Anne?" Owen asked with a turn of his head, and his stomach dropped. He didn't initially recognize her mutilated face, but now it was evident. It was Anne Dombrowski. He had failed her.

"Dear lord," he muttered and covered his mouth.

"Yes, Anne Dombrowski," Merfan yelled back and stepped in front of Owen. "Another prostitute who boarded at Miss Louise's Dollhouse! It seems like a connection to me."

Cillian lowered the letter amid their argument with a loud exhale. "Merfan, we need as many men on this case as possible!"

"I agree. Just not the Hadley's. Their valet is a suspect, and until he is cleared, which I doubt, they are too close to the case to be involved! And if they truly didn't know, which again, I doubt, they are accessories to murder!"

"Now you're just making assumptions!" Cillian snarled.

"Where is he?" Elijah shouted from a distance and interrupted their spat. He ran toward them awkwardly and yelled at the top of his lungs. He crashed into Owen's side when he came within reach and leaned over to rest his hands on his knees. He panted while he said, "Where's Gainsley?"

"He's in custody!" Merfan growled. "I already told your brother you're off the case!"

"Why?" Elijah stood at full height and grabbed his side.

"Anne Dombrowski was murdered tonight," Merfan stated as a wide-eyed Elijah glanced down at the body. "Your valet was caught red-handed at the scene! And I think you made up that letter to get attention!"

"Horseshit!" Elijah yelled, and Merfan puffed out his chest.

"He didn't do it," Owen stated adamantly and rubbed his temples, trying to ignore the immense guilt rising.

"How do you know?" Merfan barked. "Did your superior judgment whisper in your ear?"

Owen dropped his hands. There was a ghost of a laugh on his lips as he said, "Come again?"

"The three of you think you're high and mighty in this city. I already told you that you aren't welcome anymore! We aren't bringing Anne to Jackson's lab, so you can tell him to fuck off when you see him! A more trusted surgeon will do the examination, and Georges here will take over this investigation in your place!"

"You can't be serious!" Owen bellowed over Elijah's protests. Georges looked at them smugly as he turned to walk around Anne's body.

"You haven't done a damn thing on this case!" Merfan snarled. "It's time to bring in someone more competent!"

"You haven't allowed me to do a damn thing!" Owen objected. "I've been stopped at every turn!"

"Because you're too fixated on the wrong men! And you," Merfan rounded on Elijah with a point of his finger. "If you write about this, so help me!"

"What are you going to do about it?" Elijah growled with a glare.

"If you cross me again, watch what happens!"

"Is that a threat?" Owen bellowed.

Merfan shrugged in derision. His voice was haughty as he said, "I'm done with the lot of you! I work hard to protect this city, and you constantly stand in my way!"

"Is this about Peter Delmont?" Elijah yelled.

"Jackson thinks he's very clever," Merfan said. "But I won't allow him to let another murderer walk free!"

"You know damn well Christopher didn't kill Peter!" Owen snapped. He was becoming more irritated with the conversation; they were getting nowhere and fast. "Come, Eli, let's go home."

"Are you mad?" Elijah spat.

Owen ignored him and glared at Merfan. "I expect to see Gainsley out by morning."

"He won't be released!" Merfan answered with a sneer.

"We'll see about that."

"I'll make this right," Cillian promised, and Owen nodded at him before he stepped away.

He walked briskly from the scene with Elijah complaining at his back. Owen ignored his brother and shoved his hands in his pockets once again. He kept his mouth shut, fearing to say something that would later be regretted. Merfan would try to pin this on Gainsley and lock him away for life.

"Would you slow down?" Elijah demanded.

"We need to find witnesses!" Owen yelled erratically. "Merfan isn't going to let me anywhere near Miss Louise's Dollhouse, and I need to talk to her!"

"Someone saw something," Elijah said quietly. "If not the murder, someone somewhere saw her walking away with a stranger."

Owen gazed at him. "He's trying to frame Gainsley because of Jackson's testimony. This is insane!"

"He won't get away with this!" Elijah said with a shake of his head. "There is simply no way! Merfan cannot continue to fool the public when the truth is so plainly obvious! He isn't smart enough to fool an entire city and the Queen with shitty explanations and no evidence to back up any of his stupid theories! Whose side is he on, anyway?"

Owen failed to answer. He didn't want to admit aloud that Merfan already won and his fealty wasn't to the crown, but the Elite.

Owen found Jackson in his lab, pouring over his notebook, his hair sticking up at all ends. "I figured you could eat," he said. "Considering you have a terrible relationship with food."

Jackson eyed the roast and potatoes before giving Owen a grateful smile.

"How long do you expect Merfan to banish us from working on the murders?" Jackson asked.

"Until he throws someone in the bastille, I suppose," Owen murmured, "How was Calvert?"

Jackson took a bite and chewed as he contemplated. He swallowed after some time and said, "He is an incredibly irreverent man."

"We already knew that," Owen said testily.

Jackson's eyes flicked to him briefly. "The meeting lasted all but five minutes. As soon as I told him nothing was left behind, his demeanor changed, and he practically threw me out after threatening me."

"That's the second time in two weeks," Owen observed with a smile. "Will you try for a third?"

"If I could only be so lucky," he said, and his face quickly sobered. "I lied about Alexandra. I told Calvert she committed suicide so he'd talk."

"Did he?"

Jackson took another bite. "Not in so many words, but I'm convinced he knows who your suspect is."

Owen took off his glasses and rubbed his eyes. It was getting more difficult to deny that William Calvert was linked to the murders.

"I'm almost certain of it," Jackson answered swiftly. "Perhaps he didn't act out the murder because of his weakened state, but he knows who did."

"There's only one problem, he'll never be brought to justice. I have been warned to stay away from the Elite regarding any crime! Alexandra was having an affair with Abraham Kensington in the months leading up to her death. What if William discovered the alleged affair, and she was killed because of it?"

"If that were true, why would he continue associating with Abraham? Wouldn't he have killed him as well? Also, if we went to Feilding about our suspicions, William wouldn't be arrested. But, if we went to Elizabeth, then he would. We cannot allow these men to ruin this city anymore! The capital is turning closer to hell every day because the Elite are destroying one life after another! There are brothels and gambling halls on nearly every corner in Trinity Row, kids are selling drugs and being prostituted out by vile men, and to top it off, there were two brutal murders that will likely happen again! Come now, Owen! You cannot tell me this is how life is to be lived! This is not what your badge stands for!"

"And what am I to do?" Owen barked. "The Elite controls all the money in Elione! How can we stand up against tyranny when they can buy anyone off?"

"Elizabeth is a just Queen," Jackson muttered. "The gilded years are named after her reign! Just because she's getting older does not mean you cannot plead to her for a change!"

"And what if they pay her off?"

Jackson sat back and crumpled in depletion as if the thought had never occurred. "Then I suppose we're all damned."

Owen stared at him with a new sense of determination. "Not if we refuse to give up."

Jackson glanced over his shoulder with a smile, and Owen knew it appeared hopeless, but with Jackson on his side, they would never give up fighting for those who didn't have a voice in this world.

XXI
Olivette

Ollie felt nothing as Lady Ashford's casket was lowered deep into the ground. It was frighteningly cold out, and she barely registered Tellie's hand clasping her own. A headache replaced her tears, along with indifference and abandonment. Her face was puffy and red, she wanted nothing more than to curl into a ball and forget all her problems, but life wasn't so simple. Her father was not present. Whether he knew and failed to attend, or perhaps he hadn't heard, it didn't matter because he'd already abandoned them.

A loud howl forced her to look up. Kittie was wailing as her husband patted her shoulder delicately. She knew she shouldn't feel annoyed by her sister's tears, yet she couldn't help and feel incensed at the ridiculous display. Kittie was always one for theatrics and loved when all eyes were on her. Timothy gave her a tempered smile when their eyes met, but Ollie looked away quickly; fresh tears burned in her eyes.

That feeling of revulsion returned, and she trembled, breathing evenly out of her nose. She didn't feel like the same person anymore. She wasn't whole. How could she even begin to think that she could give up her body in exchange for food and rent when one man's look crippled her entire being?

Kittie was adamant that they were to stay with her for the time being, but Ollie had no intention of following through. She only pretended to avoid a fight, but she was determined to find her own way. And it had nothing to do with Timothy and how he smiled at her. It was what Lady Ashford revealed to her in the days before her death.

She was sitting in her chair by the window when Tellie said, "Mum wants a word with you."

Ollie closed her eyes. She wasn't looking forward to this conversation, though she would never admit to the violation of her body, no matter what Tellie said. She walked somberly toward the front room as the dread truly sunk in.

Lady Ashford looked incredibly awful. If possible, she was more bloated, and she was genuinely starting to reek of urine.

"Shut the door behind you," she murmured, and Ollie obliged.

She sat on the table her mother's legs were resting on and pulled her own into her chest. Lady Ashford did not chastise her for once.

"I've been unkind to you," she admitted, though she wasn't tearful. She was making an honest statement. "It was for selfish reasons, and perhaps I was even a little spiteful. But there was absolutely nothing you have ever done to warrant such horrible behavior, and I'm sorry."

Ollie's eyebrows drew in, and her heart began to quicken.

"Your father has always stepped out on our marriage, and it was never easy. It tore into my chest and made me feel as if I was worth nothing. After years of it, I thought to give him a taste of his own medicine, so I stepped out too."

Ollie's throat suddenly felt dry, but the urge to cry was overwhelming.

Lady Ashford's face hardened with indifference. "I met a very rich man and spent plenty of time with him, becoming pregnant with you not long after. I knew it was not Christopher's, and so did he. You were the reminder of my greatest mistake."

Ollie let go of her legs and let her feet drop to the floor. She suddenly felt hollower than she did before.

"But Christopher was a good man. He raised you as his own to protect you."

"From whom? Who is my real father?"

Lady Ashford dropped her gaze and sighed, "William Calvert."

Ollie's eyes widened as the sharp stab of dejection finally ripped through her chest. "I beg your pardon?"

"I had an affair with William Calvert," she admitted.

"I don't believe you!"

"I'm serious, Olivette!" Lady Ashford said dramatically. She was patting her face with her handkerchief. "I cannot apologize enough. The circumstances of your birth are not your fault, they are my own, and I am sorry I treated you differently than Kittie and Tellie. You are still my child, after all."

Ollie watched her silently. She had several curses in mind but held them back. No matter how horrible she was treated, it wasn't wise to swear at a woman on her deathbed. It did give her a sense of relief, however. She could finally let go of this life.

Ollie hadn't told Tellie or Kittie about her last conversation with Lady Ashford. She couldn't stand being looked at differently.

The rain wasn't helping her mood, especially when the thunder erupted from above, making her flinch with every clash. Her eyes raised wistfully in the distance when she spotted them.

Jackson and Avis were walking onto the grounds. He held an umbrella above them as she clutched onto his arm. Ollie released a breath of relief. It was comforting to find people with unpolluted desires who merely wished to help because it was in good faith.

Tellie went rigid next to her. "What are *they* doing here?"

Ollie wanted to shrug her off. She didn't care if her sister was annoyed about their presence because she was grateful to see them. They stood quietly on the other side of the grave, and as the priest gave his final prayer, both Jackson and Avis raised their right hands in one fluid movement to make the sign of the cross against their forehead, chest, and shoulders.

Ollie blinked with interest. She wasn't particularly religious and found it interesting that they were, at least to some degree.

"I'm sorry we're late. We stopped at our parents' graves." Avis said quietly when she stepped around to greet her. She let go of Jackson's arm and gave her a hug. "I'm so very sorry for your loss."

Despite everything, so was Ollie.

"Thank you," she answered, and when she pulled back, she glanced up at Jackson.

His face was unreadable. There was a lack of wanting to let anyone in and she could relate to that. Although, he didn't make her feel any misgivings. She felt entirely comfortable in his presence. She didn't believe him to have any ulterior motives. He didn't stare longer than necessary, nor did he make vulgar comments.

"I'm sorry for your loss," he said. His voice was deep and subdued.

She tried to smile.

"This might not be the best time," Avis said hastily. "But where are you going to stay from here on out?"

"With us," Kittie answered, and Ollie was surprised to see that she had joined them along with Tellie and Timothy.

Avis seemed satisfied by this answer, but Ollie wasn't, though she didn't say it. "My sister told me what you have done for my mother," Kittie continued, "I wanted to thank you personally for helping."

Jackson gave her a curt nod while the smile that formed on Avis's lips was somewhat strained. Ollie wondered what this meant, and she feared this was the last time she'd ever see the pair.

"It was no problem," Avis said, and she glanced back at Ollie. "You remember what I said before?"

She remembered everything.

Kittie's eyes narrowed suspiciously between the pair. "What are you talking about?"

"She told me never to give up hope," Ollie answered, but when Avis's eyes flashed in her direction, she knew that wasn't what she was referring to.

"That is kind," Kittie said, her voice cavalier. The Windsor's had joined the funeral procession. "Thank you for coming." She walked away without waiting for an answer and Timothy followed.

"It is very kind of you to show," Tellie said. "Thank you."

She turned to follow Kittie but hesitated with her arm outstretched, wanting Ollie to walk away from the Hadleys with her.

"I'll be right behind you," she said, and Tellie frowned briefly before giving them an unpleasant smile as she folded her arms across her chest and walked toward the Windsor's.

Ollie turned back to Avis. "I'm sorry."

"For what?"

"Their behavior," she answered quietly.

Jackson's cheek lifted as Avis shrugged. "You just lost your mother. I wouldn't take anything personally."

"Fair point."

"What I was meaning," Avis continued, "If you ever need us, you are always welcome to stop by our manor."

Ollie's eyes widened, and she glanced up at Jackson. He gave her a genuine smile.

"I appreciate that, especially if Theodore comes around again," she said, and she covered her mouth. She hadn't meant to say anything about him to anyone.

Avis gaped with alarm. "Has Teddy come for you?"

"No!" Ollie said louder than usual. "I only meant that if he tries to come around again."

"Are you sure about that?" Jackson asked.

"Yes," she said defiantly, but they didn't seem to believe her by the look they shared. It made her anxious.

"Come, Ollie!" Kittie yelled. The rain was no longer drizzling and truly began to pour.

"We'll see you soon," Avis said, giving her one last hug.

Jackson stood back. He seemed to understand her lack of wanting to be close to a man. "Don't forget to reach out if you need us."

She nodded once.

"For anything," he recapitulated. "And If Teddy bothers you, I want you to come to find me."

She blushed.

"Goodbye, Ollie," Avis said and grabbed onto the arm Jackson held out for her.

Ollie watched them walk away as an unnamed emotion rose in her chest. She should have asked to go with the Hadley's because she felt nothing but indifference when she glanced back at her sisters watching her expectantly.

The rest of the afternoon was a series of well-wishers and condolences paying their respects. Ollie didn't interact much with anyone who came to Timothy's, choosing to sit in the corner of the room waiting for nightfall so she could sneak away unnoticed by her sisters. She picked at her nails, her hair, and her dress. She barely ate any of the mutton placed in front of her, staring at the tablecloth instead. There was only so much socializing she could handle, and that's when she realized her sisters were perversely eating up the attention.

Christopher Ashford had not shown. He probably didn't even know that his wife had passed on. Not when he was preoccupied with the attention of a young woman. Resentment grew the longer she thought about it. She wanted to confront him, to let him know the damage he had caused. She thought about what she would say, and maybe he wouldn't care, but he needed to know.

A bouquet of flowers were delivered sometime in the evening; they were from William Calvert.

Hours later, when everyone had gone to bed, she lay next to Tellie, waiting for her to fall into a deep enough sleep to where she wouldn't stir once Ollie moved. She glanced at her sister's freckled face, committing every inch to memory. She had a good relationship with Tellie far more than she did with Kittie. Tellie was kinder and more accepting of the truth.

She arose when it was just after three in the morning when the clock ticking loudly was the only sound that could be heard. Ollie scooped up her bag, the one she failed to unpack, and crept toward the door, giving one last glance over her shoulder before leaving her entire life behind.

She wandered aimlessly for some time, long after the sun had risen, needing answers that only Christopher Ashford could give. And while she was raised on the lower west side of the indigent, on the very same side of the bridge as Trinity Row, while dire, it wasn't nearly as crime-ridden, filthy, and drug-infused as the east end.

She had never traveled to the heart of Trinity Row on her own, not remembering the poorly paved roads covered with insalubrious workhouses, but perhaps children simply didn't notice such things.

The streets were in complete disarray, yet the people were even worse. Everyone seemed to be starving and working for the bare minimum life had to offer. Children ran loose through the grimy streets. They were dirty, missing shoes, and some even were missing clothes; their parents were nowhere to be seen. Ollie felt sick as she watched them, wishing she could give them somewhere to stay to protect them from the filth of Trinity Row.

She asked around for the man who raised her, but he was either unknown, or she was laughed at for mentioning his name. One woman told her to run far away from him, while a man spit in her face for the intrusion. That's when she realized he held no amount of esteem, even in the lower class.

There was a time when Christopher Ashford had been a very well-respected gentleman. This was before he had squandered the family fortune in gambling halls, a growing dependency on liquor and opium, and an addiction to seedy women well below his age. At two and twenty, Christopher became the most affluent man to emerge from Mouveaux, ever since Adrian Von Peltier had left the city to recover relics and treasures of the ancient world. Christopher married the wealthy daughter of a Duke, doubling his fortune and having three daughters of great beauty. As a man with a deep interest in spirits and a good laugh, he hosted the most well-profited poker games still recounted today. Yes, on the surface, Christopher seemed to have it all, and for a while, he did.

Christopher was often found in the pubs, directly seated at the center bar with a drink in hand, fixing up schemes for a quick pound or betting silver he didn't have. His wife was too prudish for what a whore was willing to give, and he quickly stepped out of the marriage. He didn't care much for his daughters, often complaining that none of them were men. Christopher had no idea what to do with their three daughters and lost each of their dowries in his selfish, squandering ways. No marriage prospects came, and the only reason Kittie had married at all was that her father lost a bet.

Tellie or Ollie would arrive at dusk to gather Christopher from the bar and cart him home. Laughs and jeers would follow, and Ollie would blush and remain quiet as she helped her father discreetly. Tellie, on the other hand, would fire back and voice an opinion no man wanted to hear. Some things never changed.

Her anxiety grew as the hours dragged on. She didn't have much money; she was starving and exhausted. When her feet began to throb, she sat on the corner of Pembroke square and pulled off her slipper; the heel had worn through. Her feet were raw.

"Yew all right, lovey?"

She looked up to see three women staring down at her. One had messy blonde curls with a gap in her front teeth. The second had red hair and a sneer, while the third had blonde hair and freckles.

Ollie clenched her teeth, shaking her head.

The woman with a gap in her teeth knelt next to her. "Are yew all alone?"

She nodded once.

"Are yew touched in the head?" the redhead snapped. "Do yew know there is a killer about?"

She dropped her gaze, far too tired to care. "I was looking for my father, but no one seems to want to help."

"People will only help for money, love," the second blonde said, and Ollie's eyebrows knit together. She didn't have any money, nor was she going to try giving up her body for it. "Who's ya fada? Maybe we knows him."

"Cristopher Ashford."

The women shared a look, offering nothing more.

Ollie turned away with bitter embarrassment. "He seems to have that effect on a lot of people."

"Yew shouldn't be here alone," The redhead said quickly. "Do yew have a place to stay for the night?"

"I have four pence."

"It won't get yew a room but a spot on the bench in the boarding house," she answered while sharing a look with the other two. "We can get the money. So, yew might as well stick wit us. We can share a room wit yew. It's the safest way."

Confounded by the generosity of the people she encountered in this city, she gaped at her. "But you don't know me!"

"We knew the women who were killed," the woman with the gap in her teeth answered. "They were our friends. Trust us when we say yew should come wit us. We're safer together."

She couldn't hide the sense of relief. With the sun setting, she wasn't sure what to do.

"Very well," she answered.

The gap tooth grinned. "I'm Elizabeth Dewitt." She pointed at the redhead. "That's Melody." Then to the other blonde. "And Roslyn."

She gave them a tight-lipped grin before looking back at Elizabeth. "I'm Ollie."

"Come on, Ollie, let's get us a drink!" Elizabeth said, and Ollie quickly placed on her slippers. She knew it wasn't wise to follow a group of people she didn't know, but she didn't have other options for one, and for second, they weren't men.

Nobody really looked in their direction as they made their way through the poorly paved roads. Elizabeth and Melody chatted for the entirety of the walk as Ollie limped beside Roslyn, who remained silent. She carried herself relatively well as her eyes swept up to the buildings gone to seed, which hadn't been taken care of; decrepit-looking people were washing those that had.

Commotion ahead had Ollie shifting behind the three women. Two men were rolling around on the ground, fighting over a bone as a third tried to steal it from them.

Adrenaline coursed through her, but she wasn't sure what to do, so she stood still after a moment. The men almost seemed feral as they fought viciously with one another over the bone. She couldn't take her eyes away until one of the women tugged at her arm.

Elizabeth gave her a hard stare. "There's nothing yew can do for them. It is best if we keep moving. These men are starving in more ways than one."

Ollie glanced at her with wide eyes. She couldn't be subjected to another rape; she'd never recover. She allowed Elizabeth to steer her toward Perry's pub.

Here, they received ill-natured looks. Her company wasn't bothered as they found an empty table. Melody stomped toward the bar to order each of them a drink. Ollie hadn't drunk much alcohol before, as she'd seen what it had done to the most honorable people. So, when Melody placed a stein of ale in front of her, her nose crinkled. The other women didn't hesitate, all three sucked the liquid down greedily, and she supposed they didn't have much choice. The hard life they lived drove them to drink. She picked up her stein and took a pull; it was bitter and warm. She tried to keep her face even as she set it down, but her company noticed and laughed.

"Yu'll get used to it," Melody said as she stood, staring at someone in the distance. "Yew can get used to anyfing if yew's around it long enuff."

Ollie repressed a chill. She must be referring to sex work, although Ollie didn't think she'd ever get used to it. She never wanted to be touched again.

"How much?"

Ollie glanced up at a drunkard leering down at her. He had gray matted hair and a beard, and his four bottom teeth were missing when he smiled. He also happened to reek of liquor and human filth. Ollie placed the back of her hand against her nose to dim the smell.

"Sixpence for five minutes," Melody told him.

The man gave her a one-eyed stare. "I don't want your cunnie!"

"Well, my cunnie is all yu'll get!"

The man pointed at Ollie. "I want her!"

Her stomach turned as she sunk against the back of her chair. Distress settled in her chest, and she nearly began to hyperventilate.

"She's not for sale!" Melody bellowed.

"Says who?"

Elizabeth and Roslyn stood, blocking Ollie from view. "We say!"

"Yew sure is pretty," the man said, distracted by Roslyn. "Young too. How much?"

"She's not for sale either!" Melody said crossly with a fold of her arms.

"But yew's is whores! Yew can't deny a paying customer!"

"I'm the whore!" Melody wailed. "These girls ain't! If yew wants a good time, it's sixpence for five minutes. If not, fuck off!"

"Ah, to hell with yew!" the man huffed with a wave of his hand.

Ollie blinked back tears. No one had ever stood up for her in the way these women and the Hadleys had. Her own sisters wouldn't even intervene on her behalf.

The three women didn't sit down until the man was off harassing someone else across the room.

"Yews, all right?" Melody asked when she noted the tears welling in Ollie's eyes.

She nodded.

"Let's get sumfing stronger, eh? How about some gin?"

Ollie smiled as the others agreed. A half-hour later, Melody stood in the corner singing at the top of her lungs as a man played the piano. Anyone near threw unruly glares in their direction. Ollie sat with Elizabeth and Roslyn at a table, passing around a bottle as they watched Melody unravel at the seams.

"I knew it was too good to be true," Elizabeth muttered after some time. "A fella like Teddy Kensington doesn't want nuffing from women like us. Helena shoulda realized."

Ollie's stomach dropped at the name.

"I know one thing they like," Roslyn grumbled.

Elizabeth glanced at Ollie. "Men come to us because highborn women won't give it up, and we do! Teddy is an asshole anyway! Why does he get to take all our earnings?"

"I hate him," Roslyn said sharply. "It's unfair, he comes from a rich family, and we don't! I should be able to keep everything I make as it's my body doing the earning!"

Ollie gazed at her stoically, feeling incredibly sorry for these women and the sacrifices they had to make. It was tragic.

"OHHHHHH," Melody bellowed. "A hundred years from now, my dear, we should not care at all!"

The girls flinched at her tone-deaf voice.

"Helena loved rich men. She went from Calvert to Teddy in no time," Roslyn stated. "But I can't deny that I wasn't hopeful. I thought that if he married her, he'd leave us alone."

"Do yew suppose he lied to her?" Elizabeth asked.

Roslyn shrugged. "Of course, he did. Why would he want to wed a woman who is not only a prostitute but much older? He'll want children, they all do, and she wouldn't have been able to give him one!"

Elizabeth took another pull from the bottle and glanced back at Melody.

"I hate to say it," Roslyn murmured, "but we're losing time. Teddy will come calling tomorrow, and if we don't have his money, well…."

"It's a damn shame what they did to them," Elizabeth muttered darkly.

They eyed one another for a few beats before Roslyn and Elizabeth stood. "Come on. We will give yew money for the room. Yew can wait for us there."

"Are we going to leave her?" Ollie asked when she realized they had no intention of retrieving Melody.

Elizabeth looked at her and said, "She'd kill us if we made her leave now. We'll come back for her in a few hours. She's safe in a pub. It's public with lots of witnesses."

Ollie bit her lip as she followed the other two women to the door. But what if Melody stumbled out of here alone before they came back? She glanced back at the woman who stood up for her.

Melody's face was beat red, and she was swaying on her feet; there would be no earning for her tonight. She appeared to be having fun with no intention of leaving anytime soon. Perhaps she would be safe. Yet it didn't explain the nausea or the cloud of despair hovering in the room.

She didn't like it one bit.

XXII
Ruby

It had been three days since she had woken up in a cold sweat to the sound of a woman's blood-curdling scream. The sounds of her death still affected Ruby's every waking thought. It was too much to handle. Why did these tragedies haunt her? She'd hardly slept, and the large bags under her eyes only made her appear rather sickly. Her hair was messy, and her skin was paler than usual. She had trouble sleeping since that strange man entered her room, whether it be a dream or someone real, she never wanted to see him again. She didn't touch her food as she stared at the table. The whole family had gathered for dinner.

William was also looking in poor health. Katerina sat smugly at his side, throwing self-satisfied stares toward her siblings, appearing superior to the situation. Jet was talking loudly about his tennis victory against Peter Cavendish and ignoring his wife as usual. Ruby didn't even have it in her to be upset over the casual way her brother said his name repeatedly.

She could feel both Jade's and Esmeralda's eyes on her, which was unexpected as she had always faded into the background of her family. It was mainly due to her behavior and choices. She disliked when all the attention was focused in her direction. Preferring to be overlooked was peaceful. There was less contention when she kept out of everyone's business.

Their attention only snagged Pearl's curiosity, and she too often began to gaze over at her youngest sister. Ruby suddenly wished she hadn't pushed everyone away. It would be nice to have a shoulder to lean on, but how could she explain visions of dead women? She would be locked up for merely suggesting it.

"I don't know where Peter gets off," Jet bellowed, and their father flashed an impatient look at the boy. "To think that he believes his family to be more prevalent than ours. Well, he has another thing coming!"

"The Cavendishs have a certain patronizing manner I can't stand," William murmured in agreement.

Jet laughed in response, and Pearl threw a haughty look at the pair.

"Their downfall will be soon enough," William grunted. "Along with the Kensingtons."

Jet's smile fell ever so slightly. The resentment he held for his father was palpable.

Only Augustus found this statement hilarious and laughed loudly. Jet glared, and Pearl quickly placed her hand atop his as he said, "I'm happy to find someone who believes the Kensingtons to be as much of a hindrance to society as I do! Their loyalty is feeble and treacherous. Abraham stole my father's cattle and sued our estate when the animals were found on our property! Our own animals!" Augustus shrugged off Pearl's hand and ignored her pleas to be quiet. "The audacity is insulting!"

This piqued William's interest, and he gave Augustus his undivided attention. "How much did he sue your father for?"

"Please," Jet interrupted. "This isn't talk for women to hear."

"I don't believe I asked you," William snarled.

Ruby could tell Jet wanted to retaliate, but his jaw snapped shut, and he glared at his father. Williams' brutal stare begged Jet to challenge him. It seemed as if some things would never change. Jet would always be the little boy who would never make his father proud.

Jet's eyes flicked to her insolently. "You look awful," he hissed, disgusted, while Helena Wimple and Anne Dombrowski stood behind him. The left side of Ruby's cheek lifted of its own accord—if he only knew.

"You should be in bed."

"I'm not tired," she stated lazily.

Every head turned to her in surprise. She had never spoken out of turn.

William snorted in amusement and took another spoonful of his soup. He immediately began to cough, whether by inhaling the liquid or merely having another fit, and quickly dropped his spoon to raise his handkerchief to his mouth. Katerina watched with an unregulated amount of enthusiasm, and Jade's fist clenched. The hatred written on her face didn't go unnoticed. Both Augustus and Marian were gaping at her.

The candles flickered, and Jet said, "Jade," which sounded more like a warning than anything else. She blinked and released her fist, her dark gaze met him, and he shook his head once. Both Esmeralda's and Pearl's focus flashed between the pair with suspicion. Jade had complex reservations regarding orders, so why was she suddenly being compliant with Jet, of all people?

William was still coughing despite the strange behavior of his children. He glanced down at his handkerchief when the hacking subsided, and for the first time, he was visibly shaken. "I'm not feeling well. You'll have to excuse me."

He left the room in silence, and Katerina shared a look with her siblings. Ruby didn't like the gesture. It made her nervous, so she grabbed onto her wine glass to calm her nerves.

"Time is wasting, Ruby!" Anne wailed. "How many more women have to die until something is done?"

She dropped her glass of wine across the table and barely acknowledged the mess as she stared at Anne with disbelief. Marna hurried to clean as Katerina wailed over her ruined white linen tablecloth. Augustus sighed loudly at the interruption, and Pearl watched on with a blank stare. Only Jet and Esmeralda glanced over their shoulders as Jade followed Ruby's gaze to the space she was gaping at with fright, which was empty to all of them.

"Good grief Ruby!" Katerina yelled. "You clumsy girl! Do you have any idea how much this linen costs?"

"Why would a stain bother you when the money came from my father's pocket?" Jade snapped. "It's why you married him, correct?"

"Ha!" Anne bellowed.

"I like this one!" Helena murmured in agreement.

Stillness settled over the table, and for the first time in ages, Jet turned back with a smile saved entirely for Jade and said, "I actually agree with you."

More silence followed. Even Marna slowed her wiping motions.

"How dare the both of you!" Katerina said harshly and glanced at her brother for help.

"I won't tolerate your jealousy and hatred directed toward Katerina!" He growled. "She is your mother. She deserves some respect!"

"Shut up!" Jet barked. "You're treading on thin ice, Atwood. Your intrusion into my family is fleeting, and by that, I am referring to all three of you!"

Marian and Katerina turned to one another in panic as Augustus turned to Pearl in disbelief. Her eyes slid to him briefly before glancing back at Jet; a small smile tugged at her lips.

"What is going on?" Esmeralda demanded of her siblings. "All of you are acting... unusual."

"There is much to discuss," Jet answered vaguely and wiped his mouth. "I believe we need to have a nice little family chat," he paused to glare at the Atwoods. "Alone."

"You can't get rid of me," Katerina wailed at him. "I am carrying your little brother!"

"Watch me," he threatened and threw his napkin down on the table before stomping from the room; Marian followed him quietly. The stillness filled again, and the Atwoods were the ones left with unease this time.

Katerina began to weep loudly and made a dramatic exit. They could hear her move through the manor until she slammed a door from above.

"Highborn's sure are a fussy bunch," Helena stated, and Ruby chuckled, ensuing absurd stares from her siblings.

It was easy to see the bad omens associated with death, which had plagued Ruby for the entirety of her life. Only this time, death was refusing to let go. Helena and Anne wanted something from her that was connected to blood, which seemed to be the sole purpose of these crimes. The posing of the victims had to be for another effect, a scare tactic perhaps, and it was working. The city was outraged over the chaotic crimes unfolding.

"I think it's time for us to leave," Augustus snarled, and Pearl rolled her eyes.

"Yes, why don't we?" she said with a hint of ridicule, causing Augustus to glare. She gave them each a half-hearted hug and grabbed Jade's shoulders before she could flee. "Won't you try and act like a blushing bride? No man wants a sullen wife!"

Jade gazed at her flatly as she followed Augustus out.

"She is such a brat," Jade commented, and Ruby grimaced. She didn't like picking sides when her sisters fought, but she had to admit she was with Jade on this one.

Esmeralda gave her a perturbed stare. "She's trying to make it right between you."

Jade snorted. "She could start with an apology!"

"She did what she thought was best at the time."

Jade scoffed. "She knew what Papa would do, yet she still ran to him!"

"How would she know what he would do?" Esmeralda said with a fold of her arms. It was almost a challenge, daring her to say it aloud.

Jade bit back a retort and glanced at Ruby before leaving the room petulantly.

"What are we ever going to do with her?" Esmeralda asked and placed her arms around Ruby's frame.

"I don't know," Ruby whispered and tried to pull away, but she seemed to want to hold on for a little longer.

When Esmeralda finally pulled back, she touched Ruby's cheeks and said, "I love you, spot."

Ruby chuckled at the childhood nickname and watched as she left for the comfort of her cab.

"This is touching and all, but there is still a murderer on the loose!" Helena screeched.

Ruby glared at her before stomping up the stairs, the dead women gossiping at her back. She didn't acknowledge them, and when she reached her room, she slammed the door in their faces.

XXIII
Jackson

"She was last seen with Edward Wright," Elijah rambled. He was holding onto a shot with his left hand, and every time he was about to take it, another thought occurred, and he lowered the glass. "They aren't even pretending to lay low! They are flaunting it in our fucking faces!"

Jackson sat silently next to him, sipping on whiskey and flicking coins into an empty can. Jade was in his mind again and he couldn't pretend she ever left. He knew he should be more concerned with Elijah's words, but he wasn't.

"I know Teddy was involved," Elijah hissed. "Those two are joined at the hip!"

Jackson eyed him.

"I can feel it," Elijah pointed the glass at him before finally downing the whiskey. "She was last seen with them, and now she's dead? This has Teddy written all over it, the mongrel!"

Jackson rubbed his eyes. Elijah never shut up.

"I'm going to take him down," Elijah continued as he poured himself another shot. "Even if it means that I go down with him, I will get rid of the bastard!"

Elijah spoke of nothing but Teddy Kensington for God knows how long. He was so focused on revenge that he couldn't think properly when it came to anything else, and nearly followed Teddy down the path of the criminal world. Jackson often wondered if he was bitter because of it.

And even though he was a fantastic writer, his addictions were stronger. If it weren't for Owen, he would have been lost entirely.

Elijah managed to keep the demons at bay by repeatedly losing himself to booze and women, which Jackson used to partake in with him. That was until he fell for Isabella, and when she shattered his heart after pretending to love him, he began an emotionally detached affair with Katerina. Still, he couldn't give her what she wanted, which all seemed rather inapt now. Jade was the only woman worth anything. If he could take it all back to have her at his side, he would. But it was useless to waste time on what-ifs; it merely amplified the issue. She was something he could never have.

"Do you feel any kind of pity for these women who were slain?" Jackson asked abruptly. He was tired of overthinking.

Elijah threw him a cautious look. "Of course I do. I'm not a monster."

Jackson scratched at his chin. "But Teddy and Edward were accounted for the night of both murders. Who else could it possibly be?"

Elijah eyed him warily. "Jet?"

Jackson shook his head. "If he were a murderer, I would guess his victim type would be men, not prostitutes."

"Unless he hates women."

"It doesn't seem likely. Being a shrewd individual doesn't necessarily make one a killer. He is a product of the way his father raised him, which, I might add, is not his fault. I believe if he were allowed to live without judgment and out from under his father's heel, he would be a far different man."

"Then it's got to be Teddy. He's relatively smart for an idiot."

Jackson's face twisted in ridicule. "Your hatred is clouding your judgment. He is too much of a blundering fool, and the killer is far too calculated for his wits."

"But he's been known to sell organs," Elijah argued. "Doesn't that make him a perfect fit?"

Jackson rolled his eyes. "We don't know if Teddy actually sold any organs, and besides, I think the murderer is just a madman with a hunger he cannot control."

Elijah gawked at him.

"Don't give me that look," Jackson said. "I've dealt with far more insane individuals, and most of them walk around in plain sight. You, for example."

"Fuck off," Elijah muttered and took another shot.

"Are you going to drink that entire bottle?" Jackson snapped when Elijah gave up the glass and raised the flagon to his lips.

After chugging a good amount of whiskey and lowering his hand, he wiped his mouth and barked, "Are you going to take Jade Calvert as your lover?"

Jackson glanced at him with a high amount of perplexity. What did he know of it?

"James mentioned how you made some pretty bold statements to her." The bitterness in his voice was pronounced.

Jackson glanced down at the table and picked at it, his voice low, "She deserves a better life than to be manipulated by men."

Elijah's scowled.

"What is it?" He grumbled when the silence filled the space between them, and he could no longer bear the scrutiny.

"Since when have you ever manipulated a woman?"

"I haven't."

"Then what are you blathering about?" Elijah snapped and took another drink.

He thought of the conversation with Gainsley, understanding exactly how he felt. There was no indication of reciprocation on her end. She would never choose a life with him.

"Teddy will kill you when he finds out, and then I'll have to kill him," Elijah muttered irritably. "And then Owen will lose us both, and that will kill him!"

"Not if I leave the girl alone, and I can promise you that I will. I haven't finished my work, which is still my main priority. There is still a great deal to uncover."

"You can't beat death, Jack," Elijah snapped, and Jackson placed his face in his hands. "It won't bring them back."

"I have to try," Jackson growled bitterly.

"It's a wasted effort. You need to let it go!"

Jackson threw him a withering glare. "Don't try and tell me what to do! You have done nothing but piss and moan about Teddy for God knows how long! You've plotted and schemed against his family, which will cost us everything because *you* can't let it go!"

Elijah pointed a finger at him. "You, Owen, Avis, and James are the only meaning to my life. I would never risk that!"

"You already have!" Jackson bellowed. "We are being followed because of you!"

"Fuck you, Jackson!" Elijah yelled.

Jackson rolled his eyes and stood. "This is useless. You're completely drunk."

"And you are fucking mad! Get back here and face me!"

"You are insufferable, Elijah. Go to bed," Jackson murmured and walked from the room.

"You know what you've caused this family?" Elijah yelled at his back as he stumbled after. "What everyone thinks of you?"

Jackson rounded on him. "I'm well aware of what is said about me, and frankly, I don't give a damn! But don't act so pious, Elijah. You've done enough on your own to spread gossip!"

Elijah threw a fist at his chin, and Jackson stumbled backward, mainly because he was unprepared for the sudden attack. The act was a thinly threaded line to break all rationality and Jackson knew he should walk away, especially knowing that booze-fueled Elijah's rage. But even so, Jackson had enough alcohol coursing through his blood to fuse a short temper. He lacked the self-control to hold back. His vision burned red, and he barreled into Elijah without rational thought; they flew into the dining table, damaging it beyond repair. Nothing stopped Jackson from raising his fist and smashing it into Elijah's chin and nose over and over. He was barely aware of the screams at his back, someone tugged forcefully at his collar, but it wasn't enough to break his hold on Elijah. He ignored the pull and beat his brother, who quickly stopped fighting back.

It came fast thereafter; he was ripped away from Elijah and thrown onto the floor. He tried to stand but was kicked by Owen's boot.

He glared up at him and snarled, "Stay out of it!"

"You're going to kill him!" Owen bellowed. "Have you no sense?"

Jackson ignored him and tried to stand. Owen grabbed him by the collar, ripping him from the floor and onto his feet. Jackson's adrenaline was pumping through his veins so erratically that he began to shove Owen, throwing his fists to break free. He connected with Owen's cheek twice before the other slammed him against the wall. Jackson's head bounced off the brick, forcing him to pause.

"STOP IT!" Owen screamed as he shoved his elbow into Jackson's throat, applying enough pressure to cause him to gasp for air. "WHAT DO YOU THINK YOU ARE DOING?"

"Elijah started it!" Jackson rasped and pushed back, throwing another fist.

"He always starts it!" Owen hissed as he slammed into Jackson even harder. "That doesn't mean you beat him senseless!"

"He hit me!" Jackson roared and shoved him back once again.

"Then walk away!" Owen yelled, ducking when he jabbed.

Owen swung his fists when his words weren't getting through. Jackson teetered into the wall when Owen socked him in the eye, only hesitating when Avis forced her way between them, shouting at him and smacking him in the face. She knew how much he hated when she got in between men as they fought; it was precisely why she did it. To force him to stop because she knew he would never forgive himself if he hurt her. Therefore, he immediately lowered his fists.

Owen pulled her away, but she only tried to lunge at his throat once more. "How dare you hit Elijah!" She screamed.

"I'm always in the wrong, am I?" Jackson shouted back at her and deflected her hands. "Elijah would never dare do anything to provoke me?"

Owen pulled her back. "Avis, stop it!"

He may have stopped her from exerting physical force, but she wasn't done screaming, "Elijah provokes everyone! You need to learn how to walk away!"

"I can't!"

"You're going to learn now," Owen snarled as he let go of Avis and pulled Jackson from the wall, dragging him toward the back door.

"Don't return until you've managed to control your anger!" Avis wailed.

James was on the floor next to Elijah, begging him to open his eyes, but he wasn't moving. Jackson felt a sharp stab of guilt; he may have gravely hurt his brother. It washed over his senses, and all his rage was forgotten. Owen shoved Jackson through the door and onto the yard before he could apologize. "She's right! This is ridiculous, Jackson. You are not a kid anymore!"

He slammed the door, leaving Jackson alone in the ghastly night.

Bel Deaux was unnaturally silent, almost as if it had perished within the vast darkness. The sun had yet to break through the horizon as Jackson leaned against the brick wall next to the door he was tossed from. The back of his head ached, and his lip stung from where Elijah and Owen had hit him. He could feel the wariness pulling at his eyelids, yet he felt wide awake. It had been quite some time since he had lost control and had never once used brutality against Elijah. He closed his eyes at the guilt consuming him. Owen was right. He should have just walked away. The shift from normalcy to feral savagery was relatively thin and quite inexcusable.

Fighting used to be an outlet to release the madness within. When nothing but rage controlled his every waking thought, it impacted every relationship he had, and none for the good; it was a tiring emotion and left a heavy burden on his soul. That's when he decided to turn his life around and go to school.

It was strange to not only unleash his aggression because of the release but also to feel the culpability of his actions.

When the door opened and Owen walked out onto the steps, Jackson didn't look up. He shut the door behind him and sat down, placing his arms on his legs as he stared straight ahead.

It was awkwardly silent before Owen said, "His nose isn't broken, but he's missing a molar."

Jackson released an uneasy breath. Perhaps Elijah wouldn't forgive him after all. His face was his most prized possession.

"He'll live," Owen said as if he heard Jackson's thoughts. "It'll give him a harrowing story to tell. Women will love it."

Jackson grimaced. He was feeling incredibly ashamed of himself.

"I'm afraid it will take some convincing for Avis, of course. She is angry with you," he hedged, and when Jackson didn't comment, he continued, "What in the bloody hell happened?"

He leaned back and rubbed his eyes. "Does it matter?"

"No, I suppose it doesn't," Owen murmured. He always said that fighting wasn't an excuse, and he continually ridiculed Jackson for it. But after a pause, his tone was much lighter, "Do you remember when we fought on mum's birthday, and I shoved you through the front window?" A smile formed on Jackson's lips. It was how he attained the scar on his brow. "Pops didn't let us back in the house for weeks!"

"How could I forget?" Jackson grinned widely as he finally looked over at Owen. "I lost my virginity to Chloe Babin that night."

Owen laughed heavily at this and said, "Spending our time in brothels thereafter didn't do us a bit of good, did it?"

Jackson shook his head with a chuckle. "No!"

Silence settled over them once again. Pikitis, a stout man who never turned down a drink nor the chance to tell wild tales of his youth, strolled through the drive while whistling. He waved to them as he passed and continued on his way. Owen allowed him to live in the small hut on the other side of the vineyard rather than out on the streets. Elijah would often walk down the hill to have a drink and a conversation so that he wasn't so lonely with no one to talk to. It was one of Elijah's better traits. He even got Jackson to join at times.

"I'm sorry I threw you out," Owen said.

Jackson's brows raised in astonishment as he glanced back at him.

Owen met his gaze. "I mainly did it because you needed to calm down, but I was also very angry with you. I was afraid I wouldn't be able to hold back, and who knows what would have happened then. James and Avis wouldn't have been able to break it up."

Jackson looked back to Pikitis without a response. He never dreamed that Owen would be this serene about the matter, especially when it came to Elijah.

"I'm sorry I hit you," Jackson said.

Owen touched his cheek with a wry grin. "I need you to promise me that you'll never raise a fist to Elijah again, even if he provokes you." The clarification of his words was deafening and final. "We only have each other."

"I know, and I won't."

Owen nodded toward the door. "Come on, I'll make some breakfast, and I'm sure you want a word with Elijah."

Jackson sighed anxiously. How was he ever to explain his actions? Owen held out a hand, and Jackson took it. They were about to step inside when someone yelled, "Hadley!"

They turned to see Ryan Culpeper (a mutton shunter who worked for Merfan), jogging towards them. Jackson and Owen exchanged a worrisome look. There couldn't be another murder.

Ryan was panting and grabbing the stitch in his side with his approach. "Another woman has been found."

Owen gazed at him grimly.

"A body was discovered some hours ago near the Kinnedale Harbor. Merfan told me to fetch both of you. He wants your expertise on the matter."

"Really," Jackson drawled. "Do you mean to tell me that the snaggletooth from Berrone wasn't very competent?"

The boy's mouth parted.

Owen threw him a sharp look and muttered, "we'll be down shortly."

The boy nodded and turned on his way.

"I need to change," Jackson said as he strode through the kitchen and bounded up the stairs two at a time. He could feel Owen at his heels before disappearing into his room.

Jackson swiftly pulled the shirt from his head, unbuttoned his pants, kicked them off, and replaced them with a fresh set. He glanced at himself in the mirror. There was a bruise on his chin and a crack in his lip. Eli and Owen hit him harder than he'd initially thought. He grinned as he ran a comb through his hair. Bruises left from fighting made him feel oddly at ease. He then walked from his room and into Elijah's, buttoning his shirt as he entered.

Elijah's eyes were closed, but he turned his head at the sound of Jackson's approach and mumbled unintelligibly. He had black eyes and swollen lips.

Jackson walked around the bed and sat at his side. "I am sorry, Eli."

"As am I," Elijah murmured groggily.

"Can you forgive me?"

Elijah winced as he tried to shift. "What's there to forgive?"

"When you see your face," Jackson answered gruffly. "You'll reconsider that statement."

"It'll heal," Elijah muttered and then turned his face toward him with a grin. "You've broken your nose twice and still manage to look decent. I predict I'll be fine because I'm far better looking than you."

Jackson laughed. "Owen said you've lost a tooth. You're lucky it wasn't any in the front."

Elijah's smile faded. "I am sorry, Jack. I didn't mean to question your motives nor your desire to find answers."

Jackson shrugged. "I am at fault."

Elijah smiled. "Perhaps a little."

"Another woman's been found. Owen and I are going to inspect the scene."

"I wish I could go with you," Elijah grunted.

Jackson gave him an apologetic smile as he stood and said, "Didn't I tell you that you needed rest? Well, here's your chance."

"Cheeky," Elijah muttered.

Jackson laughed in response as he left the room.

He ran into Avis in the hallway. She pointed a finger at him and shrieked, "You stay away from me!"

"I'm sorry!"

"I don't care if you are!" she growled. "I've had enough of your insolence. I wanted you out, but Owen wouldn't hear it! Just stay away from me, Jackson. I've nothing to say to you anymore!"

She shoved passed him, and he let her go. He would have to make it up to her later.

The ride was quick and when they arrived, Merfan stood with his back toward them as they approached. Georges had his hands resting on his hips, his face twisted as he stared at the deceased. When his head raised, his lip curled at them.

Merfan turned, his face bleak. "It's happened again. I suppose you were right before."

Jackson ignored them and crouched down to get a closer look. The woman's throat had been slashed, and there were x's cut across both of her eyes. There was blood everywhere and a gaping hole in her chest. He didn't need to perform an autopsy to see that her heart was missing. She was killed in this spot and holding black flowers, but they weren't Landini lilies. They were Black Dahlia's.

Jackson made a face as he stood and glanced at Owen. This wasn't the same killer. It was a copycat because of what had been released in the paper.

"What is her name?" Jackson asked.

"Mary-Anne Stafford."

"Another one of Miss Louise's dolls?"

"Yes, and he's getting more gruesome as we speak," Merfan said and rubbed his temples. He didn't seem to notice the distinction. "And I was just about to get an award from the Queen for capturing the Dollhouse Slayer!"

Jackson glanced sharply at Merfan as Owen repeated, "The Dollhouse Slayer?"

Merfan eyed him. "He gave himself the name, might as well call him what he wants."

"I thought you said Elijah made up the letter?" Owen argued, and Merfan sneered in return. He sighed as he explained, "giving murderers an identity takes away from the victims and limits your focus."

Merfan puffed out his chest. "It was from the murderer, and you know it! Gods," he spat and looked them up and down. "How I haven't missed the lot of you!" He then looked around. "Where's that abrasive half-wit of a brother of yours?"

"He's indisposed at the moment," Owen answered.

Merfan snorted. "Sleeping it off, eh?"

"Something like that," Owen muttered.

"And you!" He snarled at Jackson. "Looks like you've been fighting again!"

He shrugged, and Owen started commenting on the woman, distracting Merfan. Jackson placed his hands in his pockets as he looked around the harbor. It was effortless for one to go missing without detection in Trinity Row. The back alleys were like a maze, endless and completely unstructured. The culprit had to be well informed on both the city and what was said in the paper. The knowledge would have to be extremely precise and very thorough.

"This means you're going to release Gainsley, right?" Jackson asked Merfan.

The constable appeared as if that was the last thing he wanted to do. "Feilding will have to make the official order."

"Get on it then," Jackson snarled when Feilding's cab rolled up.

Merfan spat tobacco at his feet and strode toward the captain.

"What a nightmare," Owen said quietly.

Jackson continued to watch Merfan as he talked to Captain Feilding and Cillian. "It seems like this is a game, and another player has entered the ring."

Owen frowned at him. "I cannot believe Merfan missed something so obvious."

"Let him think it, so Gainsley will be released," Jackson answered swiftly. "Each killer seems to enjoy the thrill of posing women in populated areas, but this one only wants the attention of one man. We're being presented with a different murderer entirely, and he's left a message for the other."

"And what message would that be?"

Jackson glanced at him. "Checkmate."

XXIV
Jade

When she woke up that morning, something was wrong. Rather, something was going to happen. It disturbed her stomach, traveled into her chest, and sat there, leaving her atrabilious and mute. She didn't offer a word to Ruby as they rode to Reignmar Abbey, and for once, she felt appreciative of a sister who preferred isolation. They were sent to the church for confession, but of all the things she was supposed to confess, she didn't feel sorry for. She was a habitual sinner, yet the God's stepped in on her behalf time and again. Perhaps they weren't what everyone said they were; maybe they were more.

Reignmar Abbey was made of iron and white sandstone with a Tri-Portal facade on the structure's north, east, and west. The north portal was for the father, decorated with the tree of knowledge. The east portal was for the mother, decorated with the tree of life. The west was for the archangels, decorated with statues depicting the seven messengers of God.

Jade glanced up at the rose windows as she followed Ruby up the steps of the Abbey to the central entrance, a favorite feature. She gazed at the steps on her left before stepping inside the cathedral. Helena Wimple was found here, a woman who would only be remembered in death.

The marble floors were checkered, and she counted the black and white tiles as she trailed behind Ruby down the pews to the kneeler where they could pray, avoiding eye contact with those in the church. The partitioners began to shuffle at the sight of them. People avoided the Calvert's like an illness, leaving her feeling tainted and unworthy.

Once she knelt, she began to recite with Ruby, "Our Father who art in heaven, hallowed be thy name. Thy kingdom come, thy will be done, on earth as it is in heaven. Give us this day our daily bread, and forgive us our trespasses, as we forgive those who trespass against us, and lead us not to temptation, but deliver us from evil."

They agilely made the sign of the cross, and when she lowered her hand, she hesitated to move. The priest was talking to Dominic Kane; she hadn't noticed him when she first entered the building.

"What is he doing here?" Ruby muttered.

She didn't care to find out and ushered Ruby in the opposite direction.

She lit candles for the father, the mother, and the seven archangels. One for her own mother, each of her siblings, and without another thought, one for Helena Wimple and Anne Dombrowski. Her prayer was simple, may they have found peace in such a vicious death. As her hand drew over the next candle, she lowered the spill over the wick and lit one for Jackson Hadley too.

"Well, look who it is," Dominic said from over her shoulder, and she froze. "It's good to see you at confession. Best be relieved of any sins before you marry Theodore Kensington."

She closed her eyes and breathed out of her nose slowly to calm the apprehension on his behalf.

"Hello, Ruby," he said.

She glanced at him sharply. Static burned angrily in her palms; he had no business speaking to her sister. "What do you want?"

He chuckled. His features were much sharper than Jackson's or even Elijah's, but that wasn't to say he was unfortunate looking. His blue eyes were devious, wild, and hiding secrets of her carnal sin. "You've been avoiding me."

"I avoid everyone."

He laughed. "That's one way to deflect any responsibility."

"I was beaten within an inch of my life for being with you, in case it slipped your memory!"

He didn't say a word as he stared at her. This used to make her heart pound whenever he gave her his undivided attention, but now she didn't feel a thing. She finally understood how he didn't deserve any of her time, words, or affections. "Leave us be!"

His brows shot to his hairline as he said, "You're angry with me?"

She glanced at Ruby, who was lighting candles, acting as if she weren't listening, but by the pale of her skin and the distress on her face, she was frightened.

He pulled her chin toward him. "How can I fix whatever I have done to upset you?"

She stepped away from his grasp. "I want you to leave me alone!"

His face crumbled, appearing saddened by this statement, but it was a false gesture. He was an excellent actor, as well as a cheat and a liar. Not anyone worth wasting time on.

"Who is ya friend?" the silky voice of a redhead said as she sauntered up beside him, snaking her arm through his. She looked to be older than him by about ten years or so.

"Melody!" Dominic happily exclaimed, and Jade sighed in exasperation. It was always the same with him. There was always another woman who captured all his attention. Call her bitter, but she wasn't one for being second fiddle.

"What did you think of the statues of the seven?" he asked her.

"Beautiful as yew said," she answered, but the woman's eyes never left Jade's face. She had a cockney accent and missing teeth. Jade's interest peaked as she glanced further at her attire that was patched, ripped at the seams, with mud caked on the bottom hem. "Are yew going to introduce us?"

"Melody, this is Jade Calvert," his voice cut through her scrutiny. "She is very dear to my heart."

Jade was so absorbed by the woman who more than likely lived in Trinity Row that she didn't snap at him for addressing her as if they were close confidants.

"And this beautiful young woman is Ruby."

That caught her attention, and her eyes narrowed at him. He wasn't going to prey on her sister.

"Calvert as in William Calvert?" the woman practically wailed. Her demeanor had changed from critical to fearful.

"But of course," he answered.

The woman snapped her mouth shut with a step back.

Jade hated this reaction from people. She hadn't done a thing to warrant fear, for she was nothing like her father nor her brother.

She glared at him for making such a fuss.

His stare turned incredulous. "What have I done to elicit such hostile behavior from you?"

"Do you confess your sins?" Jade drawled.

"Excuse me?"

"I asked if you confess your sins."

His eyebrows drew in harshly. "Of course I do."

"Are you sure about that?"

He evened her stare, but she wasn't afraid of him. "I said so, didn't I?"

She knew it was wrong to bait him, but she couldn't allow his bullying. It was the very reason the city had turned for the worse. She focused on the candles and said, "How can I take your word for anything when those rumors about the snuff films are true?"

Ruby's hand slipped, and she dropped the candle she was holding. She scooped it up quickly before her dress caught fire.

"I don't know what you're talking about," he said smoothly though the woman at his side didn't appear convinced of his lie.

"Are you ready for confession, Miss Calvert?" the minister asked from the pew.

She set her candle in a holder and narrowed her gaze. "Ignorance doesn't suit you, Mr. Kane. I believe you know exactly what I'm talking about."

"You can't prove a thing," he said without concern.

She paused. "Haven't you ever heard that things done in the dark will come to light?"

His mouth curved wickedly. "I have, but perhaps you should examine your own misdeeds before judging another. You have the whole city looking down upon you. It must be lonely."

"Because of you," she whispered.

He grinned that nasty grin she hated. "I didn't force you to do anything. You wanted it."

Her stomach turned, leaving her feeling dirty and infected. "How are you and Jackson related?" Her question was meant for herself, but his smile thinned, and his nostrils flared.

"Are you okay?" the minister asked when he noted the discomfort between them.

"We're ready," Jade answered as she grabbed Ruby's hand, and the pair walked quickly from Dominic.

They nearly made it to the confession booths when he yelled, "I'll be seeing you real soon."

Ruby hesitated, but Jade pushed her on and said, "He is just trying to frighten you."

Even though she said it to pacify Ruby, she didn't really believe it. She wasn't sure what Dominic would do or what he was even capable of. The only way for her to protect herself and those she loved was to learn how to tap into the magic in her veins.

She was sitting in the middle of her room with three candlesticks laid out in front of her. The same static she felt whenever Jackson had grabbed her hand bubbled to the surface as her mood changed. She had never thought much of it before, but these strange occurrences had only amplified as of late, and she feared what it meant.

Her mother performed mystifying acts as a child when she thought no one was watching. Her affinity for all things peculiar earned unwanted attention no matter how much she tried to hide it. The way she could manipulate lightning in the sky or summon rain out of thin air was terrifying. It was a secret kept between them, and her father wasn't to know about it. Pearl explained it off as a dream, but it wasn't a dream Jade remembered. It was magic.

She turned her hands over and stared at them; they were glowing vibrantly. It startled her just as quickly, and the light disappeared. She stared in complete shock for several minutes, her heart thundering in her chest.

Once the shock subsided, she focused on the candlesticks. It didn't take much for them to move. A simple thought and they slowly rose an inch off the rug. She gasped, and they fell to the ground, covering her mouth in shock.

The fear quickly subsided, and excitement took over. She tried again and again until the candles floated above the rug for more than a passing second. It left her exhausted and drained every ounce of her energy, and she nearly passed out. She would have to develop this ability like anything else.

A flash of memories surfaced as she climbed into bed. Her mother once tried to teach her how to harness her abilities years ago when she was a small child. She'd forgotten, and it was no wonder with the weight of grief over her mother's death and years of abuse at her father's hand. Magic came from the heart, and he tried to beat it out of her because he knew.

She gulped.

All the painful childhood experiences were because of this ability she was born with; she was damned with no hope of being saved. This only made her feel worse, and she imagined the look of disgust on Jackson's face when he found out.

The magic flowing in her veins was illicit and tainted her soul. She couldn't inflict his. Even if he accepted her, and she couldn't imagine he would, he deserved better.

XXV
Owen

He was leaning against the Ironmoore republic building and watching Dominic Kane stroll through the market court with Elizabeth DeWitt. He had been tailing a butcher named Arthur Tulley with Cillian after reports of him loitering around the harbor wearing a bloody apron near where Mary-Anne Stafford was found.

Cillian wasn't paying attention. He ate an apple while watching Arthur Tulley discuss a slab of meat with a customer. "I mean, he is a butcher. It's not that odd to see him covered in blood… He's covered in blood now."

Owen ignored him, watching Dominic whisper something in Elizabeth's ear only to have her slap his arm in return.

"Hell, half the people in Trinity Row are covered in blood," Cillian continued as he chewed. "If they aren't working in the factories, they are getting into drunken bar fights."

Dominic brazenly kissed Elizabeth on the cheek, and she grinned, looking smitten with him.

"But I guess you could argue the point because he took her heart. A butcher would know where to find it."

Owen frowned when Dominic picked out a white lily from a vendor and handed it to Elizabeth. She blushed and took it coyly.

Cillian lowered his apple with Owen's lack of enthusiasm. "Why aren't you as interested in Arthur as you should be?"

"Dominic Kane just gave Elizabeth DeWitt a white lily."

Cillian followed his gaze. "And?"

"You don't find that suspicious?"

"The killer left black Landini lilies in the victim's hand. Dominic bought his escort a lily because it is what the vendor is selling. A mere coincidence. He's a little indecorous, but he's harmless."

"I'm not so sure about that," Owen murmured.

Cillian gazed back at the butcher. "Women love Dominic. Why would he kill them?"

"You, of all people, should know that murderers aren't only committed by the unfortunate looking. Charismatic men are known to kill just as anyone else, if not more."

"He doesn't seem the type."

Owen glanced back at his cousin. "Neither does Arthur Tulley."

Cillian lowered his apple with a frown. "Now you're just being argumentative."

"Were you or were you not just stating that his profession leaves him covered in blood?"

"We have to explore all options."

Owen pressed his lips together as he gazed back at Arthur. The man appeared cheerful as he spoke to patrons passing, but that didn't mean a thing. The suspects were slim when they could not interrogate the Elite, nor anyone associated with them.

A cackle rang throughout the street. Mahala was pushing her cart of trinkets around, though she didn't seem to care much about what she sold. She was more interested in conversing with those on the street. If you wanted information, you went to her.

"She's right on time," Cillian muttered and strolled toward Mahala.

"Hiya baby!" she wailed and pulled them each in a hug. "How we doin'?" She glanced up at Owen with a rather cheeky smile. "How is you know who?"

A smile cracked on Owen's lips, even when Cillian gazed at him curiously. "Well, thank you."

"I knew it!" she beamed.

"Have you heard anything about the murders?" Cillian asked abruptly.

The smile on her face fell, and she glanced over her shoulder, pulling them in closer. "The man seen speaking to the women shortly before they disappeared wore a gas mask and a top hat. Pretty conspicuous if you ask me."

Owen glanced acutely at Dominic. His cousin had breathing problems as a child and wore a gas mask for long periods of time. The only person he knew that had worn one, and it suddenly fit. He was so focused on William, and Elijah had been so focused on Teddy, that neither had entertained the thought of a third contender. Dominic wore a gas mask, had an affinity for flowers, and went to medical school with Jackson. His stomach suddenly twisted in dismay.

"Have you seen this man walking around?" Cillian asked.

"I haven't personally, but the others have."

Owen gazed back at her. "I want to know when he's on the streets."

"I'll tell Kashi to keep a lookout," she promised.

"Will you ask the boys to help us?" Owen asked. "We need as many men patrolling the streets as we can get."

"I'll be right on it," she promised and gave him a swift kiss. He watched her walk away as Cillian stared.

"What have you figured out? You have that look in your eye, the one you get when all the pieces suddenly fit."

Owen held his tongue. He wanted to believe in Cillian, but he also didn't want to give away a lead when Merfan would thwart his efforts. He wasn't sure if he could trust Cillian anymore, and if he said his suspicions aloud, he may be told to leave his cousin alone as he had with the Elite.

"Just being cautious," he answered evasively. "Should we have a conversation with Arthur?"

Cillian's face twisted in disappointment, but he nodded his head.

Owen followed reluctantly, giving Dominic one last look. His stomach dropped when he found his cousin staring directly at him. The smile set on his narrow mouth was unsettling. He refused to return the dramatic wave Dominic gave him and focused on the butcher.

"Hello, Arthur," Cillian said with their approach. "Do you have a minute?"

The broad-shouldered man glowered at them while wiping his hands on his apron.

"'Spose."

Cillian began his line of questions, "How long have you been working as a butcher?"

Arthur glanced at Owen before answering, "Fifteen years."

"Have you always lived in Bel Deaux?"

"Yes, sir."

"Where were you yesterday, Arthur?"

He laughed once without humor. "If this is about the bang tail who was found, I had nothing to do with it!"

"Can anyone confirm that?" Cillian asked.

"Me wife," he said without hesitation. "Look, I was home all night with me family, and then I got up at four to go to work. It has been me schedule for the last fifteen years. You can even ask me, boss. I wear the same apron every day. It is stained from blood. Ain't no getting around it."

"Did you know Mary-Anne Stafford?"

"No, sir."

"You've never met her before?"

The man shook his head vehemently. "I haven't been to a brothel since before I was married."

"And how long is that?"

"Twelve years."

"So, if I ask if you had been spotted in a brothel in the past year, the answer would be, no?"

"Yes, sir."

Cillian glanced at Owen. Arthur didn't seem like he was being deceptive. He looked Cillian straight in the eye and answered every question promptly. And while they would have to confirm his alibi, it didn't seem likely that he knew anything about a murder.

Owen placed his hands in his pockets. "Have you seen anything suspicious?"

"I see a lot of things, sir, but none of them pertain to murder," he turned back to the slab of meat on his table. "Trinity Row is filled with sinners."

"Have you heard anything about these murders?" Owen asked with little hope.

Arthur shook his head. "No one talks to no one. They keep their heads down and work."

"If you heard anything, would you be willing to tell us?" Cillian asked.

"Depends on the question and who it's about."

"Meaning?"

"If you want information about the Elite and their operations, if you will, I don't have an answer. And neither do the people of the east end. They're just trying to survive, sir."

Owen shared a look with Cillian.

"We thank you for your time, Mr. Tulley," Cillian said after a moment. "We'll be in touch."

Arthur Tulley seemed to be only one of their dead ends, but that did not mean they'd give up. They'd have to risk their jobs or even their lives for the truth.

The room had been comfortably silent for some time; the water was starting to turn cold. Esmeralda sat in between his long legs that barely fit into the washbasin. His right foot was propped onto the side of the tub. She dragged her nails up and down the length of his calf while leaning her head onto his shoulder. He ran his fingers through her hair.

"What is it you want?"

He gripped her tighter. "This seems nice."

"I need you to know something before we continue with whatever it is we're doing."

"Taking a bath?"

She leaned forward. The notches of her spine were bulbous as her dark hair webbed across her pale skin. "I know I'm nothing like Clara," she said, and he stilled. "Nor would I pretend to be. My father is also a problem."

"He'll never find out, so there is no need to worry," he murmured and kissed her shoulder.

"Please don't placate me, Owen. I am being serious!"

He shrugged. "So am I."

"I want you to be happy."

"I am happy."

She turned to look over her shoulder; a devious smile decorated her lips. "I know you are, for now at least. But I don't want you ever to feel as if my father stands in your way… I don't want you to look at me with resentment if he tries to destroy your career when he finds out about us."

"I must be terrible at showing my emotions if you don't understand how much you mean to me. I know it's sudden, but it's right," he said, and her face smoothed, lips parting. "Besides, your father will never find out about us, and if he does for some reason, we'll move out of the city. I can find another job in another town."

She scowled. "I have no desire to separate you from your family."

He cupped her face. "You aren't."

"But what if he doesn't allow us to leave the city?"

"It's not a mistake being with you, Esmeralda. I would make it public if you weren't so afraid of the consequences. A life with you is better than a life without you. I wasn't exactly on top of the world when we reconnected. You found me in a graveyard."

Her brow popped. "And are you now?"

"Exceedingly."

He forgot all about the distress over the murders and her father when she pressed her lips against his, slipping her tongue into his mouth and dragging her body against his torso.

Water spilled over the edge of the tub, leaving massive puddles in their wake.

XXVI
Elijah

"Gabrielle wrote to you."

He glanced up from his typewriter to see Avis holding out a letter and looking at him questionably.

"Set it on the bed," he said dismissively and focused back on his work.

"You're wearing your glasses," she commented.

"Don't tell anyone," he muttered and resumed his typing.

"What are you writing to her for?"

Avis didn't get along with Gabrielle for petty reasons, something to do with a dress she specifically copied, a perplexing explanation. He didn't understand women.

"I write to her all the time," he answered without turning from the keyboard. "She is my favorite cousin."

He could feel her intrusive stare, questioning his motives, but he didn't answer to Avis. He was seeking help for Roslyn, and there was a definite chance Gabrielle could help him with that. Yet, it needed to be a secret.

"You should be in bed," she growled. "Jackson will be furious with you."

"Like you care what he thinks."

"Your funeral!" she huffed and stomped from the room.

He scrambled from his chair when she left him alone, wincing in pain. His head was splitting, and the pressure under his eyes was quite uncomfortable. His spectacles didn't help matters.

A grin formed on his lips as he skimmed the letter and quickly dressed. He took a tincture of laudanum for his headache and a pack of cigarettes for his nerves while slipping out of the house, unbeknownst to Avis. He limped toward the train station. He had to get Roslyn out of the city before she fell prey to the Dollhouse Slayer.

As he walked, he thought about Jackson. Perhaps he should have been more upset with him for what transpired, but he wasn't. Plenty of things Elijah had done elicited negative behavior from his family, and he couldn't blame Jackson for how he responded. He wasn't the only one growing tired of his actions.

Elijah didn't know what he wanted in life but drinking until all rational thought was gone and following sordid women home was no longer a strong desire.

After he bought a one-way ticket out of the city, he proceeded to Roslyn's rented room in Trinity Row. He knocked swiftly on the door, watching as she peered through the drapes in the broken window. A balled-up rag was stuffed into the gaping hole with no sense of security.

She seemed startled by his sudden appearance. "What happened?"

He frowned when a smile tugged at her lips as she assessed his eyes, forgetting that he was still wearing glasses. He quickly pulled them off with an exhale and glanced around her messy room. A petite blonde abruptly stood up from the bed. Her tawny eyes were wide and apprehensive, and she wrung her hands together as his gaze swept over her.

"Elijah, this is my friend Ollie Ashford," Roslyn said with a wave of her hand, forcing him to gape at the girl. "Ollie, this is Elijah Hadley."

This was the girl Avis and Jackson were helping.

"Hello," he said quietly.

Blush painted the girl's cheeks, and she averted her gaze.

"What happened to you, Elijah?" Roslyn repeated.

"I got into a fight with Jackson," he answered. "How many people know you are staying here?"

Her eyes doubled. "Have you lost your mind?"

He scratched his head. "Undoubtedly. Listen, you need to leave the city. It isn't safe for you anymore."

"And where am I to go?"

"My cousin Gabrielle is willing to offer you work as a governess."

Her face twisted in derision. "A governess? But I've never taken care of a child in my life!"

"How hard can it be?" He argued and glanced around the room again. "Anything has got to be better than this. You'll have your very own room, two to three meals a day, and all you have to do is watch over the children. You will no longer have to give up your body or be ridiculed by your brother and Teddy. You'll never have to see them again!"

She stared at him.

"You deserve so much better than this, Roslyn."

"Why are you doing this?" she whispered.

"Because you weren't born to be their pawn, no matter what your brother says." he cupped her cheek. "I'm so very sorry I didn't do more. I have been selfish and ignored what mattered, but I refuse to stand by anymore. I am getting you out of this city."

She laughed without humor and pulled his hand from her cheek. "And yet, I'm not enough for you, am I?"

He gazed at Ollie, heavily embarrassed. The girl sank onto the bed, watching their conversation unfold with tension. He didn't like how her eyes peered at him with a mix of hatred and fear. His intention was not to insult Roslyn. He simply didn't have any feelings to give her, though he wished he did. "You don't want me."

"Don't presume to know what I want," she hissed and turned to pick up a bottle of liquor. It may not be what she wanted to hear, but at least he was being honest. "What about my friends? I cannot abandon them."

"You are the only one I mentioned for work, but I can buy them tickets out of Bel Deaux if you want."

"No," Ollie said defiantly. Her steadfast decision transformed her face in captivating ways. The crease in between her eyebrows caused him to smirk. The fire in her soul had not been extinguished as he had initially thought. "There are things I have to do here."

"I didn't want to say it," Roslyn snapped. "But Christopher Ashford is not respectable, even if he is your father. There is nothing he can give-"

"Christopher Ashford is not my real father," she interrupted. "He merely raised me, and not very well, I might add. But he knows who my father is and I need that answer!"

"Be careful," he warned. "Uncovering the past isn't always the best solution."

She threw him a reproachful look.

"I'm sorry," he said while raising his hands in defense. "It's your life." He glanced back at Roslyn. "Please leave the city. My cousin will be good to you."

Roslyn appeared as if she wanted nothing more than to get out of Bel Deaux, away from the clutches of her brother and Teddy Kensington. "But Melody and Elizabeth are still out there!"

He closed the distance between them, pulling the ticket out of his pocket as well as a stack of money. "That should cover it."

"Elijah," she began, and he knew she would refuse. She didn't want to leave her friends behind, not that he could blame her, but he had to try.

"The choice is yours," he said as he turned toward the door. "Just know you can have another life. One that is not full of such pain."

He ducked out of the room before she could refuse, praying that she would make the right decision.

With his nerves getting the best of him, he limped toward the cab that was waiting for him and instructed the driver to take him to the Bel Deaux Gazette. He wasn't ready to face his siblings just yet.

"What the hell happened to you?" Philip asked when he slumped at his desk thirty minutes later.

"Don't try to pick a fight with my brother," he grumbled, rubbing his eyes. "He'll win every time."

"You fought with Jackson?"

Elijah rubbed his eye gingerly. "I was drunk."

"You're always drunk," Philip muttered as he turned back to his typewriter.

"I'm not that predictable," Elijah muttered.

"Sure, you are, and you look like death, and that's saying something. I would suggest you go back to bed."

"I'll sleep when I'm dead."

Philip snorted and threw a stack of papers down on his desk, startling him.

"Damn it, man!" he yelled as he sat up straight and began to read the first paragraph. "What's this?"

"The inquiry on William Calvert you've been relentlessly pestering me for," Philip said. "He's not right. An evil man such as him shouldn't have so much influence."

Elijah glanced up at him. "What makes you say that?"

Philip sighed as he leaned in closer. "There has been more than one account about his affair with Helena, and not only her, several prostitutes throughout the years. Word is that he has impregnated a vast number of them."

"He has bastards throughout the city?"

Philip grimaced with a shake of his head. "He never let it get that far."

Elijah raised his brows. "Meaning?"

"They end up dead long before another detects a pregnancy. It is likely they confide in him and end up losing their lives because of it."

Elijah sat back in his chair and began to chew on his lip.

Philip glanced over his shoulder before he leaned closer and whispered, "I'm starting to suspect that is the reason behind Alexandra's death."

Elijah stopped chewing and gave a hard stare. "You think she uncovered his perversions, and he killed her?"

Philip glanced around again before nodding. "She threatened to expose his secrets and turn their children against him if he didn't sign over his estate to her," Philip chuckled without humor when Elijah's eyes doubled. "It wasn't long after when she was found with a bullet in her head by their daughter Jade!"

Elijah dropped his hand from his mouth. "Owen and Jack swear it wasn't a suicide."

"And now you have the motive."

There it was, motive and William Calvert certainly had enough of it. The double standard was appalling. He fucked his way through the city, and the minute Alexandra did the same, she lost her life over it.

"I don't know," Elijah said. "There has to be more to it than that. It all seems so… impractical."

"My sources are incredibly reliable," Philip countered and stood. "Search the records of every prostitute that was murdered throughout the years and the eerie similarities of their deaths," he knocked once on Elijah's desk and turned.

Elijah pressed his lips together as he watched Philip, wishing he could go back to blissful ignorance. What was he to do with the information about William? Wouldn't uncovering the truth only bring more pain to the Calvert household? The inequity was unsettling enough, and he would have to find a way to stop it before any more women died.

He read over the report as Philip shrugged into his jacket. "I'm going to check out a few leads and grab a stein. Would you like to join?"

"No, thank you," he murmured.

"It might help that black eye of yours," Philip prodded.

Elijah merely shook his head.

"Hadley!"

Elijah looked up to see a messenger holding out a postcard. He glanced at Philip as he grabbed it. The messenger continued delivering mail to the rest of the print shop.

"Is it from him?" Philip asked quietly.

He didn't respond as he glanced down at the card. His first and last names were written across the front in the same ink and handwriting as the first letter. "Looks like."

Philip stood over his shoulder as he flipped it over and read,

Dear Mr. Hadley,

How do you think I fixed the last one? I see you made no mention of her in the paper, and I'm itching to know why. Were you told to keep tight-lipped on the matter, or are you trying to test my patience? Don't worry, I'll give you a double chance to make it up to me.

Sincerely,
The Dollhouse Slayer

His heart was thundering, but it was out of excitement and not fear. This proved Gainsley's innocence. He slapped the desk and walloped, "Well, I'll be damned! Gainsley is about to be a free man!"

"Look after yourself, Hadley!" Philip bellowed as he jumped up from the desk and hobbled toward the stairs. "You're no use to anyone if you're dead!"

It took him all of five minutes to get to the Police station, but he was surprised to find that Owen was not there.

"What happened to you?" Cillian inquired.

"I got in a fight," he answered in frustration. "Where is he?"

"He said he had family matters to attend to," Cillian stated in perplexity. "Who were you fighting with?"

"Jackson," he snapped. "Did he say when he would be back?"

"He didn't," Cillian shrugged. "Why, what do you need to see him about?"

He knew he should have waited, but Gainsley was like a brother and needed help. Elijah reached into his jacket and pulled out the postcard.

Cillian skimmed it, and a fearful look transformed his face. "He is watching you."

"I know that. Will you release Gainsley now?"

Cillian's eyes raised to meet his. "This doesn't bother you?"

"Not particularly, but I didn't come to discuss the postcard. I don't even care what you do with it. I just want Gainsley."

"This will take some coercion on my end, but I think it'd be best if you waited outside. Merfan and Fielding will be more receptive if I'm alone."

"What do you mean it will take some coercion? This proves his innocence!"

"It's your attitude," Cillian muttered. "Merfan would keep him locked up out of spite. Have a little faith and wait outside, please. I will get him for you."

Elijah ignored his rising frustration and staggered outside. He smoked several cigarettes and nearly gave up hope that Cillian had his back when Gainsley stumbled out of the police station, filthy and looking as bad as Elijah.

"Finally!" Elijah muttered and jumped up to hug him.

Gainsley pulled him in tightly. "I thought they were going to torture me until I made a false confession!"

"Thank God you didn't!" Elijah said and prodded him along. "Come on. Let's go home."

Anger settled deeply as they began their journey home. Merfan was lucky he was not feeling himself.

It wasn't until they reached the end of the street, did he look back. The constable and captain of the Police force were watching them.

XXVII
Jet

It was ten at night when the opium shipment came through. Jet overlooked the deposit as Kensington's lackeys unloaded the boat, reeling with frustration; nothing was going right. Dominic Kane was taking his sweet time when it came to Katerina because he refused to give him Ruby. He may know nothing about her, nor had he ever tried, but he was not about to give away his flesh and blood for a snuff film. She, too, had power, though there was something moderately festering about it, and he didn't know what it meant.

And now that Jade knew of her powers, he had to keep an eye on her, but she wasn't making things easy. Then again, neither was Teddy. He had been moody ever since his father shut down their plot to destroy the Hadleys.

It was not long before Teddy showed up. He stood next to him authoritatively with a glare on his face.

"Who was it?" Teddy demanded.

Jet exhaled with indignation and turned to look back at the lackeys.

"Edward and Benjamin wouldn't act so irrationally. They have enough sense not to bait me with such foolery," Teddy continued as he lit the end of a stogie. "That would leave either you or Blake."

"I don't know what you're talking about," Jet grumbled.

"Ah," Teddy said with a chuckle. "So, it was Blake then."

Jet turned his head even further from him, a scowl forming over his features. "Watch yourself, Teddy, or you'll end up with a knife in your throat!"

"Was his wish to expose us all?" Teddy pressed, unbothered by his threat. "Because of his carelessness, the Hadleys are being specifically requested by the Queen to investigate."

"Investigate what?" Jet snarled and stood at full height to face him.

"The dead prostitute!"

Jet gaped at him. "Are you mad? Why would we kill a female prostitute?"

"Jealousy."

"Jealousy of what?" He snapped. "Honestly, why would anyone tie anything back to us? And besides, no one listens to the Hadleys when they talk!"

"That isn't the point, Jet." Teddy sneered. "The point is to keep a low profile and not raise any suspicions!"

Jet rolled his eyes and turned back to the docks. "You've lost your mind."

"You better pray for your friend that no one will."

"He didn't do a thing."

"And as for the Hadley's," Teddy said with a droll grin. "I have something terrible in mind for them."

"That's even more heedless than this!" Jet cried and pointed to the docks. "They are of too much value! How is it that you and your father do not grasp that!"

"It won't happen all at once," Teddy said with a flick of his stogie. "It will go fairly undetected, and it will start with Jackson."

"Jackson?" Jet repeated slowly and stared; he knew. Still, he lied for the sake of his sister. "Of the three, I would say he is the least significant!"

"He has an eye on what's mine and needs a lesson about not messing with another man's bride."

"Jade?" he said smoothly, unsure of why he was covering for them. "What's he done with her?"

"It's only a matter of time," Teddy answered, his dark eyes flickering to him. "Your sister is far too wild and irresponsible to leave well enough alone!"

"I warned you," Jet spat with the point of his finger. "Did I not say that Ruby would be a far better match because she is quiet and obedient? But no, you completely ignored me because you think Jade is prettier! Well, that blew up in your face when she was caught running around with Dominic Kane!"

"She mocked my entire family by running to him," he snarled viciously. "She will rue the day she ever crossed me!"

Madness transformed Teddy's face, and the smile slipped from Jet's mouth. How dare he think Jade belonged to him! "She wasn't yours, and I would tread carefully around Jackson. You've seen him fight!"

Teddy scrutinized him. "With his fists, yes, but I have a gun."

Jet scoffed and gazed back at the lackeys.

"When you see Blake," Teddy finished and turned on his heel. "Tell him I want a word."

Jet watched him walk away from the docs and slip into a cab. When nothing but Teddy's words repeated in his head, a treacherous voice kept pestering for one thing.

To go home.

The manor was dark and tranquil. Jet stalked up the stairs quietly and headed directly for Jade's room. He marched straight for the bed and flipped the covers over to see a clump of pillows displayed in the shape of a body.

"Dammit, Jade!" He hissed and strode for Ruby's room.

He found her in her bed, just like he knew she would be. "Where the bloody hell is Jade?"

"Jet!" Ruby whispered in groggy confusion. "What are you doing here?"

"I need to speak with Jade, but she isn't in her room!" He snarled. "I know she tells you all about her little schemes. Now, where is she?"

Ruby frowned and pulled the blankets to cover her chest. "I don't know."

Jet took a step forward and gripped her shoulders tightly, prompting a gasp from her throat. "Don't lie to me, Ruby! Where is she?"

"I honestly don't know, Jet! The last time I spoke with her was at dinner! She made no mention of sneaking out!"

Jet shook her and hissed, "You know something! I can feel it!"

"I-I don't know a thing, I swear!" Ruby muttered. "I would have told papa! I do not want her sneaking around with a killer on the loose!"

Jet released her and cursed under his breath; she had a point. He stormed down to the servant quarters and threw open Gideon's door. He kicked the bed and yelled, "Did you know that my sister snuck away from the house?"

Gideon jumped up and let out a loud breath with a wipe of his brow. When he took in Jet's sudden appearance, he fell back amongst his pillows.

"Well?" Jet demanded. "Did you?"

"Which one, Mr. Calvert?"

"Which one do you think? Which one of my irksome sisters always oversteps authority?"

Gideon dropped his hand, looking exasperated. "No, Mr. Calvert. I did not know that Miss Jade snuck out of the house."

Jet's lips curled. "You better find her before this night is through, or my father will put a bullet in your head! Has it slipped your mind that a killer is stalking the streets?"

Gideon's face paled before he quickly found his feet and stood. "Yes, Mr. Calvert. I'll find her right away."

"Good," he sneered as Marna walked into the room. "And what about you?

"What is it, Milord?"

"Jade isn't in her room. It appears she has vanished from the manor!"

Marna clutched at her breast. "Oh, dear!"

Jet ground his teeth together when he realized that she, too, had no idea where his infuriating sister was. He stalked from the room to speak with the sentinels at the front gates, and they were just as clueless as everyone else.

He left the manor petulantly and instructed his cabbie to take him to the Hadleys in hopes of finding her there.

Jade was far better than he initially gave her credit for. If he found her with Jackson, he would kill her himself. To leave undetected from anyone came with skill, and as the Calvert manor was heavily guarded, someone was always watching.

XXVIII
OWEN

Gainsley had seen far better days and even smelled better. He chugged water from the stein Owen handed over, the contents spilling onto his chin and chest. He lowered it when the cup was empty and wiped at his face with his free hand.

"He kept saying things like, I know you did it," Gainsley grunted. "Just admit it, and the consequences won't be so severe."

Jackson was cooking eggs while Avis ground coffee beans. Elijah sat on the floor, wrapped in a blanket, and rested his head against his hand. James leaned against the wall while Owen placed bits of wood from the table into the fire. His face twisted as Gainsley recanted his story.

"I kept quiet until I couldn't," Gainsley admitted. "Begged even, but he wouldn't listen. They'd bring in water and say if I wanted a drink, I would have to admit to the murder. I refused to confess, and they'd pour it all over the floor. And damn, I was thirsty. I almost gave in for just one taste."

"It's a good thing you didn't," Owen pointed out. They wanted a scapegoat for the murders, which meant powerful men were behind them.

"I still can't believe you handed over the postcard," Jackson snapped. "They will release it in the paper, and it will cause discord throughout the city."

"What was I supposed to do?" Elijah yelled from the floor. "It proved his innocence!"

"And so did Mary-Anne Stafford's murder!" Jackson exclaimed. "You should have waited for us!"

"I'm not apologizing. I did what I thought was best!"

"You should have been in bed," Jackson growled.

"Leave him alone!" Avis interrupted. "Gainsley is free, and that's what matters! Not some postcard!"

"She's right," Owen intervened. "You were saying?"

Jackson rolled his eyes and resumed his cooking.

"Being tortured wasn't the worst of it," Gainsley said. "Augustus Atwood demanded to know why I was following him."

All five heads turned to him.

"Were you?" Owen asked with a frown.

Gainsley sighed before admitting, "Yes."

"Why?"

"I don't know. I just got the feeling I should," Gainsley answered with a shrug, and his cheeks flamed. He was hiding something.

"Did you catch him doing anything that he shouldn't?" Jackson asked.

"No, he knocked me out."

Owen's brows raised. "Augustus knocked you out?"

Gainsley nodded. "I was on the chase when he disappeared. I ran aimlessly in search of him until I spotted him heading toward Saint Julien's Park. He socked me right in the face when he noticed I was following. Next thing I knew, I was in a cell."

"He was heading to the park?" Owen asked, and Elijah blinked up at him.

"Seemed like," he said.

"But you don't know for certain?" Jackson asked.

"No."

"He's a pervert," Avis hissed. "You should see the way he hits on women in the church."

"He does this in front of his wife?" Jackson scoffed.

"Yes."

"That's disgusting," he grumbled.

Owen looked at him with peculiarity. "He could very well be a suspect. He has the temperament, you of all people should know."

Jackson gave him a wild stare. "What does that mean?"

Sensing the fight that was coming and Jackson's continuous loyalty to the Vaults, he said, "Forget it."

"Are you implying he's deranged because he fought as a youth? The Vaults do not breed killers, Owen!"

"I didn't say they did. I was merely pointing out that he was in the park where the body was found, and he has outbursts. It's very possible."

Jackson's eyes narrowed. "Then I could be a suspect as well."

Owen turned back to the fire. "Don't be dramatic."

"It's merely a coincidence," Jackson pressed.

"You don't even like Augustus!" Avis interjected. "Why are you defending him?"

"It's the inequity of the insinuation," Jackson told her. "You can't classify someone as a killer primarily because they fought in the Vaults. It is nonsense!"

Owen's gaze fell. Perhaps he was right on some level. Jackson's anger was deep within and well justified, and Owen wasn't sure he would have been any better off without fighting. The ring saved his life from addiction and perhaps even death.

"It's still worth looking into," Elijah's raspy voice broke.

Jackson shook his head as he pivoted back to the stove and Avis touched his arm.

In an instant, a loud hammering knock came from the kitchen door, and everyone jumped at the sound. It was relentless, and the person on the other side refused to let up.

Owen walked toward the door and pulled it open. Jet Calvert nearly fell through the doorway.

"Why in the bloody hell are you pounding on our door like that?" he yelled.

Jet pushed past him, and his eyes were erratic. When he caught sight of Jackson, he marched right up to him and shoved him backward. "Where is she?"

Jackson brushed him off and stepped in front of Avis. "Who do you think you are?"

Jet's face twisted as he pointed a finger at his chest. "Piss off, Jackson. Where is she?"

Owen grabbed Jet by the collar and pulled him backward. "You might want to reconsider your words and remember where you are!"

Jet pushed against him. "Don't even try to intimidate me. I want to know where the fuck my sister is!"

Owen released his collar and glanced at Jackson. Unease settled in his stomach once again. "Your sister? How would any of us know that?"

"Why don't you ask Jackson!" Jet yelled.

"What have you done?" Avis wailed as she stepped out from behind him with a glare.

Jackson and Elijah shared a look.

"What is it, Jackson?" Avis yelled.

"Nothing! I've barely spoken to the girl!"

Jet rounded on him. "Then why does Teddy seem to think otherwise?"

"Because Teddy is an absolute imbecile," Jackson grunted with a roll of his eyes.

Owen frowned, so his affection was widely known. It wouldn't be long before the consequences would turn for the worse.

"Well, she's missing, and she's here. I just know it!!" Jet yelled.

"Search the place if you're certain your sister is here," Jackson interrupted. "But I assure you, you won't find her!"

Jet glared and stalked from the room. Elijah jumped up from the ground and followed.

"Something must have happened if Teddy mentioned your name to people," Avis hissed. "It doesn't bode well to have him sniffing around! He is dangerous!"

Jackson snorted. "Let him come for me!"

"This isn't a game, Jackson!" Owen yelled.

Jackson released a breath and muttered, "At the masquerade ball, I found her hiding behind a plant to avoid dancing with Landsberry!" A smug smile tugged on his lips as he spoke. "We had a brief conversation thereafter, but that's all, I swear!"

Avis's sneer didn't vanish. She looked positively livid.

"You sort of helped her out of the pond in Saint Julien's Park," James added from the doorway.

"She's engaged, Jackson!" Avis wailed. "To Theodore no less!"

His eyes narrowed. "I know, thank you."

"Do you have a death wish?" She snarled.

"He won't do anything," he argued, but he was smiling.

Owen's lips parted. Something on his brother's face was utterly irreplaceable, like a man who had been changed entirely.

Jackson's eyes narrowed. "Why are you looking at me like that?"

Jet burst back through the kitchen door with Elijah at his heels.

"Well?" Jackson snapped at him.

Jet glared as Elijah rasped, "He tore your room apart."

"An apology would be much appreciated. And money for the eggs I burned."

Jet rubbed his forehead. "I forgot how exhausting it was to be around you all."

"I would say it's more entertaining than anything," Jackson answered, and Elijah chuckled. His face crumbled instantly, and he grabbed his stomach while muttering, "Don't make me laugh."

"When you say your sister is missing," Owen interrupted, "do you mean to say she left of her own free will?"

"Yes," Jet hissed. "She put pillows under her blanket to make it appear as if she were sleeping in her bed."

"A girl after my own heart!"

Jet pointed a finger at him. "That's what I'm talking about."

Jackson waved him off. "What if she is with Teddy? Have you thought that maybe she snuck off to see him?"

"Please, she loathes him!"

Jackson grinned and placed a hand on his chest.

It was as if Owen had never laid eyes upon his brother before. The man standing before him was not the angry boy who fought anyone who looked at him wrong. With the mere mention of Jade Calvert, he changed to a blundering fool with humor in each breath.

"Well, I've had enough of you!" Jet snarled and stalked toward the door. "I've got to find her before someone else does!"

With the slam of the door, Jackson's smile faltered.

"Perhaps we should help," Owen offered.

"Perhaps you shouldn't," Avis hissed. "Don't go messing around with that girl!"

"She could be in danger," Owen stated, and Avis threw her hands in the air with a glare and stomped from the room. James gave Jackson a grave look before following her.

Of all his siblings, he had the rockiest relationship with Avis because they were so different, yet they were alike in many ways.

"We don't know anything about her," Jackson said. "Where would we even begin to look?"

"At the engagement party," Elijah inquired, "what were you talking about before I approached?"

Jackson frowned. "Nothing of importance." His eyes then widened briefly. "She did get rather… I don't want to say excited, but she was interested in the Trinity Row murders. You saw it!"

"You don't think she'd be foolish enough to head to the east end, do you?" Elijah asked.

Jackson shrugged. “I really have no idea.”
“Well,” Owen said. “It's a start.”

XXIX
JADE

Perry's pub was crowded, disorderly, and full of spirit. The voices of many blended into one unintelligible chatter, and Jade grinned as she sipped on a stein of ale. It was remarkable to live in the moment and breathe, to not worry about the magic flowing in her veins or the significance of her father's name. There was not a soul around who gave her fussed looks for slouching, nor was there a corset squeezing her ribs to the point of blacking out. Tonight, she was like any other, an insignificant woman who held no station or expectation because of her name.

The reason she was even at a pub in Trinity Row was to see if she could. Having run from the manor some hours ago, she wondered if she should ever return. No one had come for her yet; if she had thought much about it, she should have left the city and never looked back.

She was playing poker against a few vagabonds who thought she'd be an easy way to make money; how very wrong they were. If there was one fond memory to be said about Jet, he had taught her how to gamble better than anyone would suspect. She was having such a good time that she hardly noticed Augustus Atwood leering from the corner of the room or the group of men at the bar who were scheming to follow her home.

Her attention was focused on the glaring eyes of a man named Weston Parker as she placed two pairs down on the table.

He tossed his cards and yelled, "You cheated! There is no way a low-class twit like yourself knows how to play the game and win!"

Jade smirked. She had stolen one of the maids' dresses, which was brown and torn at the seams. She blended into the crowd, appearing like another pauper.

Weston grabbed her hand and squeezed tightly when she began to take her winnings. "Now, what do you think you are doing with that?"

She whimpered and snapped her jaw together to keep from yelling out.

"You aren't taking a fucking thing from this table!"

"What's all this?"

She glanced up to see Jackson Hadley glaring at Weston. Owen and Elijah were at his side.

The man immediately released her hand with genuine fear and wailed, "I don't want any trouble, Jackson!"

But he didn't listen. He seized Weston by the collar and ripped him out of his chair. "I should break your hand for laying a finger on a lady!"

Jade stared wide-eyed, and her heart began to pound. She was cemented in her chair by the sheer force and brute nature of Jackson Hadley. She'd heard of his days fighting in the Vaults and how everyone was terrified of him; she understood why. Her father used to bet on him and boast about it.

"There is no need for this," Weston grunted. "It was an unfortunate reaction!"

Jackson cracked Weston's head against the wall to his left and snarled, "And she is William Calvert's daughter! Why don't we tell him about the unfortunate reaction and see how he finds it?"

"No!" Weston whimpered. "I'm sorry! I had no idea!"

Jackson pressed his arm into his windpipe. "I'm not the one you need to apologize to!"

Weston's watered eyes found Jade, and he grunted, "I-I-I'm s-sorry, M-miss!"

"It's quite alright," she answered.

"If you ever lay your hand on a woman again," Jackson growled, "I'll break your fingers one by one!"

"Okay!" He sputtered. "Just let me go!"

Jackson released his arm, and Weston fell in a crumpled heap on the floor. He coughed and clutched at his throat as he followed his friend, grumbling, "I'm so sorry, miss. Please don't tell your father!"

She shrunk down in embarrassment when everyone looked at her with a high amount of mistrust.

Jackson pulled out a chair and placed his arm on the back of hers, unbothered. "What are you doing here?"

"I was having a drink."

"Did it escape your mind that there is a killer on the loose?"

She frowned. "Of course not."

"Then why would you come to Trinity Row without an escort?"

Her stare hardened. "I'm not a prostitute!"

"I am well aware," he snapped with a glare. "But you are incredibly beautiful. The men who roam these streets aren't very honorable. Do you see that group at the bar? They were talking about which one would take you first!"

"I didn't think about it." She flushed as she glanced over at the men in question. They were seething at Jackson's sudden appearance.

"That is incredibly foolish!"

"No one noticed until you said something!"

"Are you mad?" Elijah cried. "You can't hide behind a dress, Highborn's stick out like a sore thumb in a poverty-stricken area! This was the worst place to have come!"

Her face burned deeper with acknowledgment, but she couldn't help and ask, "What happened to you?"

"Why don't you ask Jackson?" He retorted, and she glanced back at him.

"Elijah is right," Jackson said quickly. "You need to go home."

"No," Jade said with a fold of her arms and gave him a fixed stare.

"What do you mean, no?"

"First off, as it's my life, it's my decision!" she growled, and a smile tugged at his lips. "And secondly, who are you to boss me around?"

"I'm not trying to boss you around; I'm being rational. If you were anyone else, it wouldn't matter, but you're a Calvert!" Jackson clarified, and Elijah murmured, "Gilded cage," under his breath. She glared at him briefly and glanced back at Jackson. She was finally having a good time and wasn't ready to give it up just yet.

"I don't think you realize what will happen if your father catches wind of this," Owen muttered.

"My father will never know. He hasn't left the house in weeks! Jet would be the one you should concern yourself with, although I could take him on just fine. Nevertheless, I'll make you a deal."

Jackson gave her an incredulous look. "I will not make any deals with you!"

"Ah, c'mon, I want to hear this!" Elijah cut in, and Jackson gave him such a dumbfounded stare it was laughable.

Jade took advantage of his silence and said, "We'll play one hand of poker, and when I beat you, I get to stay!"

"What makes you so confident?"

"Jet taught me well," she answered smugly.

Elijah laughed loudly and pulled out the chair adjacent to hers. "Who do you think taught your brother?" He ripped the cards from the table. "I want in!"

Her smile fell, and her gaze turned suspicious. "Why? What do you want?"

Elijah shuffled the cards and pressed his lips together without a response. His cheeks turned a slight shade of pink, but he was so confident in his actions that she couldn't say if he was embarrassed or overheated. He then placed the deck before her to cut and glanced at Jackson. "The Chapman wedding is tonight."

"That is a terrible idea," Owen barked.

"It's settled then!" she answered with a grin. "If I win, we will go to the wedding!"

After some thought, Jackson tore his gaze from hers and nodded once at Elijah. He grinned in return and waved the bartender over. A doxy stepped up and placed her hands on his shoulders after she kissed his cheek; he frowned deeply. Jade observed him with open curiosity. If she didn't know any better, she'd say he was highly disinterested in the woman, and she wondered why he would allow her to touch him. It wasn't until his stare found her again that she remembered to cut the deck.

They put in a coin for the blind, and Elijah dealt two cards for each, one at a time. He placed two aces on the table in front of her. She kept her face neutral with the discovery of two threes in her hand. She glanced at Jackson, who stared blankly back. There was no telling what he had. Elijah's own face was incredibly reserved, making her slightly uneasy as he patiently awaited her call, perhaps expecting her to fold. She called the big blind, and they both followed suit and dealt the flop. The confidence on Jackson's face made her stomach flip, and his lips curved slightly upwards as his eyes met hers once again.

The redheaded woman mouthed, "He's bluffing," from behind Elijah.

Jade grinned, raised the bet, and tossed five coins on the table, the men at her back began to whistle. Even Elijah laughed as he met her wager and dealt the river. The final community card was another three. Her spirits soared. She had this game.

"You're up," Elijah said, and she grinned widely as she placed her cards down on the table.

He snorted loudly and tossed his cards carelessly. "I'm out."

Everyone cheered, but it was short-lived as Jackson placed two aces down. Her smile fell. His four-of-a-kind beat her full house.

"I can't believe it," she said dispassionately.

"You really didn't think I'd let you win, did you?" Jackson said with a sly smile.

Her gaze narrowed. "You cheated!" It wasn't fair.

He laughed deeply, and Elijah and Owen chimed in. "Hardly! It's just the luck of the draw! Now let's get out of the east end before your father catches us!"

"You won't make me go home?"

Jackson's face twisted as he began to stack the cards. "I thought you didn't want to?"

"I don't! But you never gave your terms of our bet."

"I didn't?" he murmured, and his eyes flashed to her slowly. He looked as if he wished to devour her whole.

Her face burned intensely with the implication of what he wasn't saying, and frankly, he need not utter a word. Her imagination was wild enough. His eyes widened and slowly wandered over her delicately flushed skin. How could someone be so terrifying yet so unbelievably fervid with one look alone? Was Cordelia correct in her assumptions? Did Jackson want her as much as she did him, and would he accept the affliction in her soul? It was too heavy of a conversation at the moment, so she tore her gaze away before saying something foolish.

The woman suddenly left Elijah's side to greet a group of women at a table not far from theirs, and she caught him staring directly at her. He looked terribly upset over the chemistry transpiring between her and Jackson. She could admit it was reckless when she was promised to another but was it still a sin if she never agreed to a union? It was a complex argument she shouldn't have at all because she should be the one to choose. Yet, she could see how she looked through the eyes of another, and she realized then that Elijah must not like her at all. It was an irrational thought as she hadn't done anything to warrant distaste. But she couldn't shake the feeling because he appeared very displeased.

She grimaced and glanced at Owen.

"Where are my manners?" Jackson laughed. "Jade-"

"Oh, she's Jade now, is she?" Elijah scoffed loudly.

Jackson frowned at him. "What is your problem?"

Elijah merely shook his head and got up from the table abruptly. He promptly yelled out to the table of doxies, who waved him over and giggled amongst themselves as he strode toward them.

"I apologize," Jackson said in her ear.

"For what?"

"Elijah. He is quite pleasant to be around and doesn't usually have such terrible manners," Jackson said, and she grinned. Was this how her siblings excused her behavior whenever she said something unrefined?

"I wish I knew what I had done to have upset him."

"It isn't you," Owen said sternly, and she glanced at him with surprise. "It's your father. He is a very powerful man and won't listen to reason."

"Owen," Jackson warned.

"She has to understand how her actions affect those around her!" Owen stated.

"That's enough," Jackson said flatly.

They needn't fight with one another on her behalf; she already felt tainted enough. She knew exactly what her father and brother would say if they saw her here. She knew what Theodore would do to Jackson if he saw him sitting as close as he was.

"I wish for so many things I can't have," she admitted softly. "I'm sorry if I've put you at risk for being here."

"You have nothing to apologize for," Jackson said, and she glanced at him sadly. "I'm not sorry. I am glad to have seen you tonight!"

His words didn't make her feel any better when his brothers hovered with judgment.

"But Owen is right," Jackson said. "It's only a matter of time before they come looking."

She closed her eyes as she leaned her head into her fingertips. "You have no idea what it's like there."

"I'm sorry it's awful for you," Jackson said after a beat of silence. "But the truth of the matter is, you belong to Teddy."

She lowered her hand and glared. "I belong to no one!"

He grinned. "I find your tenacity extremely charming and the fact that you despise Teddy all the better."

"Jack," Owen warned.

He glanced at his brother briefly and back. "I hate to force you to do anything against your will, but we can only have one drink before we need to take you home."

She recoiled from his words, her face twisting in disappointment.

"Don't look at me that way," he pleaded, his mask of apathy slipping altogether.

She despised the rules of society and the fact that her father made all her life choices.

"Jade," Jackson hedged.

A smile tugged at her lips. "I find your lack of propriety extremely charming. My name sounds agreeable on your lips."

Jackson's eyes moved back and forth between hers once again. She didn't know what he was looking for, but she hoped he wanted whatever it was.

The band was the central point of the room as people danced around. The bride and groom were full of smiles and wrapped in one another's arms. Elijah and Owen stalked off into the crowd, and several people greeted them enthusiastically. Jade grinned widely as she watched the people celebrate. This is what life looked like. The bride was absolutely brimming with love, and it was rather enviable to witness. She tried to picture it then, being happy with no care as she married the man she loved. She frowned instantly at the thought and wondered what had changed. Or rather, who changed it? Her eyes slid up to Jackson, he was watching the crowd like she was, and there was a slight smirk on his face; that irritating dimple on his cheek emerged.

He turned his head toward her, his smile blooming. "There is only one thing left to do!"

"And what is that?"

"Dance," he said while grabbing her hand.

She laughed, and the static returned. His touch vibrated up her arm again, but she didn't draw back or yell; she endured the connection. If he felt it too, he didn't allude to any discomfort. He then wrapped an arm around her waist and rested his palm on her hip as he drew her body into him. Her eyes landed on his Adam's apple. It was an odd part of the body and even stranger to be attracted to it. Her eyes raised to his face, he was staring at her again, but all evidence of humor had vanished from his lips and was replaced with something else. She couldn't give an exact name to it, but she could feel it all the way down in the pit of her stomach. The dimple formed again as he guided them, and she laughed with each step.

"This is quite different from your waltz!" he bellowed and twirled her around.

She giggled in response, and the grin on her face bloomed from ear to ear. Being here at this moment made her forget about everything else. It had been quite some time since she thought of nothing other than being alive.

After a few dances, Jackson left her at a table as he went to grab them some ale.

"Are yew Jacks girl?" a lusty voice said from behind.

Jade turned to see a woman with blonde hair and a gapped tooth grin staring at her expectantly. No, she wasn't even close to being his girl, but the thought sounded rather appealing.

"Something like that," she answered vaguely.

The blonde's smile deepened as she sat down without asking—this amused Jade.

"Name's Elizabeth Dewitt."

She couldn't give her last name, so she said, "Jade."

Elizabeth's eyes widened briefly as she held out a hand to which Jade shook. "Nice to meet ya, Jade. I wasn't even sure I'd make it! I need the money, and there is plenty to be made tonight! Many lords in Trinity Row!"

Jade's brow smoothed as her curiosity peaked. "Are you a prostitute?"

Elizabeth gave her a sure gaze. "I am and yur a lady. Can spot em anywhere!"

Jade grimaced. She had hoped it wasn't too noticeable. She didn't need anyone to recognize her or treat her differently because of it.

"So, tell me, Miss Jade," Elizabeth urged. "How long have yew been seein' Jack?"

Jade pressed her lips together, unsure of how to answer.

"He must like yew," she blurted. "Elijah says he never spends his time wiv girls anymore."

"He doesn't spend time with women?" This revelation caused a thrill of pleasure to flush through her system. She liked that far more than she should.

"Oh, he used to," Elizabeth babbled with a wave of her hand. "But not since…" she paused and eyed Jade wearily. "He just doesn' hang around them anymore."

Jade stared openly. Was she referring to Katerina or Isabella? Not that she cared for either female and completely despised his association, but there was no room for her to judge when she had her own mistakes to deal with.

She turned her head to see him standing there, holding onto two steins and watching her apprehensively. A tremor of appeal flipped in her belly, and she bit her lip to hold back a grin. What was happening to her?

The creases in his forehead smoothed, a smile tugging at his lips. Amused by Jade's interest in him, which had to be apparent by now.

He placed a stein in front of her. "Is everything okay?"

She released her lip and beamed from ear to ear. "Everything is perfect."

His eyes skimmed her face, his own interest rising. He then turned to Elizabeth. "Do you want my drink? I can go grab another."

She waved him off. "Not tonight."

He pulled out a chair next to Jade's and sat down languidly. He rested his arm on the back of her chair once again.

"Yew wound me, Jack," Elizabeth commented. "How come yew hasn' come to see me?"

Jade looked at him sharply.

"I never saw her in that manner," he explained. That damned smile was still in place. "She's always been Eli's."

Elizabeth smirked. "Oh, dearie, I wouldn' disrespect a lady! Even I have enough sense to keep me mouth closed when it matters!"

Jade forced a laugh without humor, not entirely sure what she meant by that statement.

"I wasn't going to come!" A soft brunette with wide blue eyes said as she threw Jade a disdainful stare; James was with her. She hadn't given him much thought at the park, but now that he was standing before her, she realized that he was Jackson's spitting image, only years younger. He obviously didn't have the scar on his brow, nor did his nose appear to have been broken as Jackson's had. The woman hugged Elizabeth and kissed Jackson before sitting down next to her.

"Jade, this is my sister Avis," Jackson said. "And you remember my brother, James, of course."

Avis eyed her coolly while James flashed a charming smile. "Hello again." He then tapped Jackson's arm; there was a laugh on his breath. "Gainsley just proposed to Mary Bishop!"

Jackson's smile fell. "He what?"

"Just now!" James chuckled.

"He's making a complete ass of himself," Avis thundered. "He's drunker than a mule and going on about how titles and money don't mean a damned thing when a man has a good heart!"

Jackson closed his eyes briefly and groaned.

"He really took your words to heart, didn't he mate?" Raoul mocked as he sidled up beside them. He was the one who lived with her aunt Cordelia. James sniggered even harder.

Jackson's eyes snapped open, scowling at the pair of them.

"Wait till Owen finds out!" James said in between laughs, and Raoul howled loudly, grabbing onto James for support.

"It's not that funny!" Jackson snapped, though there was a grin tugging at his lips. "Gainsley can marry whomever he wants!"

"Yeah, but Mary Bishop?" James cried incredulously, and his face twisted in disgust.

Jade knew of the girl but not enough to see what was humorous about the situation. "Why do you say that? What is wrong with her?'

"Nothing," Jackson muttered quickly, but James didn't get the hint.

"She's been with all of the sons of the Elite, and I mean all of them!"

"James!" Jackson barked, and Raoul began to tug at the cuff of his jacket as he made swiping motions at his neck.

She suddenly felt like a fool when she realized what he was saying.

"Why, just last week, she was hanging all over Teddy Ken- Ow!" James yelled when Jackson slugged him in the arm. "What was that for?"

Jade dropped her eyes and hoped her face didn't burn with embarrassment.

"Would you shut your mouth?"

"Why?" He scowled and rubbed his arm, but James wasn't stupid. He knew she was engaged to Theodore. Was this some sort of backwards warning or was he making fun of her?

Raoul touched his nose and made a motion toward Jade.

The whole table glanced at her, but only Elizabeth seemed to understand, and Avis smacked James upside the head, yelling, "You idiot!"

"Now, why are you smacking me?"

Elijah interrupted the moment by crashing into Elizabeth and kissing her right cheek repeatedly. Elizabeth giggled in response.

A wide grin lingered on his lips when he pulled away, and he asked, "Am I forgiven?"

"Of course, yew is," she told him, and her eyes doubled when she took in his face. "What happened to yew?"

"A drunken misunderstanding," he replied casually as his eyes flicked to Jackson.

Jade glanced at Jackson and he looked embarrassed as he shuffled in his seat. Was he the reason Elijah was looking the way he was?

Elizabeth tsked loudly, clearly not bothered by the suggestion. "Well, I need to get out there."

"No, you don't."

"I need to make a living."

"Nope." He shook his head. "You are going to stay here with me!"

She smacked him. "No, I ain'! I need money!"

"All you need is me!" He pulled her out of the chair and smiled down at her.

Jackson leaned into Jade's ear and said, "I am truly sorry for that."

Jade continued to focus on Elijah and Elizabeth. "You don't have to apologize for everyone's behavior."

"I don't?"

She looked at him, and his face was far too close to hers. She could feel his breath on her cheeks. "Why would you have to apologize for Elizabeth?" She wasn't about to bring up Teddy because it was embarrassing. The other was a safer topic. "She is very kind, and I'll admit I wasn't expecting that. I've never spoken to a prostitute before, but I must say, it was a high point."

His eyes rounded in wonderment. "You are incredible. Do you know that?"

Her mouth began to rise again, and that was the thing about Jackson. She felt happiest when he was near. It was wrong to be attracted to him for more reasons than one, but there was this desire to memorize his face so she may never forget it. She wanted to remember what it was like to have someone look at her as he did now, genuinely affected without malicious intent.

Avis watched them openly with a frown on her face, but Jade ignored her. She wasn't going to waste her time with Jackson feeling sorry for herself.

She danced with Elijah and Owen, laughed so much that her cheeks ached, and conversed with everyday people who didn't have an alternate agenda. She consumed far more alcohol than she ever thought was possible, and she even held Jackson's hand. The friction sparked between them, but he didn't pull away. If anything, he squeezed her tighter. The night continued that way for some time, drifting by faster than she liked.

The sun was rising when they exited the dancing hall.

Jackson placed his jacket over her shoulders when she began to rub her arms from the chilly morning air.

Elijah and Owen walked side by side with their arms slung over each other, singing loudly.

Jade exchanged a genial glance and a laugh with Jackson.

He placed his hands in his pockets. "We were supposed to get you home, not keep you out later."

"I'm glad you did," she said.

"I fear the consequences."

"If anyone suspected my absence, my father would have torn apart the city by now. But as no one came, no one noticed. Not with Katerina around, anyway. I can say I spent the night at Esmeralda's, and it'll never be questioned."

"Fair enough," he said.

A feeling of closure hovered between them, and it caused an efflux of anxiety to emerge. She did not want this to be the last time she ever saw Jackson Hadley.

"I haven't enjoyed myself like that in quite some time."

Jackson smiled. "Nor I."

"It's nice to be around people who aren't scheming," Jade said and looked out to the horizon. "Everyone that surrounds my family seems to want something. Almost as if you owe them for a mere conversation."

"That's society for you."

A sudden thought occurred, and her head cocked to the side. "Why is it you never married?"

His brows raised as his eyes slid to her.

She grinned sheepishly. "I apologize. I suppose it's none of my business. I just find it odd. Your father was influential when he was alive. I remember seeing him around, the name Hadley was spoken freely with respect, and when he died, it's almost as if you three turned your back on Bel Deaux."

Jackson's face smoothed as he thought about it.

Guilt struck her, and she wanted to smack herself. Strange to feel it only when around him. "I'm sorry. You don't have to explain anything to me."

He glanced at her. "We dealt with loss in the worst way imaginable. Our parents were the most incredible people. How is that easy to accept? I know you understand. Your mother was quite different from your father."

"She was."

"I became obsessed with death after my parents passed," he admitted, and his eyes flashed cautiously. "The desire to find a cure plagued my mind, and I was so consumed by it that I never looked for a wife."

She gave him a sympathetic gaze.

"I'm not upset by the fact," he added, eyes trained ahead. "I could never have given what was needed."

"Somehow, I doubt that," she countered with a wide smile.

He gave her a sloppy grin. "Do you have any hobbies?"

Astonishment transformed her features at the sudden change in conversation. "I beg your pardon?"

"Is there anything specific you enjoy doing?"

"Oh," she answered quietly. No one had ever asked her that question before. "I love music. I used to play the piano and the violin every single day, but it annoyed my father. He said it was disruptive noise and never allowed me to practice when he was in the house." She paused to rub her lips together. "I also like to read and paint and play chess. I even enjoy a tantalizing game of poker when the occasion calls for it." She gave him a wink, and he chuckled. "But Theodore won't allow it either. He doesn't like it much when my attention is focused on anything but him."

Jackson stopped walking, his hands were still in his pockets, and there was a deep frown on his face.

She paused. What had she said to cause him to look at her so gravely? She quickly averted her gaze. "It's not much, I suppose, but I've grown up in a very sheltered environment. Perhaps if I were given a chance to go out and explore, my hobbies would be grander."

"Your hobbies are well enough," he murmured, and his face twisted with concern. "They're even admirable. Especially if they make you particularly happy."

She couldn't hide the confusion on her face. "Then why are you looking at me that way?"

"I'm growing rather tired of Teddy Kensington," Jackson answered truthfully after a moment of thought. "What a shameful person he is, and how narcissistic to think he is interesting enough to captivate your entire life!"

She wasn't the only one who saw through him, which was refreshing.

Longing ripped through her chest—they would never be more than this, and it simply wasn't enough. She would never be able to reach out and touch him. He would never be hers.

"I don't think you should marry him," he said after a moment.

She blinked in surprise.

"And I don't mean to say that you should choose me instead, although I'd follow you anywhere," he admitted, and her mouth parted with a rapid beat of her heart. He ran a hand through his hair with an embarrassed laugh. "But that's beside the point. The point is he is an absolute mongrel, and Elijah was right. You deserve far better than him."

"I don't intend to marry him," she whispered.

He exhaled in relief.

"I'm going to flee the city," she said, and he gaped in surprise. "I'm going to run as far as I can, and I'm never going to look back."

A myriad of emotions crossed his face—relief, pride, confusion, but the most discernible of all, anguish.

"I want to be with you," she said confidently. Even though she didn't feel confident at all, she was ready to jump out of her skin.

He stared at her for what felt like an eternity, and the longer he failed to answer, the more embarrassed she became. Perhaps he was only physically attracted to her and lied to her face just now. That seemed to hurt more.

"Never mind," she said quickly and averted her gaze. "I suppose I'm still a little drunk."

"Jade."

"I shouldn't have said anything. I'm sorry." She turned to run away, but he grabbed her arm before she could flee and pulled her back toward him.

The intensity of his stare had static not only erupting in her palms, yearning for his touch as if his hand only belonged in hers, but in her stomach as well. She craved to know what the rest of him felt like.

"I want to be with you too," he finally said, his voice low.

She grinned widely, her heart threatening to burst. Waves of euphoria coursed through her veins, and she never wanted to forget this moment. He was all she ever needed. Fuck all the rest.

He grabbed her face and evened his breath. She could feel his hands shaking, a harsh wave prickling against her skin, forcing her to comprehend the gravity of their feelings for one another. She pulled back when their lips were about to connect and grabbed onto his wrist. It only amplified the static, causing him to wince in pain. She instantly let go. "I have to show you something before you kiss me. If you still want to be together once you have truly seen me, then you can have all of me."

"I see you now," he said and kissed her anyway. When their lips met, a surge of frisson accelerated throughout her entire body, especially when he placed a hand on her neck, leaving her adust. Her lips parted, and he tasted the inside of her mouth, which was incalescent and better than she could have ever imagined. Their lips moved simultaneously with the desire to be much closer than they already were.

When she drew away for a breath, he hauled her back, consuming her unmercifully, unafraid, and with ebullience. If this were what she was meant to live for, she would never question the Gods again.

Yet, just as she let go of every concern life had to offer and gave into Jackson completely, the static burned unbearably, producing white spots even with her eyes closed. Heat burned deeply in her chest as a hot ember, flowing down her limbs and sparking within her palms.

"Ah," she whimpered and pushed him away, leaving burn marks in the shape of her hands against his navy-blue shirt. His eyes doubled as they traveled down her chest, which was fading from white hot to a dull orange. She glanced wildly around, but they were alone on the street.

She panted as she looked back at him, tears filling her eyes; she was exposed, but he wasn't running away. His face softened as he held up his hands. "You're safe with me. You just don't have control yet."

Her voice shook as she asked, "What do you mean I don't have control?"

"Of your power," he said casually. The tears she was trying to blink back spilled down her cheeks. He knew. He knew, and yet, he was still standing here. His face crumbled with her distress, and he wiped away her tears with his thumb. "I will never let anything happen to you."

"You say that now," she whispered, twisting her shaking hands, which were no longer glowing. "But you will run away when you see me for what I am."

His brows pinched. "Would you like me to?"

"No," she said and swallowed the lump in her throat. The only thing she wanted was to be free with him. She dropped her eyes to avoid the disappointment on his face and whispered, "But what if I'm wicked?"

"Have you hurt someone?"

"Of course not!"

"Do you lie, steal, or cheat from others?"

"No."

"Then you aren't evil," he answered with finality.

She dared a glance at him. He was looking at her in all seriousness, but his face, the most remarkable one she had ever laid eyes upon, wasn't repelled. He gazed at her as if she were the only woman in the city. The only woman worth looking at. "And how do you know?"

He placed a hand on his chest. "Because I can feel you here."

She tried to smile. "They say witchcraft is evil."

His face smoothed. "And what if they say that so demons can walk free in disguise?"

Her mouth parted. She had never thought of it that way. She never thought of witches as good when they were taught to be pure evil.

He looked behind her when his brothers called for them and murmured, "We better get going before they wonder." He grabbed her hand despite the returning current. "This isn't the time for this conversation anyway."

She pulled her hand away when it started to glow, holding it tightly against her chest. His face hardened as she shrugged out of his jacket, handing it over before Owen and Elijah noticed the sudden burn marks on his shirt.

"You're safe with me," he repeated.

She dropped her gaze, blinking back more tears. He had to be a figment of her imagination. An entity she made up to come to terms with her insanity.

This time, he let her walk away from him.

Owen and Elijah were still singing when they reached Esmeralda's chateau. They went through the gates and around to the servant's quarters.

"Shut it, will you!" Jackson hissed; aggravation was heavy in his voice.

The boys turned.

"It was a pleasure!" Elijah said while grabbing her hand. If Jackson's touch was wildly unpredictable and erratic, driving her power to the surface and threatening to expose her for what she was, Elijah's touch was like the calm in the middle of a storm. Such as the steady flow of a river streaming through her veins, calming her heart, nerves, and mind. He gave the back of her hand a quick peck and let go without a second thought. She grimaced when Owen tipped his hat, not daring to touch him.

When she glanced up at Jackson, his brows pinched briefly, but his face quickly smoothed over, and he gave her an uneven grin.

Esmeralda opened the door then. Her eyes flashed in utter surprise at the lot of them. "Where were you?"

"Esmeralda!" Jade wailed. "What are you doing up at this hour?"

"I've been looking for you!"

Jade threw up her hands. "Here I am!"

Jackson laughed.

"Where were you?" Esmeralda insisted. "Have you been out all night? And drinking, mind you! Don't even try to deny it. I can smell it!"

"You act as if it's a bad thing!" Jade muttered. "You should try having fun for once!"

Esmeralda glowered at her.

"We are just returning your sister safely home," Owen said as he swayed on his feet. A mischievous grin lingered on his lips.

Esmeralda's eyes narrowed at him. "And where were you exactly?"

"We went to a wedding and ate some cake!" Elijah explained loudly. "You know Jonathan has exquisite taste in wine despite his carelessness when it comes to bathing."

Owen laughed. "This was the cleanest I've ever seen him!"

Jade smirked at Esmeralda's bewilderment. How peculiar it must seem with everyone still reasonably pissed. Jackson chuckled at the pair, and she, wholly smitten over said man, peered at him in adulation. The thought made her cringe. She needed to get away before she confessed her growing fixation with him. She stepped forward but was pulled back almost instantly.

She glanced down at her hand in Jackson's, and the spark returned. "Goodbye, Jade."

Her eyes raised to his. Why did it feel as if he were telling her goodbye for good? She sighed as anguish settled in. How was she to walk away now that she knew of him?

"Thank you for the wonderful evening, Jackson."

He placed a hand on his chest and watched her go without a word. Esmeralda quickly shuffled her inside as she shut the door, trying to grab onto her arm when Jade headed for the stairs to lie down. A headache was forming.

She halted in her tracks when she spotted her father sitting with Pearl and Ruby in the kitchen. His left arm rested casually on the table while one leg was crossed over the other.

Pearl looked grave when their eyes connected, and Ruby was distressed, but nothing was to be said. Jet was leaning against the wall in the far corner. The glare on his face was to be expected, although it was nothing compared to the demoralizing stare her father gave her.

"Jackson Hadley, eh?"

Her heart exploded with rapid beats as she watched him. It sobered her quickly.

"It seems as if I could have saved myself a lot of arguments had I chosen Jackson as your suitor instead of Teddy," he muttered with a gruff laugh, and Jet threw a look of perplexity. "We could have been royalty!"

Esmeralda stepped beside her and wrapped an arm around her shoulders. Pearl's brow pinched at the pair.

"Unfortunately, you never learn," William said as he tapped his fingers on the table.

"Papa," Esmeralda said.

"I didn't tell you to speak," William hissed, and her jaw snapped shut with a glare. He took the air from the room. She should never have come here; she should have run away with Jackson instead.

"It's a good thing Jet came to me when he did because Augustus ran straight to Theodore, and unfortunately for you and Jackson, Abraham and his thugs are out for blood."

"Papa, please," Jade whispered, but he held up a hand.

"Do you believe me to be stupid?" he asked, and she lowered her eyes. "I know when you leave the house and what you do." His eyes slid to Ruby, and she shrunk in her seat. "Even when you think I don't!"

Jade's shoulders sank in discouragement. She would never be able to escape. "So, what will my punishment be?"

"Thirty-six lashings should do the trick."

Her jaw went slack; she couldn't take another lashing. Her siblings began to protest immediately, but he slammed his fist on the table, which quieted them all. The silence that followed was deafening as he glowered at each of them. "You think I am being unkind?"

None of them answered.

"Adultery will not be tolerated under my roof."

"I didn't sin with Jackson!"

"It will only be a matter of time," William growled with a glare directed toward Esmeralda, who opened her mouth to speak. "I don't understand why the five of you bait me with such foolish behavior! I have given you everything you could possibly dream of, but it isn't enough! Well, I'm done trying to mold you into respectable people!"

Her father had a way of quieting them all into submission, but her hand twitched. Esmeralda grabbed it to still her.

"I didn't become the man I am today by allowing indecency and disloyalty to thrive in those around me, and that applies to you all. I'm tired of having this conversation with you!"

She took even breaths to calm her erratic heart and nerves.

"This is where you would apologize," Jet barked, and her father merely blinked, waiting for her response.

Jade pressed her lips together. She refused to apologize for something for which she wasn't sorry. She would never regret meeting Jackson Hadley or spending the evening with him. She wouldn't let them win and would fight for the day when they could live unapologetically in love. Until then, she would hold her tongue, no matter how many scars they inflicted upon her skin.

She raised her chin defiantly. "I have nothing to apologize for!"

"Is that so?" William barked, waiting for her to respond. When she didn't, he continued, "Ruby will also receive fifteen lashings for sneaking off with James Hadley."

Everyone but Pearl gaped at the girl. "But-"

"But nothing," William scoffed.

Ruby held her breath to quiet a sob.

His words sparked a flame of anger. He had destroyed every one of their lives and taken all hope from within. Well, it wasn't going to happen anymore.

She flexed her hand and was surprised when the static didn't return to her fingertips.

"Control yourself," echoed through her head fiercely, and her nose twitched. It was Esmeralda's tight grip that held her together. "You don't know how to wield your power just yet."

It was true that she didn't have full reign, and there was a chance she could hurt her sisters in the process. She quickly accepted defeat for now, but there would be a time when she wouldn't back down.

"I will take them," Jade said adamantly, and Esmeralda stiffened beside her.

"What do you mean you'll take them?" her father spat.

"I will take Ruby's punishment on top of my own," she answered, not bothering to look away from her father's terrifying face to see what the others thought. She made Ruby a promise, and if there was a possibility her sister could get out of this nightmare unscathed, then Jade would give up her freedom to make it happen. She wouldn't give in to fear.

XXX
Ruby

Jade didn't initially make any noise, but the sound of a whip smacking against her back had Ruby cringing inwardly. She sat in the silent hallway with Esmeralda and Pearl, listening to the sound of their sister being punished behind a closed door. William called for Adam to administer the blow.

Ruby jumped with every crack, closing her eyes when Esmeralda grabbed her hand tightly. The brutality was relentless, intensely increasing as she counted each whip. The seconds were agonizing, especially when Jade began to whimper. Guilt washed over her entire body. She shouldn't have allowed her to take the fall. It was gut-wrenching, and the moment Jade screamed aloud, Marna cupped her mouth to stifle a sob. Even the three prostitutes following Ruby were downcast. It was far too much; all four of them left the hallway.

After the twentieth strike, Jade's screams failed to cease at all and vibrated into Ruby's very soul, a sound she would never forget.

"Why isn't she stopping it?" Jet asked no one in particular.

Ruby glanced over with uncertainty; Esmeralda met Ruby's stare with consternation.

"She doesn't have an ounce of control," Pearl answered as more screams followed. She was staring at the wall ahead as if she were concentrating heavily. "She wouldn't even know where to begin."

"We could stop him," Jet suggested, and Ruby's face twisted as she frantically looked between the three of them, all of whom seemed to agree on something. "We're stronger together. He won't be able to stop us!"

"It's not the time," Pearl dismissed, and another scream echoed.

"You always say that!" Jet snarled. "When will be the time?"

"Not now. Papa will retaliate."

"So?" Jet barked. "We have magic in our veins!"

Ruby froze, grounded by his words. He couldn't possibly mean witchcraft. The implication was deadly.

"It isn't just Jade," Esmeralda snapped. "None of us know what we're doing!"

"Blake will get killed if we act now," Pearl added as if to shut him up, and it worked. Jet faltered; fear evidently rippled over his face. "We cannot act impulsively, not when we're heavily influenced by emotion. If we do what you are suggesting, then we need a plan. We also need Jade's help; she won't be of any use in a weakened state. Papa is powerful, and he is smart. He may not be able to touch us, but he will harm the ones you love."

"You want us to do nothing?" he snapped and held out his arm to the door.

Pearl shook her head. "He will kill her!"

"Father wouldn't dare, and we aren't the ones she needs," Pearl hissed. "Jackson Hadley will come for her. He is integral to her power."

Ruby's stomach dropped. "Power, what power?"

"Are you certain about that?" Esmeralda asked, ignoring Ruby's question altogether.

"Yes."

Jet stood back carefully, Ruby was still trying to digest their words when the cracking finally stopped, and all that was left was Jade's screams.

Esmeralda stood from the bench and stormed into the room without permission. Adam practically ran the moment he was dismissed, looking as if he'd be sick.

"That needed to happen," Pearl explained. "He will help her escape."

Jet glanced over his shoulder at the guard running to the door at the far end of the hall.

"What are you talking about?" Ruby cried and clutched Pearl's arm with sheer hysteria. If her siblings shared a similar likeness, she wouldn't have to endure insanity alone.

Pearl merely shook her head instead of answering her question and followed Jet into the room. Ruby was left staring at the wall in silence, her heart was beating furiously in her chest, and all the fear she had felt in the last year had vanished. She wouldn't have to be crippled by death any longer.

Ruby halted in the doorway when she spotted Jade. She was hanging by her wrists from a rack above her. Her back was sliced open and dripping with blood, and so was the floor below her.

"This is a warning," William barked. Ruby turned her head; he was staring directly at her. Fear washed over her entire body, and she stepped backward in distress, ready to bolt if he was so much as to strike her. "If you ever entertain James Hadley again, I will give you forty-two lashes."

She tried to swallow, but there was still a large lump in her throat.

"Get her out of my sight," he sneered and turned toward his desk, unbothered by the daughter he had brutally beaten.

Tears fell down Ruby's cheeks, and she could barely breathe. Jet's face slipped the moment their eyes collided, in complete understanding of the wickedness of William Calvert and the destruction of their lives. It was evident by the sheer unspeakable pain displayed across Ruby's face.

Marna handed Esmeralda a fifth bowl of hot water by the time they got Jade's back to stop bleeding. She was lying on her stomach while Esmeralda and Pearl cleaned the wounds.

"I didn't have a choice. Augustus ran straight to Teddy!" Jet bellowed as he paced in front of her bed. "If I didn't involve father, there is no telling what he would have done!"

Jade blinked. She was gazing at the windows in front of her.

"I don't think you understand how spiteful Teddy is over Dominic Kane, and now that Jackson is a threat, he's going to draw blood. Father is the only person in the city they're afraid of!"

"That's enough, Jet," Esmeralda snapped.

"Why can't you obey?" he roared over her. "And why do you have to go running around with Jackson Hadley, of all people?"

Jade closed her eyes.

"For the same reason you run around with Blake Emerich," Esmeralda answered. Jet stopped pacing to look at her spitefully.

"What do you mean by that?"

She rolled her eyes. "You act as if we care."

Jet flushed in embarrassment, but Ruby knew it wasn't because he was ashamed of his love. It was how society made it seem filthy, and he would have to overcome a world of judgment if he wanted to live freely.

"I wasn't going to say a word," Jet glossed over the situation. Ignoring the truth was easier for him. "Because as much as I dislike the person, you can be, you are still my sister!"

Esmeralda finally turned to look at him. "Why don't you go home? You've done enough damage for one evening."

He wasn't one to be dismissed, and he began to argue, but Ruby didn't want to listen to his petulance. "Tell me what's going on! What power were you talking about before?"

Marna halted, and Jet barked. "Leave us!"

She sped out of the room, and once the door was closed, the three of them glanced at one another cautiously. Ruby was about to scream when Pearl blurted, "I can see things, and I don't know why!" She covered her mouth quickly and shook her head.

"What do you mean you can see things?" Ruby asked. She felt like she was crawling in her skin, and relief was hanging on the horizon.

She lowered her hands. "I can't explain why, but I knew about Jade and Dominic's affair long before I exposed them."

Ruby glanced at Jade; her eyes were still shut.

"He was going to hurt her," Pearl said quietly. "I saw him slitting her throat, although I don't know why … I almost felt as if it was on behalf of someone else, but I couldn't be certain, and I didn't know what to do! I couldn't go to the coppers, they would have arrested me for speaking about a murder that had yet to happen, and I wasn't sure if any of you knew about your power. I reacted just as Jet did! I had to ensure Dominic would never get close to Jade again, and father was the only way!"

Jade didn't stir. Perhaps too shocked by this revelation.

"I didn't mean for it to be at your expense!" she said fretfully, but there were no tears in her eyes; she didn't even seem that apologetic. It was as if she was telling a well-rehearsed story. "I'm sorry that you've taken the brunt end of papa's hatred and abuse! And I am sorry that I have turned my back on you. I don't know how to make it right!"

Jade continued to lay motionless, not attempting to respond.

"I'm so sorry," Pearl repeated.

Jet rolled his eyes disdainfully and walked to the window.

"So, if you saw this happening," Esmeralda asked as she stood from the bed. "Then what else have you seen?"

Pearl glanced at Ruby for far longer than expected. It made her feel self-conscious like she had done something terrible.

"Ruby can see the dead," Pearl finally said, and she froze. Jade's eyes finally snapped open and met her stare. Esmeralda and Jet peered at her with… fear, perhaps? Or was it disgust?

"Is that what you can do?" Jet boomed. "I could never figure out your gift, but now I can see the decay inside you. It festers deep within!"

Ruby flushed in embarrassment. His tone was that of revulsion and judgment. She was rotting from the inside, wasn't she? No wonder she never felt right. She wanted to curl into a ball and wither away.

"It isn't a curse. It is a gift!" Pearl snarled at him, and his eyes widened at her ill-mannered tone. "Death isn't what you think it is!"

"What do you mean by that?" Jet asked slowly.

But she was already shaking her head. "I'm so tired of trying to deny it! I ignored Jade whenever she talked about magic because I didn't want it to be true. If she believed it was an absurd dream, she wouldn't try to strengthen her power and expose us. But it doesn't matter anymore because they've already returned to the city. They can feel it in the air. It is the very reason the prostitutes lost their lives."

Ruby glanced at the dead women. They were watching Pearl closely.

"What are you talking about?" Jet growled.

"Do you know how a Vampir feeds?"

Jet sighed loudly and pinched the bridge of his nose. "Well, of course, I do. But Vampirs are not real. They're a myth."

"No, they aren't," Pearl argued.

"It is written that Tannith De' Valles bound all creatures of the night from consuming blood," Jet reiterated. "If you're subjecting yourself to ridiculous tales, you might want to consider how they cannot feed!"

"We are Tannith's direct descendants," Esmeralda interjected. "The same magic that bound these creatures exists in our veins! If Vampirs and Lycans are freed, then all of humanity will cease to exist!"

"You expect me to believe that three angels were cast from heaven for their crimes against God and mated with human women who birthed these creatures to destroy the very people who worship him?" Jet argued, and Pearl nodded vigorously. "It's hard for me to hold faith in a fifteen-hundred-year-old book. Perhaps if there were more evidence to back up these theories, I would become a believer. Take a look at the witch trials. Sixty women were crucified because they were intelligent or questioned the word of men. It's all fables, Pearl. Men make up stories to appear far greater than they are or give meaning to a meaningless life."

"If magic flows inside us, then what is to say they don't exist?"

Ruby thought she had a point, but wouldn't there be more evidence of these creatures? Perhaps Vampirs and Lycanthropes didn't exist, yet it was feasible to say that a group of men fit this narrative into their own lives. It wouldn't be the first time a man had twisted the word of God for his own nefarious purpose.

"There's somefing not right about this," Helena blurted. "One of them is lying."

Ruby would have to wait until they were alone to ask what she meant. Something held her back from exposing them.

"They're in the room with us, aren't they?" Pearl demanded.

Ruby glanced back at her, smoothing her face to remain as neutral as possible.

"I fink it's her," Anne said.

"What are you talking about?" Jet hissed.

Pearl turned to the corner Ruby was focused on. "The prostitutes. Tell them we mean them no harm."

"Lie," Helena said. "They aren't to know 'bout us."

"They're here?" Jet yelled and glanced around the room wildly.

Pearl ignored him and grabbed her arm. "Will you tell them?"

"I really don't know what you're talking about." Ruby lied.

Pearl sighed impatiently. "He said they followed you."

"That's what I'm talkin' about," Helena wailed with a point of her finger.

"Who?" Esmeralda asked.

But Pearl shook her head, refusing to answer.

"Well, now that we're all on the same page," Jet drawled. "I need you all to help me take down the Kensington's and Atwood's."

Ruby's brows puckered. He never asked for help.

"Our power draws them in," Pearl pointed out.

"It doesn't matter. We are more powerful than a fiend if they even exist!"

Pearl threw Ruby a furtive look as if she had done something.

"Do you want the Atwood's to destroy our family? Because that is what's happening!"

Esmeralda's stare turned very grave as she stood from the bed. "Then you're going to kill us all."

Ruby tried not to show any fear; she had to be completely wrong. The devil wasn't real. Only men were.

XXXI
Jackson

"Are we actually going to meet with Adam while we are hungover?" Owen asked.

"I still feel drunk," Elijah admitted.

They exchanged glances and began to laugh mercilessly, but Jackson didn't find humor in the situation. Jade possessed magic. She was in more danger than anyone in the city. He had to get her out.

"What a night to remember," Owen bellowed after the humor faded, and he looked at Jackson behind him. "And what's the matter with you?"

Jackson shoved his hands in his pockets and stared at the cobbled road, deep in thought.

Owen placed a hand on his shoulder. "Come now, Jack, Jade was in your arms all night! How can you be upset about that?"

Jackson shook his head and looked away. "You don't understand."

Elijah threw an arm around the both of them and swayed an inch from his face. "Take her then if you want her!"

Jackson glared. "She isn't the type to be kept hidden."

Owen studied him carefully. "Perhaps you're right in a sense, but not everything needs to be shared with the world either."

"Exactly," Elijah blurted. The whiskey on his breath was overpowering.

"You are way too close to me right now," Jackson muttered with a wry grin.

Elijah and Owen laughed.

"I met Esmeralda in the graveyard," Owen stated in all seriousness.

Both Jackson and Eli looked at him in confusion. "What was that?"

"I was visiting Clara and Charlie when she walked up behind me," He admitted. "I- I've been meeting her in secret."

Elijah's smile dropped with a flat stare, but Jackson smiled. "I can see you together. Quite perfectly."

"She understands," Owen said. "And that is what it all comes down to, right? Someone to understand your pain and not judge you for it."

"See," Elijah blurted. "And I love booze. We all have passions in life!"

"Yes, but you can have Esmeralda," Jackson said dismissively, and a curious thought emerged. What if she possessed magic as well? "She can remarry within time. Jade is not a free choice."

"We can always kill Teddy," Elijah suggested, a petty laugh escaping.

He chuckled.

"I'll help you get her," Owen promised.

"We can't seriously kill him," he responded quietly.

Owen's lips curved. "I wasn't implying that we should, but he can be arrested for a fair number of daily crimes. We just need to expose him for the low life that he is."

Having Owen on his side meant everything, but there was still Jade's ability of magic. She was in danger.

"Hear, hear!" Elijah boomed.

Owen groaned.

"What is it?" Elijah asked.

"I really don't want to meet Adam today!" Owen admitted. "I just want food and a bed."

"Ah!" Eli gasped. "Kippers sound amazing!"

Jack's mouth twitched. "We could always visit Ms. June."

"We've been awfully rude lately," Elijah pointed out. "She may not want to see us at all."

"Even so," he answered brightly. "We should make it right."

"Look who decides to show up after a month!" Ms. June wailed when she opened the door, one hand perched on her ample hip. Her mouth dropped when she caught sight of Jackson and gasped, "You're back!"

She flung her arms around him and gave him a tight hug and a kiss on the cheek. "How are you?"

"I'm great," he answered smugly. "And you?"

She glared at Elijah and Owen. "Better when I'm not ignored! What do you want, Hadley? And what have you gotten yourself into? Who have you been fighting?"

"It's nothing!" Elijah remarked. "We've just been so busy with the recent murders that we've barely had time to sleep!"

"You know we love you, Junie darling!" Owen added.

Jackson pulled her in tightly. "Don't be angry with them!"

She leaned her head back and eyed him. "You're completely pissed and want food, don't you?"

He chuckled. "Perhaps a bit, but that doesn't mean we don't miss you."

She giggled when he nuzzled the side of her face and swatted his hand. "All right, sit down and shut up, will you? I've got babies sleeping upstairs!"

Ms. June took care as always. She poured them each a cup of coffee, placed cigarettes in front of Elijah, and filled their plates with eggs, kippers, and bread.

"What else have I missed?" she asked after sitting down with her own cup of coffee.

"Jack is in love," Elijah blurted as he shoveled a spoonful of eggs into his mouth.

Ms. June gasped.

He lowered his fork and threw a very vexed glare in Elijah's direction.

"You are?" Ms. June gushed.

"No, I'm not," he answered quietly.

"Yes, you are," Owen challenged, causing Elijah to yell, "ha!" in triumph.

Jack's eyes cut to him. "I never told you I was in love!"

"Perhaps love is a little preemptive," Owen admitted. "But I have never in my life seen you happy until last night. Not even when you were smitten with Isabella, which was more toxic than anything. There is a strong connection with Jade."

"I hardly know her!" Jack protested in defense.

"You know enough," Owen answered dismissively.

"Oh, darling," Ms. June said and grabbed his arm. "I'm so happy for you!"

"Don't be," Jack said and returned to his plate. "I can't have her."

"And why is that?" Ms. June snapped. "Did she deny you? The tramp! It's her loss, love!"

His lips raised as he said, "She is engaged to another."

Her face went slack. "You've gone and fallen in love with a taken woman? Are you stupid?"

Owen and Eli sniggered.

"I am not in love!" Jack cried indignantly, but he wasn't fooling anyone. "It's not possible!"

"Says who?" Owen objected. "Can it even be measured?"

"I'd say no," Elijah muttered through bites. "It is different for everyone, and you said you wanted her for yourself. If the intention weren't to love, she'd be the mistress you kept hidden."

Ms. June's eyes narrowed. "And just who is this girl?"

Jack refused to meet her eye as he mumbled, "Jade Calvert."

"As in William bloody Calvert's daughter?" Ms. June yelled, which caused Elijah to tap her arm and say, "Shhh… babies are sleeping upstairs!"

She smacked him.

"I'm not in love," Jack repeated darkly.

"That sounds exactly like something someone would say when they are trying to deny their feelings," Elijah disputed through another bite.

Ms. June stared at him incredulously.

"Owen is also in love," Elijah revealed carelessly.

Owen punched him in the shoulder.

"Ow!" he whimpered with a laugh in protest.

"That is not even close to what I said!" Owen snarled.

"Oh, don't act like that isn't where this infatuation is headed!" Elijah grumbled.

She placed a hand on her hip and rounded on him. "Don't tell me she's married!"

"She was," Owen replied hesitantly.

Her fingers tapped on the table. "Widowed?"

Owen nodded.

"It's the other one, isn't it?" She cried. "The eldest Calvert girl?"

When Owen failed to answer, she pointed a finger. "How dense can the two of you be! Those girls are not to be messed with! You may as well put targets on your backs because if any of those blokes catch onto your mindless behavior, you'll end up six feet under!"

"If Eli kept his mouth shut, no one would suspect a thing!" Jack muttered with a scowl.

"Is that why the pair of you are banged up? They are starting to suspect, aren't they?" She rubbed her forehead. "My gods, you will get yourselves killed over women!"

Eli reached for her hand and pulled it from her face. "No one suspects a thing."

Owen raised his brow at the blatant lie.

"He's right," Jack agreed. "Elijah and I had a drunken misunderstanding, is all."

"Oh! Is that all?" Ms. June wailed. "You are turning on yourselves now, and it's not a problem?"

"We haven't turned on each other," Eli said. "It was a stupid fight that will never repeat itself." He glanced at Jack. "Right?"

He nodded. "Right."

She rubbed her forehead. "The lot of you are going to make my heart stop!"

The conversation thereafter was much calmer. They laughed while recanting the memories of youth and how June came into their lives. Her cheeky grin met them each time they praised her affections, and despite her initial rebuttal, she would never turn the boys away. They connected in ways that couldn't be entirely explained. Some people enter your life and simply become your heart and soul. And for the Hadleys, June was irreplaceable, even if they didn't see her every day.

A busty brunette quickly entered the kitchen with a fearful look. "I don't mean to interrupt, but something terrible has happened on Piscott Avenue and High Street."

"What is it?" Ms. June barked.

"Emily and Julianne swear there's been another murder!"

All three Hadleys stood without further explanation, each kissing Ms. June on the cheek with their thanks.

"I hate to eat and run," Owen began.

She waved him off. "Just promise you'll catch the bastard!"

He nodded before the three headed out the door.

"He's getting more confident," Owen commented as they briskly walked.

"I'd say!" Elijah said gruffly. "Back-to-back murders?"

"He's spiraling," he stated. "Whatever control he had is slipping."

"That could be good or bad," Elijah said. "The tendency to make a mistake is greater, but so will the body count."

Thunder suddenly crashed above, and their heads turned upwards. The sky was as procellous as the sea before them and full of chaos, an ill omen.

Gone was the start of a beautiful morning.

They fell into a bout of silence as an angry mob met them. A group of Merfan's men pushed people aside as others carried a body wrapped in a sheet.

"What do you know?" Owen asked promptly.

"There were seven witnesses," Merfan answered as he ripped the wig from his head and scratched the sparse hair in its place. "Your suspect is of average height and well-built; all noted his fine clothing."

Jackson folded his arms. "Did anyone get a good look at his face?"

"Every one of them did," Merfan answered. "He had dark hair and a cleft chin."

"Teddy," Elijah muttered under his breath.

"He wasn't wearing a mask?" Owen asked.

"A mask?" Merfan repeated. "What kind of mask?"

"Never mind," he said. "None of them recognized the suspect?"

But Merfan was staring at Elijah with a haughty smile formed on his purple cheeks. "Did your brother finally snap and beat the piss out of you?"

Elijah pursed his lips.

"Did anyone recognize the suspect?" Owen reiterated.

Merfan huffed. "Would I be here talking to you if they did?"

"Have you identified the deceased?" Owen pressed, not in the mood for light banter given the current situation.

"Charlotte Dubois."

Elijah cursed under his breath.

"Her heart was missing. Just like the other one."

They shared a look.

"Were there any flowers in her hand?" Jackson asked.

Merfan nodded. "The same as before."

"Which?"

Merfan sighed. "Black Dahlia's, I think. They weren't like the ones left in Helena's hand. They were the same as the last murder."

Jackson gazed at Owen. This deadly game between these sadists was going to claim a lot of victims.

"One takes their blood and places Landini lilies in their victims hands. The other cuts out their hearts and places black dahlia's," Owen murmured. "It's very peculiar, I almost think..."

"You almost think, what?" Elijah asked when he trailed off.

Owen's voice lowered, "There is something otherworldly about it. Men cannot simply be this evil."

Jackson swallowed the fear that was tempting his faith. Men were evil, and Bel Deaux was no doubt worse than hell itself.

"Thank you for coming on such short notice," Adam Riley said as he fumbled with the papers on his desk, searching for the correct file before handing it over to Owen. "I don't even know where to begin or how to elucidate the subject."

"How about you start at the beginning," Jackson suggested. He was annoyed they were even here. Why Owen agreed to this meeting when there were multiple murderers on the loose was confusing as hell. But his brother seemed to think there was something vital with Adam's inquiry on patient sixty-one.

The doctor sighed. "I have never been a man of God, but there is no denying the existence of an afterlife with patient sixty-one. How else would you explain a man living in stage three decomposition?"

"What do you mean?" Owen asked while glancing up from the folder.

"He's a walking, talking corpse," Adam blurted with evident fear. "And he's extremely intelligent."

Jackson blinked several times over. "Are you on drugs?"

He sighed impatiently. "No, I'm not on drugs! He doesn't have a pulse, and he's decomposing, yet he's alive."

Jackson didn't know what to say. He couldn't gauge whether Adam was being truthful; he turned to his brother for an answer.

"There must be some mistake," Owen concluded. "He probably carries some disease to make one appear on the verge of death, like the plague."

"There is no mistaking this, he is dead, and he is alive!"

Owen was stunned into silence, but Jackson wasn't in the mood for the doctor's games any longer. The man was clearly bitter over their lack of accommodation toward Leonard Holloway. "You're wasting my time," he snapped and stood from his chair. "I'm not going to feed into your delusions."

"Why don't you at least take a look at him before you leave," Adam's voice shook with terror. "Then you'll be able to determine if I'm acting delusional or not!"

"You're the expert," Jackson murmured. "What do you need my opinion for?"

"I'm no expert in death," Adam replied wearily. "And frankly, patient sixty-one scares the hell out of me. I have spent all month in the abbey praying to God for forgiveness, for only he can absolve my sins, which I can see you understand." He nodded toward the cross hanging from Jackson's neck.

Jackson and his siblings were raised devoutly, and while he didn't necessarily keep up with his faith, he continued to wear a cross around his neck to remind him that not all was lost, but this wasn't about his beliefs. This was about stopping a murder before it happened again.

"You should know that begging God every night for forgiveness, knowing full well that you are inflicting pain on addled minds, again and again, won't save you from hell!" Jackson snarled, and Owen swore under his breath. "You're only cementing your fate!"

"And what do you know of God?" Adam snarled. "Wearing a crucifix won't save you either!"

"Perhaps it won't, but of the two of us, I'm not the one torturing innocent people for financial gain!"

"I'm not torturing them," Adam argued. "I'm helping them."

"I think you missed a few crucial lessons in life."

Adam sneered at him.

"Sit down!" Owen ordered, causing Jackson to give him an incredulous stare. "Just listen to what he has to say! Why does everything have to be a fight with you?"

Jackson bit his lip as he sat back down.

"Where did you find patient sixty-one?" Owen inquired, giving Adam his full attention.

Jackson leaned languidly in his seat, placing one foot on the opposite knee. He was becoming bored and disinterested in Adam's lies. A man couldn't be alive and dead at once, and it annoyed him that Owen was playing along.

"He's been here as long as I have," Adam admitted. "And he was here for the entirety of Dr. Schull's career."

Owen glanced over, and Jackson rolled his eyes.

"What did Dr. Schull have to say about him?"

Adam rubbed his chin in contemplation. "He said he was a demon, and I agree with him, but I think you should ask patient sixty-one yourself. He will be happy to answer your questions."

"Five minutes," Owen answered before he could deny him, and Jackson held back what he truly wanted to say.

"Thank you," Adam replied with a sigh of relief. Jackson frowned when Adam began sticking cotton balls covered in petroleum jelly in his nose. "Patient sixty-one is rather smelly."

Owen grabbed two petroleum jelly balls and began stuffing his nostrils.

"I'm fine," Jackson muttered. He wasn't going to feed into the deception.

"Suit yourself," Adam replied.

He led them down two flights of stairs, far enough to make him realize they were stepping underground. Patient sixty-one was locked in the basement, far away from anyone else.

He repelled backward when the distinct smell of death hit his nostrils, there was a fresh body decaying, and he immediately raised his hand to cover his nose. The smell was so overpowering he almost upheaved. "You keep your dead down here?"

"No, that's patient sixty-one, as I've said."

Jackson gave Adam an appalled look, but the doctor held out a small jar. "It will only get worse."

Jackson didn't hesitate and plugged his nose, although it only seemed to dim the smell as they continued down the dingy hallway. It wasn't as pristine down in the basement; the walls were yellowed from cigarette smoke and death.

Adam didn't hesitate to unlock the rusted door with a large crucifix hanging from it, and when he flung it open, it took several seconds for Jackson's eyes to adjust. There was a figure hunched in the corner of the room. He stepped through the doorway with Adam's assistance and was about to berate him for leading them to a corpse when the creature's head turned toward him.

He jumped backward when the sunken eyes reflecting his silver cross traveled upwards dully. "Ah, Dr. Hadley, I presume."

Jackson couldn't form any words. Patient sixty-one's entire face was putrefied, exposing his teeth and hinging on the grotesque. Even the skin from his arms had decomposed, uncovering muscle tissue and bones. Yet, that was nothing compared to the smell; the jelly couldn't hide the rotten and revolting scent of death. Adam was right. Patient sixty-one was a walking corpse.

"My appearance is quite appalling, I know," he admitted and ran a hand through his hair that had yet to be touched by the decay that inflicted his body. "My deepest apologies that you have to meet me in this state when my natural form is far more pleasing to both the eyes and nose. Yet, I cannot hide my excitement and fascination with your presence, for I have followed your work, and I find you quite interesting for a human. As are you, Owen."

Jackson glanced over at Adam, who had yet to step in the room, and then at Owen's frigid stance and bulged eyes.

"Aren't there some patients for you to torture?" the creature snapped at Adam.

"T-there is no need for, uh, theatrics, Caelum," Adam stammered and wrung his hands tightly together. "J-Jackson and Ow-Owen h-here won't know that you're j-joking."

The creature's eyes widened briefly, and his attention shifted back to Jackson. "Where are my manners?" He was standing directly in front of him in one swift movement. Jackson stumbled backward into Owen, and they slammed into the wall behind. "I apologize," the creature said quietly and stepped back. "I forget myself sometimes, even in my weakened state. However, my name is Caelum Black."

Jackson pressed himself further against Owen, shielding him; death had quite a terrifying face.

"I won't force you to shake my hand, of course," his steely gaze dipped to Jackson's crucifix, and a wry smile formed on his blistered lips. "You are a man of God, how peculiar. I wouldn't have guessed by your work."

"Old habits die hard," Jackson finally found his voice, and the corpse merely laughed. His canines and lateral incisors were elongated into a definite point.

"There is no need to worry," Caelum stated calmly. "I couldn't hurt you even if I wanted to, and I assure you, I don't."

"And why is that?" Owen asked, and Jackson was surprised at how calm his voice sounded when he could feel Owen's heart beating against his back.

"I am bound," he explained as he leaned against the far wall. "It is strictly forbidden."

Jackson blinked. Something stirred in his memory, but he could not quite recall what it was.

"Are you insinuating to be a creation of one of the Elders?" Owen demanded.

Caelum's daunting gaze landed on him. "What do you know of the Elders?"

"Our father was a historian and an archaeologist," Owen explained with some ease. "We were taught everything there is to know about this damned country!"

"Then you know how Julien Athos and Tannith De Valles saved their people from genocide," Caelum dared.

Jackson's brows knit together in confusion as Owen stepped out from behind him and walked toward the creature.

"It is written that Vikings invaded Valcour and eradicated the royal house of De Valles. They threatened to consume the entire continent of Sildione, a war ensued," Owen answered, and Caelum appraised him. "But my father didn't believe it was the Vikings at all. He believed the fallen angels Malachai, Obel, and Eliel eliminated the house of De Valles and took claim of the northern country, Valcour. Jebriel, the first Vampir, and Kael, the first Lycan, and Azrael, the first of the Nephilim were sent to create a Perennial world by order of the fallen. These immortals were referred to as the offspring of the sons of God and daughters of man. All who are cursed for eternity for their crimes against God."

"Your father is a very intelligent man," Caelum answered vaguely.

Jackson sank against the wall as the creature glanced back at him. He should remember everything his father ever said, but unfortunately, a vile man destroyed his childhood. He retained nothing but abuse and, thereafter, rage.

"So… what are you?" Jackson asked foolishly.

"I am long forgotten in your world," Caelum answered. "I have not heard the name whispered in quite some time. They say I'm a demon, and perhaps to an extent I am, although I never possessed a soul. I simply drank the blood of my prey, for I am a Vampir."

It simply couldn't be. Jackson paled, and his heart started to beat emphatically. But with a talking corpse standing before him, was it hard to believe that he was a demon who had survived for over a millennium?

Caelum's face crumbled, and he groaned painfully. His eyes turned black, and he bawled his shaking hands into fists.

Jackson and Owen glanced at one another.

"You need to control your emotions," Caelum grabbed his ears and bent over. "I cannot stand the sound; it's bending my sanity!"

"We aren't doing anything," Owen said.

"Then why are both of your hearts pounding?"

Caelum could hear their pulses, and he didn't know what was more terrifying, the reality of his words or the creature standing before him.

"He tortures his patients," Caelum nodded toward the forgotten doctor. "I can hear their screams."

Jackson and Owen turned to look at Adam, whose gaze was unfocused and glazed over. When they looked back at Caelum, he was laughing, exposing his elongated teeth once again.

"I want to go now," Owen muttered, and Caelum ceased at once.

"I can no longer live in this state!" he snarled. "The one who has the power to save me from this hell resides in the city, and I am unable to seek her! But oh, how I can feel her! She is in the ground, in the air. Taunting me, beckoning me to find her!"

Jackson paled as Jade's face came to mind. "What do you mean by that exactly?"

"If she only knew how I could protect her if she simply let me go."

Jackson suddenly felt ill. He, too, wanted to leave and never think of Caelum again.

"Are you trapped here?" Owen asked.

"As a creature who is bound, any symbolism of God confines me," he said with a nod toward Jackson's necklace. "Your old habits have unwittingly protected you, as does the cross hanging on my door; it is why the doctor refuses to set foot in the room and douses himself in holy water."

"Are you the last of your kind?" Owen asked.

Caelum laughed. "You must be wildly naive to think there is only one Vampir left in existence. Every single species of the night survived the crusades, which is why we were bound by Tannith De Valles."

"Then how many are there?" Owen demanded.

"There are about a dozen Vampirs left and a handful of Succubus, which wouldn't take long to repopulate should we become unbound," he answered swiftly and sure. "That is not counting the countless Lycans scattered across Sildione. One of which is my brother."

"Lycans?" Jackson repeated.

"One who suffers from Lycanthropy," Owen answered under his breath. "The ability to transform into a wolf at whim." Jackson opened his mouth when Owen added, "I believe they differ from werewolves who have no control of their mind and are ruled by a full moon."

"Some werewolves survived, and so did the Nephilim and their kin, the Shedim, frightfully terrible creatures. I must warn you, if I am unbound by the witch who lives in the city, so will all of the Perennial race, and the Shedim are mindless creatures with no conscious. They are the nasty ones written about, who rip flesh from bone and you'll be alive when they do it." Caelum admitted as he assessed Owen. "It will only be a matter of time before we are freed. Tannith's direct line survived after all these years, and they reside here in Bel Deaux. They can, and they will save us!" He started laughing when Jackson grabbed onto his knees and breathed out slowly. The creature was referring to Jade; there was no other rational explanation.

If heaven and hell truly existed, then Caelum could never be released from this asylum.

The cab was silent between Jackson and Owen once again. He held onto the crucifix hanging from his neck in a tight fist and released an unstable breath. The hair on his skin rose with every detrimental thought; he had never felt fear to this extent in his entire life. A nagging feeling in the back of his mind told him Jade was the object of the creature's desire, a terrifying thought. His chest constricted when he pictured her at the Vampirs side.

"One of those things had to have killed Helena and Anne," Jackson said just as his thoughts threatened to destroy him.

"They are bound by magic and unable to feed," Owen answered dismissively.

"Someone helped it!" Jackson screamed, forcing Owen to look at him. "All of the blood from Helena and Anne's bodies were drained! Don't you find that odd, considering how they feed?"

"It's Dominic," Owen said flatly before glancing back out the window.

Jackson gaped at him. "How do you figure?"

Owen closed his eyes. "Helena and Anne were last seen with a man wearing a gas mask. He used to wear one daily; the only person I've ever seen do this besides a plague doctor or sick patient. He also has an affinity for rare flowers, and he went to medical school with you."

Jackson paled. His cousin never once crossed his mind, yet it made sense. He was caught torturing animals as a youth, though the Queen brushed it off as a boy acting like a boy. He has also been accused of rape.

"I don't believe he is acting alone. However, I cannot point the finger by mere circumstance as Merfan does. I have been tailing him in secret. I want to trust Cillian, but I'm worried."

"So, what do we do?"

"We?" Owen repeated. "We aren't going to do anything. I will tail him while you act none the wiser."

"What?" He scoffed.

"We have to tread carefully. We aren't the only ones watching."

"Then what about the Vampir?"

He shrugged. "We will never mention him again."

"Were you not in that room with me just now?" Jackson wailed. "How can you not be worried?"

"Because he is bound."

"But he said-"

"No one is going to release a demon. Even if there is someone in Bel Deaux who possesses magic, as he says, they wouldn't release a creature whose very purpose is to drink blood to live!"

Jackson held his tongue, unsure why he could think of nothing but Jade. She may not release him intentionally, but she has no control over herself. He tightened his fist once again.

"We aren't going to talk about it to anyone," Owen barked. "I don't want to cause an unnecessary panic."

"The city has been in a panic for the last month!" He hissed.

"All the more reason to keep quiet on the matter."

Jackson gawked at him.

Owen sighed. "Look, I don't have the answers, and quite frankly, I don't have any words for what transpired. I simply… do not know."

"So, we do nothing?"

"What can we do, Jackson?" Owen yelled. "Caelum is bound for now, which is the safest circumstance, and unless you wish to track down this supposed person with magical powers, there is literally nothing we can do!"

He breathed out, pinching his nose, still hesitant to bring up Jade. And in all honesty, he didn't owe her a damned thing. His silence made no sense, but he had to be sure before he made his brother aware and accused the girl, which could lead to her death. "What about Elijah?"

"What about him?"

"Are we keeping this from him?"

"Of course not," Owen muttered. "I suppose we have no choice. We should have a family meeting. Create a plan of action in the case Caelum does get released."

His words did nothing to ease Jackson's mind. With hell hanging over their heads, it was only a matter of time before everyone he loved would be at risk.

"I don't even know where to begin, so I'll just come out and say it," Owen stated from the head of the table. Elijah, Avis, and James were seated beside him as Jackson stood in the doorway stoically. "Dr. Adam Riley from Bellevue asked us to look at a particular patient." He glanced over at Jackson, and the others followed his gaze. "A patient known as sixty-one resides in the depths of the asylum and has for quite some time."

Elijah's brow puckered. "Why are you telling us this?"

"Because he isn't…he isn't human. He is a Vampir."

Elijah scoffed as Avis and James looked stupefied. When neither Jackson nor Owen smiled or had a joke to follow, Elijah bellowed, "You're serious?"

"I know it sounds ridiculous."

"And made up," James muttered under his breath.

"You were too young to learn the history," Owen said. "And I don't have the time to explain, but I highly suggest you read father's journals."

James sat back. He hated not knowing the past, and that included their parents.

"This isn't some joke, although it sounds like one," Jackson interjected. "Patient sixty-one, or Caelum Black as he introduced himself, looks as if he has been dead for weeks, but he isn't. And that's because he is bound."

The collective breath from the table made him still.

Elijah sat back in his chair. "Bound as in bound by Tannith De Valles in the eighth century?"

"Yes," Owen answered.

Elijah and Avis didn't even bat an eye. "What do we do?"

"What, no further questions?" Owen barked. "You're not going to ask if Jackson and I are sane?"

"You seem to forget what father instilled in us," Avis answered. "How much of a threat is Caelum?"

"As of right now, he isn't."

"How probable is it that there will be a day when he is?" Elijah asked.

"That I cannot answer. He seems to believe someone in this city can unleash him."

"Then we have to find this person before he does," Elijah stated.

Little did he know they already had, and for the first time in his life, he held the truth from his siblings. He had to get to Jade first.

"We will keep on as if nothing is out of the ordinary," Owen stated. "We will continue to look into the Dollhouse Slayer murders, although there is a chance that these creatures may be connected somehow. How? I am not sure. But we will keep quiet on the matter, and if by some horrible chance, these things get released, we will flee to the house in Berrone and plan from there. Agreed?"

“Agreed.” they murmured.

When Owen looked back at him, he looked positively terrified. A reflection of how he felt, but he wasn't as concerned about the creatures as he should be. He had finally comprehended the weight of the power Jade held. It was so much grander than he originally came to terms with.

Caelum talked about Tannith De Valles direct line, which meant there was a possibility Jade wasn't the only one in her family who possessed this power. If Jet had similar abilities, that would be a very frightening aspect indeed.

XXXII
Elijah

"She was seeing him." Genevieve Smith confirmed as she glared at Elijah from the bed, her arms were folded over her chest, and her sister Antoinette stood by her side. They were suspicious of him when he paid for an hour of their time, yet it didn't involve getting undressed. The red-headed twins were very popular and often bought together. They earned far more than anyone else in the Dollhouse.

Elijah asked, "Which room did he use?"

Genevieve huffed.

Elijah's eyes raised from his notepad with her refusal to answer. He dropped his hands in annoyance. "I told you I'd pay double for a simple conversation. This should be the easiest money you have ever made!"

"A simple conversation?" Genevieve hissed. "You want me to spill Lord Calvert's secrets! Lives have been taken for far less regarding him!"

"I won't tell anyone," Elijah said. "As far as anyone knows, we are having a good time!"

"Doesn't sound like it," Antoinette muttered.

Elijah rolled his eyes and tucked his notepad into his jacket. He walked over to the bed and pushed against its back so that the frame slammed against the wall repeatedly.

The twins giggled in response, and Antoinette began to fake a moan.

Genevieve shook her head, but a smile lingered on her lips. She jumped from the bed and stood next to Elijah to whisper in his ear, "He never sees anyone here. He takes them away and brings them back."

"How long?" he grunted through his actions.

"Depends," she said. "On some occasions, it was just a few hours. On others, it was for days at a time."

"Days!" he repeated. "I suppose I shouldn't be surprised. He wouldn't be the first lord to have a separate flat from his manor."

"She was sick right before she disappeared," Antoinette said suddenly, and the pair glanced at her. Genevieve looked furtively at the door and mimicked her sister's false moans. Elijah continued to push against the bed as Antoinette walked closer.

"Miss Louise was worried she might have a babe in her belly, but Isabella never said a word, and when she disappeared, we were instructed never to speak of it."

Elijah frowned. "Why?"

"The Lords in this town are very dangerous, Mr. Hadley," Genevieve answered curtly. "And we like our teeth right where they are!"

Elijah bit back a curse.

Genevieve began to muss up her hair, then stated loudly, "I'd heard of your expertise, Mr. Hadley! But now I know! How will another man compare?"

"Yes, that was the best we've ever had!" Antoinette followed her actions.

Elijah nodded with the realization that they were done sharing information.

Both girls began to plant painted kisses on his cheeks and neck. Antoinette reached up and ruffled his hair as she whispered, "You need to speak to a man by the name of Cromwell. When he shows up, the girls never return."

As she pulled away, Elijah's eyes followed her.

"He lives in the Gas-light district with his mistress, or so they say," Genevieve added and untied his trousers before giving the door a pointed look. "She works for the opera house. It's where he spends his nights when he isn't getting rid of strumpets for Calvert."

There was more he wanted to ask but decided not to push it. He gave them a bow and handed over paper money. "My thanks, ladies. I do hope we can meet again."

He then strode to the door and opened it. A few prostitutes and a chap named Donovan Scotts lingered in the hallway. He flashed a roguish grin and began to tie his trousers for effect as he stalked passed.

Duke drove him to the opera house, where he acquired tickets for the upcoming show and the guest list. It took some negotiating and bargaining with the vendor to attain the highest-priced tickets, but Lady luck was on his side, and he slipped back into his cab.

He couldn't ignore his anxiety, wishing to go back to ignorance. Before Owen and Jackson told them about the Vampirs hidden in the city and how they may or may not be the very reason for the killings of these women. Though, William Calvert had some explaining to do. Owen told them to carry on and pretend as if nothing was out of the ordinary. Live as if they didn't know a thing, which was easier said than done.

He found Jackson and Owen in the library. Owen stood over their father's oak desk, looking at the dozens of papers that littered the surface. Jackson was throwing darts at a target to the left of the fireplace roaring with a fire.

"Have I got a story for you!" Elijah yelled when he entered the room.

Jackson smirked at his appearance and turned back to the dartboard.

Owen gave him an irritated look. "I really don't have the patience to listen to another sex story, Eli."

Elijah paused with a frown and quickly recovered when he realized what Owen was referring to. "This is nothing. It's all for show." And pointed to his face where Antoinette and Genevieve left red-stained kisses; he must have looked ridiculous to the ticket vendor. "I was questioning the Smith twins, and they were frightened someone would overhear, so we pretended to shake the sheets."

Jackson barked out a laugh.

"And what did the Smith twins have to say?" Owen asked as his eyes dropped back to the papers on the desk.

Elijah delved into the story, first with Philip Preston's version at the gazette and ending with the man named Cromwell.

"Derrick Cromwell?" Jackson said swiftly with a turn. "As in father's old business associate?"

Owen stood at full height. "I'd forgotten about him."

"I doubt it's Derrick," Elijah countered. "They mentioned that his mistress worked at the opera. Derrick would be well into his eighties by now, and he was overly frail when we last saw him! How could he keep up with a mistress and murder prostitutes on the side?"

"It must be their son, then," Owen answered and began to pet his beard. "So, Calvert is having prostitutes murdered when they become pregnant with his bastards?"

"Philip certainly believes so," Elijah said. "And while the twins couldn't confirm Isabella was with child, it was suspected, and they were told to shut up about it. Calvert has direct ties to two prostitutes who are now dead!"

"He may not be the Dollhouse Slayer," Jack murmured. "But he definitely has some incriminating evidence stacked against him."

"It's starting to come together," Owen agreed.

"What are you talking about?" Elijah hissed. "William is our main suspect!"

"I think it's Dominic," Owen countered.

His stomach dropped. "Dominic?"

"I cannot say for sure," Owen answered. "But there have been subtle coincidences in regard to him. I would like to catch him in the act, although it seems unlikely. I've been tailing him in secret. I don't want to be instructed to stay away from him as well."

"The flowers," Elijah muttered. Their cousin bred rare flowers and plants; he was very well-versed in botany.

"And the gas mask," Jackson added.

"A man in a gas mask was seen with Helena and Anne before they disappeared," Owen explained at his confused expression.

"Then who do we investigate?" Elijah asked.

"Both," Owen said. "I will continue to tail Dominic while you interrogate Cromwell."

"As I said before, it doesn't matter," Jackson huffed. "He has gotten away with murder for years. He's far above the law, and I cannot see how we can stop him!"

The room stilled except for Jackson's darts. Elijah nodded with his acceptance or lack thereof. He refused to give up. "How do you feel about going to the opera tonight?"

"I can't," Owen said. "I'm going to patrol Trinity Row."

Elijah pursed his lips, focusing on Jack. "What about you? Are you up for the opera?"

Jackson hit the bullseye and glanced at him briefly. "That depends," he then walked to the board and plucked the darts from it. "Are you going to buy me dinner first?"

"Depends," Elijah answered with a grin as he joked, "Are you going to get drunk and fight Teddy Kensington?"

Jackson laughed once until Owen threw a sharp glare in his direction. He rearranged his face and said, "The opera doesn't interest me."

"It would be nice of you to assist me, Jack," Eli prodded, and he was starting to suspect there was one way he could get his brother to go. "The Calvert's are attending, and I mean all of them. His daughters, Jet, and their spouses."

Jackson lowered his hand and stared. Owen huffed as he turned back to the papers on his desk.

"Okay, I'll go," Jackson answered suddenly and placed the darts on the mantel.

"That didn't take much," Owen murmured and picked up a piece of paper to examine it.

Eli couldn't suppress the scowl that formed on his face. There was no denying that his brother would take the chance to see Jade. He just wished it didn't bother him so much.

"Are you going to bathe?" Jackson asked as he stalked past. "You smell like cheap hookers and booze."

Eli smiled as he followed him to the stairwell and boomed, "My two favorite things!"

"Please behave yourselves!" Owen called at their backs. "You don't need to get locked up for running your mouths!"

"We'll be on our best behavior!" Elijah yelled back.

Jack threw him a wry grin.

"Well," Elijah laughed and said, "better than usual."

"And for the love of God, NO FIGHTING!" Owen shouted from below.

"Did you hear that?" Elijah asked Jackson.

He chuckled, and they turned to their separate quarters to get cleaned up.

Jackson was standing in the foyer and tying his white tie in the mirror when Elijah came down. He stood behind Jack and began to straighten his suit. As he looked over his reflection, he muttered, "God damn, I am one handsome mother fucker."

Jack's cheek lifted as his eyes slid to meet Eli's.

"You're not so bad yourself!" he said and lightly smacked his arm.

Jack's eyes wandered back to his reflection, and the smirk dropped.

"Did Owen leave yet?" Eli asked as he turned to slide on his jacket and top hat.

"Yes," Jack answered before giving his appearance one last approval and faced Eli as he adjusted his cufflinks. "I'm to watch over you. He was adamant that I forbade you to get pissed and make a mockery of yourself amongst the lords and ladies of this city. Ladies being the main objective, but he seems to forget what happens when you and I are out together."

Elijah laughed once. "Remember when you lost father's horses to a mule with a bum leg in one hand of poker!"

"Bessie was a fine enough animal," Jack reasoned as he slipped his hat on.

"Jack," Elijah said with a touch of irony in his voice. "Those horses were some of the finest bred horses in Bel Deaux!"

"That's quite debatable," he mumbled, hardly bothered.

"And then you drugged Merfan and posed as a mutton shunter to steal the horses back from Richard Beauregard!"

"Oh, yeah!" Jackson snorted in mirth.

Elijah paused and looked at his brother once over. "You really aren't any better of an influence than I am."

"I never said I was."

Elijah chuckled. "We should be fine as long as we don't have more than two glasses, maybe four." he said sensibly as they walked out of the door. After a pause, he insisted, "Six at the most."

"Don't worry," Jack assured with a grin and opened his jacket to reveal a flask. "I brought provisions."

Elijah mimicked his brothers actions and said, "As did I."

Jackson laughed deeply as they slid into the cab.

"I find it interesting that the twins were willing to speak about Calvert," Jackson stated after taking a swig from his flask. "Most shut down when his name is mentioned."

"Can you blame them?" Elijah rasped and grabbed the liquor from his pocket. "They are being targeted. Wouldn't you want it to stop?"

"I want it to stop, and I'm not in the victim's profile," he admitted, and his long legs bounced up and down. He drummed his fingers on his knees.

Despite his rising jealousy, it was refreshing to see Jack interested in a girl again.

"You seem different," Elijah observed.

"I feel different."

"How so?" Elijah asked.

"I don't know."

"How about we start from the beginning?"

"I don't want to talk about it," Jackson muttered, closing his right hand into a fist.

Elijah observed him but said no more on the matter.

When they arrived at the Opera house, it was flooded with people making their way through the doors. The nobles were out for a night of frivolity, ignoring truths and pretending all was well in Bel Deaux. Elijah and Jack waited until most were inside before entering the building. They relieved their hats and coats outside of their box and stepped inside. They were on the upper deck amongst the wealthiest of citizens.

Elijah glanced over at Calvert's designated booth, but they weren't present. Instead, Katerina, Adelaide, Theodore Kensington, and Edward Wright were there.

"Where are the Calvert's?"

Jackson's gaze drifted to the booth, landing on Teddy for the briefest moment before settling on Katerina. "I haven't a clue."

As they watched, Pearl and Augustus joined them in the booth.

"It's so strange," Elijah muttered. "Why did the Calverts marry into them? Two years ago, the Atwoods were unknown members of society. What's the draw?"

"It's got to be blackmail," Jackson answered as he tore his eyes away from Katerina. "William wouldn't have agreed to the marriage with anyone other than the Elite without some damaging evidence."

"That's what I said, but Owen thought it was ridiculous."

"You know that's because Owen could care less about their tawdry lives, and let's face it," Jackson stated flatly as he pulled out his flask again. "If prostitutes with a connection to Calvert weren't being murdered, we wouldn't either. We should leave them alone for tonight. Our mission is Cromwell, not the Atwood's."

Elijah's eyes slid back to the booth, and something piqued his interest when his attention landed on Pearl's husband. "Augustus has dark hair and a cleft chin."

Jackson's eyes doubled as he glanced back at Atwood.

"Everyone knows Teddy, but Augustus drifts into the background. What if he is the other murderer?"

"Gainsley was following him for whatever reason," Jackson answered. "He could have interrupted him as he was posing Anne."

Their conversation evaporated as the players began. He positively loathed the opera. He ripped the flask from Jack's hand and took another drink; this would be a long night.

Jack shared his sentiments on the theater; they couldn't get out of the booth fast enough at intermission. Elijah grabbed two glasses of champagne from a passing waiter and took a sip as he handed the other to Jack, who declined.

"That's fine," Elijah said after he swallowed the liquid. "I'll drink for the both of us."

"We need to keep our wits about us," Jack muttered as his eyes befell Teddy and Edward; the pair were stomping toward them. "Now, what do they want?"

Elijah took another drink.

"What are you doing here?" Teddy spat with his approach.

Elijah lowered his glasses and gave a frothy look. "We live in Bel Deaux. Why are you suddenly so surprised to see us about?"

"Because you two are up to something!" His glare settled on Jackson, who rolled his eyes. "You hate the opera. You wouldn't be here if you weren't scheming!" When Elijah opened his mouth to protest, Teddy said, "I've known you my whole life, remember?"

"We aren't scheming," Elijah snapped. "Now fuck off!"

Teddy took a step toward Jackson. "I should pulverize you for keeping my wife out until ungodly hours of the night!"

"She isn't your wife yet, and I didn't force her into anything. You are the one who likes to prey upon women, remember?" Jackson said, and Teddy's lip curled. "It was her choice to attend the wedding. I was merely looking out for her."

"She will be my wife in due time," Teddy snarled and took another step forward. "And I'll kill you if you so much as look in her direction again!"

Jackson shoved him backward with one hard push, and he stumbled over his own feet. Edward caught him, and they crashed into the opposing wall. Several people loitering in the hall glanced in their direction.

"You don't frighten me at all, you fucking ratbag!" Jack snarled. "You're a vazey meater who hides behind his father's name and power! I should pulverize you for assaulting Ollie!"

Movement caught Elijah's eye, and he glanced over to see Merfan heading their way. He muttered, "Coppers," under his breath.

"Why should I care about that little whore?" Teddy fumed, and Jackson's nose flared, his jaw clenching with anger. "I think the only way for us to settle this is down in the Vaults!" Elijah snorted in mirth, and Teddy threw him a murderous stare. "You think it's funny, do you?"

"I do, actually," Elijah admitted.

Teddy looked positively livid as if he wanted to punch Elijah but didn't dare with so many witnesses.

"Do it," Elijah taunted. If he wanted a fight, they would give it to him.

Teddy smiled slowly and glanced back at Jackson. "What do you say?"

"I don't fight anymore."

Teddy's eyes narrowed on Elijah's black eye. "Really? Considering how you sucker-punched me, I would say otherwise!"

"Go the fuck away!" Jackson hissed with a careless toss of his hand.

Teddy shook his head slowly and glanced at Edward. "That's a shame. I will have to take my aggression out on Jade!"

Jackson grabbed him by the collar before Elijah could make a move. "If you touch her, your sweet old mum will have to bury you in a closed casket!"

Teddy grinned nastily as Merfan and two officers crept up with their weapons drawn. "How about you and I settle this tomorrow night in the Vaults? Right after Oliver Beckett slaughters your little brother!"

Jackson slowly began to smile maniacally.

"Put him down, Jackson!" Merfan yelled, but Jackson didn't immediately release him. A dark shadow crossed his face. Elijah knew better than to intervene. It didn't take long for Merfan to lose his patience and yell, "I mean it!" It was only a pity that Teddy didn't comprehend what he was in for.

"I'll see you tomorrow night," Jackson muttered, shoving him back into Edward.

"Get out!" Merfan yelled.

"We're paying customers!" Elijah wailed.

"Not while you're out here assaulting people!" Merfan croaked and placed his gun back in the holder. "Get out, or I'll throw you in the bastille for the night!"

Elijah opened his mouth, but Jackson grabbed his arm and pulled him along, even when Teddy and Edward laughed at their backs.

"Dammit," Elijah hissed and ripped his arm back. "We're here to interrogate Cromwell!"

"Well, I suppose I fucked that up, didn't I?" Jackson muttered.

"Don't do this!" he bellowed, following Jackson resentfully down the stairs. "He isn't worth it!"

"That's rich coming from you."

"Do you really want to get into this again?" Elijah snapped.

"No, I don't."

"Then what are you doing?"

"Walking away."

"Don't tell me you're going to fight him!"

"I am."

"Owen won't tolerate it!"

"Yeah, well, Owen isn't my father," Jackson muttered, and he didn't turn back when Elijah stopped chasing him. There was no reasoning with him when he made up his mind. It was a wasted effort, just as this evening seemed to be. And while Jackson could handle himself no matter who provoked him, he couldn't let him go to the Vaults alone. There was no telling what would happen.

He cursed under his breath and followed his brother. Cromwell would have to wait until another time.

XXXIII
OLIVETTE

"Go then," Melody told Roslyn. They were sitting in the pub and passing a bottle, a daily ritual. "There is nothing in this city for yew."

"I can't leave you behind," she said.

"Yew don' need us, lovey," Elizabeth answered. "We can take care of ourselves."

"You won't try and make it?" Ollie asked with incredulity. Elijah Hadley gave Roslyn more than enough money to make their way.

"For what?" Melody snapped after lowering the bottle. "I won' survive in the country where there is no work. No one will hire an old whore like me for nuffing. Nah, I will stay right here."

"Yeah, this is my city," Elizabeth added. "It's where I belong."

Ollie could respect and admire them, but that wasn't to say they should endure the harsh environment of Trinity Row.

"Yu'll make a good governess," Elizabeth hedged. "I can see yew wiv children. Yew has a nice gentle way 'bout ya."

"It's for the best," Melody prodded. "Blake and Teddy won' be able to hurt yew no more."

Roslyn's lip quivered, and they hugged her, leaving Ollie to blink back tears. How none could see the humanity in these women was ridiculous.

When she pulled back, she looked at Ollie expectantly. "What about you?"

"I'll be just fine," she said, trying her best to give a genuine smile.

"We'll look out for her," Elizabeth added and winked when she gaped at her with astonishment. "Yur one of us now."

She smiled. It was nice to feel acceptance for once in her life.

They took a cab over the grand bridge to the gaslight district, spending the afternoon in the west end. Roslyn bought them each a new dress with Elijah Hadley's money, a warm meal, and a trinket to remember her by.

After saying their goodbyes, they watched Roslyn board a railcar, waiting until the passenger car sped off before they made their way back to the bridge.

"Yew shoulda went wiv her," Melody said after nearly ten minutes of silence.

"I have to find my father," she said adamantly.

The woman huffed when they neared their room. "Yew best gets in. We'll be there shortly."

Ollie trudged toward the door, giving Melody and Elizabeth one last look before disappearing into the night.

The following evening came like any other, the air was frigid, and fog hovered in the streets like the plague—a clandestine setting for the macabre events unfolding in the city. The citizens of Bel Deaux were in a state of shock and vigilance toward the unknown danger lurking in the darkness.

Ollie was kicked out of the boarding house in the early morning hours. Neither Elizabeth nor Melody ever returned. She wandered the streets all day looking for them, but as the daylight hours were ending, she was filled with anxiety about what may have happened and prayed it was nothing wicked. The women were far harder to track down than she imagined, and she feared what it meant.

"Melody was here this morning. She got into a nasty fight with another prostitute," one barman growled. "The other one dragged her out of here."

She sighed in relief. At least they were seen today, which meant they were okay. "What about Christopher Ashford? Do you know him?

"Oh, yeah, I know him but you won' find him around here," the barman said as he locked the door of his pub. "You won't find anyone here. Jackson Hadley is returning to the ring tonight. Everyone in the city will be down at the Vaults."

"Jackson Hadley?" she repeated, and her heart began to race. "He is fighting tonight?"

"Yes."

"Where can I find the Vaults?"

The barman looked mortified that she would even ask. "Oh, you don't want to go down there. It isn't safe for a young lady who is all by herself."

"Please, I need to find him!"

"Why? What do you want with a man like Christopher anyway?" the barman asked, not realizing she was referring to Jackson. "Does he owe you money?"

"I'm not a prostitute!" she growled. "Christopher Ashford is my father!"

"Oh, yeah," he muttered after some thought. "I remember you."

She grimaced, unsure if it was worth finding him anymore. He would probably turn her away.

"Can you please tell me where I can find the Vaults?"

The man was already shaking his head. "I told you the Vaults aren't safe for little girls like you."

"I'm not a little girl, and I have a knife."

He laughed. "So does the Dollhouse Slayer!"

"Please," she pleaded, and a sob nearly escaped. She couldn't take it anymore. She couldn't handle the constant ill-natured behavior from others. She just wanted to see some decency as she had with the Hadleys.

Whatever the man caught on her face tore the smile from his lips, and his shoulders sagged. "The Vaults are down in the warehouses by the Kinnedale Harbor, right off Milton Street."

"Thank you," she said with a swift turn.

"Look after yourself, would ya?"

Ollie glanced over her shoulder. He appeared genuinely concerned for her well-being. "Don't trust anyone, no matter how good they look."

Ollie gave him a swift nod and went on her way, although she felt more at ease.

The Kinnedale Harbor was six blocks from the pub. The night was terrifying, and the closer she got to Milton Street, the darker it became. The fog was thick, and it grew colder. She couldn't help the sharp glances over her shoulder or what sounded like footsteps behind her. She didn't know if she was being followed or if her mind was playing tricks on her. She gripped her knife tightly and sprinted toward the large warehouse when it came within sight.

A flood of people entered the building, and she gave her very last copper to the doorman for entrance. She was exhausted and hungry, and her teeth were chattering as she followed the mass of people heading toward the stands.

The warehouse itself was dark and had a pervasive smell about it. She slowly descended a flight of stairs behind a line of people. Water dripped from the ceiling, and there were grimy puddles everywhere. A stadium with brilliant lighting illuminating from its center was on the ground floor.

When she stepped through the break in the enclosure, she gasped. The amphitheater for the Vaults themselves looked as if it could fit hundreds of people, and it appeared as if there were that many here, laughing, drinking, and smoking. She sat down abruptly on the first row, not wanting to draw too much attention as she scanned the crowd. She was completely astonished by the Vaults themselves. It was like a whole other world down here, which caused her anxiety to heighten, afraid of what someone may do with their inhibitions lowered. She didn't see her father anywhere. She didn't see Elizabeth or Melody either. There were simply too many people to sift through.

"Ladies and gentlemen, boys and girls," a booming voice rattled through the speakers secured in each curve of the coliseum. "After a month of waiting, our returning champs from the double duel are here to take a jab at one another!" The crowd cheered as Ollie watched silently, shaking her leg strenuously as a distraction to calm her unsettled nerves. "May I introduce Oliver Becket and James Hadley!"

The crowd erupted, and Ollie's stomach dropped. Oliver was Timothy's brother. She didn't know he fought in the Vaults, but she didn't dwell on the thought. James Hadley walked out onto the ring with an arm held high. He was shirtless, and his hands were wrapped in white cloth.

"But I have a gift for you, ladies and gentlemen. As for our main event, for one night only, a new contender challenged a long-remaining titleholder! Theodore Kensington will stand against the iron fist himself… Jackson Hadley!"

If the crowd had gone wild before, it was nothing compared to the explosion when Jackson walked out onto the ring; he was shirtless, and his hands were also wrapped. People jumped up from their seats and screamed. Ollie rose from her seat, staring at Jackson wildly. Christopher Ashford was long forgotten. His torso, chest, and arms were sculpted, but he was covered in scars, looking more terrifying than ever. She would have felt bad for Theodore if he wasn't such a shameless person.

"Who will fate smile upon this night?" the announcer bellowed as Jackson and James walked toward their opponents, standing heads taller.
"Will the Hadleys stay undefeated, or will they be ripped from their thrones once and for all?"

Some jeers followed, but Ollie didn't look to see at whom they were booing. Jackson looked positively frightening as he glared down at Theodore. And at that moment, she prayed to God that he would win.

Jackson turned from the ring and joined Avis, Elijah, and two other men on the far left. She immediately ran toward them, shoving people out of the way and not giving a damn about the insults hurtling at her back.

She nearly made it to the Hadleys when a bouncer stepped in her way. "Not so fast, missy. Only fighters are allowed down here."

"Please, I know them," she begged, pushing against his hold. "AVIS!" she screamed, but it was too loud. Avis didn't glance in her direction.

"If you don't return to the stands, I'll throw you out on your ass!" the bouncer threatened as she continued to push against him and scream for Avis.

The bouncer whirled her around and grabbed her by the back of her hair, dragging her away.

"Let me go!" She screamed and tripped over her feet. Though it didn't slow him, he continued to drag her.

They came to a sudden halt, and the bouncer ripped out a fistful of her hair. She grabbed the back of her head and whipped around; relief came instantly. Jackson had pulled the man off her.

"She's with us!" he snarled.

The bouncer shrugged off Jackson and pointed his finger. "You keep your hands off me!"

"Ah, fuck off!" Jackson grumbled and pushed him on his way.

Avis held out her hand. She nearly started crying as she grabbed onto it.

"Are you okay?" Avis asked, pulling her to her feet.

"No," she muttered and wiped her skirt.

"Did he hurt you?" Jackson growled.

She shook her head vehemently, though the back of her head pulsed from where the bouncer ripped out her hair.

"Where have you been?" Avis asked. Her voice was gruff; she was furious. "You're sisters came looking for you!"

Her stomach dropped, never once thinking Kittie and Tellie would ever search for her, and suddenly, she felt mortified. "I've been looking for Christopher Ashford!"

"What did I tell you? If you need anything, you come to us!"

"I didn't want to bother you any more than I already have."

The lines on her face creased more prevalently, but she wasn't allowed to express what was on her mind because Jackson tugged at her arm. "The fight is starting!"

"Come on," Avis said and grabbed her hand. "I cannot believe you've been wandering the streets alone!"

Of course, it was stupid, but Avis wouldn't understand. "I couldn't stay with my sisters."

"Then why didn't you come to me?" Avis hissed.

"I don't know!" Ollie yelled, and Avis stopped in her tracks to gaze at her. Ollie couldn't bear the scrutiny and peeled her eyes away, her focus landing on Elijah. He was long-legged like Jackson and focused on the ring, as was the man standing beside him.

Elijah was, in a word, beautiful. She almost wished she could appreciate the fact. The structure of his face was uniform and well-defined. Every line and curve complimented the next. His hair had been slicked back with pomade, yet it didn't stay that way. It could be seen as endearing, but the pub owner's words flooded back: 'Don't trust anyone, even if they're good-looking.'

"Elijah, this is my friend Ollie," Avis muttered with little interest. Her eyes were trained on James. "Ollie, this is my brother Elijah."

His head whipped in her direction, eyes widening a fraction before giving her a curt nod. He looked away when she began to blush, and she was relieved by this. He may be attractive, but it still didn't change the fact that she had been raped and didn't want to be leered at. Tears threatened to spill down her cheeks as she snapped her teeth together to keep from crying out. Distraught that Theodore had taken her life. She wasn't sure she would ever feel normal again.

She glanced further at the man standing beside Elijah. He had dark hair, spectacles, and scruff on his face. "Owen, this is Ollie. Ollie, Owen."

"Nice to meet you," he said without taking his eyes from the youngest Hadley.

She gave a tight-lipped smile as Avis pointed at the others.

"This is our driver Duke," she said about the old man standing by Owen. "And our neighbor Pikitis."

They both tipped their hats at her.

A petite woman, who was at least a foot and a half shorter than the Hadley men, was dressed in trousers and a button-up jacket, sidled up next to Owen, and bellowed, "I thought we were going to miss James's fight!"

"Just on time!" he said and hugged her.

An average man followed. He had a round belly and a mustache. "I never thought I'd see the day you'd step into this ring again!"

"Neither did I." Jackson agreed.

After the woman gave them each a hug, she looked at Ollie questionably. "Elijah?" she asked with a raise of her brow.

"She isn't with me," he protested.

The woman gave Jackson a sharp look.

"She's Avis's friend," Jackson explained with a smirk. "Ollie, these are my best mates, Cordelia Calvert and Raoul Cheron."

"It's a pleasure to meet you," Cordelia said with a raise of her hand to shake.

Ollie felt the hair on the back of her neck rise. This woman may or may not be her aunt, which was a terrifying thought; the Calvert's were incredibly powerful and dangerous. Her eyes traveled down the woman's arm, and she stared at her hand disdainfully with no desire to touch it.

"Whatever you've heard about my brother," Cordelia snapped, dropping her hand and placing it in her pocket. "I'm the exact opposite."

Ollie blushed when everyone turned to look at her. "I'm sorry."

Cordelia shrugged, hardly bothered. "I'm used to it."

This made her feel even more foolish. It wasn't like her to offend anyone; it's why she kept to herself. She preferred being overlooked.

"Well, ladies and gents, this truly is a special evening. Let us all give a warm welcome to the ELITE!" An older man with white-blonde hair dressed in his best led a group of men, one of which was Abraham Kensington, to the boxes directly in the center of the stadium. They each had a woman on their arms. She stared at the older man sitting as head of the group. Was he truly her father?

Ollie didn't look away until the announcer yelled, "Let the fights begin!"

James raised his hands as Oliver charged him and threw a fist. James barely slipped the punch and swung his own, jabbing with his left hand, which connected against the man's chin with little impact. He took a quick step forward and threw a right hook. This time, Oliver's head flew in the opposite direction, and he stumbled.

"That's it!" Owen bellowed with a clap of his hands.

"C'mon, James!" Cordelia yelled.

He hit Oliver a third time, and Elijah placed his thumb and pointer in his mouth, whistling loudly. Raoul thrust his arms in the air while Avis jumped up and down. Their excitement was undeniable. Ollie got caught in the moment, yelling out her own support for the youngest Hadley.

James was sure-footed, despite being so tall. She figured Oliver would have the advantage to jump around, but James swatted him down like an irritating fly every time he came within reach.

Oliver charged toward James, who grabbed him by the hair and threw several fists into his head. Oliver barreled into his side, trying to pull his legs out from under him. James lost his grip on Oliver's hair and wrapped his arm around his neck and shoulder. James pushed back as Oliver tried to lift him off the ground unsuccessfully. Oliver gave up trying to throw him down and cocked his fist, swinging it directly into James' stomach. He lurched forward, releasing his hold, and an uppercut slammed into his jaw. He hurled backward, twisting to catch himself before he fell. But Oliver had taken the upper hand and kicked James in the stomach. The crowd groaned as his legs and arms gave out, and he fell flat on his face.

Ollie gasped and covered her mouth. Her heart was in her throat.

"GET UP!" Jackson shouted.

Oliver kicked him in the side twice as he tried to stand, coughing and dry heaving. Avis screamed.

A third, fourth, fifth, and sixth time he kicked James directly in the stomach with all his might.

Jackson yelled in frustration and flew into the ring. No one disputed this. The announcer encouraged him to annihilate Oliver, who didn't stand a chance when Jackson threw a combination into his face and landed with a devastating right into his jaw. He fell sideways, motionless on the ground. The crowd exploded, and the noise was deafening.

James propped himself on his knees, teetering back and forth. Jackson held out his hand, but he smacked him away after some minutes and stumbled onto his feet. He tried to push Jackson when he offered another hand; his words were completely unintelligible, but he looked positively livid. He raised his finger in Jackson's face, sneering as blood dripped from his lips and chin.

Jackson shook his head while saying something slowly, he was trying to keep his cool, but James wouldn't listen. He shoved against his shoulder again, and Jackson finally smacked his hand away. They instantly began shouting at one another.

"Uh oh," Cordelia uttered as Owen and Elijah rushed into the ring.

"Do we have another round between brothers?" The announcer asked, and the crowd chanted, "FIGHT, FIGHT, FIGHT, FIGHT!"

Ollie stopped breathing when Owen grabbed onto James and pulled him back. He struggled against his hold and continued to hurl insults at Jackson.

Oliver was dragged off the ring, but no one was paying attention, all hoping for a fight between Jackson and James, making Ollie feel sick.

Owen didn't allow James to go anywhere near Jackson, and once he pushed him out of the ring, James ripped his arm from his grip and limped down the hall. People were booing him and throwing trash at his back. Ollie instantly felt sorry for him. Avis and Duke rushed to follow.

"He's embarrassed," Elijah told Cordelia, who was rubbing her chin. "He just needs to cool off."

Ollie glanced up at him. There was a crease in between his eyes, torn between which brother to stay with. She peeled her gaze away and looked back at Jackson. He was beckoning Theodore onto the ring. The crowd was still chanting, "FIGHT!" while the announcer introduced Theodore Kensington to the floor.

"Who will come out on top for our main event?" The announcer asked, and Ollie let out an uneasy breath. "Will it be Jackson Hadley, who has never failed to showcase his insanity? Or will it be Theodore who has proved his strength in this ring?"

"He has a decent left hook, but he's not as good as Jackson, and he knows that," Elijah stated.

"It just doesn't make any sense," Owen said with a frown, but his face suddenly smoothed. "Do you think he is trying to gain sympathy from Jade by losing to Jackson?"

"I wouldn't be surprised if he was." Elijah huffed.

"Why would he do that?" Cordelia interrupted, and he averted his gaze. "Why would he do that, Elijah?"

"Because Jackson returned to the ring for her."

Cordelia blinked up at him. "What did you just say?"

He exhaled and shared another glance with Owen. "We escorted her to the Chapman wedding. Teddy didn't like that, so he threatened her."

Ollie swallowed back bile.

"Threatened her how?" Cordelia bellowed.

"His objective was to get Jackson into the ring," Elijah said with a wave of his hand. "And he initially said no, but when he mentioned Jade…"

"He made up his mind," Cordelia finished with exasperation.

"What did you expect him to do? Let Teddy violate her?" Owen barked.

Ollie flinched. Not all men were evil. She just wished she had met one of the Hadleys before Teddy found her.

"Oh, my," Cordelia whispered under her breath. "If William finds out about this, and I'm sure he has, he will strike her!"

"Strike her how?" Elijah asked through clenched teeth, and Ollie finally glanced back at them.

"He whips her to keep her compliant."

Ollie's stomach dropped again, and she suddenly felt ill. This city was full of savages.

"Bloody hell, what is it with these people?" Elijah snarled.

Cordelia didn't have anything to say to pacify him, but she didn't need to explain the origin of their iniquity. Everyone knew about the Elite and their odd practices, even if they mostly sounded like wild conspiracy theories.

"I need to check on her," Cordelia said abruptly. "And the only way I can is when they're here." She was scrutinizing William and the young woman wrapped around him. Presumably, his wife. "How long do you think they'll drag this out?"

"There is no telling with Jackson back in the ring," Owen stated. "He's knocked people out in less than two minutes, but he's also fought for well over thirty."

"I'm going to risk it," Cordelia dared. "Marna will let me in the house."

"You can't go on your own!" Elijah howled.

"I'm not a child, Elijah," she said reproachfully.

"He's right," Owen agreed. "Normally, I wouldn't worry, but there is more than one killer on the loose."

She pressed her lips together and gave him an even stare. She seemed as hard-headed as Avis was and didn't like being told what to do.

"I can go with you," Raoul said, but there was a touch of reluctance in his voice.

"No, you stay," Elijah muttered. "I'll go with her."

Raoul instantly shook his head. "I can't let you leave. Jackson's your brother!"

"He's your brother, too," Elijah stated. "It's okay. I have seen him fight a hundred times. I'll go with Cordelia." He glanced at Pikitis. "Will you come with us?"

"Of course I will!" The stout man bellowed.

Elijah turned back to Raoul. "We'll meet you back at the house."

"Are you sure?"

"Yes," Elijah said briskly before glancing at Owen one last time and disappearing down the arch behind Cordelia.

The crowd drew Ollie's attention back to the center of the ring. Jackson and Theodore were circling one another. Theodore's lips were moving, but none of them could hear what he was saying, and she prayed to God that Jackson would rip him apart for what he did.

Jackson eyed him steadily and raised his fists as Teddy continued to sneer under his breath. Jackson jabbed with his left hand, but Teddy swiped him, and a laugh followed. Teddy kicked his side, yet Jackson didn't flinch much.

Whatever Teddy said next had Jackson gnashing his teeth and jabbing again. This time, Teddy fell prey to his fists. Jackson twisted his body and threw a cross punch right into Teddy's cheek; his head snapped back. Jackson threw a lead hook into his ribcage and then a left. Teddy grunted and thrust in a few feeble jabs before kicking his leg again. Jackson raised his knee to deflect it. Teddy lost his balance and fell on his back, his legs flying in the air. Jackson grabbed his feet and tossed them out of the way. Teddy rolled onto his hands and feet, to which Jackson dropped to his knees and wrapped his left arm around Teddy's waist, punching his face persistently. Teddy tried to sway him but couldn't, and Jackson maintained his swing.

Teddy finally got up on his feet and thrust Jackson upwards, but he instantly lost his footing and fell backward again, Jackson slammed his knee down onto his chest, and his right arm continued to administer the blow. Owen and Raoul started yelling. The whole crowd was roaring, including Ollie.

It wasn't long before the referee ripped Jackson off Teddy. He coughed and spat blood onto the ground beside him as he rolled onto his side. Abraham Kensington was screaming in the offense. Jackson's cheek lifted when Abraham met his stare, thoroughly enraged. This made Ollie laugh; Teddy deserved what he got, and perhaps Abraham should have raised his son better.

When Teddy swayed onto his feet, his face was covered in blood, and his eyes were puffed and starting to swell. This could end quickly, but she wished it wouldn't.

"I thought you wanted your chance," Jackson yelled loud enough for them to hear, and Teddy glowered at him. "I'm waiting for it!"

Teddy threw a punch, except Jackson blocked it. He threw a combination, hitting Teddy three times in the face.

He rushed Jackson with his arms swinging, not paying attention to what he was doing; it was his only defense, and it worked. His left fist caught Jackson's cheek.

Jackson threw all his weight and struck back continuously until Teddy dropped to his knees and fell face-first into the filthy ground. The referee pulled him back before his kick connected with Teddy's head.

Ollie stopped jumping and covered her mouth.

Teddy rolled over, his arms flopping at his side. He was disoriented and knocked out for a brief instant. Abraham was up on his feet again, yelling for the referee to interfere. He ignored the fop and began to count. Jackson glanced over his shoulder at his brothers. He smiled and turned back. Teddy had raised his legs unaided. He wasn't going to give up just yet.

"He only needs one good hit," Raoul muttered. "Jackson has knocked more people out cold than anyone I know."

Owen's eyes flicked to the Elite. "I wonder what Abraham will have to say about that."

Ollie followed his stare. He was seething in his seat, but William Calvert, Joseph Cavendish, and Micha Wellington were on their feet, clapping.

"Are they clapping for Jackson?" Ollie wondered.

"It would seem that way."

The woman in the seat next to William looked surly, and so did Edward Wright. It was clear which ones were there for Teddy and those impressed by Jackson.

Teddy stood after some minutes, his face swollen and covered in blood. Ollie smiled in satisfaction, it didn't take away the pain entirely, but it certainly helped.

Teddy took a second to talk to his father when Abraham demanded it. His head was bent over, and Abraham had his hand on his neck. He was berating him in front of the crowd. After a few grueling minutes, he stepped away from his father and nodded at Jackson.

Teddy charged him as soon as the ref stepped out of the way. Jackson blocked him and threw a few punches, but what he wasn't prepared for, what anyone wasn't prepared for, was the knife Teddy swiped into his abdomen.

"WE HAVE ENTERED A DEADLY FIGHT, LADIES AND GENTLEMEN!" The announcer roared.

Jackson yelled loudly and shoved Teddy away from him. The blood drained from Ollie's face, her stomach dropping; he couldn't die! Raoul grabbed Owen's shirt, clutching it tightly as they both screamed; the noise emanating from the crowd had Ollie covering her ears.

Teddy swiped again, and Jackson jumped far from his clutches. Teddy charged him after swiping a third time, the blade's tip connected with Jackson's abdomen. Jackson twisted his body and slammed his elbow into Teddy's head.

Jackson kicked him once in the chest, and he stumbled before falling on his back. Jackson jumped on top of him, throwing a fist. If he was going easy before, he didn't hold back now. Blow after blow, Jackson administered punches to Teddy's head as he yelled. It wasn't long before Teddy's body went limp; he'd kill him if he didn't stop.

The referee didn't pull him back until Abraham jumped from his box. Jackson clutched his side as the referee thrust his arm in the air. Blood was spilling through his fingers, and he glared up at the Elite. Abraham continued to hurl insults at Jackson. He was a rotten cheat. The only way his son could win was with a weapon, and while there weren't necessarily any rules stating you couldn't have a knife, you had to declare them beforehand so that both parties knew.

The announcer was yelling into the microphone, "There you have it, folks. A knife couldn't even stop him! The undefeated champion of Bel Deaux... Jackson Hadley!"

XXXIV
Owen

"How deep did he stab him?" Owen howled as he grabbed a fistful of his hair.

"Considering the fact that Jackson hasn't crumbled over," Raoul said. "I don't think it pierced a lung."

"It still could have hit an organ," Owen argued.

Jackson ripped his hand from the referee and stalked toward them. Owen held out his arm when he was within reach, but Jackson brushed past him.

"Are you all right?" Raoul wailed.

He waved him off and walked down the alcove. Raoul ran after him, and Owen held out his hand, suggesting Ollie go ahead of him. She practically ran to keep up with Raoul and Jackson.

"How deep is it?" Owen demanded once they were enclosed in one of the back rooms.

"I'll live," Jackson muttered. He looked down at his side. Blood was oozing from both wounds in his abdomen.

Raoul crouched down to inspect the damage. "This is superficial, it sliced through the skin, but it didn't pierce directly through the intercostal muscle."

"The tip of the blade slammed into the bone," Jackson groaned, his face twisted with pain.

Raoul looked at him. "Then you may have a cracked rib. We need to stitch this up and wrap it before it gets a chance to get infected." He then placed his fingers above and below the wound in Jackson's stomach. "This might be a little deeper. I can see your muscle, but it doesn't appear to have pierced an organ."

Jackson took a step back and balled up his shirt, pressing it against his side. He exhaled heavily and leaned against the wall. "It fucking hurt like hell!"

"Better your ribs than a lung or heart!" Owen muttered.

"I don't know if the bone is any better!"

Owen inhaled sharply. He should arrest Teddy for what he did, but the Elite would never allow it. Feilding would never allow it. "We need to get out of here before the Elite decides to pay us a visit. Can you make it to the house?" He didn't like the way Jackson leaned against the wall for support.

"I'm confident Teddy merely grazed his rib meat," Raoul said with a gravelly laugh, and Jackson's cheek lifted.

"Then why even try it?" Ollie asked meekly.

The three men glanced at her.

"Because he was losing," Owen murmured. "Abraham wanted to make a statement, and he's going to get away with it because you were in the ring."

Jackson exhaled heavily.

"But he didn't declare any weapons. That is against the rules!" Raoul cried.

"Well, he wasn't planning on using one until Abraham gave it to him," Owen answered. "Teddy was losing, and he's embarrassed about it. He wanted his son to be the one to come out on top, and yet he didn't. He didn't even get a decent hit in, and why any of them thought he could stand a chance against a trained fighter is mind-boggling. The only solution I can come up with is he is vying for Jade's compassion."

Jackson glowered. "I don't think that will get him any."

"Unless this was his chance to kill you," Raoul interrupted, and Owen froze. "He challenged you to a fight to get you into a vulnerable position and one that if he stabbed you, he wouldn't get in trouble for. It's a brilliant plan, and we heard them say it. They want you all dead."

Jackson grinned. "How upset do you think Abraham is now that Teddy couldn't even throw a proper punch?"

Raoul chuckled.

"It isn't funny," Owen snapped, and he stopped laughing immediately. "He could have killed you had you not beat the piss out of him first. You are very fortunate to be standing!"

"I guess it's a good thing I have iron fists, as they say," Jackson said with a wry grin.

"This isn't a game, Jackson," Owen growled.

"I know it isn't, but I'm not afraid to die."

"I AM!" Owen yelled gruffly, and the room fell silent. "Do you have any idea how much you mean to me?"

Jackson pressed his lips together as he looked away. Owen knew that Jackson could admit to being genuinely happy only a handful of times. It was why he didn't mind the thought of death, but it didn't make it any less painful.

"Or what it would do to us if you died?" Owen pressed. "Do you even care?"

"Of course I do!"

"You certainly don't act like it, and what about Jade? Isn't she worth living for?"

Jackson hesitated, his mouth hanging open.

"The cards may have been in your favor tonight, but it won't always be so easy, and you need to realize that! The Elite want us dead, Jackson! It is not safe for us anymore! Feilding is loyal to them, and so is Merfan! Cillian is the only reason I hold any sway at the yard, which could change at a moment's notice."

"Cillian wouldn't betray you," Jackson said.

"He wouldn't?" Owen countered. "Money talks!"

Silence followed once again. Owen and Jackson watched one another closely.

"So, what should we do?" Raoul asked.

"I don't even know anymore," Owen said warily and glanced at Ollie. "We will take you home safely. It wouldn't feel right if we left you alone wandering the streets."

"I don't have a home," she explained. "I was looking for my father."

Owen grimaced and looked at Jackson, who was wincing. When he met Owen's stare, he nodded once. Owen glanced back at Ollie. "You better come with us for now. I can help you find your father at a more prudent time."

"You will?" she asked with a frown.

"Once we get Jackson patched up," Owen said. "I'll take you at the first sign of light."

She looked on the verge of tears. "I don't understand any of you!"

Owen glanced at Jackson, but he didn't meet his gaze. He was looking at the girl. "I know it's hard to trust when you've been subjected to maltreatment. I understand your pain because I have felt that pain. It's the reason my brothers and I offer a helping hand. No one was there to save me, but I promise to be there for you."

Her lips quivered as she watched him. Owen felt pride swell once again. Jackson was turning out to be quite a decent man.

When Ollie found her voice, it was barely above a whisper, "Watching you pelt Theodore was quite satisfying. He deserved every minute of it."

"Yes, well, despite getting sliced with a knife," Jackson answered. "It was rather satisfying to do."

She gave him a grateful smile.

"I hate to interrupt," Raoul interjected. "But we need to get Jackson sewed up."

"He's right," Owen murmured. "Let's get out of here."

As they shuffled out, Jackson asked, "Where's Cordelia and Elijah?"

Raoul gazed at Owen.

Jackson frowned between them. "Where are they?"

"They went to check on Jade," Owen said flatly, watching as confusion and unadulterated fear transform his brother's face.

"How could you let them go to the Calvert manor?" There was heavy criticism in Jackson's voice as he spoke. "They are going to get killed!" He was sitting on the examination table of his lab as Raoul stitched his side.

"Will he be all right?" Owen asked Raoul.

"He's fine," Raoul answered as he threaded the needle through Jackson's flesh. "Both wounds are superficial."

Owen relaxed, walking to the whiskey decanter.

"Are you ignoring me?" Jackson demanded.

"Stop being dramatic. The Elite are preoccupied," Owen snapped. "I bet fifty stacks they will recede into their underground lair to plot our murders until morning." He poured himself some scotch and held up the flagon to Ollie. "Would you like some?"

She shook her head in response. He placed the topper back on the bottle and turned to look at Jackson while sipping his drink.

"I'm being practical, Owen!" he roared.

"You really need to sit still!" Raoul chided him.

Jackson exhaled heavily.

"I'm serious, Jackson!" Raoul badgered.

Jackson leaned back against the table with his arms behind his head. Raoul pulled his chair around the side of the table to finish his work.

"It's been well over an hour," Jackson fumed when the silence was suffocating; the clock was ticking slowly.

"Stop talking!" Raoul ordered, and Jackson dropped his head against the table.

"The Calvert's live on the other side of town," Owen pointed out. "It probably took them forty minutes just to get over the Grand bridge. If they haven't shown up within the next hour, I can head over there."

"I'm coming with you," Jackson said adamantly.

Owen didn't protest because it was no use, opting to light his pipe instead.

"Have you uncovered anything about the Dollhouse Slayer?" Ollie asked after a moment.

Owen ignored her use of the ridiculous nickname and said, "Two names have come up more times than I can count, and I'm starting to feel as if it's necessary to interview them. Feilding can't protect them forever."

"Who are you talking about?" Raoul asked.

"Dominic Kane and Augustus Atwood."

Raoul glanced at him briefly as he pulled the string tightly. Everyone thought William Calvert was their only suspect.

"Gainsley wasn't the only one who's noticed Augustus's movements, and I hate to say it, but there seems to be some truth to Dominic's stag films."

Jackson glanced at Ollie.

"I failed Anne," Owen admitted sadly, and Jackson gazed back at him. "When Elijah and I spoke to her, I promised to protect her, but I couldn't even do that! Now there is a chance this may be the work of our own blood!"

"To be fair, none of us have ever considered Dominic part of the family."

"Still."

"Bad things happen all the time, Owen. You cannot blame yourself for it. You have absolutely no control when someone decides to use violence against another. The only control you have is how you serve those in need. So, when someone makes an awful decision, be the hope when others fail to see it."

Owen observed him for a length of time. It was an extraordinary thing to watch how far he had come. "You're a good man, Jackson. Mum and Dad would have been proud of you."

"It's because of you," Jackson said, and his face twisted with doubt. "I know I wasn't always the easiest to live with, and I repeatedly failed to show an inkling of appreciation. But I should have, and I should have been there when Clara died."

Owen clenched his teeth. He was not expecting the conversation to turn to her, and he dropped his gaze.

"My last words to her shouldn't have been so harsh. I should have told her I loved her because she was like a sister to me."

Owen shut his eyes. Many terrible things were said that night, but he knew Jackson didn't mean any of them, and neither did he. Clara didn't hate Jackson for what happened. She loved him just as much as Owen did and was distraught that he may never return. It was devastating that she never got the chance before she passed.

"I think about that a lot. I think about how I acted and how it affected every single one of you. It is why I came back. I wanted to make it right."

"I know," Owen admitted.

"But you need to understand that all of us are who we are because of you."

Owen finally looked at him.

"I know you think you fell short somewhere, but you didn't. We just needed to figure out who we were, and I'm sorry you were never given that chance."

He never felt as if his youth had been taken from him. He loved his childhood… well, certain moments at least, and it was because of his siblings. He would do it all over again. He didn't need to experience anything else.

When Owen failed to respond, Ollie said, "That's sweet of you. I wish I had a family like yours."

Owen glanced at her curiously. "Who did you say your father was?"

"I didn't," she said and cleared her throat. "His name is Christopher Ashford."

Owen blinked at her. Christopher Ashford worked for Dominic. He was the man behind the camera.

Jackson shook his head once. She did not need to know what her father had been up to.

"I'll ask about him tomorrow," Owen said. "You can stay with us as long as you need."

Her lip quivered, and she tucked hair behind her ear as she said, "I appreciate that."

"Anytime."

As soon as Elijah returned with Cordelia, he would visit Dominic. He didn't want to wait any longer. He had produced plenty of excuses to avoid interrogating his cousin and didn't need the justification for another day.

"I want to go-" Owen began, but a clamor of noise suddenly came from above, and shouting followed. "Down here!"

Gainsley tore down the steps. He was wild-eyed, frantic, and incredibly peakish. "There's been a double murder!"

They made their way through the city on a trolley. Duke had yet to return with Avis and James, but Owen tried not to let it bother him. The killer was spiraling, which was a terrifying thought; it had been less than a week since Anne had perished.

"How is he posing dead women throughout the city without anyone noticing?" Raoul asked.

"Everyone was either down in the Vaults or at the opera," Jackson murmured. "He had the whole city to place them without any witnesses."

Ollie gaped up at him. Fear had taken hold of her features. Jackson refused to leave her alone, worrying that the Elite would come knocking on their door in retaliation.

"It will be okay," he told her. "We won't let anything happen to you."

She didn't look convinced, nor did she seem to like being the center of attention. Owen tore his gaze from hers and landed on Gainsley. He was not in the Vaults with them tonight, which was most unusual.

He blurted, "Where were you?"

"Justina needed a friend," he explained as he shuffled on his feet. "I sat with her all night."

Owen glanced at Jackson, a reflex he couldn't shake. It didn't matter what situation they encountered. He would always look to his brother for an answer.

Jackson's eyes flashed briefly with a shrug.

"It's good you were there for her," Owen amended, and Gainsley swallowed as if he was ashamed to have missed the fight, but it didn't matter. The commotion of the crime took precedence over his failure to turn up at the Vaults.

Owen peeled his eyes away from Gainsley to the distressed crowd. The opera had just been released when the public found not one but two bodies greeting them on the steps of the reception hall. After jumping from the trolley, Owen shoved through the horde. Some women were crying, but the overall feeling wasn't sorrowful. There was a buzz of excitement and inquisitiveness. People were smiling and laughing as they strained to look at the murdered victims. Owen suddenly worried about the future state of humanity and stopped short when he spotted the deceased women draped over one another. Jackson stepped into his back.

All the blood was devoid from both of their bodies, and their faces had been carved with a knife. They each wore a beautiful dress that had been pulled up to expose their privates while flowers rested in each of their hands; rigor had set in deeply.

Owen stepped toward the pair and paled as he realized who they were.

It was Melody Andrews and Elizabeth DeWitt.

Jackson cursed from behind him.

The crowd suddenly pushed back against them. His fellow coppers began to blow their whistles and shove back with their batons, waving them in the air as a threat.

"They're losing control," Jackson murmured in his ear. "The bloody hell?"

"What is it?" Owen asked, but as his eyes drifted upwards, Jackson need not explain. Someone had painted a message on the side of the opera house in what looked like blood.

Where is your God now?

XXXV
Elijah

The sirens of police cabs howled through the streets, disrupting the peaceful night as they strode in the opposite direction toward the Calvert Manor. A whole foot shorter than Elijah, Cordelia and Pikitis kept up with his stride; her hands were shoved deep into her pockets as Pikitis smoked a cigarette.

"What is that about?" Elijah muttered.

"My money's on Jackson," Pikitis said through a cloud of smoke. "The Elite will have him arrested if he wins."

"They can't do that," Elijah grumbled.

"My brother will never allow them to be together," Cordelia said after being entirely silent for the duration of their walk. "Jackson represents everything William is not."

"The good in the world?" Pikitis offered.

Cordelia paused, a wry grin on her lips. "He is far better than all of us, but that's not what I'm referring to. William gave up his soul to achieve the success he had acquired, and the wheel of his empire traps him while Jackson is free. And thus, he will not be able to control Jade once she stands beside your brother. William has exerted quite a bit of effort to keep her under his heels. He won't give up that power for Jackson."

Elijah gave her a wild look. "Why would he need to do that?"

She sighed. "Alexandra left a letter in the event she was to pass. I didn't read it until I realized Jackson was invariably infatuated with Jade."

Elijah held his tongue. Why did the thought of her rip through him so viciously? Was it merely because he would never find love and happiness with another? Or was something far worse begging him to betray his brother, something he couldn't fathom? The devil tempting him to sin…

"It's too complicated to explain at this moment," she said hastily as it began to rain. "But I am certain now that she needs to get out of the city. William and Teddy will destroy her if she doesn't break free."

"Jackson won't let it happen," Elijah assured.

"That's what I'm afraid of," Cordelia admitted. He threw her a keen stare, unsure why it would bother her.

Once they arrived at Eaton Terrace, their communication ceased entirely. There was a sentinel on either side of the front gates of the Calvert manor, and they were both holding firearms.

"I'll distract them," Pikitis whispered as he retrieved a bat strapped to his shin. "You go check on the girl."

"Pik-" Elijah began, but the man had already started dragging the bat against the fence and singing at the top of his lungs while running in the opposite direction. The guards quickly gravitated toward the noise.

Elijah tugged at Cordelia's elbow and nodded his head. They crept around the far side of the manor. He was grateful for the drizzle and darkness to cloak their presence. As two guards walked by, he jumped behind a pillar, pulling Cordelia into a tight embrace. She clutched onto his arm as the guards talked loudly, not paying the slightest bit of attention to their surroundings.

When their voices became muddy, he held out his hand so Cordelia could step into his palm and hoisted her up over the wall. He held his breath as she climbed over the spikes, releasing his relief when she dropped to the other side of the fence. They stared at one another for a measured second.

"Hurry," she whispered when no guards came calling.

He gripped the wrought iron and pulled himself up the wall of the pillar. Once he reached the top and placed a leg over the spikes, gunfire went off on the far side of the yard, but he still flinched. He hurled himself over the fence and clipped his right leg on a spike. He fell on his shoulder and grit his teeth as he scrambled to get away before the guards shot him dead, though he had trouble standing.

Cordelia helped haul him to his feet, and they ran in the opposite direction of footsteps, despite his searing leg and shoulder. They nearly reached the front door when a man stepped in front of him and pointed a barrel at his nose.

Elijah held up his hands, his heart hammering in his chest along with the ache of never having truly lived.

"You're not Jackson Hadley," the man hissed.

His eyes widened slightly. "I'm his brother Elijah."

The man lowered his weapon. "She said Jackson was going to come."

"He's fighting in the Vaults," Cordelia said. "We're here to check in on Jade."

"Miss Calvert!" the man murmured. "She didn't say anything about you either."

"Jade wouldn't know that-"

"I'm not talking about Jade," he hissed. "Pearl said…look, it doesn't matter. You have five minutes to get her out of here."

Elijah backpedaled. "Pardon?"

"You have to get her out of here before Mr. Calvert returns!"

Elijah hesitated.

The man stepped closer and his voice was a harsh whisper, "Listen, I can hold them off for five minutes, but that's it. Save her!"

Elijah blinked in surprise and shared a look with Cordelia.

"You're wasting time," the man snarled, pushing him toward the back door. "Go!"

Cordelia was already ten steps ahead of him as the back door opened. Pearl was standing on the other side of the door next to a disheveled-looking woman, ushering them in quickly.

"Elijah?" Pearl said in genuine surprise.

"Sorry to disappoint. I know you were expecting Jackson," he grumbled.

"I…" she began but shook her head in dismissal and grabbed Cordelia's hand. "Hurry now." She led them up the servant stairwell.

"What is going on?" Cordelia badgered.

"Jade isn't doing well. She has a fever, and Katerina refuses to call a doctor!"

"She's sick?"

"No," Pearl whispered as they reached the top of the stairwell, her eyes landing on Elijah. "My father punished her for sneaking out."

He swallowed slowly with chagrin, which was difficult with a lump in his throat, but he didn't say a word as she led them to Jade's bedroom. Upon entering, her cries filled the room. Esmeralda was holding one of her hands as she wiped her head with a damp cloth. Cordelia ran straight to her side. Sweat rolled down her forehead, and she was shaking uncontrollably.

The sheer panic that flooded his senses nearly threatened to cripple him as Cordelia cried out, "What happened?"

"Marna can explain later. You must leave now!"

Esmeralda threw the blankets off Jade and jumped out of the way, she was in a nightgown that hung off her shoulder, and there was blood. Lots of it.

Cordelia barked, "Help me, Elijah!"

As he scooped her up, she cried out. He could feel the dampness and welts on her back. He clenched his jaw; her father had whipped her mercilessly, and it was all their fault.

He followed Pearl and Cordelia out of the room, down the hall, and through the servant's entrance. Once they reached the back door, the commotion on the other side of the yard stilled them.

"A carriage is waiting at the end of the street," Pearl said, and he glanced down at her. "You have until the end of the day to get her out of the city. Marna will look after Jade."

"I will look after her," Cordelia muttered.

"You have to stay here," Pearl said. "If anyone can hold off, William, it is you."

Cordelia gaped at her. "I can't talk to him!"

"You have to. You are the only one he will listen to!"

"He won't listen to me! He hates me!"

"That's why he'll trust you."

Cordelia glowered at her.

Pearl turned to Elijah. "Marna can explain, and Jade will fill in the gaps when she's more coherent. We will hinder my father for as long as possible, but as I said, I would not linger in the city. My father isn't a forgiving man, especially when it comes to his children."

Elijah hesitated while looking at Cordelia.

She looked severely troubled, but she whispered, "Take care of her."

He opened his mouth to argue when Pearl yelled, "Go!" and Esmeralda pushed him out of the door. Marna stepped around him, and he followed her through the yard. The same guard that let him pass held open a gate for them.

Marna granted, "Thank you, Adam."

He didn't say anything as they strode onto the pavement and practically ran to the end of the street. Marna threw open the door and allowed him to enter first.

He settled himself and held Jade tightly. She was moaning and shaking violently, clutching onto his collar as unintelligible noises escaped her lips. She was in a high amount of pain. "You're safe now," he murmured while looking at Marna expectantly.

"I don't have answers," she said. "I was merely told to take care of Jade while ya separated. Esmeralda was goin' to come at first, but Pearl said it wasn't wise. William will put a bounty on ya heads once he discovers that she is missin'."

"But how does she know this?"

"Pearl saw yew," Marna said. "Well, she saw Jackson."

"Saw him how?"

"She has… visions," Marna answered shakily. Elijah's face hardened at the thought; the fear was scathingly evident.

He thought about the omniety of her touch and the Vampirs wanting to be freed. "Do they possess magic?"

"I fink so," she said, her hand covering her mouth.

Elijah huffed, hating that he was caught in the middle of this. He shouldn't be here holding Jade; it should be Jackson. He wouldn't let his jealousy overcome his thoughts anymore; it was ridiculous. He simply wasn't going to interfere. "Well, she's not too accurate, is she? So perhaps she's wrong about this."

"She's predicted other fings that have come true."

He breathed out of his nose once, unprepared for the weight of this situation. He would rather continue with the simple things of life, like drinking at the pubs and going home with women whose touch wasn't consolatory and remarkably healing to his mental state. Ones who didn't come from fucked up families that were far richer than the Queen.

One that clearly wasn't meant for him.

He lusted. It was true, a severe problem he seemed to have, but it didn't mean he would do anything about it. He should have stayed at the Vaults and let Raoul deal with this.

Yet there was no turning back now. He'd seen Jackson stitch wounds a thousand times and even helped with James under the instruction of his brother. This wasn't the time to worry about his problems; this wasn't about him and his fixations. It was about Jade, and she needed help from one person to another. She deserved to be treated as a human when no one else gave her that right.

She was still shaking in his arms. "The fight should be over by now. Jackson will know how to fix it."

"Fight, what fight?" Marna asked.

He glanced down at Jade's mass of dark hair. Her round curls had flattened with sweat and matted blood, most of which fell out of the pins in the back of her head. "There was a fight in the Vaults tonight."

"Is Jackson fightin'?"

"Yes."

"Who's he fightin'?"

"Teddy," he huffed.

The silence in the cab left the pounding in his head louder than ever, wishing he could see Jade's face to know if she heard him. He wondered if he should have lied instead. If any of them had a reputation, it was Jackson. When he fought, he was a mad dog, and many still avoided his gaze.

"What if Teddy hurts him?"

Elijah rolled his eyes. "Teddy is a pussy."

Marna's face twisted cynically. "Yew musta never saw him angry."

He exhaled and gave her a dubious look. "You have clearly never seen Jackson angry! Teddy is absolutely terrified of him despite what he might say. He runs his mouth to make himself appear a certain way, but he cannot fight. He will not be a problem."

"I hope ya right," the woman muttered.

He felt paralyzed in his assertion of the situation; he wasn't careful enough. Yet he wasn't given a chance to dwell on the thought for long because the cab came to a complete stop. There was a commotion outside and a lantern bobbing in the darkness.

His heart was beating emphatically when the door opened, and Dominic Kane's sharp face peered into the cab. A nasty grin formed on his lips as he spotted Jade in Elijah's lap. "Well, well, well, what do we have here?"

XXXVI
Jackson

When more people discovered the message, the crowd began to riot, and a shot was fired. He looked wildly around to see Merfan pointing his pistol in the air; he was red-faced while screaming at the mob of people. Jackson pulled Ollie in front of him and caged her in between himself and Owen's back when the mass of people pushed heavily against them; she whimpered when more shots were fired.

"Get off me!" Raoul yelled in his ear.

Jackson glanced over his shoulder to see him and Gainsley shoving people backward, but the crowd shuffled closer, which was constricting. People were beginning to get smashed and screaming ensued.

"We've got to get out of here!" he yelled, pulling Ollie closer to his chest. "Don't let go of my hand, okay?" She eyed it hesitantly. "I won't let anything happen to you. I promise!"

Her tawny eyes gaped up at him, she looked positively frightened, yet she clasped onto his hand tightly.

Owen tried to push forward, but there was no gap between the bodies ahead of them; they were too compacted against one another. Insults, screams, and complete chaos emerged.

"We can't go forward," Owen called over his shoulder. "We have to go around the side!"

Jackson took a step back slowly, pulling Ollie along. He groaned every time he was elbowed in the abdomen and could feel blood seeping from the wounds. He had never witnessed a riot of this magnitude, wondering if the rowdy horde from the Vaults had wandered into the Gas-light district to look at the Dollhouse Slayers work. It didn't feel as if the crowd would ever thin.

Jackson glanced at Gainsley. "Take Ollie back to Cordelia's, would you? And do not let her out of your sight!"

"All right," he said, but Jackson harshly grabbed him by the scruff of his jacket. "I mean it, Gainsley! Don't go sneaking off for whatever bullshit nonsense you were doing during the fight! She doesn't leave Cordelia's, and you don't let anyone in. You got that?"

"I got it!" Gainsley yelled and grabbed onto Ollie's arm, but she gave him an inexplicable stare and ripped her arm from his.

"You can trust him," he said. "I promise."

She looked as if it was the last thing she wanted to do.

"He'll keep you safe," Jackson assured. "Go with him."

"I hope you're right," she muttered before disappearing behind the valet. He whipped back around, hoping he wouldn't later regret the decision.

"Come on," Owen hollered, yet the sea of bodies failed to part when he tried to move on.

"On three!" Raoul bellowed from behind. "One!" He placed his hands on Jackson's arms. "Two!" he yelled. "Three!"

Jackson pushed against Owen, propelling him through the entangled mass with the help of Raoul. They stormed through to the edge of the group, yelling at people to turn around and go home.

The opera house was a massive structure, an extension of Dragon's Keep, though it was two blocks over. Ten floors high of white marble, painted ceilings, a grand foyer, a grand staircase, and the auditorium that seated nineteen hundred people with an eight-ton chandelier hanging from above.

The first officers they encountered allowed them instant passage, and Merfan looked relieved to see them. "Thank God!" He muttered. "We need all the help we can get! We need to get the crowd under control so we can get the bodies out of here!"

Gunfire to their right interrupted him, and when they glanced over. A young officer was holding a pistol with a shaking hand as he stared wide-eyed at what he'd just done. A man was sinking to the ground as he clutched his stomach. More screaming dispersed; the crowd pushed forward.

"Get back!" Merfan yelled as he pulled out his baton and threatened the group in front of him.

"They're losing control," Owen muttered to Jackson. "I'll help with the crowd. You help with the bodies."

Jackson didn't answer as he and Raoul stepped through the line of police officers. A sheet was being strewn across the columns as a photographer took pictures of the victims. Feilding eyed them steadily with their approach. He wore a dark uniform and helmet. His toothbrush mustache twitched as his dark eyes landed on him with suspicion. His voice was profound as he said, "If it isn't Jackson Hadley."

Jackson didn't acknowledge him, his attention drawn to the dead women he had known on a personal level.

"You've ruffled quite a few feathers since you've returned home."

Grief struck him in the most primal way, and he blinked back tears, his throat constricting with each breath. To see them torn apart was utterly devastating, especially when Elizabeth had spent the night dancing with them at the Chapman wedding.

"Damn," Raoul muttered at his side.

Their mouths, once full of laughter and spirit, were now sliced upwards. Their eyes, which had once gazed beyond the decline of the east end, now had giant x's slashed from above their brow and down to their cheeks. And their throats, so fearfully cut and cavernous, the point of which had most likely drained them.

He finally released the breath he'd been holding, fluctuating with his rising anxiety. There were two sets of black flowers in their hands, Landini Asiatic Lilies and Black Dahlias.

"Melody was last seen around nine this morning," Feilding stated. "And Elizabeth was last seen around eleven. Some chaps at the Dollhouse thought she left in Dominic Kane's cab."

Jackson glanced at him sharply.

"He has thus far denied it."

"Of course he would," Raoul barked, and Jackson gazed back at the women. "Why would he implicate himself in a murder?"

"We didn't ask about a murder," Feilding revealed. "Just if he had seen her."

"Which in itself is a rather obvious question," Jackson murmured. "Naturally, he'd deny any association. And besides, his mother wouldn't allow him to take the fall even if he were behind this."

Feilding gazed at him steadily.

"If you want the crowd to disperse, then we need to get the bodies out of here immediately," Jackson said insipidly, forcing Raoul to glance up at him with a frown. "And the murderer is definitely here. He wouldn't have left the bodies in such a public space if he didn't want to cause an uproar. The sole purpose of this horrific display."

Feilding turned to the chaotic mob.

Much to his dismay, it didn't seem like any of the Elite were involved. They were all accounted for on this very night, and even if they ordered someone else to pose the bodies, none of them were here to witness this grotesque arrangement. Owen's theory about Dominic was seemingly more plausible with the passing of time.

He finally met Raoul's stare and muttered under his breath, "Owen was right. We need to visit Dominic."

Raoul's brow puckered. "What is his motive?"

"Perhaps there isn't one," Jackson said while eyeing Feilding, who had joined Merfan and Owen's ranks to keep the crowd at bay.

"There isn't always a reason behind every decision. Some people are compulsive and act without a thought in mind because it fuels their desire. I'm sure you can relate to that on some level."

"Yes, well, when I fuel my desire," Raoul grumbled. "I'm pleasuring a woman and not killing her!"

"Touché," Jackson murmured.

They wrapped the bodies and placed them on stretchers, carrying them to an awaiting cab headed for the morgue. The knot in his chest never once dissipated, and it wasn't until they had fled the scene did his thoughts stray to Jade.

He thought about her words and how she wanted to run away. His resolve was easy; he'd run away with her. They would never be able to be together in this city, and he was willing to walk away if it meant being at her side. Between the murders and the Elite, there was no chance of happiness for either of them.

They were unenthusiastically welcomed back to the morgue but welcomed back, nonetheless. Under the heavy eye of Doctor Malik, they conducted the autopsies of each woman.

"Melody was likely killed from a blow to the back of the head," Raoul muttered as he glanced over her cranium through a microscopic brass lens. "Her skull is concaved; a piece is even missing. The blow is severe enough to have overwhelmed her. He must have taken her by surprise."

The sound of Raoul twisting the lenses of his glasses replaced the sounds of his words.

"It appears as if Elizabeth was strangled," Jackson murmured after some minutes and adjusted his own lens. "There are petechial hemorrhages on her forehead and conjunctiva in each of her eyes. She has cyanosis on her face, lips, and fingertips. And while he tried to cover up her ligature marks with a knife, I can see evidence of it on both sides of her neck that were not brutalized by the blade."

As much as he tried to focus, he could not wipe the image of Elizabeth celebrating along with them, dancing, smoking cigarettes, and laughing with Jade. It really didn't take much for her to find a soft spot for Jade. And Jade! What if he hadn't found her? What if…

"Stop it," he whispered and dropped the knife. He walked from the table and wiped his hands on his apron. His eyes landed on the wall ahead of him, his sight becoming narrow with each breath. It had become immensely difficult to focus on any given object. He rubbed his eyes harshly and looked back at the table. His vision was now blurry and chattered. His heart rate began to elevate, and the lump in the back of his throat made it difficult to breathe. He walked backward until he nearly collapsed over the back counter. His cheeks burned so warmly that he knew his legs would give out at any second.

He closed his eyes and slowly began to count his breaths.

"Are you all right?"

"No."

When his nerves abated, he grabbed an Erlenmeyer flask, throwing it against the wall, and then another; it shattered against the cement loudly. He glanced back at Elizabeth; a mess of scraggly curls matted with brain matter lay on the table in the most grotesque manner. Her gap-toothed smile was lost in the knife wounds on her cheeks. Each side was sliced upwards as if the killer thought to give her a twisted smile, ridiculing her once soft face with a vile touch of evil.

He placed his hands on his hips and gazed back at Melody with eyes that burned furiously; her broad smile came to mind. He slowly counted each breath to quiet the delirium threatening to break free.

It was personal now. Whoever was behind these murders implied they were watching the Hadleys every move. And that suggested association, perhaps someone who knew them on some level. Someone who knew their patterns and thought process.

They were interrupted by Owen flying into the dissection room. He had a letter in his hand and a very grave look on his face. "We have a serious problem."

He loaded five .44 caliber rounds into a single action six-shooter with a nine-inch barrel before jumping on a trolley toward Kensington Air. He lowered the hammer over the only empty chamber and tucked a revolver in the band of his trousers. There was also a hunting knife attached to the sheath on his shin.

Edward Wright sent a letter stating that the Elite had Avis and James tied up at the docks, and they would be dead within the hour.

"Something is going to go wrong," Owen muttered. "I can feel it."

"Nothing will go wrong," Jackson assured, but there wasn't much conviction in his voice; they could only do so much. James was young and impulsive, and to be honest, so was Avis. Not that she would be any help if she were tied up, although Jackson taught her how to throw a mean right hook. She'd get one in if she could. "We have the advantage with the rain."

"I've never told you how sorry I was," Owen started, but Jackson rounded on him in anger. "Don't you fucking start!"

Owen's jaw snapped shut as he gazed out beyond the window.

"There is no need to say our goodbyes just yet," Jackson said. "We've gotten out of far worse situations!"

"With the two of us, yes," Owen reminded him. "But it isn't our lives that are at stake. The Elite would kill Avis and James just to prove a point!"

"They know I'd kill them all," Jackson said with ease. "Teddy and Edward value their lives too much to risk it."

The color drained from Owen's face, and genuine fear replaced his anger. There wasn't anything left to say.

They jumped off the trolley a block from Kensington Air and ran the rest of the way. Jackson skidded across the slippery dock before righting himself and pressing his back against the side of Kensington's Warehouse. Owen wasn't far behind, and when he motioned that all was clear on his end, Jackson sighed in relief. Thankful for the rain, they were cloaked in darkness and nearly impossible to detect. The storm extinguished the gas lamps, and Kensington's patrol skirted the harbor and the empty lot in front of the warehouse.

He peered around the corner facing the west end; a guard was standing with his back to him. Jackson covered the man's mouth with his hand and swiftly sliced across his throat. The guard gurgled and sagged against him. Jack dragged the man from view and laid him on the ground. He glanced back at Owen, who was still guarding the east side of the building and ran back to the corner to look. The dock was barely visible, but he could hear the guards calling to one another over the deluge. He glanced behind again to ensure that Owen was still there, and when he got a thumbs up, Jackson placed his knife in his belt and reached up to the window. As he hoisted himself far enough to see through the small casement, Edward and Peter Cavendish were standing in front of Avis, James, and Duke.

Jackson dropped to the ground and turned to Owen. "They're in there. How should we proceed?"

"They'll take our weapons if we walk through the front," Owen answered and gazed up at the wall. "Perhaps we should climb up and in."

Jackson didn't hesitate as he placed his foot against the crevice on the edge of the building and hoisted himself farther up the wall. He climbed to the second story and looked through another casement to ensure the room he was about to climb into was empty. It was not only dark but vacant as well. He slid his legs through first and crouched into the room, pausing to listen. His heart thrummed in his head and throat with short and shallow breaths. He could hear them talking, but the words were indistinguishable. He ran swiftly across the room and peered out of the door. He could only see Edward and Peter. Jet and Blake were nowhere in sight, and Teddy must be indisposed still.

He could feel Owen at his back, yet neither said a word to one another as they watched the scene.

"They won't let you get away with this," James rasped.

Edward punched him across the face, and he groaned in discomfort; Avis winced, turning her head.

Owen gripped Jackson's arm when he went to move forward and muttered, "Wait a minute."

Jackson's anxiety flared, but he didn't make another move.

"And as for your fucking brother," Edward declared as he watched James spit. "I'll remove each one of his limbs one by one."

"I'd like to see you try!" He yelled, which caused another punch to the face.

"No!" Jackson whispered. "Be quiet!"

One of the lackeys ran into the middle of the room and began to whisper rapidly to them. The silence stretched; Avis began to mouth something to James.

"They're here!" Edward finally shouted. "You might as well show yourselves! We know you are hiding!"

Owen's grip on Jackson's arm tightened. They'd be shot dead if they revealed themselves now. The silence stretched on as the group peered around the warehouse.

"Enough of this!" Edward yelled and pulled out his gun; he aimed it directly at James. "You have three seconds before I put a fucking bullet in his head!"

James closed his eyes as Avis hurled insults at them all. Edward cocked the hammer of his gun and yelled, "One!"

"All right!" Jackson bellowed when Owen let go of his arm. They stalked down the stairs, and every head in the warehouse watched as Edward and Peter pointed their revolvers directly at him. "We're here," he barked. "What is it you want?"

"Oh, what I have planned for you will be incredibly satisfying."

"Enough with the games, Edward," Owen snapped. "O'Brien and his men are on their way as we speak."

His smile faltered.

"You lie," Peter challenged.

"Do you believe that I would come without backup?" Owen inquired.

Edward hesitated and lowered his gun just so.

"Out with it!" Jackson yelled. "What do you want?"

Edward stared a little longer than necessary before tilting his head with a smirk and asking, "Who do you value more?"

Jackson frowned as he gazed in between the two. Even Owen seemed perplexed by the question, was he truly asking Jackson to define his love for his brother and sister?

"Is it your brother?" Edward growled and pointed his gun at Avis's head. "Or is it your disobedient sister?"

Jackson's eyes widened, and he dropped to his knees. "Take me! I'm the one you want. Spare them and take my life!"

Edward scoffed. Clearly, he wouldn't offer his life in the place of anyone, and he wasn't expecting Jackson to sacrifice himself for his siblings.

"Please!" Jackson repeated. Avis and James were worth so much more than he was. They had their whole lives ahead of them and deserved to find out what they were truly made of. "I won't even hold it against you! Take my life, Edward!"

He faltered and lowered his weapon once again. Jackson couldn't tell if he was accepting this course when a shot rang through the air.

James gulped as blood sprouted from his neck, and he took more bullets through his cheek and chest before Avis's scream ripped through the warehouse. Both Jackson and Owen aimed at Jonathan Cavendish, who had crept into the room unbeknownst to them all. Jackson emptied all five of his bullets into Jonathan, and Owen shot two rounds into Edward after he clipped Jackson in the shoulder. He fled like a coward, and someone yelled, "The coppers are here!"

Jackson slid across the floor and quickly untied James. He was struggling to breathe as blood gushed from his wounds, his eyes were wide, and he began to shake violently.

"I d-don't want t-to die!" James grunted against his hand with wild eyes, but the blood never stopped. "I w-wan-nt t-to-"

"You want to, what?" Jackson asked as Avis and Owen wrapped themselves around the pair.

"James!" Avis whimpered.

James grunted and fell against Jackson; he never answered the question. Jackson applied more pressure to his neck and muttered, "Hold on." But it was apparent he could not as his eyes slowly glazed over, and he sagged against Jackson forcefully.

"Stay with me, James!" Jackson said through clenched teeth, and the tears began to fall. He continued to gurgle, but his words became more indistinguishable with each passing second, and within minutes, he bled out. James's lifeless body completely slumped against him with one last gargled breath.

"NO! PLEASE, GOD, NO!" Jackson screamed as Owen and Avis gripped them tightly.

James's body rested on the couch in the library. Jackson sat with his head in his hands, still wholly engulfed in blood. He ignored the bullet wound in his shoulder, which throbbed and seared relentlessly. He covered James's mangled cheek and eyes, not wanting to remember his brother in death.

Merfan had tried to keep them all at the docks, but for once, Owen ignored orders as the three of them carried their brother to a cab. Duke stood in the far corner and held his hat as he stared somberly at the ground. Avis sat in front of the fireplace. She hadn't spoken a word; her eyes were glazed over and bruised. Owen stood in the hallway with Cillian, who had commanded the entire force to leave them alone.

Shame sat heavy with the knowledge that he had let James down. He would never have let him out of the house if he hadn't been so distracted. James should have never been in the Elite's company, yet Jackson never once tried to stop it. He was selfish and despicable, a poor excuse for a man.

Owen returned with Cillian at his back, who removed his hat and said, "I'm truly sorry for your loss. If there is anything I can do, I will."

"Why don't you do your fucking job and arrest the members of the Elite for once?" Avis hissed.

"It's not that easy!"

"Like hell it isn't!" Avis spat as she jumped up from the table. "You come into our house and act upset while those bastards walk free!"

"Avis," Owen muttered.

"And where is Elijah?" She yelled.

"I don't know," Cillian said quietly.

"Well, you better find him because our fucking brother is dead! And if Elijah's body turns up, I will hunt you down and gut you myself!" Cillian glanced at Owen dubiously, but Avis wasn't finished, "Right after I hunt down the men that did this to James!"

Cillian waited for Owen to reprimand her, and frankly, so did Jackson. But when Owen placed his hands in his pockets and stared evenly back, Cillian shook his head. "I can't protect you if you choose to retaliate."

"Then find him," Owen enunciated slowly.

If Jackson wasn't so upset, he might have clapped Owen on the back for not thinking like a cop and taking their side.

Cillian glanced between the three of them before saying, "I see that we simply won't agree, and I'll leave you to grieve in private, but I'll only give you one warning. Stay away from the Elite." His eyes settled on Jackson, almost begging him to challenge his statement. "I will find Elijah before the day is through."

Jackson didn't say a word, and Owen walked him out.

When the door shut, Avis rounded on Jackson. "This is your fault!"

Jackson closed his eyes. Of course it was.

"You two had to go messing with those Calvert girls!" Avis growled as she stalked toward him. "The Elite found out and took James because of it! I will never forgive you for what you have done!" She slapped him across the face, and he couldn't blame her. Again and again, she smacked him until his cheek felt raw.

At last, he grabbed her hands and yelled, "STOP IT!"

"You killed him!" She wailed and thrashed against his hold. "You killed him!"

Jackson didn't let go of her wrists until she sagged against his chest and screamed.

"What would you like to bury him in?" Raoul asked from James's closet.

Jackson rubbed his forehead. He was weary and not in the mood to talk, let alone plan the burial of his brother. He sat on the bed as his dearest friend lent his support. Raoul arrived within the hour of the shooting and treated his shoulder thoroughly, which was a clean shot and not life-threatening.

After returning with two bottles of liquor, Avis refused to leave James' side and had been drinking herself into a stupor; no one bothered to stop her. Owen hadn't been left to grieve and fought with the police force on Jackson's behalf. Merfan and Joseph Cavendish wanted him arrested for the murder of his son Jonathan. O'Brien took Owen's side and wasn't allowing anyone near the Hadley residence. His claim of self-defense didn't matter to Merfan nor Joseph, who wanted him behind bars before a swift execution. They were pleading with Feilding to decide. If that wasn't enough of a concern, Edward Wright survived his wounds.

And to make matters worse, Elijah and Cordelia still hadn't turned up.

"I can't believe Feilding is allowing Edward to walk free," Raoul said.

"He wasn't the one who shot James," Jackson said quietly.

"Still," Raoul argued. "Look at what they do to people!"

Jackson blinked; he was tired of arguing. He was so very tired of everything.

"You are a lot calmer than I was expecting," Raoul admitted as he walked out of the closet with a blue blazer in his hands.

"I don't know how to feel."

"There isn't a proper way to grieve," Raoul answered and laid the jacket next to him. "I'm sure the anger will come once the shock has worn off."

Jackson bit back a scowl. He was already so distraught with himself; he should have stopped it before it ever started. He tried to let go of the anger because it only made him act in repulsive ways.

"It's my fault."

Raoul stopped what he was doing to address his statement with a string of denials and lies. He didn't want to listen to his words of encouragement or his sincerest apologies any longer. It was stifling and astounding that no one aside from Avis realized his accountability in the situation. He stood from the bed without a word and strode from the room, Raoul's voice quickly ceased with his departure, but he didn't care.

He didn't feel anything at all.

XXXVII
Ruby

"Ruby," came a whisper from the darkness. Not again! She pulled the covers up over her head and curled into a ball.

"Ruby," another whisper, and she pressed her eyes tightly together. "Ruby." She was startled awake by someone shaking her shoulder. She rolled on her back and blinked several times over. The person who awoke her wasn't a stranger nor was he terrifying.

Confusion immersed. "James?"

He was dripping wet and giving her a sloppy grin.

She jumped up, not bothering to cover her chest with a blanket. "What are you doing here?"

His eyes wandered over her face, and he whispered, "I wanted to see you."

Her anxiety was replaced with nerves. The kind that twisted your stomach and left you tongue-tied.

"How did you get past my father's guards?"

He gave her a somber smile. "The rain."

She wished she knew what to say to make him not so sad, but he made her nervous. Without alcohol, she didn't have a bold bone in her body. Her mind was completely blank.

"Did I cross a line?" He asked, and she frowned at him. "I broke into your room uninvited, but I just wanted to see you one more time."

"I'm not upset," she said with a reassuring grin. He was alluring, and she liked how his stare roamed every inch of her face with intrigue. Her nerves were erratic. She had to make a move before she lost any self-confidence. She leaned forward, but he pulled back.

"This isn't why I came," he admitted. "I want to know who you are."

"You know who I am," she answered.

"Do I? I don't know what interests you… what makes you happy or what makes you sad," he said with a glance around her room. "What your favorite song is or even your favorite book? Those are important things."

"Are they?"

"Yes," he replied and met her stare once more. "They tell you everything you need to know about a person. I do remember you like the color blue. Has that changed?"

"No," she said with a grin. "What is your color?"

His smile bloomed. "I like gold because of the way it looks against your skin." She blushed with his confession. "And pink, how it brightens your freckles. And your freckles… the most discernible feature. I remember how you hated them. I never understood how you wished not to have any like the other girls. Those girls were so common. They would blend into a room full of people, but not you. I'd notice you in any crowd on any given day."

Her voice caught in her throat, and she blinked back tears. When she found her voice, she whispered, "Why are you so good to me?"

"Because you're everything I never was," he said. "You're astonishingly kind-hearted and vibrant despite being so sad. I would have liked to have been the one to have made you happy. To have made you smile."

She blinked back tears. She wasn't rotting from the inside, as Jet said. James was proof of that, and she realized then that she wanted to make him happy too, but the way he stared at her caused butterflies in her stomach.

He let her speak for what felt like hours. No one asked her about her life or her feelings, and he wanted to know all of it. She told him about her past, what it was like growing up as William Calvert's daughter, and most importantly, what she wanted for the future.

She spoke until her voice began to slur from exhaustion, and when she blinked back sleep, he asked, "Would you mind if I lay beside you?"

She nodded meekly. "I would like that very much."

He wrapped his arm around her and pulled her into his chest. His arms felt natural and sound. The first time she had ever felt calm and content. The nerves subsided, and she allowed the rhythm of his breathing to lull her to sleep.

Yet before she fell under, she swore he whispered in her ear, "I promise we'll meet again one day, but please don't forget to truly live."

She had awoken abruptly and had been sitting at the foot of her bed for an hour now. Something was terribly wrong, yet she couldn't place it. There were now six dead prostitutes in her room, but that wasn't it. Elijah Hadley left with Jade some hours earlier, although that wasn't it either. There was a sense of death, although, no other woman came to her room. This new death made her feel as she did the day her mother died.

Melody asked, "How are yew gonna stop the devil?"

Ruby glanced at the woman. She wasn't sure of that either. Pearl was insistent that Vampirs lived amongst them, biding their time until they were able to feed once again. It sounded utterly ludicrous, but then again, there were six dead prostitutes in her room.

"Yew has to stop the men helping him," Elizabeth said and sat down on the bed next to her. "Yew has to make Owen Hadley see reason! He's a good man, Ruby. He needs to know what happened to us."

Ruby frowned. "You said you didn't know what happened to you."

"Yews right. We were drugged, but I can tell yew we got into a fancy cab. One from a rich man."

"That does not tell me a thing. There are a lot of rich men in the Gaslight district. I need a name or even a face."

"It was dark," Helena said. "His face was hidden behind a mask, and he never said what his name was. He gave me a drink the moment we were in the cab. I don't remember anyfing after that."

"You told me," Ruby said as she bit her nail. All six women recanted the same story. They followed a seemingly harmless man into a dark cab. He offered them a drink, and nothing could be recollected after.

This conversation did nothing to appease her ill feeling. The murders weren't the reason behind her distress which was sitting heavy in her chest. It was akin to grief; only she didn't know who she should be grieving for.

"Why didn't you want my sister to know you were in the room?"

"I told yew," Anne said. "She is lyin to yew!"

"Innit odd she can see the future, but she holds yews back? Tells yew not to use ya power cause yew don' know what ya doin?"

"She said Jackson was comin for Jade, but it was Elijah," Elizabeth whispered. "She lied."

"Even ya step mutha is up to sumfing," Helena added.

Ruby clucked her tongue. She was still reeling over an encounter between her mother and Augustus from the day before.

She had left the library after retrieving her favorite novel when she heard voices rushing to Katerina's quarters. She paused to listen because it was bizarre to hear another man inside the manor aside from her father or Jet.

"It's in there!" She heard that woman wail.

"Calm down," Augustus said. "I told you I'd get rid of it!"

Ruby hid around the corner to listen.

"What am I going to do, Augustus?" she said frantically. "He is in no condition to make another, and when they find out, I'll have no claim whatsoever!"

"I have enough of a claim," he growled.

"Not if Jet has a say! He absolutely loathes me, and he is standing in the way right now! If I bore William's son, no one can contest it!"

"Stop worrying," he growled. "We can rectify the situation immediately!"

Ruby looked around the corner apprehensively to see Augustus leave the room, holding a bundle of blankets in his hands.

"She lost the baby!" Anne Dombrowski yelled from the end of the hall as Helena and Elizabeth peered inside the room.

"What are they gonna do?" Melody screeched. "Make another?"

Ruby slouched against the wall when Helena shrugged. She made the decision to wait for Jade because she would know what to do, but she was never given a chance to ask her sister about it.

"I think we're in trouble," Ruby said, and when the women spoke of their confusions, she clarified, "I believe the Atwood's and Kensington's are up to something, and I'm becoming rather suspicious of Pearl."

"She was very uncaring when speaking to yew all," Helena said. "But I thought that's just how she is."

She had a point, and she didn't even know Pearl. But neither did Ruby, not really. She needed Jade here to help her.

"I wonder if Jade left anything behind," Ruby said to no one in particular as she rose from the bed and strode to Jade's room. She closed the door quietly behind her as if she were frightened that someone might hear.

The room felt cold and abandoned, as if Jade had been gone for ages and not just a few hours. Ruby fell back into the door and sighed heavily when she spotted the blood-stained sheets, the tears she could not shed before spilling onto her cheeks. She felt utterly trapped, entirely and utterly trapped.

She clenched her teeth to avoid making any noise as she could not control her weeping. She clutched onto her chest, and her knees threatened to buckle; she slid down the door and fell to the ground.

She was uncertain how long she sat and cried, but when her tears dried and her head began to throb, she pushed herself up and walked over to the vanity. Her eyes found a brush, some jewelry, a book by Adrian Von Peltier, and a diary.

She didn't know Jade kept a diary.

Ruby touched the leather-bound book lightly. It was tempting to fish out her sisters secrets, but it was her mother's name that was engraved at the bottom, not Jade's. She snatched the diary from the vanity, and on a whim, she opened it. A letter with "My dearest Alexandra" was written on the front.

Frowning, Ruby opened the letter.

My Dearest Alexandra,

The days become more dire the longer I stay in this wretched village. There is no solace nor hope left within me. I fear I will be unable to come back to Bel Deaux. To you. It is here that I must remain; it is the safest for everyone, including you. Please do not take this as an omission of my love, for I must stay away because of my love for you. Trust me when I say it is you and only you. I will think of you every day and night and know there will come a time when you love another, have children, and create a good life, and that comforts me when my thoughts turn dark. Do not try to come to me. There is no use anymore. It is not safe for you here. I cannot stress that enough. Please stay away.

Yours eternally,

V. Burgundy

The door opened abruptly, and she shoved the letter back in the journal and placed it under a book. Esmeralda's head popped into the room. She frowned deeply when she noted Ruby's tear-stained cheeks. "Have you been crying?"

"Yes."

Esmeralda stepped into the room and shut the door behind her. "Why?"

"I'm frightened because I don't know what's going to happen," Ruby admitted. "And I'm worried about Jade."

"I know it's hard not to worry, but she will be okay, and so will we."

"Then why do I feel this way?"

Esmeralda placed her hands on her shoulders. "Because none of us know what we're doing. We've been suppressed for a long time, and the future of our house is being challenged."

Ruby's stomach twisted as Cordelia stormed into the room with Pearl behind her. "It's now or never. The Elite are preoccupied at the moment. They'll never notice if we sneak out."

"Come on," Esmeralda said.

"We should split up," Pearl suggested. "It will be harder for them to track us. Ruby, you can come with me, and Esmeralda can go with Cordelia. We will meet back in Bellmere."

Esmeralda hesitated and glanced at Ruby.

Her stomach turned. The prostitute's warnings came back to mind, but she didn't know if she should feel this way. What would Pearl have to gain exactly? If any of them were to betray one another, it would be Jet.

"If you're certain this is the best choice," she said quietly.

"I'm certain," Pearl encouraged.

Cordelia urged, "Let's go!"

Ruby followed the others and took one last look at Jade's room. Before long, everything about her sister would be forgotten in this house and erased as if she had never even existed.

XXXVIII
Jet

Edward was nursing a liquor bottle after the doctor stitched him up. Henry Wright was hurling a multitude of threats toward Jackson's very life.

"I want him dead!" He seethed while looking over at his son. The group of Elite men had convened at William Calvert's home an hour after the incident at the docks.

"I can send a firing squad to their house," Abraham proposed. "He'll be dead within the hour."

"We cannot kill him now. The Queen is watching," Teddy answered. He was leaning on his elbows in the chair next to his father and covered in bruises. "She sent her guards to watch over their house when she caught word of James's death."

"Then we'll do nothing," Abraham muttered. "We killed one of theirs; we're even. An eye for an eye, eh?"

"No!" Joseph Cavendish and Henry snarled viciously together,

"I want Jackson dead!" Joseph wailed. "He killed my son! What more reason is there?"

"They all need to be killed," Henry concluded. "How dare they attack us and think they can get away with it!"

William glanced at him. "Jonathan killed their brother. Did you honestly believe they would not retaliate?"

"James Hadley was an insignificant fool! No one will even mourn the loss!" Joseph growled, his voice shaking violently. "Had you allowed our sons to kill them in the first place, they'd all be dead, and Jonathan would still be here!"

"I will not wage a war with the Queen!" William barked. "The city will riot!"

Joseph sneered at him.

"Jackson will want revenge!" Teddy said quietly, but there was apparent fear in his voice. "It won't be long before they come knocking."

"You want us to wait for him?" Wright asked. "What if he takes his time?"

Jet glanced at his father. He didn't believe Jackson deserved death, for he would have done the exact same under the circumstances, as would everyone in this room, but he wanted this done with. He had other plans to execute. "It won't be long before he shows up on our doorstep. We have something he wants."

"And what is that?" Abraham drawled.

"Jade," Jet answered, all eyes on him. When he looked over, Teddy was glowering at him. The Kensington's had taken enough liberties when it came to his family, and it was enough. Abraham was just one of the many men who took advantage of his mother, though he wasn't aware Jet knew. "He'll want to avenge his brother, of course," Jet continued. "But when he finds out Jade is in danger, he won't be able to help himself."

"What makes you think that?" Henry asked.

Jet glanced at William, yet he didn't seem as angered by this insinuation as he was when he punished her for it.

"She spent the night with him at that wedding," Jet answered. Teddy's lip curled, and so did Abraham's. No one made fools of the Kensington's, especially a woman. "They were near one another all evening. There is obvious fondness there. And if there is one thing about my sister, she does not like anyone."

All the air was taken from the room, yet William laughed. Teddy and his father shared a look of anger.

"I truly made the wrong decision regarding her," William said in humor.

"How dare you!" Abraham yelled as Jet blinked at him in surprise.

"She is mine!" Theodore growled, and Jet stared at him with indifference; it was pathetic how he couldn't let her go.

"You keep saying that, but I no longer wish to hand her over," William hissed.

"You cannot take back your word now!" Abraham bellowed.

"I can do whatever I want," William snapped. "The wedding is off. I have no desire to tie our families together anymore."

Jet nearly laughed when Abraham choked on air. He wanted to applaud his father for seeing reason for once.

"I didn't want it to have to come to this," Theodore said, pulling the revolver from his jacket.

"No!" Jet screamed and took a step toward Theodore as he pulled the trigger and shot William in the head.

Jet halted with the gunfire, wide-eyed and stunned. Blood poured from William's head and nostrils. He instantly slumped in his chair; death was quick.

Theodore chuckled and scratched the back of his head with the barrel of his gun. "It looks like suicide runs in the family."

Jet faltered as he watched the most terrifying man he had ever known fade into complete darkness. His father always seemed otherworldly and far too powerful to succumb in this mortal coil.

"Are you out of your mind?" Henry yelled and jumped up from his seat. "How do you expect to get away with this?"

"Feilding will cover it up just as he did before," Theodore said with a dark smile, and Jet blinked at him.

"I'm glad that's well and done with," Abraham drawled with a puff of his stogie. "He was starting to get on my nerves."

Jet's hands were starting to shake. He closed his eyes and breathed out slowly. He couldn't very well unleash his power. He was outnumbered and wouldn't be able to control them all at once. He needed Jade for that.

"I told you women couldn't be trusted!" Abraham barked at Teddy. "You better get that girl under control before another scandal breaks and she insults you any further!"

"Don't fret. She will no longer cause any disruption in society or to my name."

Jet turned back to the fire and wiped his mouth, he could not arouse any suspicion just yet, but he realized now that Teddy intended to take his whole family down.

"Good," Abraham growled. "We better get on before anyone sees us."

They all began to file out one by one as Abraham's henchmen entered the room and began to clean it of all evidence.

They moved William so that he was sprawled across his desk and placed the gun in his hand. Jet glanced over his shoulder and watched as Abraham barked out orders.

"He'll know you moved the body," Jet said as he walked toward the door. "He'll know it wasn't a suicide just as he knew my mother hadn't taken her own life."

"Who will?" The elder Kensington growled at his back.

"Owen Hadley," Jet answered and stepped from the room. He didn't know how to feel about his father's passing. There was a sharp pain in his chest, and he placed his hand over his heart. There was a time when he wanted to please his father, but those years had long since passed. There was no love in his heart for the man who raised him.

Katerina was hovering in the hall. "What happened? I heard a gunshot!"

"Go up to your room and lie down," Teddy ordered.

"What happened, Teddy?" Katerina demanded.

"It's best if you don't know until the coppers arrive," Teddy said, and Jet almost made it to the door when he realized he couldn't leave his sisters alone with the Atwood's and Kensington's.

He tore up the stairs with Teddy screaming at his back and bursting into every room, only to find each empty.

"Where are they?" Teddy roared.

"Don't look at me," Jet barked. "I've been with you all day!"

Teddy grabbed him by the collar. "You better find Jade, or I'll put a bullet in your head too!"

It was enough. Jet wasn't going to allow Teddy to threaten him any longer; he wasn't going to let him take over his father's empire. Jet shoved Teddy backward with a snippet of magic. Teddy flew across the hall and slammed into the wall just above the stairs, shattering the mirror that was placed there.

Footsteps barreled up the stairs, no one had witnessed the blue light that erupted from his hands, but Teddy had. Cut up and dumbfounded, he gaped at Jet in complete and total fear.

It wasn't hard to find his power, with anger driving him. He raised his hand toward Teddy, stripping him of his senses completely. He writhed around on the ground, scared and alone.

Blake yelled, "Stop it, Jet!"

His justice was short-lived. Jet watched for a few more breaths before he lowered his hand, and Teddy gulped. "You won't be marrying my sister. You will spend the rest of your days in prison for murdering my father and mother!"

Teddy stared at him with wide eyes.

"You better run, Teddy. Time is ticking," Jet snarled. "Now get out of my fucking house!"

Teddy scrambled to his feet without any prompting and hightailed it down the stairs. Blake and Micha Wellington were gaping at him with alarm in their eyes.

Jet's hands were shaking.

"You need to breathe," Blake said, placing a hand on his shoulder. Jet smacked him away, not wanting to be touched. A myriad of emotions left him anxious; he had just exposed himself to the one person who wouldn't hesitate to turn him in. He also just witnessed his father get shot. His father was dead.

"BREATHE!" Blake screamed.

Jet inhaled loudly. Anger and anguish bubbled to the surface, and he exploded, punching the wall repeatedly. Blake ripped him back, and he struggled in his hold.

"Let me go!" He yelled.

"Stop and breathe," Blake said.

He continued to struggle but wasn't as adamant as before; tears spilled down his cheeks.

"Breathe," Blake repeated. Jet cried out as he met Micha's stare, looking grim and forlorn. He had not noticed when he showed up, but he hated showing himself tearing at the seams. He could not show any weakness, but he could not breathe either. Apprehension sat heavy in his chest; everything he feared was coming to pass. He may not have had any warm feelings for his father, yet it did not mean he wasn't affected. He just watched a man die. He was the only man that protected his family, and now they were free game.

Memories of youth came to mind, running around the yard with Esmeralda and playing in the mud with Jade. He held tea parties with Pearl and adored Ruby, the most forgotten memories. Yes, there was a time when he was inseparable from his sisters; this was before his father stomped it out of him. And yet, he still cried for him. With William Calvert gone, nothing held the Kensington's and the Atwood's back now.

He hoped that wherever his sisters were, the Hadleys would protect them from the likes of Teddy and the Elite until he could reach them, and they could devise a plan of action.

They would have no choice but to expose their secret. It was the only way they could protect themselves from death.

XXXIX
Jade

She slowly blinked as consciousness sunk in. There was a sharp pain in her head and it grew as the minutes passed by, rendering her to groan. Her head lulled to the side as she tried to move, but her limbs were confined and immobile. Every inch of her body ached, seared, or was numb. As she slowly lifted her head, blurry, indistinct shapes were moving about the room. The only sound to be heard was the clock ticking, the only thing keeping her grounded when her body and mind felt like slipping under.

The minutes turned into hours before she finally could raise her head with clarity. The room was large, dirty, and cold. Large pulleys and chains hung from the ceiling, with steel stacked upon each other. She was being held captive in her father's warehouse. A foul stench threatened to upheave her stomach. Someone stood with their back to her as he fumbled with the contents on the table in front of him. There were knives, jars of a thick red substance, and different sets of black flowers strewn across the top. The man may have his back to her, but she knew his blonde mane and long slenderness from anywhere. It was Dominic Kane.

She turned her head in distress as she tried to move against her restraints. She couldn't remember much of what happened before or how she got into this predicament, but she knew that she had to break free before something terrible came about. Yet the magic in her veins was nowhere to be found. She couldn't feel her hands at all.

Within her struggle, she spotted a blonde woman and the sandy-haired man she had seen with Jackson tied into a chair on her left. Elijah Hadley was tied to a chair directly in front of her. He was hunched over, and spit fell languidly from his mouth.

She tried to say his name, but the words that formed in her mouth were unintelligible.

Dominic turned then, not paying the slightest bit of attention to her, and touched Elijah's face. "He's a bit of a pretty boy, isn't he?" A terrifying laugh came from behind her, raising the hair on her neck. The sound did nothing to quiet the pounding of her heart or the fear that had swallowed her entirely. Pearl was right. Dominic intended to kill her.

Elijah tried to pull away, but Dominic secured a tight hold on his chin. "How far you've fallen from the tree, dear cousin. I would have killed you immediately under any other circumstance, but you see, I need a bit of blood from you."

Dominic released Elijah's left arm from the ties and pulled it straight in front of him. She tried to repeat his name, yet it was as if she had no control over her tongue. He appeared as groggy as she was, but when the tip of a blade reflected in the light, he jerked his arm back, causing Dominic to stumble forward. In a split reaction, he smacked his forehead against his cousin's, and he fell to the floor. Elijah yelled out, and his face crumbled in pain before falling unconscious.

This had awoken her senses and loosened her tongue, allowing her to scream, "ELIJAH!" explicitly.

Dominic whipped to her, a devious smile forming on his lips. "My dearest Jade."

His angular face slowly became more distinct. He no longer held a face she admired. His eyes were bloodshot against his pale, waxy skin. The snarl on his mouth was one she had never seen before. A crazed expression took hold of his handsome features like a true monster.

She glowered and thrashed against her restraints. "Let me go!"

Dominic rose from the ground slowly. His unbuttoned shirt exposed his ghastly skin. Like a spider's web, his veins were blackened and woven across his chest like an infection of the illest kind. The poison encompassed his heart and the color of his eyes; there seemed to be not an ounce of humanity left within. It frightened her.

"What have you done?" she whispered harshly.

His head cocked to the side. "I offered my soul for immortality."

Her eyes widened in fear.

"I've seen what death has done in this city, as well as old age," he said as he walked to the table where the weapons lay. With his back to her, she pulled against the ropes confining her wrists, cutting into her skin. She was far too weak and could no longer feel the magic in her veins. "I am not one for either. And with the discovery of the bones of the four great dragons, I opened my mind to the possibility that Tannith DeValles was an actual figure in history, as was every myth surrounding her. I searched far and wide for her bloodline," he paused to look at her. She stopped pulling against the rope and mimicked the expression ever written on Jackson's face when he wanted to give nothing away. And yet, it was evident that Dominic knew what she was. "As you know, Witches are born and could not make me into an immortal in the way a Vampir could. So, I went looking for the Nephilim. The ones who were bound by her magic and enslaved by their immortality. If I could find a Witch and a Vampir, I could beat death forever!"

"You're mad," she bellowed and struggled against the ropes again. "Those creatures don't exist!"

"Ignorance doesn't suit you," he said, throwing her words back at her.

"You'll never get away with this!" She promised.

He grinned at her. "I already have. No one suspected that it was I who killed those women! The police task force thought it was the Elite, yet they did nothing! They let the murders occur because of their wealth and power!" He grinned madly. "I could go on killing forever, and no one would look in my direction!"

She froze. "You enjoyed killing them?"

"The blood was for Jebriel," he explained with satisfaction. "The mutilation was for Augustus and for me. You cannot believe the relief I felt at finding another who held the same murderous desires as I did. I pledged to help the Vampirs, and he pledged to help the Lycans."

Her stomach twisted; Pearl was married to a monster.

Death hit her nostrils, and she coughed at once. It saturated the room, infecting every inch and her eyes began to water. She heaved as the putrid smell came closer than before, and she was trapped in fear's terrifying grip when a corpse walked into her line of vision.

Skin rotted off his bones, yet he stood before her as if alive. His red eyes bored into her soul. "Hello, Miss Calvert."

She gaped at him, at a loss for words.

"It's a pleasure to meet you finally," the creature said.

She leaned back in revulsion. She couldn't say that she felt the same about the beast before her.

"Tell me, how does it feel to meet a Vampir?"

She was at a loss for words. The only thing she could do was scream, which left her lips and permeated the room.

XL
Jackson

"How much longer are we going to sit here?" He yelled.

Owen was staring out of the window and driving Jackson out of his fucking mind. It had been four hours too long, and neither Elijah nor Cordelia had turned up. And what was worse, Gainsley and Ollie were also missing. He sent Raoul to check on them, but Cordelia's house was vacant.

"Something is very wrong," Jackson prodded as if to entice Owen out of his thoughts. They had placed James' body in a coffin sitting in the entranceway. He had taken Avis to bed when she was too drunk to walk, and he found Owen gazing out at the drive as if a carriage would suddenly appear. "We have to find them. We already lost James. We cannot lose Elijah too!"

"Do you think I don't know that?" Owen snapped.

"Then what are we waiting for?"

Owen finally turned from the window and met his eye. "I was hoping they would turn up by some miracle, but I can see now that they won't. I didn't want it to come to this…" he trailed off, though Jackson knew what he was thinking. "We will never be invited into William's home without an invitation, especially after what transpired in the Vaults and the docks. Not to mention what may or may not be done against his daughters in retaliation. To tread carefully, I suggest we ask Elizabeth for assistance."

He nodded, knowing he wouldn't be able to avoid his aunt any longer.

A sound of horses interrupted their conversation, and Jackson glanced over Owen's shoulder, anxiously watching as the cab came to a halt. Of all the people he was expecting to exit the cab, Micha Wellington was not one of them.

"This isn't right," Owen said aloud. "The Elite wouldn't show up at our doorstep unannounced," he muttered and walked to the front door.

Jackson followed, carefully avoiding the coffin in the hallway. It was hard to accept the fact that James was dead. It was almost like he didn't believe it, a never-ending nightmare.

When Owen opened the door, Micha halted when he saw the coffin and took his hat off his head. "I'm so very sorry for your loss."

"Thank you," he murmured.

"Had I known what would have happened, I would have tried to stop it," Micha admitted, and Jackson bit back a nasty retort. "I don't agree with any of their choices. I don't think it's right how they believe themselves to be untouchable and commit atrocious crimes."

"Do you know something about the murders?" Owen inquired.

He shook his head. "They aren't involved as far as I can tell, but I'm also not in Kensington's and Wright's inner circle. Although, if you want my honest opinion, I do not think it to be them. They are too arrogant to get away with such a crime."

"I agree with you," Owen said.

"How is Jade?" Micha asked.

"Jade?" Jackson repeated. "How would I know?"

Micha's brows knit together. "She isn't here?"

Fear trickled down his spine. "No."

Micha's eyes bugged from his head. "She isn't? Elijah left with her hours ago! Jet sent me to check on them. Teddy Kensington shot and killed William Calvert!"

The world shifted under his feet, and he had to grab Owen's arm for leverage. He wasn't fond of William Calvert, but this meant the end of an era. A terrifying reign indeed, but that's not what bothered him. Elijah and Jade were missing.

"What did you just say?" Owen barked.

"William Calvert is dead," Micha repeated.

"You know this for a fact?" Owen asked.

"Yes, I witnessed it with my own eyes. They are going to set it up as a suicide."

Owen cursed under his breath.

"If the Elite doesn't have them, then it's Dominic," Jackson snarled and headed back into the house to get his gun.

"What do you intend to do?" Owen asked, following at his heels.

"Bring them back!" Jackson snapped as he began loading his revolver. "It's Dominic. It has always been Dominic. He is the one behind the murders, and he is the one who kidnapped Elijah and Jade!"

"I know he looks like a good suspect-"

"He did it, Owen, and you know it!" Jackson roared. "He is helping one of those demons feed! They might not be able to hunt, but Dominic can! You know he is the type of person who wants power and even the chance at immortality! He has always been worse than William and the Elite!"

Owen took off his glasses and sat on the edge of the couch.

"I can't lose them too!" he said, hearing the panic in his voice. "I'll tear apart the entire city if I have to!"

"We failed, James," Owen said, wiping the first tears he finally allowed to fall. "I still can't believe he's dead."

Jackson released an uneasy breath.

"It's not enough that they took him from us," his voice shook. "If he kills Elijah too…"

Jackson's heart was in his throat. The amount of anger rising was problematic, he would do anything to save them, but they might not be in as much danger as one would think. Jade had the power to fight them off.

It was time to come clean. "There is something about Jade I haven't told you."

Owen glanced at him.

"Are you sure you can trust him?" Micha interjected, and Jackson frowned. What did he know of it? "Her very life will be at stake, so you better be sure she will be kept safe."

"Did she tell you?" Jackson asked.

He chuckled without any humor. "I've known her my whole life. She was once one of my dearest friends, and for a time, I wanted to marry her."

Owen gazed at Jackson, perhaps worried he would snap. Yet he couldn't drag up any jealousy toward the past. Whatever happened or what was thought to occur had nothing to do with him. For even he thought his life would have a very different outcome.

"I no longer have romantic feelings for her," Micha said hastily. "But I'm starting to suspect you do."

"I would never put her life in danger," Jackson said. "I just want her to be happy. Owen can be trusted."

"Ah," Owen muttered. "She's the one Caelum spoke of, isn't she?"

"Yes," he answered with a hint of defeat. It still frightened him to imagine her at the Vampirs side.

"Do you have any reason to believe she would unbind a Vampir?"

"Wait, what?" Micha barked.

"I can't see why she would, but Caelum spoke of a direct line. She may not be the only one in her family who holds an ability for magic."

"I know Pearl does," Micha said. "But she isn't one for it. She would rather live as a pauper than admit there was anything different about her."

Jackson pressed his lips together. He didn't really know Pearl at all other than she was egotistic.

Owen rubbed his face and placed his spectacles back on. "We're wasting time. We need to get to Dominic's flat before anything dire happens." He glanced at Micha. "Would you be willing to stay here until we return? My sister is sleeping off alcohol, and I don't want to leave her alone. Raoul and Pikitis should return within the hour."

Micha's cheeks went red as he nodded.

Owen turned to Jackson. "Are you ready for this?"

Jackson tucked his revolver into the waistband of his pants and grabbed two more off the table. "No."

He only hoped that bullets could injure a Vampir who was bound.

XLI
Elijah

Elijah was awakened by a blade piercing against his skin, a vertical slash against his arm. The minutes passed into an hour, maybe more (or less), before he was coherent enough to understand his surroundings. The straining in his head was pronounced, and it didn't help that his vision was already touchy, making it nearly impossible to focus on who was standing in front of him. Time passed slowly as blood ran down his arm into a bowl on the ground. He thought back to how he got into this predicament and how there was a chance he wouldn't be able to get out of it.

Dominic's voice drifted in and out, and he could only catch snippets of his words. He was talking to someone, a woman, by the sounds of it. Something about how she came the closest out of anyone, but it didn't make a difference because he was brainsick. There was something very wrong with him.

He thought back to his moments of youth. Elijah hadn't spent time with Dominic in recent years, not since they were teens, and he was right. There was something very wrong with the way his brain worked. He remembered how Dominic was very interested in dead things, particularly animals. Sure, most boys would poke a dead animal with a stick when they saw one and move on, but Dominic obsessed over the corpses. He wanted to see what was inside and rip it apart from morbid fascination. All the nasty things that were said about Jackson were the honest to God truth about Dominic.

Jackson just wanted to find a cure for death, while Dominic wanted to watch things suffer and die.

They cut ties with their cousin about ten years ago. He was accused of raping a girl, and he was never charged because of who his mother was. No one believed the girl except Owen and Jackson. She was ridiculed and taunted throughout society; most thought she made it up for attention. Owen couldn't believe how the city would take the side of an accused man because he was rich and good-looking. No one bothered with the girl, and her family never recovered.

The girl was Roslyn Emerich. It was why they looked after her or at least tried to.

He was failing in all aspects of his life, and he couldn't believe they never concluded that Dominic Kane might be their prime suspect. They were so obsessed with William Calvert and the Elite that they completely ignored what was right in front of them all along.

He watched the red substance drip from his arm until it clotted and dried on his skin. It was a crippling reaction, but it wasn't what grounded him in sudden fear. He wasn't alone when he was abducted. The thought that Dominic had taken Jade's life took the wind from his lungs.

He tore his gaze from the bowl and raised his head. She was hanging by her wrists not ten feet away; her feet barely touched the ground. He scanned the room; they were in a warehouse. Lifts, sheaves, rings, pistons, flywheels, and large headstocks were strewn about the room; they were inside Calvert Steel.

Gainsley, Ollie, and Marna were strapped to chairs unconscious, but there seemed to be no one else inside.

"Jade!" He hissed. "Jade, look at me!"

Whatever Dominic had done to her, she wasn't rousing.

"Jade!" He repeated through clenched teeth, yet she still didn't move. He glanced at Gainsley, who didn't seem to be conscious either. He kicked his leg out, connecting with Gainsley's shin. His head bobbed, but he didn't rouse. Next to him, Ollie and Marna began to stir. He continued to kick Gainsley until he finally raised his head, eyes doubling and gazing around in complete confusion.

He slurred, "Wh-whasss goin on?"

"We need to get out of here before Dominic returns!" Elijah hissed.

Gainsley continued to blink as he took in his bearings.

Elijah sighed in frustration. There was a small table to his right; the knife that injured him was sitting there as if by design. He took the bait, grabbed the blade before Dominic returned, and sliced through his ropes.

He quickly sliced through Gainsley's ropes before he ran to Jade and placed his fingers on her neck, feeling for a pulse. It was beating steadily.

"Oh, thank God!" He murmured and began to twist the knife in the locks securing her. Yet he was having trouble with it. He could never find the latch in the way Jackson or even Owen could.

"Elijah," Jade murmured.

"Hold on," he said. "I will get you out of here."

"This is a trick," she croaked and raised her head. A severe bruise covered her cheek and left eye. "You need to get out of here!"

"Like hell I do! I'm not leaving you here!"

"You need to get as far away as possible," she murmured. "The devil is here!"

He repeated, "I am not leaving you!"

"ELIJAH!" She suddenly screamed.

He didn't feel it at first, not until the knife twisted aggressively into his side. He grunted against the searing pain and glanced down, a hand violently gripping the blade's hilt, veins protruding as it turned even further. His eyes flicked back to Jade, and he coughed once; it was severe and grating. His eyes widened when blood flew from his mouth and splattered across her face. She was screaming, but he couldn't hear the sound, just his breath, and heartbeat. He blinked a few times as her agonized eyes pleaded with him. It was the last thing he remembered before the world went black.

XLII
Olivette

Ollie gaped in fear as Jade Calvert's restraints snapped in half, and her hands dropped to ease the blow of Elijah falling forcefully against her. She took several pronounced steps back and wrapped her arms around him as she fell along with his dead weight. She began to slap Elijah's cheeks earnestly.

"Open your eyes, Elijah!" Jade begged, her voice quivering. "Look at me!"

Blood was spurting from his side and all over her dress. She hastily placed her hands over the wound and applied pressure. Ollie could have sworn her hands glowed briefly, but it must have been a trick of the mind.

Laughter caught both of their attention, and when Ollie tore her eyes from Elijah's unconscious form, Dominic Kane was holding a knife and grinning wickedly at Jade.

"How could you!" she gasped.

He turned the knife in his hand and looked at it; that crazed smile was still in place. "What do I care about, Elijah?"

Jade's eyes narrowed. "He is your cousin!"

He shrugged. "He's far more troublesome than he's worth."

Jade's breath caught, and she dropped her head against Elijah's chest, her shoulders shaking in protest.

"I can't believe I almost wasted my time on you! I am going to tell your father that you were a little slut who couldn't help herself! I'll tell him that you ran around with Jackson and Elijah. And when Jackson caught you and Elijah in bed together, he lost his fucking mind and killed you all!"

Jade lifted her head and said, "He won't believe you!"

"Not if I corroborate the story," a soft voice said, and all the color drained from Jade's face as she watched the woman walk towards her. "It won't be hard to tarnish your name. You have practically done so your entire life!"

There was a sharp intake of breath from the bedraggled woman sitting beside her.

Jade gasped, "Pearl!"

Ollie's stomach dropped; she felt helpless at the recognition of the name. Jade's sister (Ollie's half-sister) was betraying the family. She suddenly felt someone tugging at her restraints and looked over her shoulder to see Gainsley slicing a knife through the rope. He held a finger up to his lips.

Ollie glanced back at Jade.

"What are you doing?" Jade wailed when Pearl placed her hand atop Dominic's shoulder.

Pearl smirked. "You can't be this dense. Do you know how long I have watched you throw your life away, and for what? An inclination for being a pest and slumming around with men all over the city? I never understood how you could never listen. You are, if not worse than mum ever was, and will end up six feet under just as she! But not before Ruby releases Jebriel from his imprisoned state, and I rule by his side!"

The smell of death overpowered Ollie's senses as a grotesque creature entered the room, and she shrank in fear against Gainsley, who pulled her from the chair and tucked her behind his back along with the other woman.

She stilled as a near skeleton with flapping skin and decaying muscles walked into the room. His body may be dead, but his eyes, so brilliant and red, bored into her soul with one glance, and she shielded her gaze into Gainsley's jacket. He squeezed her arm.

When she dared to look around, the decaying demon knelt on his knees, a wicked smile curved on his blistered mouth. A girl was dragged into the room, kicking and screaming against the men restraining her. They tossed her to the ground and pulled the burlap sack off her head. When the freckled girl found the demon in front of her, she started screaming.

"Not Ruby!" The woman whimpered.

Jade's chest suddenly glowed with the sight of her, a faint orange at first, yet it instantly burned into a blinding white light. Gainsley froze at the overwhelming illumination and grasped Ollie's wrists tightly. The radiance traveled down her arms and into her fingertips, and her hands began to glow as heat pulsated through, projecting luminosity into Elijah's stomach. The light swam into his veins and didn't die out until she removed her hands. Blood was no longer oozing from the wound at his side.

"Holy shit," Gainsley muttered.

She was knocked back, and the light from her chest and limbs dimmed.

"And what do you think you're doing?" Pearl hissed as Jade tried to sit up again, but she waved back, and Jade's head smacked against the ground. "You are only here to watch!"

"Why are you doing this?" Ruby wailed as she shuffled backward to get as far from the corpse as she could.

Pearl chuckled. "There is a pecking order in life, Ruby. We are at the top of the chain, and so are the immortals. We should live unafraid and in the open, no longer under the heel of William Calvert and his despotic reign. I need you to release Jebriel for me so that we can be freed from the rules of society!"

"Don't listen to her, Ruby!" Jade yelled.

Pearl flicked her wrist again, pressing Jade back into the ground. "Jackson Hadley was killed tonight." Ollie's stomach dropped as Gainsley tensed, and Jade stopped struggling, her eyes doubling. "Jonathan Cavendish shot him dead."

"You're lying!" Gainsley yelled.

Pearl glanced at him, her eyes darkening. "It's not a joke. They lured him down to the docks for the very purpose."

"I don't believe you!"

"He was shot in the cheek, neck, and chest. He died in Owen's arms."

Gainsley began to shake, and Ollie gripped his arms tightly to still him. He was shaking so badly that the ground was moving beneath her feet. She tried to push her weight against him so he could fall back against her if needed. That was until she realized it wasn't Gainsley shaking at all. He stopped trembling and was looking at Jade.

Her chest was glowing again. Only this time, fire erupted in her palms.

"Jade, stop," Pearl yelled. "You need to calm down!"

Dominic doubled back and tripped over himself while the demon started laughing.

"Jade stop it!" she screamed. "This isn't funny!"

Gainsley took a step back, forcing Ollie to move with him. Only Ruby tried to proceed toward her, but Pearl held her back.

The ground shook violently until the force of Jade's magic hurled them all into the far wall of the warehouse, a rippling wave of impact. Ollie screamed with the collision, her back struck with pain, yet it was nothing compared to the overpowering noise. Both she and Gainsley placed their hands over their ears.

Ollie dared to glance up. Jade trajected in the air ten feet above the ground, fire erupting from her mouth and down through her feet. The bedraggled woman slowly lowered her hands, aghast. The fire obliterated the floor below and the ceiling above.

There were simply no words. Jade, Pearl, and Ruby possessed magic.

"RUN!" Ruby yelled at them.

Gainsley quickly regained his senses and slowly crawled on his hands and knees toward Elijah, unconscious on the ground. Ollie was suspended, her eyes locked on Jade. She was the girl Owen spoke of, asking Jackson if she was worth living for, and now he was dead. He spoke of death so flippantly when most people shied away from it; he wasn't afraid. His loss would have a terrible impact on his family. A family she wished she was a part of.

Ollie was so transfixed on Jade she didn't notice that Gainsley was dragging Elijah by his feet toward her until he nearly knocked into her.

"Help me!" He screamed. "He's still alive!"

She stumbled as she tried to find her footing. Gainsley ran around Elijah, placed his hands under his armpits, and hoisted him up. His head bobbed to the side; he might not be dead, but he was out cold.

"Grab his legs! We need to get out of here!"

She grabbed one of his shins and tried to haul him without much impact. Gainsley took the brunt of Elijah's weight and dragged both of them away from the blinding scene behind them.

"Don't look back!" He hollered.

She did not intend to. She refused to be in the crosshair of those with magic, especially those who were at odds with one another. Something crashed from above and smashed into the concrete behind her; she screamed and dropped Elijah's legs. She covered her ears and glanced over her shoulder; the large pulley hanging from above was swinging dangerously. Jade was no longer in the air. She was crumpled in a heap on the ground, and the warehouse had caught fire. Ruby had taken her place to square off with Pearl; green flames erupted from her palms.

"Ollie!"

She turned back around. Gainsley and the woman had dragged Elijah away from her. "I need you to help with Elijah! I must get Jade before they kill her!"

She scrambled to her feet, grabbed his arm, and dragged him along with the disheveled woman. His dead weight was heavy, and it took all her energy to pull him away from the chaos ensuing. She tripped over her feet, panting and crying as she hauled Elijah inch by inch.

"C'mon," the woman said. "Yew can do this!"

"I'm trying!" she wailed and slid on her dress; the woman reached out to steady her.

She pulled her skirts out from under her feet as Elijah was suddenly lifted off the ground. She turned her head to see Owen and Jackson Hadley, of all people holding Elijah.

"You're alive!"

"We've got him!" Jackson bellowed and nodded toward the coiling doors. "Get out of here!"

She tore after the woman, through the doors and out into the black night, which greeted them with the effluvium of the Kinnedale Harbor. Ollie's heart was in her throat, and she didn't take a breath until they were away from the sudden inferno of the warehouse.

Quick footsteps sent her anxiety over the edge. A svelte woman with long dark hair and even darker eyes approached. She was accompanied by Cordelia Calvert, leaving Ollie to sigh in relief.

"Gainsley!" the dark-haired woman said, and Ollie turned to see him shuffling from the door with Jade's unconscious form in his arms. She was wrapped in his jacket, and her bare legs were exposed. Her nightgown must have burned off completely.

"Esmeralda!"

She touched Jade's cheek. "What happened?"

"I don't know how to explain it," he said with a turn of his head as Owen and Jackson followed, carrying Elijah in their arms.

Esmeralda yelled, "Owen!"

"Ruby and Pearl are fighting with magic!"

Esmeralda gaped at the burning warehouse when screams ensued. She turned to run through the coiling doors, but Cordelia stopped her. "You can't risk it!"

"Yes, I can! My sisters are in there!" Esmeralda shrieked. "I hold the very same power they do. You must leave! This is our fight now!"

Owen hesitated as she gave him one last look.

"C'mon!" Jackson yelled and pulled Elijah, forcing Owen and the woman to move along with him. "She'll be okay!"

Cordelia was the only one who watched Esmeralda run into the warehouse. Ollie jogged to keep up with Gainsley. He swiftly pulled them toward the row of carriages parked along the street.

"This way!" Cordelia ordered, running up fast behind, and they followed her toward a red hansom cab on the end of the street. She flung the door open, and Jackson stepped inside, hauling Elijah with him. Owen stood just outside the door, helping with his feet and stepping aside so Gainsley could follow. He held out his hand for the harried woman and then to Ollie when an explosion from the warehouse expelled into the night.

She ducked and screamed. Owen grabbed her by the arm and pulled her between the cab and his chest to block any debris that might fall.

Gainsley ducked out for a better look. "My god!"

When the seconds ticked by and nothing fell upon them, Owen helped Ollie inside before slamming the door behind her.

"Owen!" Jackson yelled, and his long legs were bent up awkwardly into his chest. Elijah was folded on the ground, and Jade was curled in a ball on the bench. Yet no remark followed as the cab shifted when someone jumped onto the stoop and quickly began to roll away thereafter. Ollie fell forward along with the tousled woman.

"Dammit!" Jackson yelled.

"What is it?" The woman asked.

"Owen ran back to the warehouse… although I can't blame him." He glanced down at Jade and felt for her pulse.

"Is she alive?"

"Yes," he murmured and shrugged out of his jacket to cover her further. He glanced at Ollie. "What happened?"

"Pearl told us you were dead. She said you were shot to death and died in Owen's arms. It is why Jade's like this. She lost control, and fire streamed out of her."

His eyes widened, and he glanced back at Jade.

"Why would she lie?"

"Pearl sees fings," the woman answered. "She musta got it wrong. Although, she usually doesn't."

"My brother James was shot," he murmured. "He was the one who died."

Ollie's stomach dropped. She had only seen him once, yet she could feel the heavy grief in the air. "I'm sorry."

Jackson's jaw clenched as he brushed the hair off Jade's forehead. Ollie understood he couldn't talk about it and she couldn't blame him.

The woman folded her arms. "She must not be able to tell yew apart."

He gazed at her.

"She said yew was coming for Jade, but it was Elijah. She said yew was the one who died, but…."

He closed his eyes and grabbed the bridge of his nose.

"I'm sorry," the woman blurted. "I didn' mean any disrespect."

He dropped his hand and said, "I know. I wonder why she cannot tell us apart. That's an interesting facet of her power." He looked at Ollie. "How did you get here?"

Ollie recanted the story of being ambushed by Dominic's henchmen. Christopher Ashford being one of them. He didn't even care, which hurt worse. She may not be his actual daughter, but he still raised her.

Marna, the woman she learned to be, also recanted her tale. She realized how lucky they were to have survived such a strange and cataclysmic turn of events. It was a miracle, and it was shocking, and it was numbing all at once. She didn't know how to feel about her half-sister tucked into Jackson's side, nor her abilities, but she knew that Jackson was a good man. If he vouched for her, she could open the door for a possibility.

Marna asked, "How did yew know where to find us?"

"We didn't," he admitted. "It took us way too long to suspect Dominic when our sights were set on the Elite. We searched his house, which was empty, and every single pub in Trinity Row. There was no sign of Dominic anywhere, and we decided to ask the Queen for help. As we were about to head over the Grand bridge, we saw an explosion in the sky, so we followed it."

"I'm glad you did," Ollie said.

"It's good to see you're safe," he murmured. "Thank you for helping my brother. Both of you."

"Ya welcome," Marna said.

"Where are we going?" Ollie asked when she noticed they were crossing into the city's far reaches.

"Berrone."

She frowned at him.

"It's our safe point," He answered. "If anything should happen and we are split up, we are to convene at the estate in Berrone; it's heavily protected. My father built it in case this very scenario ever played out."

Ollie had never been out of the city before, but she didn't have anything to keep her here. If walking corpses were vying to break free, then the only option was to follow the Hadley's wherever they went.

XLIII
Ruby

The fluctuation of magnetic energy interlaced with anger was inordinate. Her vision burned, and no rational thought came. One betrayal after another, Pearl intended to hand her and Jade over to the fiends that fed off the living. Which was enough to drive the power from deep within her, but she also expected Ruby to free them so she could control them as her father had.

It drove her power to the surface, and she expelled green flame after green flame in Pearl's direction. Dominic had fled, yet the demon stayed, waiting for his chance at freedom. Pearl was controlled. Having discouraged them from using their power, she was the only one who knew how to wield it properly. Yet, there was enough enmity thrumming in Ruby's veins that she could keep up. Pearl may have been able to wield and manipulate her ability, but she wasn't stronger.

The ground cracked open every time she pulled energy deep within, splintering across the ground and dividing the room. The warehouse was crumbling around them, yet the fire didn't affect her well-being. She was made from fire, just like Jade.

Pearl's magic was made of air. It rippled through the room in waves; had she been ordinary, it may have been a true source of injury. Ruby deflected every blow; her limbs glowed vibrantly with every pull.

"I am not your enemy, Ruby!" Pearl screamed. "Stop this now!"

"You started this!" Ruby yelled. "You attacked Jade!"

"She brought it on herself!" Pearl snapped and flicked her wrist. Ruby rose off the ground with an influx of air, startling her.

"Put her down, Pearl!" Esmeralda yelled.

She dropped an inch when Pearl's head inclined toward their sister. Esmeralda was standing with Owen Hadley at her back. Another crash from the ceiling had Pearl lose focus, and Ruby fell to the ground. The warehouse was nearly engulfed in flames.

"We need to get out of here!" Owen yelled.

Ruby locked eyes with the Demon; his red eyes watched her calmly despite the chaos ensuing around them all. The six prostitutes were at her side, encouraging her to summon her strength. Ruby had been a wallflower her entire life, and now she was anything but. Jade had protected her from pain, and now it was her turn to protect her sister. She was going to destroy the demon.

She summoned all the energy within and sent a current of electricity from her palm directed at the creature. Levin surged into the chest of the fiend, and he arched backward. The surge sifted through his body and into the sky, illuminating the entire skyline with green lightning.

Her arm vibrated violently, but she couldn't pull away. There was screaming from behind, perhaps even her own, but she couldn't think as time stood still. Her power connected to the Vampir, soldering with the beast, and she could no longer control what she had moments ago. Tears poured down her face, and her arm felt as if it would break in half.

Esmeralda could not get close enough to help, and Owen pulled her back. Her screams were soundless. Owen engulfed Esmeralda in his large embrace, and they cowered on the ground.

She could hold on no longer, feeling as if this was the end and accepting her fate. She was going to die and hopefully bring the Vampir down with her. It was the least she could do.

At last, a shockwave sent her backward, a discharge of Pearl's power and vanquishing the fire into ash. She was disoriented from the blast, staring up into the sky. She blinked slowly as smoke from the demolition continued to pollute the air; stars were scattered around a perfect moon, round and nearly full. She couldn't remember the last time she looked at the night sky.

Sounds were coming from somewhere off, which was distorted, and it seemed dire. She turned her head. The creature was biting Owen's neck, though it was short-lived. Esmeralda sent the demon flying back. Electricity stemming from her hands.

The Vampir fell flat on his back, though he no longer looked like a walking corpse. His face and skin were restored. Ruby blinked several times as she leaned up on her elbows. He was the man who had visited her in her room; he had been after her all along.

A howl rang through the air, and the fiend began laughing. A second wolf joined, and their cries to the moon echoed throughout the streets. She didn't kill him as she intended; she set him free.

Pearl ran toward the devil with a manic smile on her face.

The desire to escape overpowered every other thought and she hastily jumped to her feet. Owen had his arm around Esmeralda, leaning on her for support as they stumbled from the crumbled building and ash. Ruby faltered as she ran toward them, her head seared with pain, and her knees threatened to buckle; yet she had to get away. She didn't want to be left alone with the Vampir or any other creature that might be stalking the streets.

Owen's neck was torn and covered in blood. The vulture had attacked him and drank his lifeline, which was worrisome. Ruby grabbed his arm with the intention of helping shift his weight, but she herself was not steady, and the pair leaned into Esmeralda.

She whimpered as she continued. They skirted through the wreckage as quickly as possible toward the nearest carriage. The horses secured to the hansom cabs were rearing back on their legs and neighing loudly. When a third howl sounded, the horses took off into the streets.

Owen's legs gave out, and he fell to his knees, taking them down with him. Esmeralda cried out. "Don't give up on me, Owen!" she pulled on his arm, and tears streamed down her face. "We are not going to die tonight!"

He grunted.

"I'm sorry," Ruby said. "I'm so sorry! My intention was to kill him! I did not mean for any of this!"

Owen glanced at her. "I know."

She cried out for what had happened and covered her eyes. She single-handedly destroyed civilization. These fiends would kill and annihilate anyone they encountered.

"C'mon, Luv," Helena said in her ear. "Yew have to find the strength. They need yew."

With the help of Esmeralda, Owen shuffled to his feet and held out a hand for Ruby. She grabbed it, and he swiftly pulled her into a standing position. Her bearing was out of sorts, but she pushed on.

She glanced over her shoulder. Pearl and the fiend were nowhere in sight.

Flight finally kicked in, and they scrambled down the cobbled streets awkwardly. Police sirens and screams echoed throughout the streets.

As they rounded the main road, a man was crouched over a motionless person on the ground, eating his entrails.

"I don't think so," Esmeralda muttered and raised her arms. Electricity stemmed from her palms and connected with the demon, sending the fiend into the air. It screeched and landed on its back. Esmeralda skirted toward the person lying motionless on the ground.

She yelled, "This one's dead!"

The fiends were finding their victims because of what she did. She was a murderer.

The rabid man rolled over and hunched up on its heels, teeth gnashing at her, and a growl rumbled low in its chest.

Ruby felt the static pull in her palms as she held onto Owen, itching to strike the demon. Esmeralda must have felt the same energy because she raised her hands in the air, and electricity ensued in the sky, lighting up the city as if it were the middle of the day. The demon cowered back slowly as Esmeralda lowered her arms with its retreat, daring the beast to strike her.

The fiend turned on its heel and ran in the opposite direction.

Esmeralda didn't return to Owen's side for several minutes. Ruby watched anxiously, wondering what her sister thought of her now.

She blurted, "I didn't mean for this to happen!"

"How could you have known?" Esmeralda said as she returned to Owen's side and pulled him on. He was still queasy, and she wondered how much blood he had lost. "Let's get out of here!"

Ruby didn't have time to think about how much damage she had caused. They moved through the streets with more ease, and they met no other creature on their way. Several police cabs flew by, heading in the direction of Calvert Steel. It sure took them long enough.

They walked for another twenty minutes before the Gaslights came within sight, and she could feel the adrenaline finally coursing through her, pushing her not to give up. The illumination gave hope to all of them, and they began to run, not stopping until they reached the nearest trolley. Once they were secured in the moving car, she felt for the first time that evening as if she could finally breathe.

Owen sagged against one of the railings. It seemed like he exerted all his energy to make it to this moment.

"Stay with me, Owen," Esmeralda said. "We're almost there."

"I'll be all right," he said. However, he didn't sound very convinced. "Where are we going?"

"I figured your house is the safest," Esmeralda answered.

Owen winced. "Okay."

"I'm so sorry," Ruby whispered.

"Quit apologizing," Esmeralda said. "You had no way of knowing what would happen. I cannot believe Pearl was helping Dominic and that thing! What is wrong with her?"

"It promised her something she isn't getting in her everyday life," Owen said.

"Do you suppose Augustus knew?"

"I don't see how he wouldn't," Owen said and shifted back in his seat. "I don't hear any more screams."

"Hopefully, the fiends have enough sense to stay away," Esmeralda answered and placed the back of her hand on his forehead. "They know what will come for them if they tear apart the city."

Owen's mouth twitched. "You are terrifying."

She grinned. "Remember that."

Ruby couldn't find comfort in their humor. She unleashed immortal beings that had been bound for a millennium. Bound for their crimes against God and man, the thought left her feeling ill. She may have very well just caused the destruction of humanity.

The Hadley manor was relatively close to the Grand Bridge. Ruby and Esmeralda helped Owen hobble down the drive, which was pitch black. She tried not to give in fear as every noise made her jump, waiting for a Vampir to strike down upon her.

There was a commotion in the distance, and light came from the windows in the manor.

Owen halted in his tracks, forcing the girls to stop along with him. "My brothers wouldn't hesitate. They should be long gone by now."

"Who do you think that is?" Esmeralda asked as a group of men stood outside of a cab conversing with one another.

"I don't know."

"We should tell my father. He will know what to do."

Owen grimaced, and Ruby felt his hesitation deeply. She hadn't spoken to her father since he punished Jade, and she was not inclined to ever again.

XLIV
JADE

When she had stirred from heavy sleep, feeling as if every inch of her body had been broken, a flood of memories returned. Her eyes snapped open, thinking perhaps she had the worst nightmare to date, but she didn't recognize her surroundings. She was wearing a very large shirt and lying in a four-poster bed with a black duvet. Her fever had broken, and her back wasn't nearly as sore as the day before; she could feel the burdening scabs with each movement.

The wounds on her back were the least of her worries, she wasn't sure how she came to be in this room, and the further she looked, the more confused she became. The room was massive, with vaulted ceilings and a chandelier hanging from it. There were cathedral-sized windows surrounding two French doors that led out onto a balcony. There was a desk littered with pages of fine handwriting, and several had fallen onto the ground, as were drawings pinned on the wall.

Where the hell was she? The last thought she could recall was Pearl stating that Jackson was dead. She covered her eyes and cried until there was nothing left but a headache, not bothering to keep quiet or hide her grief.

Someone touched her back. "You're safe now."

Her eyes flew open. Jackson was leaning over her. Her heart began to pound emphatically, and she sat up to touch his face. "You're alive!" she croaked.

His mouth curved. "I'm alive."

She flung her arms around him, and he pulled her into his chest. She buried her face in his neck and wept. He tightened his hold on her, and for the first time ever, she felt safe. He was alive, and they were together. He didn't care that she held power. He didn't care about her indiscretions of the past. He saw her for what she was and made her feel as if she was worth something when no one else had. He saw beyond the exterior and left her complete in herself. She didn't have to be anything other than herself, which was very beautiful.

Touching him now wasn't as overbearing as before. There was no more static, no more undercurrent of discomfort. It was even; an influx of pleasure that belonged.

She placed her lips on his. He was initially hesitant, perhaps waiting for the static to return and pull them apart. When it didn't, he gripped her tighter. Their lips moved flush with one another. She could feel it in the pit of her stomach and beyond; euphoria flared in every nerve. She had to be closer, to feel every bit of his body. She thought she had lost him, and she wasn't going to waste any more time. She unbuttoned his shirt as his hands slid down to her thighs, and he began to lift her shirt—which was probably his shirt.

"I can make whateva yews is hungry for," a voice wafted through the door.

They pulled apart, and she leaned back on her heels. Marna and Cordelia stepped into the room. "Oh, thank God!"

Cordelia eyed them suspiciously as she entered the room, and Jackson blushed.

She reached out for Marna then and squeezed her just as tightly. Her sob reverberated in her ear. "I didn' think we was gonna make it!"

Jade closed her eyes. "We did. We're alive!"

Marna held her face with a wide smile. "I'm so happy to see yew made it."

She smiled. "Me too."

She hugged Cordelia when Marna pulled away. "You've been holding out on me. I cannot believe you never told me about the ability you have!"

She grimaced. "Can you blame me? My father thought he could beat it out of me, and the law forbids it."

"I must have been a terrible aunt for you to think you could never confide in me."

"It's a big burden to unload on someone," Jackson interjected. "Don't be angry she hid the truth. She was probably terrified."

Jade gave him a grateful smile. How did such a wonderful person fall on her path?

His smile widened, and he winked at her.

"There is still much to discuss," Cordelia stated, and Jade tore her eyes from Jackson. "We were debating on what we should make for dinner. Gainsley has returned with the food."

"Gainsley?" Jade said, and that's when she remembered Elijah getting stabbed. "Did Elijah survive?"

"You saved him." Jade looked toward the door. The blonde who was tied up in the warehouse stood awkwardly in the archway as if she were intruding on something she shouldn't. She was folded into herself, and this made Jade think of Ruby. It was a jab in the chest, and she prayed in vain that her sister made it out alive. "He was stabbed and bleeding out, and when you touched him, mag-" she paused with a heavy sigh. "You closed the wound somehow."

It was an interesting revelation, but as she watched the girl, she felt a pull in her energy. There was something familial about her. "What is your name?"

"Ollie."

"It's nice to meet you, Ollie."

The girl tried to smile, though it seemed very forced. The curve of her lips, or lack thereof, was distinct and familiar.

"He's been out cold," Jackson interrupted her thoughts, and she gazed up at him. "I don't know why or when he will wake up, but I believe he will pull through. His heart is strong and steady."

"Where is Owen?"

"He went after Esmeralda," he said. "He knows to meet here if anything happens. I expect them to turn up within the next few hours."

They pieced the story together one by one, and she felt grateful that they had all pulled through. Pearl clung to her thoughts. It was incredibly disheartening to think that her sister had deceived them. Her motives were selfish and incredibly wicked. She knew what Dominic was doing to those poor women and still allowed it to happen.

Jade didn't know what transpired, but she hoped Ruby had escaped the warehouse unscathed. Ruby was stronger than she believed. She just needed the confidence to uncover her power.

"I'm a bit peckish," Jackson said to lift the somber mood. "Let's get some food going, eh? I brought one of Avis's dresses for you to try on."

He pointed at the end of the bed as he wrapped an arm around Cordelia, and she did the same to him. She watched as they walked from the room. The silence was another reminder of what occurred. Pearl betrayed them, Vampirs existed, and their magic had been exposed.

She couldn't begin to fathom the reason or make sense of it. She was too tired for much else. She tried to help Marna fill the tub, but the woman brushed her off. When the bath was ready, she recoiled slightly from the heat until she was used to the temperature and lowered herself in, submerging her whole body, hoping, if nothing else, to cleanse herself of the dreadful night.

She found Jackson in the kitchen with Ollie, Cordelia, Gainsley, and Duke.

Jackson was cooking food on the stovetop; he grinned when she entered.

"Are you feeling better?" Cordelia asked as she chopped garlic.

She smiled over at Jackson. Knowing he survived made all the difference. Marna handed her a piping cup of coffee, and she took a sip, preferring black coffee over a cup of sugar. "The coffee is superb."

Gainsley grinned at her. "Jackson and Elijah are the chefs in the family, but if there is one thing I don't mess up on, it's the coffee."

Jade asked, "How long have you been with the Hadleys?"

He blew out of his mouth loudly and gazed at Jackson. "Let's see…twenty years now, I think."

Jackson nodded.

"Really?"

"Mrs. Hadley brought me home from the Reformatory school for juvenile delinquents when I was five. My father died when I was four, and my mother could not take care of six kids on her own, so she gave us up. We each went to a different orphanage, and I haven't seen one since. I can't even remember their names."

"That's awful," Marna said, and he gave her a rueful smile.

"It wasn't ideal, but I gained four brothers and a sister. The Hadleys are the only family I remember aside from Reformatory; the nuns and priests don't treat children very well. I still have the scars and saw a lot more than any child should. To say I was grateful when Mrs. Hadley brought me home was an understatement."

"How did she find you?" Jade asked. She was fascinated when others spoke of their childhood, and she often fantasized about growing up in Trinity Row. As crazy as it sounded, she would rather have lived as a pauper than be born of privilege. Being rich didn't make her life any easier, and she could empathize personally with his treatment at the Reformatory. Sympathy came easy at the thought of him being separated from his birth mother, but to grow up with the Hadleys must have been something incredible.

"She was a social worker," he answered as he set the table. "She said I reminded her of her boys. Her heart broke when she found me crying about how no one loved me or would feed me. She took me home that very day."

"Gainsley, I'm so sorry," Jade whispered.

He shrugged. "I don't remember much. Elijah, Avis, and I became inseparable. Jackson and Owen were a few years older, they played with us sometimes but not very often, and James was just a baby." He gazed at Jackson as he said this, but he didn't have a remark.

"That sounds like an ideal upbringing," Jade commented. "We had moments when our father wasn't around, but it never lasted long."

The scrutiny was evident. Perhaps Gainsley would like to contradict her words, but he would never understand. Money may not have been a struggle, but the abuse was, and she envied him. She would rather struggle to find food or a place to stay than deal with being beaten for who you are.

"William was never one for affection," Cordelia agreed as she dumped garlic and onions in the pan Jackson stood over.

"Never," Jade repeated.

Ollie watched Jade a little too carefully for her liking. It was as if she had done something to the girl, and she was, in turn, apprehensive of any further misgivings.

Jackson's cheek lifted when she met his stare. His hair was messy, and he was wearing glasses, her favorite way to find him. He was shaking the pan he held back and forth before tossing the ingredients in the air. He gave her a wink when the contents fell back into the pan.

She grinned. "I could watch you cook all day!"

He laughed.

Horses interrupted their serene morning. The carriage had rolled around to the back of the property. A stout man was sitting on the stoop, and a coffin was strapped to the top. Jade's stomach dropped.

"Finally," Jackson stated as he walked to the window.

Raoul jumped from inside the carriage and held out his hand for Avis.

Watch that will you?" Jackson asked Cordelia as he stepped outside to greet his sister, who jumped in his arms. Duke followed him out of the house.

"I didn't know what happened to any of you!" Avis wailed. "Something terrible happened in the city, and I thought I lost you too!"

"Who is in that coffin?" Jade asked.

"James," Gainsley answered grimly. "Jonathan Cavendish shot him right after the fight at the Vaults."

"The fight?"

"James fought in the Vaults, and so did Jackson," Cordelia answered, causing Jade to slump back against her chair, grief and anguish rising heavily in her chest. "He fought Teddy."

Jade's jaw slackened.

"Yeah," Gainsley laughed as he strode toward the door. "And he beat the ever-living piss out of him!"

"But not before Teddy stabbed Jackson in the side," Ollie added, and Jade gaped at Jackson through the glass doors as he untied James' coffin. "It wasn't deep as he is still standing."

"It's good to see we all made it out!"

Jade whipped around. Elijah was standing in the doorway looking rough for wear.

"At last!" Cordelia beamed from the stove. "We were wondering when you were going to wake!"

Elijah rubbed his head. "I feel like shit, but I'm-" he faltered when his gaze caught Jackson, Gainsley, Raoul, Duke, and Pikitis lowering the coffin from the cab.

"Who died?" he bellowed.

Jade covered her mouth as Cordelia said, "James." Somberly.

"WHAT?" He screamed and ran out of the house. Avis grabbed him as he continued to shout and pull away. "HE CAN'T BE DEAD!"

They lowered the coffin, and Jackson grabbed him, holding him tight. Elijah's legs buckled under him as obscure noises emanated from his mouth. Avis wrapped her arms around Elijah's back, and together, they cried for the brother they had lost.

The atmosphere had turned grim as the afternoon wore on. The anticipation of Owen returning with Esmeralda and, hopefully, Ruby dragged on. It was the primary source of her anxiety as well as being in this village. She had never been to Berrone before, and quite frankly, it scared the hell out of her. The land was hallowed, and she could feel the ancient magic vibrating in the ground. It caused her limbs to twitch restlessly. She didn't enjoy feeling as if she was crawling out of her skin or the mania threatening to take over her mind. Jackson was never far; he held her once they were seated on the couch, and she let him.

Pikitis walked into the library with Duke at his back. A gun was slung over his arm and a bandolier strapped to his chest. "The perimeter is secure. No one will get close to the house, but whatever you do, do not wander the property alone."

"Why?" Raoul asked. "Do you think the Elite will sneak onto the property?"

"I sure as hell would like to see them try," Pikitis said casually as he lit a cigarette. "I've placed boobie traps all along the yard."

Marna's eyes widened at him, and Gainsley laughed loudly. "Would you care for a bowl of soup, Bob? Duke?"

"Yes, please," Duke said.

"I'd love some!" Pikitis answered with vigor and inhaled his cigarette. "Hey, did I ever tell you about the time I almost got killed in Etra?"

"You haven't," Jackson replied as Marna jumped to give them food. The pair hadn't joined them for dinner.

"So, there I was," he said and held up his hands. "Our convoy was headed straight for Ibis. We fought through the trenches of Ryok, and we had won a battle that didn't look so promising; loss wasn't in our hearts anymore. We were on the up and up, and the war was on our side for once. So anyway, as we were trudging through the countryside of Antunes, which is beautiful, by the way… we stopped to catch our breaths and have a cuppa. So, I walk to the hill to look over the valley, and I am thinking about nothing in particular when I notice something out of the corner of my eye. I look straight ahead and see three steers staring directly at me, and their horns are massive!"

He held up his hands to make his point; the ash on his cigarette was growing. "So, I look to my right, there isn't a place to hide, and I look to my left, still nowhere to go, and if you know anything about animals, you don't run away from them. I made a decision at that moment."

"What was it?" Jade asked, thoroughly captivated by his story.

He grinned wickedly. "I ran straight for the oxen."

Gainsley laughed loudly, and Ollie finally cracked a grin. Jackson smiled at Jade, and she giggled under her breath.

"Did it frighten them?" Cordelia inquired; there was wry amusement in her voice.

"Of course, it did, and I was close to getting snagged on a horn as I ran past, but I made it through them and kept running on down the hill!"

"Were you yelling as you ran?" Elijah asked. His face was puffy and red. He cried all afternoon with Avis, which was gut-wrenching to watch. She was seated next to Elijah and staring at the fire. As her attitude wasn't very warm toward Jade initially, it was a surprise when she gave her a hug, thanking her for saving Elijah's life.

"Hell, I don't know," he bellowed, and the longer he talked, the longer his ash grew. "Probably."

Marna returned with a bowl of soup and held up a bottle of whiskey.

"Do yew drink Pikitis?" Marna asked as she held up a bottle.

"Oh, I've been known to take a nip or two in my day," he said with a cigarette hanging out of his mouth. "Boy, I'll tell ya, the first time I ever met James, he was about fourteen and liked to sneak into the old liquor cabinet, if you know what I'm saying. So, there he was, taking shots of whiskey at Christmas dinner while Clara was making pudding and Elijah was pouring a little more into his cup after each snort," he chuckled, and everyone around the room laughed. "So, James gets this hair-brained idea to help her pluck the turkey and mind you, he can barely even stand up straight. The poor bastard! And for forty-five minutes, he was chasing this turkey around the yard while Elijah was hooting and hollering at him!"

"Clara was mad as hell," Elijah answered raspily. "I got a real whopping for that!"

"Yeah, you did," Pikitis laughed. "And then she kicked you out of the house!"

"Didn't you wake up in the barn?" Jackson added with a Cheshire grin.

"Yeah," Elijah said, and his smile evaporated instantly. "I'm really gonna miss that kid."

That one statement took the humor from the room.

"We all are," Avis whimpered.

Elijah turned and squeezed her hand. When he looked back at Jackson, he asked, "What are we going to do with James?"

"We have to wait for Owen to bury him," Jackson answered.

Avis let out a sob, and Elijah placed his arm around her and pulled her into his chest.

"I heard you uncovered the Dollhouse Slayer," Pikitis said as a distraction from James.

"Yes."

"Dominic has been killing those prostitutes for a Vampir, and Pearl knew about it," Ollie interrupted from the other side of the couch. "What if Ruby freed it?"

Jade closed her eyes.

"That would explain the green lightning in the sky," Jackson murmured.

Jade's eyes snapped open, and she gazed at him. "What?"

He gripped her hand. "The entire horizon was green for several minutes."

Her anxiety threatened to consume her, and she placed her head in her hands. Taking deep breaths to calm her nerves, Jackson rubbed her back.

"So, what do we do?" Raoul asked.

"If Owen hasn't returned by morning, I'm going to find him," Jackson said.

"I'm coming with you," Elijah stated.

Jade lowered her hands with determination. "I have to figure out how to bind them once again. If Ruby has the power to unleash them, then I might have the power to reverse it."

Jackson was giving her an unreadable stare once more.

"If those things are on the loose, there is no telling how many more people will die."

He pushed his glasses onto his forehead as he rubbed his eyes.

"When are we going to get Ruby?"

"We?" Jackson repeated and lowered his hand, clearly confused.

Her eyes narrowed. "Yes, we. You cannot expect me to stay here while you go back to Bel Deaux!"

Jackson snorted and bellowed, "Oh, yes, I certainly can!"

She glared at him.

"Don't give me that look!" he snapped. "Dominic and Pearl intended to kill you!! I will not allow you to step foot in that city as long as he breathes!"

She pointed a finger at his chest. "I don't need your permission!"

"Jade," Cordelia intervened. "Stop it."

"I know you don't!" Jackson replied, "You can do whatever you set your mind to! I don't wish to rule your life, Jade. I just want to be a part of it!"

She dropped her finger and folded her arms. "Then what's the problem?"

He gave her an annoyed look. "The problem is, I cannot sit back and watch you walk into the lion's den! I will not be able to think rationally while trying to protect you!"

She pressed her lips together, clearly unamused.

"Someone could get hurt," Ollie added. "And then how would you feel?"

Jade flashed her a reproachful look.

"We will get your sister out of that city," Jackson promised. "Don't you trust me?"

She frowned at him. "Unequivocally."

"Then let me do this and put your faith in me."

How could she not trust him? He saved her life without realizing it. "Okay."

He exhaled in relief. Maybe it was because of what they shared; her feelings were now a myriad of something tangible, solid, and clear. She was okay with having a disagreement as long as they understood one another in the end. And despite everything, she felt relieved. They were here together on the same side. No matter what happened, they would deal with what the night would bring together.

She jumped up in a cold sweat; her heart and head were pounding vigorously. She dreamed of her mother and blood.

It took several breaths to realize she was lying in a bed alone, and it was fairly dark out. She glanced out at the French doors that were opened; it was raining. She slouched back on the pillows and listened to the deluge. Her thoughts were too detrimental, and hysteria threatened to ravage her mind. She didn't want to be alone. She wanted to be with Jackson.

She threw the covers off her and headed straight for his quarters before losing the nerve. There was light coming from under his doorway. She walked over to it slowly, raising her hand to knock with uncertainty, pausing in hesitation while her heart threatened to beat out of her chest. "Oh, for god's sake!" she whispered after a few beats and opened the door. He was sitting shirtless on the edge of the bed and writing in his notebook.

He gave a dubious stare when he turned his head. "Is something wrong?"

She hesitated in the doorway. The only man she had ever seen shirtless was Dominic Kane, but he was soft and round. It was far different staring directly at a man who was very full of life and the epitome of masculinity; it caused her to forget why she even came in the first place. "Um, no. Are you uh," she cleared her throat. "Alone?"

His brows knit together. "Yes."

Of course he was. She shut and locked the door behind her.

"What are you doing?" he asked while standing slowly.

Her eyes dropped to his bare chest; it was absorbing and well-defined. His abdomen was wrapped from where Teddy had stabbed him, and a surge of annoyance rose. Her eyes lowered even further to his stomach, where his hips jutted out, and a line of dark hair fell from his navel and dipped into his trousers.

He cleared his throat to divert her attention.

She raised her eyes to meet his gaze. "I need you to make me feel something other than grief."

His face twisted in perplexity.

Her hands were shaking, and the static was electrifying, but she continued, "I need you to make me feel."

He blinked several times and uttered, "What do you mean by that?"

"I cannot live this way anymore," she nearly whispered. "I'm tired of feeling so fucking numb and so fucking shattered all at once! Watching Elijah getting stabbed brought back these memories of my mother that I don't want to remember!"

His eyes traveled the length of her face.

"And I am sorry, I'm sorry you lost your brother. And I'm sorry for my sisters, for Pearl knowing about the murders, and for Ruby, who may have released the fallen. Unintentionally I might add, but she could have possibly released them all the same!"

"You have nothing to apologize for. It's not your fault."

"I'm surprised you haven't run away from me," she said quietly and dropped her gaze.

"Nothing could ever make me change the way I feel about you," he said firmly, causing her stomach to flip in a pleasing manner.

"I want you," she whispered.

He exhaled heavily before saying, "Jade."

"I don't need a lecture on what's right and what isn't!" she argued and took a step toward him. "You are all I want. Isn't that enough?"

He stared rigidly, eyes dipping to her exposed shoulder and back to her face.

Her brow popped; he was nervous. "Haven't you ever thought of it?"

He barked out a gruff laugh, turning his body and rubbing his eyes. "You're going to be the death of me, woman!"

She grinned idiotically, and with three seconds of insane courage, she pulled the nightdress over her head and dropped it on the ground.

He lowered his hand and said, "And what of-" he abruptly stopped when he caught sight of her stark form. She had the satisfaction of watching his eyes bulge from his head as they swept over her body.

Her heart never quieted, but she refused to feel shame as she slowly walked toward him. His chest was visibly rising and falling with her approach, his eyes never leaving hers.

Her smile fell when the nerves began to rise. She lifted her hand to touch his bare stomach, and his lips parted; a current pulsed between them. She raised her other hand to trace his mouth.

His eyes traveled the length of her face. "Are you sure about this?"

Her voice caught in her throat, so she nodded.

"I don't want you to rush into something you can't take back because you are upset about what happened to my brother."

"I want this," she said adamantly, her eyes flashing to him. "I want you."

He breathed forcefully out of his mouth once as his eyes shined with acceptance. He then placed his hands on either side of her face and dipped his head to meet her lips. When they connected, it surged throughout her entire body. His lips were vital and imperatively soft as they moved against hers. Slowly at first, before gaining velocity with rapacious intensity, she pressed her body into his, eliciting a moan from him that vibrated into her mouth. He reached down and lifted her into his arms, and she wrapped her legs around his waist as he walked them toward the bed.

Their lips disconnected as he laid her down, and she went to scoot backward, thinking he would closely follow, but he grabbed her legs the second she began to inch away and pulled her down to the edge of the bed. "You can't run from me now."

Her eyes widened under his primal gaze, which was mesmeric and supernal. The ustulation sparking in her stomach was lucent as he knelt on his knees, eyes never breaking her stare. He kissed the side of her knee. His breath and lips burned in their wake as he trailed kisses down her inner thigh. This alone threatened to unravel her fundamentally, and he had yet to kiss the most sensitive part of her.

His eyes flashed at her. "I'm going to eat you alive, girl."

She gulped.

"Do you still want this?"

"Yes."

She bit back a grin when his mouth lowered over her sex, consuming her with temerity. His right hand gripped her thigh as the other hand trailed up the side of her hip and ribs toward her breasts. The static that normally prickled her palms erupted all over her body with every pull of her nerves, evoking a scream from the back of her throat. She arched off the bed as the intensity grew with every sweep of his tongue, the overwhelming sensation threatening to consume her wholly. She withdrew her hips from his mouth before she peaked; the magnitude was far too inordinate.

He gripped her hips tightly, holding her in place so she could feel exactly what his mouth intended to do. The fluctuation of pleasure gradually built once again; this time, he released her hips and placed two fingers inside of her to help his unmerciful mouth. She relinquished control, allowing him full access to her body.

His tongue and fingers moved rhythmically, giving a new sense of freedom she had yet to expand upon. She would take full advantage of what Jackson offered, and never would she dissipate into darkness again. Her magic bloomed from her heart and traveled down every nerve and vein, illuminating the room. Only this time, she didn't cower in fear, and he didn't pull away.

Her muscles tensed around him as her climax ripped through every inch of her, seizing hold of her limbs as his name escaped her lips, leaving her aflame. He didn't pull away until she relaxed and melted into the bed, trailing kisses up her stomach and taking a nipple into his mouth.

"Jackson," she whimpered. Her legs were shaking, and her heart was beating rapidly. She couldn't even form a coherent thought.

He chuckled against her skin. "Had enough, have you?"

Her eyes shot open, and she gripped his hair, pulling his head up to meet her gaze. "Never!"

He gave her a self-satisfied grin as she placed her lips against his and slid her tongue into his mouth, tasting her own arousal. This simple action showed her how incredibly powerful and desirable she could be. Emotions she couldn't care less for, except with him alone. Being with Jackson was earth-shattering in every sense of the word, and never would she take a moment with him for granted. She wanted to return what he had given her until he begged her to stop… until he was the one left breathless and panting.

She reached for the buttons on his pants and hastily released them one by one. With this, he helped her effortlessly remove the garment until he was as naked as she.

He was built significantly better than her other frame of reference, which wasn't even comparable. The years of fighting in the Vaults shaped his muscles and left him ravaged with scars, the result of an untamable youth. But even as the years had passed, he was far more cut than she realized, not to mention his length.

"I want you to fuck me," she said when her eyes raised to his.

The smile carved on his ample lips slowly faded as his eyes traveled between her stare and her mouth until she grabbed onto his neck, drawing him closer. He pushed her into the bed with force at her request, his tongue promising to ignify her body once again.

She only pulled back from his mouth when he slid into her, which was more substantial than she anticipated. "Ah," she moaned.

"Are you-"

"Yes," she said and grabbed onto his ass, pulling him in as she thrust upwards.

"Oh my god," he grunted, his breath erratic.

Together they moved quicker and faster, finding one rhythmic motion. He kissed her neck when she turned her head, placing her lips on his biceps. The heat sent shivers down her body. She tasted his skin, inducing a howl of his adherence to her touch—the friction of unadulterated passion passing between them in one fluid movement.

She closed her eyes, savoring the moment. Every stroke was transcendent, building the pressure of another release.

He pushed up onto his hands, giving each thrust more depth and extremity. She gripped his arms firmly on either side of her head, static pulsating through the contact.

"Look at me," he said.

Her eyes flung open, falling prey to his transfixing stare. The color was intensely blue, yet these facets of white and green were in the mix. She once thought he was unobtainable, and now she understood he was amative to her soul. Never having found solace in life, he was a nepenthe of relief, grounding her body and mind.

"Come for me, Jade."

His words split her in two, and she arched her back, stomach pressing into his. He wrapped an arm around her waist, pulling her closer as warmth spread between them and static pulsated through her core, rippling through her entire body.

He slammed into her with more ferocity, moaning with each bated breath. She was utterly captivated by his face, saturated with pleasure, transforming his features devoutly. His eyes were closed, and his mouth parted with every thrust.

"Come for me, Jackson," she demanded when she sensed his climax drawing near.

His eyes snapped open at her words, doing just that. She grinned in satisfaction when it was her name he moaned with his release. His entire body shook involuntarily, and she could feel his heart thumping wildly against her chest. He buried his head into her neck, entirely out of breath.

She wrapped her arms around his shaking form with her own limbs threatening to dissolve into nothing but fragments of their kinetic energy.

XLV
OWEN

He was weak. The Vampir took far more blood than he initially realized, leaving him woozy and disoriented. He was lying on a relatively small couch in the Calvert manor as Esmeralda and Jet argued over the information in an ancient book. Blake Emerich stood silently in the corner, and Ruby sat in a small chair, her eyes unfocused on the ground. She had apologized a hundred times for unleashing the Vampir, and once Jet revealed the death of their father, she hadn't spoken a word. Ruby covered her mouth and turned away from them. She began to sob quietly, holding her breath to stifle the sound. Before long, Esmeralda wrapped her arms around her. He couldn't comfort either of them; it was too difficult to focus. Much of what they said was lost on him.

This information they were discussing was vital, yet he couldn't retain any of it. After much of their arguing, he gathered that they were trying to uncover if he himself would turn into a Vampir or not. He wanted to tell them he wouldn't. The only way to be transformed is if he drank from the Devil.

He couldn't find the energy to speak. He was far too tired and debilitated. It would take hours for him to recover. He knew Jackson was safe with the rest of the group at the house in Berrone, so there was no need to worry about their well-being. He would get to them in due time.

"How long are we to sit here before Pearl returns with the Vampir?" Esmeralda shrieked.

"I'm not giving up the estate!" Jet yelled.

"A new house can be bought, and the money isn't here! If Pearl doesn't come for us, the Elite will!"

Owen turned his head to look at them. They were standing chest to chest, arguing about two entirely separate issues. Esmeralda was concerned about the immortals, while Jet was worried about his material possessions and wealth.

"We can't stay here," Owen interjected.

Jet's eyes bugged at him. "Aren't you concerned with the fact that Teddy killed my father?"

"Of course I am, and I'm sorry for your loss," Owen answered groggily. "But that isn't the issue at the moment. I don't think you realize what is stalking the streets. Your money won't mean a damn thing if you're dead."

"I thought Vampirs couldn't enter a house without an invitation," Ruby said.

"Pearl could invite him in, and she will," Esmeralda answered dismissively. "We have to go where she can't find us. We have to go to Berrone."

"What's in Berrone?" Jet asked.

"It's our safe point," Owen answered and grabbed the bridge of his nose. He was beginning to feel queasy.

"That's great," Jet said with heavy sarcasm. "You know the Kensingtons wanted you dead, but my father put a stop to it?"

"Yes," Owen answered and breathed evenly out of his nose. How his body reacted to the circumstance, he would relate it to being hit by a trolley. Not that he had ever been hit by a traveling car; he could only imagine. It wasn't getting any better; it was getting worse.

"What's wrong?" Esmeralda asked.

"I don't know."

"Shhh!" Jet hissed. "Do you hear that?"

Owen dropped his hand and strained to listen. It sounded as if there was shouting coming from outside. His vision was beginning to trace, and his brow pinched as he struggled to gaze at Esmeralda evenly. She sat at his side; he was seeing double of her.

"Owen!" she said urgently.

"I don't feel so well," he murmured.

Shuffling forced him to look over his shoulder. Jet and Blake were looking out of the window. "Oh, look, a mob. How quaint."

"A mob is headed this way?" Esmeralda repeated, and Ruby jumped from the couch for a look.

"They even have torches and pitchforks," Jet stated calmly. "What an idyllic scene. I would take a guess and say this is Teddy's doing since I used my power against him."

"I suppose this is our queue to leave," Blake answered, and they both turned from the window. They stood over Owen. "Can you walk?"

"I can try," he replied and held up his hand. Blake hoisted him from the bench, and he swayed into them.

"You're not going to make this easy, are you?" Jet barked, and they steered him from the couch. Esmeralda grabbed his hips, trying to help support his weight as he could no longer make much use of his legs.

"We got him! Get down to the cellar!"

Esmeralda grabbed Ruby's hand, and they ran ahead. Owen couldn't do much as they dragged him toward a large painting of William Calvert. Esmeralda pulled it open, revealing a stone staircase leading below the ground.

They shuffled in the crevice, and Blake pulled the painting shut behind them. His disorientation was getting the better of him, and he tried relentlessly to get a hold of himself.

"You're a long-limbed fellow," Blake grunted as Jet gave up trying to drag him down the stairs and ordered him to grab his legs.

"My apologies."

"Remind me never to get bitten by a Vampir," Jet commented through the winding staircase.

Once they reached the bottom wine cellar, they propped Owen against one of the racks and ran down the rows of wine.

Esmeralda dropped to his side and touched his face. "My love. You aren't well, are you?"

He closed his eyes when diplopia took over once again.

"Do Vampirs have some sort of poison in their fangs?" She asked.

"I have no idea."

A bang from above silenced him, and the three of them glanced at the ceiling. Jet and Blake jumped into action when several footsteps entered the house. He grabbed Owen's arm and hauled him upwards.

"He needs a doctor," Esmeralda told him.

"Are you mad?" Jet hissed. "What fucking doctor would take a look at him without turning us in?"

"Watch your language," Owen hissed.

"There must be some sort of poison associated with a Vampirs bite. Can't you see how unbalanced he is?" Esmeralda argued.

"We can't take him to a doctor; we'll be reported. Did you not see the mob up there?"

"Adam Riley," Owen said.

"Who?" Jet asked.

"Adam Riley knows about Vampirs. He will not turn us in. He works at Bellevue," he explained with his eyes closed. "That is if you can get us out of here."

"He doubts me!" Jet hissed.

"The nerve." Blake retorted.

Owen grinned. He would be more amused by Jet and Blake's antics had he not felt so terrible.

They carried him through row after row of wine racks. He retained bits and pieces of the darkened space as they carried him toward a door on the far side of the room. The noise from above heightened and became louder with each passing second.

When they reached the door, Jet opened it slowly, pausing to listen for any commotion on the other side, yet it seemed to be above them and not outward.

"Be on the lookout, girls. I can deflect their attention, but if they come after us, you need to be ready to stop them," Jet ordered.

"We're ready," Esmeralda answered.

They dragged him up a small set of stairs. Blazing light from behind forced Owen to open his eyes. The Calvert manor was on fire.

"And Teddy says I'm one for theatrics?" Jet snapped.

"They've got to burn the witches," Blake muttered as they turned back around and began shuffling in the direction of the nearing cabs.

Jet raised his hand. Blue light traveled into the ground and moved toward the mob; his deflection as he said. They hoisted Owen in first before filing in one by one.

"I can't believe you're not losing your mind over the destruction of that house," Ruby stated while gazing out of the window.

"We have others," Jet said. "We just need to make sure we get the money before Teddy does."

"Or Pearl," Esmeralda added.

As they began to roll away, he could barely keep his eyes open.

His thoughts drifted to Clara, as they often did, to the last peaceful day they had together. The last memory he had of her smiling face. They were in the library, he at his desk working while she paced and read a book, their most common hobbies.

The room was reasonably quiet, and he gazed at her often in worry. Her due date was nearing, and she complained of abdominal pain each day.

"I really wish you would stop leering at me," she said, although her gaze hadn't lifted from her book.

"I really wish you would sit down," he countered.

Her eyes met his, and a crafty smile lit her face. "I know my body, Owen. I need to walk."

He sighed and glanced back down at his work. He was an up-and-coming detective for the justice of the peace in Bel Deaux. The Duchess of Jendoux wrote when her niece Georgina Peck turned up missing five days before.

"Tell me about her," Clara said to deflect his anxiety. "Where was Georgina last seen?"

Owen sighed. "Clara, this isn't the time. You need to focus on rest."

"Don't patronize me, Owen," Clara chided. "Tell me about her."

He watched her apprehensively. He wasn't sure if talking about a missing girl was the best thing for a woman, let alone a pregnant one.

The longer he stared, he realized how beautiful she truly was. Her red hair fell around her frame, and her green dress complimented her blue eyes. He wanted to remember her at this moment, with a big belly and bare feet.

"Owen," she pressed.

"I don't want to upset you," he said quietly and pushed his spectacles up the bridge of his nose.

"Then why don't we talk about Jackson."

Owen glanced out of the window and grumbled, "I don't want to talk about him either."

"And why not?"

"You know why, Clara," he snapped.

"Don't you use that tone with me, Owen Hadley," Clara bit back, and he gave her an apologetic grin. "For someone who says they despise the man he has become, you were the first out the door to defend him today. And not only that, but he also saved Elijah. You know, if Gerald found Elijah first, he would have been too drunk and incoherent, making it nearly impossible to shoot correctly. We would be burying Elijah right now if Jackson hadn't intervened."

Owen took off his spectacles and carelessly tossed them onto the table, rubbing his temples. "I know."

"When are you going to let go of that male pride and speak to him?"

He glanced out of the window again. "I have nothing kind to say to him."

Clara stopped pacing and lowered her book. "A thank you would suffice."

"That could be said in a letter," he grumbled.

"Your obstinate behavior is aggravating." she snapped. "Utterly and completely aggravating."

He sat back in his chair with folded arms. "If my memory serves me correctly, you weren't overly thrilled with Jackson either."

She glared at him. "Yes, because he is my brother too! I am mad at his choices and want him to be a better man! It is not out of hate that I am upset, and I do not hold any negativity in my heart for him! I think it's time you release it because you know damn well he is your favorite!"

Owen's jaw snapped shut, yet he didn't deny it.

"Thought so," she muttered and returned to her book.

Despite the subject, Owen smirked and rubbed his chin.

"You know where to find him," she hedged.

"He also knows where to find me," he grunted.

"Aggravating," she said under her breath, and he chuckled.

She would be happy to know they had patched their relationship and that they were getting along. He hoped James would join her wherever she and Charlie were. Clara would take care of him until they could meet again.

XLVI
Jackson

"JACKSON!"

He was startled awake and lost the dream just as soon as his eyes snapped open. The only thing he could recall was that it was very dark, and it was James who had screamed his name.

He sucked in a deep breath, almost as if he had forgotten to in his sleep. His heart thundered furiously against his ribs, and he began to pant heavily. He closed his eyes and leaned back against the pillow, slowing his breath and rubbing his eyes. His lips were severely raw, yet his body was oddly at ease.

There was pressure against his side; a leg and an arm were draped across his body. He turned his head to see Jade's sleeping form, her lips lightly touching his shoulder as her dark hair flowed down the side of her face and onto his arm. He pushed the lock back with his finger and stared. She was beautiful in this peaceful state of sleep, even with a large bruise across her cheek, and why wouldn't she be? His heart was still pounding, only now he was confident it was because of Jade and not some nightmare.

He'd spent the night kissing her heedless mouth as their bodies scraped ardently against one another. Never had he experienced anything quite like it, quite like her. It was unexpected yet significant. She herself was beyond significant and completely life-altering.

He lifted his arm over her frame, shifting her weight so she could rest her head on his collar, her nose nuzzling his neck. He tightened his arm around her, feeling the fresh scabs on her back against his forearm, and pressed a kiss into her hairline. Her arm and leg tensed against him.

He whispered, "Are you all right?"

"Yes," she said, tracing a finger down his Adam's apple. The static burned, but it no longer hurt; it was staggering.

"Did I hurt you?"

"No."

"Do you regret it?"

"Never."

He smiled in relief and pulled her in even tighter.

"Was it…" she began and trailed a finger down his chest; his breath caught. "How was it for you?"

He gasped as her hand traveled down his stomach, stopping at the base of him when she realized he wasn't able to answer. She looked at him with a raised eyebrow.

He finally let out a breath. Did she honestly not understand? How could he even begin to explain so that she would?

"It was," he paused to search for the right word before settling with, "Intense."

"Intense," she repeated. Her voice was light and playful.

"Nothing would ever compare," he admitted. "And I know you felt it too."

She gave him a sly smile.

He wasn't a poet, he couldn't explain it properly, but he could properly show her. He pushed her back into the bed and began to kiss her lips. And to his immense satisfaction, she hungrily reciprocated and clutched onto him. Perhaps she did understand.

He had never loved with someone the way he had with her. The amount of pleasure consumed him entirely, which was overbearing, leaving him shaking and out of breath. She was unmerciful as she devoured him, an act of her adoration. The frisson left him complacent that she deeply wanted him alone.

It was a frightening thing to have so much to lose. Life rarely awarded him with the delectations of life, and a nagging feeling tore at his thoughts, taunting him with fear and grief that it would all be taken away. Yet, he would not permit a bitter thought to ruin the moment, not when she was demanding all of him.

He allowed her to push him into the bed, taking complete control. He reciprocated her grin when she settled on top of him and began to move her hips.

Even if he died tomorrow, it was well worth this moment.

They were watching the rain from bed and blatantly ignoring dawn on the horizon, pretending there wasn't any danger hovering. He held her close and leaned his head against hers as she trailed his skin with her fingertips; static followed.

"I want you to know that I don't make it a point to do this," she said after some time.

"Do what?"

"Fall into a man's bed."

"I never thought you did."

She sat up fully and turned to face him. "You need to understand something about Dominic Kane." He frowned as she looked at him in a pleading sort of way. "I have not been well for some time. I wasn't well when I met you at the mask. I was suffocatingly numb, wandering through each day with this weight sitting heavy in my chest. It threatened to smother me, and I thought if I found an outlet, something to distract me from the pain, I would be able to survive."

Jackson's face crumpled. How could someone so ornate be so despondent?

"But he was all wrong for me, and I wish that I could take it back. He didn't make me feel any better about myself, not in the way you do. I wish I had found you sooner."

"We are together now. That is all that matters."

Her face twisted in confusion. "You aren't mad?"

"How could I be?" he asked with a dry laugh. "That part of your life had nothing to do with me."

Her face smoothed. "You are quite different from Teddy. He took it very personally, and I wasn't even with him then."

"That's because he was raised to believe the world owes him."

She pressed her lips together and a crease formed in between her eyes.

"What's wrong?"

"You know how you said you wouldn't be able to think rationally with me in Bel Deaux?"

His brows pinched, and he said, "Yes."

She blinked a few times before looking up through dark lashes. "I need you to come back to me," her voice was low and demanding.

"I will come back to you," he promised.

Her lips raised, but they didn't quite reach her eyes.

He sat up and grabbed her face. "I will always find my way back to you."

He didn't want to leave, but when there was still no sign of Owen, the decision was made for him. Raoul agreed to assist them back to the city. Breakfast was a heavy affair, though he was sitting in a state of ecstasy. Jade grabbed his leg every now and again, a reminder that she was here at his side. It was incredibly overwhelming to have something worth so much, something he had never shared with another woman. Once they returned from Bel Deaux, he would start a life with her.

"I'll see you in a few hours," he told her as he was about to leave.

She nodded solemnly and wrapped her arms around his waist. When he placed his lips against hers, the kinetic energy returned. Their kiss was possessive and heady. If this was his last by some terrible chance, he wanted to make the most of it.

When he pulled away, he placed his forehead on hers. "I will bring your sisters back to you."

"I know you will," she said.

Everyone came out to the porch. He said his goodbyes to Ollie and Cordelia, thanking Gainsley and Pikitis for staying behind to watch over the girls.

"You better return," Avis told him and Elijah. "Don't do anything stupid, and please bring Owen back whole. I cannot lose one of you. Promise me."

"I promise," Jackson said.

He gave Jade one last smile and ducked into the cab. Raoul rode on the stoop with Duke to provide them with privacy. It was quiet for some time before they began discussing James. Elijah needed to get it all out, and Jackson let him. He never thought he would lose one of his siblings, and without knowing where Owen was or what was happening to him, fear elevated his unrest; they may lose the patriarch of the family.

They spoke of the best days when James was a child. He was the one who hadn't spent much time with their parents. He was one when their father died and three when their mother passed on. All James knew was his siblings and Gainsley. They took his upbringing seriously, and Jackson felt extremely guilty for missing the last five years of his life. He would never have left if he knew it was all he had.

"What are we going to do?" Elijah asked in all seriousness. "How are we going to go back?"

"I don't intend to come back once we find Owen," Jackson said. "If anyone catches wind of Jade's ability, she will be imprisoned. They all will."

"You're going to give up your entire life for her?"

"I'm not giving up anything," Jackson snapped. "But we can't stay here with her father and Teddy. We'll never be left alone."

"I know that. It is just a lot to take in."

It was the truth, but perhaps he should spare his brothers this burden and take on the task himself. He was the one in love; he would go wherever Jade went. He didn't mind leaving the city behind as long as she was at his side.

"You don't have to go," Jackson told him.

"Yes, I do," Elijah answered without question. "The Elite control the city with fear and violence. We can't protect its citizens when Merfan and Feilding work for them! Everything we stand for is corrupted by money and greed. There is not anything worth fighting for anymore. We were forced off the Dollhouse case, and why would that be unless Feilding knew who committed the crimes? We've been stopped at every turn from doing our jobs!"

"Well, it's not a wonder as to why," Jackson answered dryly, "The Elite will stop at nothing to remain hidden in plain sight."

"That's always been the problem," Elijah answered. "They've always orchestrated the lives and deaths of the citizens of Bel Deaux."

He exhaled, there was nothing left to say on the matter.

It took an hour to ride back to the capital, and his anxiety flared in his chest the entire ride. His unease failed to settle when the city came into view. The sky was overcast as always; smog settled in between the buildings and train tracks. Airships slowly passed across the skyline, causing dread to encompass his lungs.

"Well, it's not burning to the ground," Jackson said as he gazed out of the window.

"Do you think Ruby truly unleashed the Vampirs?" Elijah asked.

"Maybe she didn't," he answered while gazing at the grand bridge. "I expected the city would have been torn to shreds. Something we would have heard, even from Berrone."

"I cannot believe they hold power and Vampirs exist!" Elijah muttered. "What a wild revelation! Am I dreaming?"

Jackson laughed. "I wish I could say that you are."

They stared out the window, expecting complete chaos in the streets, but all was normal. If they hadn't experienced what they had in the last forty-eight hours, it would have seemed like another day in Bel Deaux.

Raoul drove them to the Hadley manor. It was here that they came upon a cavalcade of Policemen.

"What is happening?" Elijah blurted.

The carriage slowed, and Raoul knocked on the window. Jackson slid it open.

"What do you want to do?"

Something turned in his stomach, but they had to proceed, especially if this intrusion had anything to do with Owen.

"We have to find out why they are here."

"I don't think we should!" Elijah protested.

"What if something happened to Owen?"

Elijah clenched his teeth together as Duke snapped the reins, and the horses trudged forward until they reached the front of the drive. Jackson shared a look with Elijah before hopping out of the cab. All the police officers standing on the stairs turned to them expectantly, Merfan being the head of the group.

"What is going on?" Jackson asked with Elijah at his side.

"You are under arrest," Cillian said as he grabbed Jackson's wrist and slapped a handcuff on it.

"Whatever for?" He bellowed as Elijah was handcuffed and shouting obscenities. Raoul and Duke were dragged from the cab and slammed into the ground as officers detained them.

"For the murder of Roslyn Emerich!" He yelled. "And every other prostitute who lost their lives these past few weeks!"

"Are you fucking mad?" Jackson bellowed.

"You clearly are!" Merfan yelled as he stalked up to Jackson and poked his chest. "I knew it was you, you son of a bitch! We've had the Dollhouse Slayer under our nose this whole time, and when I find Owen, I will arrest him for aiding and abetting a criminal!"

"With what proof?"

"Roslyn's body was sliced from end to end in your laboratory! I believe that is damning evidence if you ask me!"

"I haven't even been here!" Jackson wailed.

"Sure, you haven't," Merfan sneered with a raspy laugh. "I have you now, and I'll hang the lot of you!"

"We were set up!" Elijah screamed.

"Sure, you were," Merfan hissed.

"Where's Owen?" Jackson bellowed as Cillian shoved him toward a police cab.

"Beats me, but I'll throw him in the brig with you when I find him!"

Cillian shoved him toward the carriage Elijah was tossed in, protesting, and kicking against the officers restraining him.

"C'mon, let's talk about this!" Jackson pleaded. "You know us! You know we had nothing to do with this!"

"I thought I knew you," Cillian answered. "I don't know how you can explain away Roslyn's slain form. She was hanging in your basement, along with Landini lilies scattered around the room."

"Doesn't that sound suspicious to you? How did you even know to come here?"

"Augustus Atwood reported it when he came looking for his sister-in-law. It seems as if you have some explaining to do! Pearl Atwood reported the kidnapping of her sister Jade, and she claimed you had her!"

"This is madness!" Jackson yelled. "She set me up!"

"Pearl Atwood framed you for murder?" Cillian asked cynically.

"Yes!"

"You're not the person I thought you were!" Cillian muttered before shoving him toward the awaiting cab. Jackson protested and shoved back. He wasn't going to go down for these crimes. Dominic Kane and Pearl Atwood were not going to frame them for murder.

Merfan pulled out his baton and smacked Jackson across the back, causing him to stumble. Cillian shoved him into the cab and slammed the door.

"I told you we shouldn't have come!" Elijah yelled.

"Well, I'm fucking sorry I ruined your night!" Jackson snapped as he adjusted himself. "I had to be sure it was nothing to do with Owen!"

"Whoever was murdered wasn't Roslyn," Elijah stated. "At least I don't think it was her. I bought her a ticket to Jendoux to work for Gabrielle, although I'm not sure if she went. She was concerned about leaving her friends behind."

"Well, if she has any sense, she left."

"Where the hell do you suspect Owen is?" Elijah grumbled.

"He must have gotten away from the warehouse if Pearl hadn't already turned him in. I just hope he's okay."

Elijah's jaw snapped shut.

"How are we going to get out of this?" Raoul barked. "They'll hang us!"

"I don't know," Jackson murmured. There was truly nothing they could do at this point. Merfan fixed him for the Dollhouse Slayer murders, and Cillian was no longer on their side, a prediction Owen had made. Only this time, Owen wasn't here to save them, and he hoped, by some fucking miracle, Queen Elizabeth would step in on their behalf before Feilding made the decision to have them swing.

XLVII
Jade

Cordelia poured everyone a glass of wine, but Jade refused. She didn't bother to partake in the distractions of her aunt. She stood by the window and waited. "I knew I should have gone with them," she said. They were more than likely ambushed; she only hoped he had found Ruby and Esmeralda. They would protect them.

"There is no use dwelling on it now," Cordelia said. "We cannot undo what has been done."

"You're right," she answered. "We need to return to the city right now!"

"We can't go after them!" Cordelia roared.

"We don't have a choice!" Avis interrupted. "I already have to bury one brother. I would like not to have to bury another!"

"I agree," Gainsley said. "We should have gone after them earlier. I will drive you to the city."

"It's settled then," Jade said and sprang from the window. She wasn't wasting another moment here while Jackson was gone into the unknown.

"I don't want to return to the city," Ollie admitted. It was the first time she had spoken since they entered the front room for a drink. "I would rather remain behind than put myself in danger again. There is nothing I can do to stop those fiends."

Jade glanced at Cordelia. Her aunt didn't seem happy, but she wouldn't argue. "Marna and I can stay with her…and Bob?"

"You can count on me!" He bellowed. "We'll take care of things here while you get our boys!"

Jade smiled. It was the first time in her life that she felt welcomed and substantiated within a group of people. They were on the same side, and that was all that mattered.

She let her anxiety get the best of her. The ride was miserable, and she felt on the verge of throwing up. Her thrumming heart was beating wildly, fearing something terrible had happened to Jackson. The carriage rolled down from the Perican hills and into the Val Haven wood, bringing along with it mist that seeped in low and a harsh bite to the air that stung. There wasn't a cloud to be seen. Thousands of stars scattered the blackened sky as the moon hung large and bright. It was mostly a quiet night, and the ride was smooth.

Gainsley whistled softly as he pulled a pipe from his tattered jacket and stuffed it to the brim with tobacco. His eyes darted to the thick trees that were looming nearby.

She tried to shake off the ill feeling that began to rise in the pit of her belly and continued to listen to Gainsley's whistle as a distraction from the trees that had enveloped the carriage entirely. With each step into the enclosed forest, the horses began to have fits and stalled every few feet. Gainsley yelled at the creatures, though they ignored all commands by neighing and rising on their hind legs.

She paused to listen. Her ears peaked as she strained to hear the commotion outside. The horses had begun to walk backward, causing the carriage to jilt and shake.

Jade peered out of the window. "What is going on?"

But before Gainsley could respond, a gnarly screech echoed throughout the trees, vibrating to the core of each of their bodies, sending a shrill of panic that would never be forgotten. Jade gazed out into the distance. Her eyes widened in fear as her breath puffed like smoke in the frozen air. After a few beats, the screech came again, closer and more menacing this time.

"Get us out of here!" Jade yelled.

Gainsley didn't need to be told twice; he pulled out his whip and smacked it against the horses. They must have gotten a sense of urgency, for they began to run. Jade flew back against the seat, heart pounding in her head. She looked out of the window; this time, she could hear snarls behind them. Her head whipped toward the back of the carriage, and amber eyes glowed back at her.

The horses were erratic as they ran. The carriage swerved and hit a stump sticking out near the road. The carriage was separated from the harness and crashed into the trees, Jade was knocked out cold, and Gainsley was thrown from his stoop. The horses ran forth without them, leaving nothing but destruction and horror in their wake.

The raw air was frigid and clung to Jade like a disease. Her jaw tightened and teeth clenched as she grunted loudly, eyes popping open and rolling back. She barely registered the pounding in her head or the irritating burning sensation that shot up her legs; the bone-numbing temperature canceled any other sense of thought or notion. She rolled to her side, grunting and blinking in the faint light that broke through the destroyed cab she had comfortably sat in. She pushed herself up and cried out when it felt as if her brain smacked against her skull. Her arm buckled, and she fell to the ground, losing all thought and consciousness.

Her face twitched at the bright light that annoyingly kissed her cheeks. Her brow furrowed when the agonizing pain in her head became clearer with each breath of awareness. Moaning in the back of her throat, she lifted a hand to rub her temple. The world was extremely blurry when she dared to open an eye. Rays from the sun shined in directly, causing her to quickly turn her head and groan in pain with the sudden whiplash of movement.

"What in the bloody hell," she murmured. She was still inside the cab, recalling the memories from the night before as she struggled to sit up fully. Her legs were halfway out of the cab and into the open. Unable to get out any other way, she slid down through the gap at her thighs, coughing and squinting as she looked around. There were broken wood panels and blood scattered along the dirt path. She ignored the pounding in her head and heaved herself upward.

"Gainsley!" she tried to yell, but her voice croaked instead. She cleared her throat and yelled, "Gainsley!" More intelligibly.

Gainsley never answered. Nothing came but the birds that called to one another.

She hobbled around the cab and called once again for him. A bloody heap halfway in the road made her halt. Her heart began to pound at the sight. She slowly hobbled forward as the unrecognizable body that was once a man lay discarded. The entire rib cage had been ripped open and hollowed, the insides nowhere to be seen. The smell emanating from the body was starting to rot with the warmth of the rising sun.

She lurched forward and threw up bile, her hands resting upon her knees. She breathed in slowly, one calculated breath after another.

She spit on the ground every so often, taking several minutes to regain her composure before flight kicked in, and she began to run. Stiff from the accident still, she had trouble finding her footing and fell against the ground, scraping her palms and knees. She yelled out, wanting nothing more than to wake up from this hellish nightmare. However, it only got worse when the rotting smell of death found her nose again. She opened her eyes to see the bodies of the horses scattered along the trail.

She jumped to her feet, and this time, she ran until her lungs gave out.

The sun was descending, and the night began to make its presence known. Two men on horses rode quickly through the Val Haven wood and came upon a figure slumped in the road. Halted with their approach, they discovered a woman lying on her stomach. The skirt below her knees was shredded entirely, exposing scabbed over skin. The first rider jumped off his horse to take a closer look.

"Is she dead?" The second asked.

Dirt near Jade's nose moved with every shallow breath.

"Nearly," The first offered. He cocked his head when he noticed the large gash on her forehead, which had been scabbed over.

"Wonder if she was in that crashed carriage."

"Must have been."

"Has she been wandering the woods alone?" The second asked.

"Dunno," the first shrugged.

"Reckon we should take her into town?"

"Reckon so."

The first looked up at the bright orb that was rising in the sky. It glared down at them as a warning. "Quickly, we don't have the time."

The second jumped from his horse, grabbed Jade's legs, and heaved her onto the back of the first rider's horse. "We'll never make it to Vendekk if we don't hurry."

The first wiped his brow. "I know."

The second man opened his mouth but was interrupted by a howl coming from within the thick forest. His eyes widened at his companion, who was staring ahead. Another howl made the second rider run to his horse and jump on. Both men turned their animals and kicked, picking up speed when a third howl rang from behind; the men drove as far and as fast from the forest as possible. They pushed their horses to the verge of exhaustion and didn't relent until they reached the gates of Vendekk, pounding against them with vehemence. Their fervor didn't stop until the gates opened, and they burst through to help the gatekeepers shut the night out. Only when the gate was locked once again did they relax and laugh with one another at their narrow escape from the evil that stalked the Val Haven wood.

XLVIII
Ruby

"It's been a year," Esmeralda said.

Ruby turned her head in reflex, but her mind was completely blank.

"Today marks the one-year anniversary of Mother's death," she explained when Jet also failed to say a word.

Instead, he pressed his lips into a hard line and gazed dismissively out the cab window. He held secrets more than anyone, and Ruby craved to know the dark basis of his mind, yet she could only speculate.

His reaction must have been the devastating effect of grief, for she knew he loved their mother beyond.

When they reached the gates of the Bellevue asylum, Owen looked on the verge of death. Esmeralda had started crying, and this is when Jet realized there was more than meets the eye. He watched disdainfully as she wiped Owen's forehead, which had been resting in her lap.

"All three of you have a thing for one of the Hadleys?" he snarled, but she ignored him. He then glanced at Ruby.

"You can admit, they are quite handsome," Ruby repeated Esmeralda's words from what seemed like ages ago. Esmeralda tried to grin, but her lip quivered instead.

"You know that James-" Blake suddenly smacked Jet, and he rounded on him. "Have you lost your mind?"

"Now is not the time," Blake hissed, and for once, Jet snapped his loudmouth shut.

Ruby was not one for secrets; it made her anxiety rise. "What about James?"

Blake glared at her brother, and it was evident that it was usually the other way around. Jet watched him appreciatively for a few seconds before turning back to her. "It's nothing. It's none of my business who you end up with."

Ruby's eyebrows drew in harshly with his blatant lie. For one, Jet made it his business to order them around. And second, there was something he was going to reveal about James. She wasn't sure if this was a good thing or not. It put her in an even more foul mood than she already was. Using her power drained her energy. If she laid her head down on the bench, she would fall asleep instantly; but her father's death had her wide awake. She wasn't sure how to feel about it. He was never affectionate or even paid much attention to her. In truth, she should feel relieved. She couldn't explain why she didn't.

And that's when she realized she hadn't seen Helena, Anne, or any of the other prostitutes since she released the undying. It was what she had dreamed of since Helena entered her life, yet it was empty without them.

"We need to figure out how to bind the immortals once again," Blake interjected. "I realize this was unintentional, and I'm not blaming you. However, that doesn't change the fact that those creatures are on the loose."

"All I did was project my power against it," Ruby said, realizing how strange it was to discuss magic openly without penitence. "My intention was to kill it."

"Well, if necromancy is your power, it may be the cause," Jet said. "You can conjure the dead, and they were the living dead. Therefore, it brought them back to life in a sense."

"That would imply a healing power would work against them," Esmeralda proposed. When she finally raised her head to look at them, she looked tired, as tired as Ruby felt.

"Then all hope is lost. None of us have healing powers." Jet stated. "If we did, Owen wouldn't be in the state he is in."

"You aren't helping!" Esmeralda snapped as the carriage halted in front of the hospital. "Can we please focus on Owen for now? The Vampirs can wait!"

"Can they?" Jet barked.

"If an angry mob showed up at our door, then no Vampir has yet been discovered!"

He rolled his eyes and jumped from the cab, helping Blake haul Owen up the steps of the asylum.

The structure was as long as it was wide, with a white clock tower looming overhead. It wasn't as impressive as the sky tower in the heart of the city, but it still made a point. The grounds were vacant and detached. No trees or bushes to decorate, perhaps so no patient could hide while enclosed in its gates. Ruby grabbed Esmeralda's hand, gripped her skirt, and ran up the steps.

The halls were stark white and quiet. The Gaslights were nearly extinguished, and the further they walked inside, the eerier it felt. They didn't run into a single person down the long hallway.

"It seems abandoned," Jet commented.

The administrative office was behind a steel door at the end of the hall. Ruby followed despite a voice in her head screaming at her to turn around and run. Her unease only grew when Esmeralda opened the door to the office and froze in her tracks.

"What is it?" Jet barked, but when his head turned down the hall to the right, he muttered, "My god."

Esmeralda stumbled backward and glanced down the very same hall Jet and Blake were looking at in incredulous fear.

"What do you see?" Ruby asked and carelessly took a step forward to examine the hall for herself. Several bodies were discarded on the floor, and the hair on the back of her neck rose when Jet hissed, "We need to get out of here!"

She whipped around with the intent to run and halted in primal fear. A man stood in the middle of the hall with a devilish grin. Blood was smeared across his chin and dribbled down his neck and chest; his lateral incisors and canines were defined into a sharp point. He had dark hair and eyes that were reflective in the dim light, appearing silver. "At last, we meet," he said, his eyes never wavering from Ruby. "I cannot thank you enough for freeing me from my prison."

The static hit her palms with the sudden adrenaline coursing through her veins. She would have run before but no longer felt meek and timid. She was a force to be reckoned with, and she would no longer sit back and wait for someone to save her.

The Vampir wavered, and the smile fell from his blood-stained lips when Esmeralda stepped beside her. "I mean no harm to you. You are my savior. I will protect you from the others."

"Do you really expect us to trust you?" Esmeralda said as she took another step forward, placing herself in front of Ruby.

His eyes flicked to her. "No, I don't. The city is no longer safe with us unbound."

"The city wasn't safe with you bound," Esmeralda countered.

"Fair point, but there is good and evil in us, too," he said, backing away from them slowly. "I have been bound for a very, very long time. The men I killed here tonight deserved it. And perhaps, some of them did not. My bloodlust is far too overwhelming now to think rationally. My intent, however, is not to inflict harm. The Hadleys come from a line we protected many centuries ago."

"Who is we?" Ruby asked, thinking of James.

"My brother and I," he answered with another grin. "He is what you would call a Lycan. Ironic, is it not? Two brothers bitten by two different creatures of the night."

"There are more of you?" Jet bellowed.

The Vampir grinned. "Absolutely there are, and when the Nephilim and Shedim come for you, you'll want extra protection for the ones you love." His eyes widened when they dropped to Owen in Jet and Blake's arms. "What happened to Owen Hadley?"

"He was bitten."

Alarm took hold of the Vampirs face before he stepped forward. In a blink, he was gone. Ruby and Esmeralda whirled around to see him bending over Owen.

"Stay away from him!" Esmeralda screamed.

"Relax," the Vampir said with little interest. "What bit him? A Vampir, a Lycan, or one of the Nephilim?"

"What is the Nephilim?" Jet demanded.

"One-third of the children of the fallen," the Vampir answered, relaxing as he did so. "They are the vicious ones spoken about in the removed texts of your holy book. The further removed from the original bloodline, the more rabid. In the days of old, they used to call them flesh-eaters or the walking dead. The venom they hold is deadly, even to us."

"It wasn't the Nephilim," Esmeralda said anxiously. "He was bitten by a Vampir, another male with dark hair and an aquiline nose."

His eerie eyes landed on Esmeralda; his nostrils were flaring. "Jebriel bit him. He is the first of our kind and my sire. Our venom is not poisonous. It merely paralyzes our prey for a few hours. He will feel ill when he wakes, and he will retain some of Jebriel's memories. He is living through them now. See how his eyes are rapidly moving?"

"Are you serious?" Esmeralda inquired as she leaned over Owen.

"I'm afraid so."

"He's too heavy! I must set him down," Jet snapped impatiently before Esmeralda could answer, and they carried him into the nearest room, propping him on the bed.

"Is there anything we can do for him?" Esmeralda asked, but the Vampir refused to enter the room.

"I have no control of my bloodlust at the moment. You have no idea the effort I am exerting not to-" the Vampir whipped around, staring straight at the door ahead. "He's here."

"Who is?" Jet barked.

"You need to hide Owen and the mortal. Jebriel has come with the other witch."

Ruby's heart sank. He must be referring to Pearl and the Vampir she unbound. The result of her actions left them all at risk, even if her intent was for the good.

"Where can we hide from a Vampir?" Jet asked.

"You can't," he answered. "But I can hold them off while you run."

"If Pearl is with him, she'll know our every move," Esmeralda said, and the Vampir had yet to look back at them all. "She is a seer."

"Ah," he finally faced them once again while sniffing the air and cocked his head to the left. "I understand now why he would create an alliance with a witch rather than destroy her. To see the future is a very powerful gift."

Ruby glanced at Esmeralda in confusion; she didn't have any more answers.

"Follow me," the Vampir said.

"What about Owen?"

"Leave him," the Vampir answered as he left the room.

Ruby shared a look with each of them.

"I say we leave before he leads us into the depths of this place forever," Jet murmured, but Esmeralda had already run after him.

"Looks like that plan is fruitless," Ruby said and followed her sister. She couldn't keep up with the Vampirs strides. He was inherently fast and agile.

Adrenaline flowed into her system, quieting the fear that had always taken hold of her entire being. She felt brave here and now, wishing Jade was here to see it. She wished Helena, Anne, Mary, Elizabeth, and Melody were here to see it.

The Vampir strode to one of the rooms facing the grounds. He pointed toward the window once they were all inside, implying they should look. Ruby trailed behind Esmeralda and gazed over her shoulder to see exactly what the Vampir wanted them to see. There were four people slowly making their way across the expansive lawn. A man led the group in the middle, with two women and another man trailing him; one was Pearl, and the other was Dominic.

Ruby's chest tightened at the sight of her.

"Now, what do they want?" Jet barked as he peered over her shoulder.

"Jebriel will want me to bend the knee to him," the Vampir said. "But that was never in my nature."

Ruby gazed at him. He spoke of texts removed from the holy book. These texts talked about the fallen angels who defied God and mated with human women, thus resulting in Vampirs, Lycans, and the Nephilim. While she hadn't read any removed texts or the holy book itself, Jade had. She recalled her sister explaining about the ranking amongst the immortals. Jebriel was the first Vampir, and his original creations were Amelia Rolfe and Caelum Black; Tannith DeValles had destroyed the rest.

Vampirs were expected to obey Jebriel whether they wanted to or not. He had complete control of the species, except for Caelum. It was said that Caelum drank Tannith De Valles blood in a lapse of control, leaving him far more powerful than before. He joined the ranks of the Athos army, and when he was attacked by one of the Nephilim, he didn't die as expected. Tannith's blood had saved him, and he became the only Vampir/Nephilim hybrid. Thus, allowing him to defy his creator's orders.

"Are you Caelum Black?" she asked, and her siblings gazed at the Vampir.

His eyes widened with surprise. "I am."

"Do you think Pearl intends to attack us?" Jet barked. He clearly was not interested in the Vampir or his name.

"I have no idea," Esmeralda answered and stalked toward the door. "But I'm certain this isn't a friendly visit."

Ruby was left in the room with the Vampir. He watched her intently. "I can see the sadness set deeply in your eyes. Do not fret, for you will no longer be alone."

Her defenses suddenly rose, and she glared. "I do not need to be consoled by a Vampir!" She practically ran into the hallway, as far as she could from the fiend. Esmeralda had already stepped outside, standing on the steps facing their sister. Jet joined her while Blake hung back in the doorway.

"And what do we have here?" The Vampir Jebriel said. He had a well-defined widow's peak and red eyes. When Caelum joined them, Jebriel's malicious mouth curved at the sight of him. "Every single person I wanted to see is here! Ah, my dear Ruby. You saved us from our misery and torment.

I have been bound for a thousand years, which was an agonizing time. Do you know what it is like to crave something you can never have?"

Of course she did. She had loved a man who wanted nothing from her. She was overlooked and pushed to the side her entire life as her siblings prevailed.

"I thought my existence would remain in agony. I nearly gave up hope, all the witches were burned alive almost four hundred years ago, and not a whisper or hint of magic could be felt. I accepted my fate, for I was not a creation of God. In his eyes, I deserved a life of punishment, but then, the magic returned; Tannith DeValles' line had survived. I watched, and I waited. Each of you were born with extraordinary gifts. But my chance for freedom came when I could sense the necromantic ability within you."

Ruby stood her ground, though she wanted to run; she didn't ask for this. She didn't want to deal with Vampirs or dead souls. She just wanted to be in love and live a quiet life.

Her gaze found Pearl, astounded that her sister would associate herself with such a demon. Pearl watched unaffected. She found it odd that it was Jet standing here with them on their side and not Pearl. If she could have made a prediction, it would have been that. Jet was incredibly shrewd; she never accounted for his capacity for love and loyalty, while Pearl hid her evil ways very well. Yet again, perhaps she didn't. Ruby never went out of her way to have a relationship with her and find out who she actually was. She assumed Pearl was just uptight.

"I can never repay you for what you have done for me," Jebriel continued. "I am forever in your debt."

Pearl's head turned to Jebriel with a sneer. She must've thought it was she who should be in his favor. She was at his side, speaking of the pecking order in society and how they should be at the top.

"Is that all you want?" Caelum asked, and she jumped at his booming voice. "Our unwavering devotion to you?"

Jebriel rolled his eyes. "Your defiance tires me. How long must you object to what I have given you?"

"Given me?" Caelum roared. "You've taken everything from me! You took my life and expected me to do your bidding no matter how indifferent I felt! I don't want to be a murderer. I don't want to drink blood to survive. I have suffered because of you!"

"Be reasonable. Being immortal is not a terrible fate."

"And yet it was!" Caelum snapped. "Tell us, what is it you came for?"

Jebriel gazed over at the women standing next to him. Amelia's gaze met him with a smile; Ruby would describe her as akin to royalty. She appeared far more regal than Queen Elizabeth herself. She wore an elaborate diamond necklace and an expensive silver gown, and her dark hair was twisted on her head with ringlets falling down her neck and cheeks.

"I am not here to offer death," Jebriel explained as he looked back at them. "I want to offer a life of religious freedom. I want to ensure that the rich and the poor coexist peacefully without judgment or starvation. I want to save the people of Bel Deaux from their misery and torment. From persecution and the boundaries of humankind."

Ruby's stomach twisted. It seemed like a well-thought-out plan and even favorable. Yet there was something menacing lurking in his words. Something you wouldn't get back if you offered your soul.

"And what would we have to give in return?" Jet asked.

Jebriel grinned at him. "Don't you wish to live with your lover without judgment and hatred? I can offer that."

His words were too improbable. No one offered complete peace and freedom without stipulations. Jet glanced at Blake with far too much intrigue, pleading with him to see reason in the Vampirs words.

"He's lying to you," Caelum stated, and Pearl raised her hand. Caelum clutched at his throat as he raised slowly in the air. Adrenaline seeped into Ruby's pores, and the static returned to her palms.

"All of this is unnecessary," Jebriel answered. "Caelum just needs a reminder of his privilege."

"If we chose to side with you," Jet said, causing everyone to gape at him. "What do you want?"

The Vampir grinned. "Take my mark and give all of your worries to me. I will protect you."

"Don't listen to him!" Blake yelled when Jet took a step toward the devil. "He's merely telling you what you want to hear, so you'll give up what you can't take back!"

"We can be together with him!" Jet cried.

For once, Ruby felt the need to fight for her family. "Don't go to him, Jet!"

"Stay out of it, Ruby!" He yelled.

"Yes, Ruby, remain in the background as you've always done!" Pearl hissed. "Jet, come with us, and you will no longer have to live your life ashamed!"

Jet was easily persuaded. When you've been told your whole life that the way you feel is wrong and immoral, anything objective to that seems like paradise.

She understood, but it wasn't genuine. "How can you not see the deception? This fiend only wants to feed on your soul! His motives are selfish!"

"You wound me!" Jebriel said mockingly as he placed a hand on his chest. "I can save you! That mob that burned down your father's house will never come for you again. Pearl took care of that."

"What did you do?" Jet asked.

"I destroyed their house as they destroyed ours."

Ruby had never been more terrified of her sister before, but not Jet. "With them in it?"

"Do I look like an amateur to you?"

Who was this woman? She had the same face as her sister, but Ruby didn't recognize her.

"So, what do you say?" Jebriel asked.

He appeared torn as he gazed down at the Vampir, although it was easy to see where his thoughts were heading. He would choose the Vampir if it meant he could live freely.

"Jet, you don't need him to live as you want," Esmeralda hissed. "He can't change the minds of everyone in the city!"

"I can't?" the demon countered. "I can offer what the Queen can't. What the Elite can't."

"And what is that?" Esmeralda asked.

He grinned at her. "Immortality. I can hear your friend's heart thrumming in there. I can finish his transition if you'd like."

Esmeralda raised her hand and struck Jebriel with a surge of electricity. The Vampir flew onto his back. Ruby's heart was pounding as Pearl glowered in their direction. Her bravery was faltering, and her stomach twisted with bile. Who was she kidding? She couldn't do this.

"Don't give up, Luv."

She whirled around to see Helena, Anne, Mary, Elizabeth, Melody, and Charlotte stepping from inside the asylum. A seventh person joined the prostitutes, and it hit her like a ton of bricks, completely breaking her heart.

James smiled down at her.

"No!" she whimpered.

"Don't be sad for me, Ruby," he said. "I am not hurting. None of us are."

"How?" She managed to cry out.

"Don't worry about me. Focus on yourself and do not give any power to them. Your life is worth fighting for. Keep going!"

"I don't know if I can," she muttered. He couldn't be dead.

"Yes, you can," he told her. "Your emotions drive your power. Use it to your advantage, and you'll never falter."

Tears stung her eyes as she turned back, rage and grief oscillating through her. Pearl staggered with what she saw on Ruby's face. Screeching in the distance peeled their attention from one another. At first, Ruby thought it might be a wolf running on all fours toward them, but they were too small. The closer they crawled, the more distinct they became. Rabid humans foaming at the mouths were moving at an alarming rate; this must be the Nephilim, or perhaps it was the Shedim.

Caelum fell on the ground when Pearl began using her magic against them, as did Esmeralda. Jet jumped in front of Blake as protection.

With their awareness elsewhere, she decided to take out the Vampirs. She projected at Jebriel and Amelia, throwing them from their feet. The amount of anger rising within her didn't give out. She continued to pour her magic into the Vampir until green flames entirely consumed her. Her body began to vibrate with the amount of energy flowing through her. The ground split beneath them, forcing Pearl and Esmeralda to fall on their backs. The ground shook so forcefully that the building behind them started to crumble in its foundation. The closest Nephilim fell deep in the crevice, but it didn't deter the others. Ruby directed the effluence of her magic toward the rabid creatures, striking any that got too close.

The ground split wider and wider the longer she projected her energy outwards, halting the Nephilim that were left standing, forcing them to run in the opposite direction. The female Vampir fled after the creatures, and so did Pearl. Anger drove her magic to the surface. Anger for her mother, anger for her father, anger for her sister's betrayal, and the most damaging, anger for James's death. When Jebriel began to scream out in pain, her senses were utterly stripped from her, and she was thrown back.

Her head smacked against the ground with her fall, hindering her vision. She rolled on her side and blinked up at her brother standing over her.

"I cannot allow you to kill him. I need him."

"No, you don't," Esmeralda snapped as Ruby tried to sit up. "You don't need to follow a Vampir that can be bound! He is destructible. Why would you even listen to him?"

"Because he is the only one who has ever offered a life without judgment."

He left her to run after the Vampir, and Blake followed.

Esmeralda ran to her side. "Are you alright?"

"James Hadley is dead," she whispered, and Esmeralda's eyes doubled. "James Hadley is dead!"

"Are you certain?"

"Yes, I just saw him!"

Esmeralda wrapped her in a tight embrace as she cried for some minutes. Shouting brought her into the present moment, and she pulled away to see Jet and Blake on the other side of the yard, dipping into the night.

"What a fool," Esmeralda stated. "We'll deal with that when we get to it, but for now, we need to help Owen."

"How does he not see the deception?"

"Because he is being offered something no one else has provided," Caelum answered and held out a hand for Ruby; she eyed it hesitantly.

"I won't hurt you," he hedged.

She didn't know the reason, but she trusted his words. He lifted Ruby from the ground and instantly let go of her hand when she was standing. Esmeralda wrapped an arm around her for support, and they followed Caelum back into the asylum.

There was a large knot in her chest with the knowledge of James's death, and she peered around anxiously. But it seemed as if the dead were no longer with them, which somehow felt worse.

"I can't believe Jet went with that monster!" Esmeralda said after she collected herself. "And Pearl! What are we going to do?"

Ruby didn't have all the answers. She usually waited for Jade to decide, but her determination was final.

"We fight."

XLIX
Olivette

Ollie took up a game of chess with Avis, who was barely paying attention. Jackson and Elijah had left first thing the day before, and Jade had left the previous night. It was nearing fourteen hours later, and they had yet to return. Everyone was anxious, most of all Avis.

Cordelia came in from sitting on the porch with Pikitis; a cigarette hung from her mouth. She sat on the piano bench and placed her fingers upon the keys, playing a soothing song for them.

Sorrow submerged the unease in one swift moment. How different her life would have been had she grown up in the Calvert home. Would she have been braver? More confident? Or would she have ended up as Pearl had? Their magic obviously didn't come from William Calvert, or she herself and Cordelia would also possess an ability. She had four sisters and a brother she never knew she had. Which was a saddening thought, and she suddenly missed the sisters she grew up with, hoping they were safe.

Cordelia instantly whirled around and stared at Ollie. She dropped her gaze, not looking back until the feeling became unbearable.

"Why are you staring at me?" she asked meekly.

Cordelia's face was pinched. Whatever she was looking for was starting to feel uncomfortable. It left her feeling inadequate, wishing she was someone else who had never been violated.

"I sense something in you," she answered after a pause, causing Avis to follow her stare.

Ollie averted her gaze. She wasn't ready to have this conversation just yet. "I must have one of those faces," she said abruptly and stood. "I think I'll go for a walk."

"I'll join you," Avis said. "I can't sit idly any longer."

She was glad when Cordelia didn't agree to join. She didn't want to have to explain herself.

The floors in the spacious hallway were lined with embroidered rugs, and the walls were carved into great detail of the Hadleys sigil, a roaring Manticore. A massive chandelier hung in the middle of the ceiling, although it looked like an opera house that had long been abandoned. There was a blue hue to the hallway from the shadow of all the other unlit rooms.

They pulled on shawls and walked out on the porch, yet it didn't seem like a cover would be necessary. The sun was out, and it was exceptionally warm—a rare occurrence.

The substantial manor was more like an intricate, gothic castle on one hundred and seventy-two acres of land. It was encompassed by innumerable trees and hedges that were still being taken care of. Countless stairs led up to a white sandstone structure with numerous fountains and statues decorating the property.

"Well, well, well," Pikitis said. "Come for a smoke, did you?"

Avis smirked at him. "We're going to walk the grounds."

"Don't go too far now," Pikitis warned. "And whatever you do, don't go near the fences. You will be blown to bits!"

Ollie rounded on him with a widened gaze. "Are you joking?"

Pikitis shrugged and raised the butt of his cigarette to his lips. "Take a walk and find out."

"We're just going to get an apple," Avis giggled and pulled her along.

They trudged down the steps, sixty-two to be exact. Avis steered her to the left when they reached the bottom, and she didn't know which avenue was worse. The orchard, with its gaunt scarecrow watching over the grounds as several crows squawked loudly. Or the graveyard with its large dead willow tree hovering over the rows of gravestones.

"I really wish they'd hurry," Avis muttered, and Ollie did too. "I had hoped Micha would have come, but he was worried about my brothers."

"Why would he worry about them?" Ollie asked as her heel sunk into the grass the further they walked.

Avis reached up and picked two fat red apples from the nearest tree. "We've been seeing one another in secret. He fears what they will do. What Jackson would do when he finds out."

Ollie's face twisted. "He wouldn't allow you to be happy?"

"Of course, he wants me to be happy, but no man is good enough in his eyes." She held out an apple for Ollie, and she reached for it. "He's right. There aren't many good men in Bel Deaux except for Micha and my brothers."

Her stomach sank with the thought of James. She had yet to express her condolences with everything they had been through. "I'm sorry about what happened to your brother."

Her lips quivered. "Me too."

Ollie bit her lip. She didn't want to talk ill about anyone but wanted to know what Avis thought of the Calvert's.

"What is it?" Avis asked with a bite of her apple.

She turned the apple in her hands. "What do you think about Jade?"

Her mouth curved slightly as she chewed. "I've never seen Jackson happy in my entire life. Content maybe, but never happy. And while this time is certainly chaotic and full of grief, he is happy, and it's because of her. How could I despise that? I could never thank her enough for saving my brother. Both of them."

Ollie tried not to frown as she realized that some small part of her was jealous.

"Why do you ask? Is there something to Cordelia's words?"

If she could tell anyone her secret, it would be Avis. "My mother revealed something before she passed, and I don't know why she would lie about it."

Avis never answered; she had stopped walking entirely. Ollie turned to look at her. Avis's blue eyes were gazing upwards in dismay. Ollie gazed up at a wooden cross. The scarecrow was no longer hanging from his perch and her stomach twisted. She could have sworn it was there just minutes ago. "What happened to the scarecrow?"

"I don't know," Avis said apprehensively. If Ollie didn't know any better, she would say Avis was terrified. "Let's get back. I don't dare walk any further with Bob's boobie traps around the yard."

Ollie followed her without complaint, ignoring the urge to look over her shoulder and run.

They ate dinner and returned to the library for a game of poker with no sign of Jackson, Elijah, Owen, Jade, or Gainsley. Pikitis recanted various tales of his ventures across the continent to soothe their anxiety-ridden minds. The stories would have been more enjoyable had they not been staring at the clock, restlessly waiting for their arrival.

"Something is wrong," Cordelia muttered. "It's been twenty-four hours since Jade and Gainsley left."

No one commented.

Avis jumped up from the table some minutes later, wringing her hands together, and stalked toward the front window, anxiously gazing out of it.

"Well, I'll be."

"What is it?" Pikitis asked as he placed two threes down on the table.

"I think they're coming," she muttered and ran toward the front door. "I can see something in the distance."

Ollie followed the others as they stepped out into the night. The air took a shrill dive from the blissfully warm day, mocking the sun by sweeping throughout the earth and sitting heavy in one's chest. Ollie could see her breath and movement in the distance.

"What is that?" Avis asked, her gaze narrowed.

"I don't know, but I don't think it's a carriage," Cordelia said as she turned toward the house. "We should arm ourselves."

Something large and wide jumped onto one of the pillars at the end of the drive. It snarled viciously. A second beast jumped onto the second pillar, rearing its head into the sky and howling at the moon.

"Get to the bunker and stick to the trail!" Pikitis ordered as he pulled the gun off his shoulder. "Barricade yourselves in, and whatever you do, don't open the door until I come for you!"

One of the wolves jumped off the pillar. It made it five feet before an explosion went off.

Pikitis laughed. "They'll be sorry they ever thought to cross Bob Pikitis!"

Cordelia returned from inside the house with two rifles in her hands and one slung over her shoulder. "You know the drill, Avis."

Ollie could not feel her limbs. She was numb with fear. "You aren't going to run for it?"

"We can't have wolves running around the property in case Jackson and Elijah return. They'll get ambushed." She aimed her gun at the beast sitting on the other pillar. "We'll meet you in the bunker."

Cordelia herded them inside and shut the door. Ollie stared in shock and awe as Marna grabbed her hand, and together they ran down the expansive hall after Avis. Several gunshots were fired, and Ollie screamed, ducking as she ran. Marna's grip was her lifeline.

Avis led them down a small flight of stairs and to a hallway on the left. She entered a study, and she shut the door quietly when they were safe inside. Ollie stood suspended, her heart slamming in her chest. Avis and Marna ran to the east wall, where several guns were displayed.

"Come get a revolver," she instructed. "These hold silver bullets. It's the only protection we have against them."

"What are they?" Ollie fretted.

"Werewolves," Avis answered. She didn't even sound frightened. She sounded readily prepared. "Hurry now!"

She didn't know what Werewolves were, but she sprinted for a gun with the urgency of Avis's tone. She thrust a revolver in her hand. "All you have to do is cock the hammer, point the barrel at your target, and pull the trigger. Silver slows them, but I'm not sure if it will kill them."

There was a crash from the windows in front of the house, with more gunshots and yelling.

"There is a bunker in the forest behind the house. They will not find us hidden within. We could hide for days, and no one would know. We must run out of the back door quietly. There is a grouping of bloodwood trees in the elder wood; there is a hidden door next to the one with an H carved into it." Ollie did not realize she was hyperventilating until Avis grabbed her face. "You need to be strong, and you need to run. If one of those things tries to jump at you, shoot it! You understand?"

"Yes," she whispered.

Avis dashed to the door, tensing as she listened. She opened it moments later and poked her head in the hall. She motioned for them to follow, and she picked up her feet. There was a struggle from above. She could hear Cordelia shouting, snarling wolves, more gunshots, and Pikitis laughing.

"C'mon!" Avis hissed.

They wasted no time running into the kitchen that was down another flight of stairs and raced to the back door.

"What about Pikitis's boobie traps?" Ollie wailed.

"He knows about the bunker," Avis called over her shoulder, running without fear down the pathway toward the forest. "Keep on the path, and don't look back!"

Ollie ran as fast as her limbs could take her, though she could hear snarling at her back. She whimpered as the beast gained upon them.

"AVIS!"

"KEEP RUNNING!"

Once they made it to the woods and into the enveloping trees, Ollie could not see a thing. She tried to follow Avis's footsteps and even heard Marna panting behind her, and before long, they split up.

Her bare feet smacked against the forest floor in haste. Ollie ran for her life as howls cried in the distance. Her breathing came in rapid spurts, and her eyes darted around the surrounding area for a space to conceal her body from the fiend. But the snarls were closer than ever, and a scream sprouted from the back of her throat. How she found herself in this particular situation was one she could not explain within reason, even to herself. Still, she ran as the beast was upon her. Perhaps it was toying with her mind before it consumed her flesh. It was much larger, much faster, and far more deadly than any monster she had ever encountered in life or book.

Her feet were raw, her lungs burned, and tears welled in her eyes. The snarls surpassed and round, amber eyes reflected in the darkness ahead. She stopped short, panting as sweat rolled down her temple. Her heart was pounding furiously, and her breath was visible. The beast came into view from the shadows of the trees and into the moonlight. Her eyes widened with its growls, and fear swept down her entire body in a paralyzing way, making her lose all control of bodily functions; she was trapped. How terrifying it was to stare death in the face, for she did not want to die at all. It stopped just before her, its vitriolic eyes shined, and its teeth bared.

She raised the gun in her hand and aimed it at the massive wolf. She cocked the hammer just as Avis instructed and pointed, but nothing happened when she pulled the trigger. Her eyes widened in disbelief.

"P-p-pleas-e-e" she sputtered, her heart thrumming in her chest.

The monster gnashed its teeth as it jumped forward. Another wolf intercepted it just before it ripped her apart.

Her legs gave out, and she fell to her knees, astounded by the fact that she was still alive.

The attack of Werewolves, they learned, was as terrifying as one could imagine. It wasn't until the Lycans Orion Black and Thackeray Mueller came to their aid, did she realize how incredibly fortunate they all were. Pikitis beckoned them from the bunker some hours later, and she was relieved everyone had made it out alive.

She hid behind Cordelia and Avis to listen to the Lycans tale. She trusted their judgment, especially when Cordelia urged them onward.

The Lycans were relatively controlled for being newly unbound, and she couldn't imagine being confined in her skin. She had already felt like she had been a prisoner her entire life, but this was on a grander scale. They were imprisoned in their own bodies.

The Vampirs could not feed nor sire; vein contact was strictly forbidden, disrupting the madness from within. The Lycans were unable to transform into their wolf-like state, leaving them on the verge of psychosis every full moon. The Nephilim failed to consume the flesh of their victims, wilting away into inevitable darkness and derangement. And the Shedim lost their element of manipulation and possession, which left them in a constant state of delirium.

As she listened, she couldn't grasp what being bound truly meant. Their bodies ate away while they were unable to transform, to feed. They wasted away while there was nothing that could be done. They had to endure death day in and out.

"How did you know where to find us?" Avis asked in Orion's silence.

He glanced at her. He had heterochromia, just as Jade did. One of his eyes was blue, and the other was predominantly brown with the tiniest fragment of blue filigree. His weren't as prevalent as Jade's, but they still stood out. She had never met another person with this affliction, and she watched him curiously, wondering if he was ever ridiculed for it, considering he grew up in the Middle Ages.

It was odd to meet two different people with two different colored eyes. It was a strange anomaly, yet their faces were entirely favorable. She could see what Jackson saw, what everyone saw as their eyes swept over Jade in appreciation because she could see it in Orion as well.

She dropped her gaze when Orion caught her staring. He was the larger wolf attacking the smaller one in the clearing. Despite how much blood was spilled, he didn't seem affected.

"We've always been here," he said, his accent thick and heavy. The Black brothers were speculated to be from Benschland, and by the way he was gurgling his r's and over-pronouncing his a's and u's seemed to have some truth to it. "We watched the grounds for centuries. Protecting the Hadley line was our duty when we were human. It was only natural to remain doing so."

"You were the scarecrow?" Avis asked.

"Yes."

The scarecrow was absolutely terrifying, but Orion looked nothing like the decrepit creature that was watching over the grounds.

Marna placed a blanket around her shoulders and handed over a cup of tea. She nearly died at the hands of a Werewolf, and she didn't know if she could recover. Marna stuck close to her, offering a helping hand to subdue her fear; it was a nice feeling.

"Where are the rest of the Hadleys?" Thackeray asked.

"Bel Deaux," Avis answered. "They went in search of Owen. He never made it out of the city after the attack at the warehouse."

"Is that where the witch went?"

"Yes."

The wolves began speaking with one another in a different language. However, their dialect was too far removed from modern Bensch, a language Ollie could understand. This was ancient, proving just how old they truly were.

"My brother Caelum will help," Orion stated after a moment. "Although there is only so much he can do. Jebriel is the first Vampir. He is cruel and vain and will stop at nothing to conquer once again. Even if that means destroying everyone in his path."

Ollie swallowed, unsure if she could handle the supernatural beings that were threatening to destroy mankind.

L
Elijah

Elijah was sitting in the far corner of a dingy prison cell, as far away as he could from the other man locked inside with him. The man was pacing and continuously smacking his head as he spouted nonsense. He hadn't taken his eyes away from the man since he was thrown in by a very pleased-looking Merfan, who had taunted them since they had been arrested. The minutes passed slowly, and his thoughts lingered heavily on Owen and if he was safe. They were being picked off one by one. The papers already dubbed him and Jackson as the culprits for the Dollhouse slaying murders, and the city ate it up. Dominic and Pearl orchestrated their downfall and were very clever; they would get away with it if Merfan had his say.

Shouting swerved his attention from his cellmate. Merfan was protesting loudly as several footsteps came barreling down the hall. He jumped up from the ground and walked over to the bars of the cell. Cillian was striding toward him with a large set of keys in his hands.

"He assisted in the murder of those prostitutes!" Merfan yelled at Cillian's back. "He shouldn't be given any privileges!"

"Go tell that to the Queen then!" Cillian snapped. "She has every right to see them!"

"I'll have you fired for this!" Merfan bellowed.

"Go ahead and tell Feilding," Cillian spat and shoved the keys back in his hands as soon as the door was locked once more.

"What's going on?" Elijah asked him.

"Queen Elizabeth is here to see you and Jackson."

Relief came in an instant. She could get them out of this mess and make it right. He followed Cillian down the hall, up a flight of stairs to a floor with several doors. He stopped just behind one marked with a five.

Cillian pointed. "She's in there."

Elijah opened the door. Elizabeth and Jackson were sitting in the room, waiting. It always hurt to look at Elizabeth; she looked just like his mother. Blonde hair, blue-eyed with the exact same smile.

The one she gave him now, however, was anything but friendly. "Elijah."

"You have no idea how good it is to see you!" he admitted as he leaned down to kiss her on the cheek and pulled up a chair next to Jackson.

"Is this a good visit?" she barked.

He frowned and glanced at Jackson. His brother didn't look any more pleased than the Queen. "Well, you're going to clear our charges, right?"

She snorted. "Is that what you believe?"

Elijah's eyes doubled. "You're going to let us hang for this? We had nothing to do with these murders! We were in Berrone!"

"You know I love you, even though you never visit me!" she threw Jackson a stern look, and he dropped his gaze. "The very reason you returned to Bel Deaux was by my request, and you have yet to find out why!"

"I avoided you because I don't want to be your successor," he said.

Elijah closed his eyes. They had always gotten along with their aunt, but she was stubborn and didn't enjoy being told no. As Queen, many wouldn't disagree with her, and now wasn't the time to provoke her.

"And why not? You would make a good King."

"Power isn't something I strive for. I just want to live my life quietly and help those in need. Give a voice to those who don't have one."

She smiled. "That's the straightforward attitude of a good ruler—one who doesn't want it. I wanted to be Queen, but for all the wrong reasons. I never had the patience for the needy, helping them when hungry. I don't care for politics, either. I want to enjoy the pleasures of life with no disruptions. Your mother would have made a better Queen than I ever did." Elijah glanced at Jackson. What did she want from them then? "It pains me to say that I will not be able to get you out of this rubbish."

Elijah's stomach dropped, and he gaped at her.

"The papers have already outed you," she explained when Jackson shook his head. "The whole city believes you to be the killers, and it doesn't look so good when your valet was already arrested for this."

"And released," Jackson snapped.

"Watch your tone with me, Jackson!" She hissed, and he murmured his apologies.

Elijah couldn't even focus when she began to explain the expectations of the city and how none of her people would respect her if she helped wanted murderers. She would rather save her reputation than save the lives of her nephews.

"Perception is a funny thing," she continued. "You could do right your whole life, but you associate yourself with the wrong person, taking all your credibility away, and no one believes you no matter what you say."

"What are you suggesting?" Jackson asked.

"You should have never entangled yourselves with the Calvert's. A mob burned down their house some hours ago. There were whispers of witchcraft. Teddy Kensington claimed Jet used magic against him after killing his father."

"William Calvert is dead?" Elijah bellowed.

"Unfortunately," she said. "And I've ordered a warrant for the arrest of the children. I cannot have witches running around the city casting their magic against people! I'm sorry to be the one to tell you that my people are screaming for their execution," she said, causing Jackson to tense up. Elijah could see the veins in his arms. They were far from Berrone to warn them, to help them.

Elizabeth may be a monarch, but her duty was to listen to the people and do right by them. If they wanted witches to be crucified, she had no choice but to follow through, especially when she didn't know their intentions. He could agree to a point; Pearl and Jet were unpredictable.

"I know you are trying to make a point," Elijah growled. "But they aren't the danger here, and neither are we. It's Dominic!"

Elizabeth eyed him evenly.

"He is the one who has committed these crimes. Therefore, he should be the one who pays for it!"

Elizabeth gazed at Jackson, who had yet to say a word about it. "Is that what you believe?"

"It's what we know, and I am starting to suspect you do as well," Jackson answered.

"I know nothing," she hissed. "You cannot blame your cousin to deflect your crimes."

"And you cannot allow us to take the fall to save your son!" Jackson argued.

She glowered.

"I sent Roslyn to serve as a governess for Gabrielle," Elijah blurted, and she gazed at him in surprise. "Whoever was found, if there was anyone, wasn't Roslyn Emerich."

"A body was found," Elizabeth answered. "I saw it in your lab with my own eyes, and while your actions toward Roslyn are admirable, if they are true, it doesn't change the fact that a woman was ripped apart in your house. My people are screaming for your deaths."

"What?" Elijah bellowed. "But we didn't do it!"

"All proof was found in your house! Try convincing the city of your innocence with the evidence stacked against you!"

"Can't you remove the death penalty?" Jackson asked.

"No, unfortunately. My people want you to swing. You are scheduled to hang tomorrow morning at dawn."

Elijah melted in his seat. She wasn't even going to try and save them. The least she could do was to protect them from execution, but by her sour demeanor, she wasn't even willing to do that.

"What about Raoul and Duke?" Jackson asked.

"They will hang too."

Elijah swallowed. They were going to die for atrocious acts they didn't commit. He looked at Jackson, but he had no words of comfort. Jackson looked even more terrified than he felt.

LI
Jet

"The Hadleys have been arrested," Pearl said.

He glanced up from his plate. Pearl was reading the paper while sitting next to her droll of a husband. "For what?"

"The murder of those women," she answered smugly, and Blake frowned at her.

"You're barking!" Jet bellowed. "How did they come to that conclusion?"

"Roslyn was found in Jackson's basement," she answered coldly, detached. There was no feeling nor compassion in her voice as she gave the information. Jet glanced at Blake, breaking under the news. "She was ripped from one end to the other." She paused and looked at Blake. "Did no one tell you that your sister was murdered?"

He shook his head. "You lie!"

"Why would I lie to you? It is here in the paper!"

"You are trying to pit us against one another!" Blake yelled, pushing Jet away when he reached for him. "You are trying to create contention in our hearts so we will fight with one another!"

"Is that what you truly believe?"

Blake stopped struggling in his arms, and they gazed over at the Vampir, Jebriel. His red eyes penetrated the soul, and Jet found he could not hold the Vampirs stare for long.

"Those monsters killed your sister brutally, and I am the one putting contention into your heart?" Blake sagged in Jet's arms, a sob escaping his lips. "They will be rightfully dealt with. I made sure of that. Your Queen was going to let them walk free! She argued with Captain Feilding for hours until he finally convinced her that the people would riot against her reign if she cut them loose. Is that the type of leader you want? To let murderers walk free simply because they are her kin? Or do you want a leader who will stand up for what is right?"

"And what is right?"

"Perfect justice for criminals and complete and total freedom for everyone else. Don't you despise the confinement of society and how they have ridiculed and judged you for wanting to live your life happily and in love? Why should you be punished for that? Who are you hurting?"

The more the Vampir spoke, the sweeter his words sounded. No one had ever offered him the choice to live how he wanted. He understood Jade's wish to run away, and some part of him envied how she had done just that. Now it was his turn to create the life he wanted.

"We've lived in the shadows for far too long. Why should we shy away and fear the mortals who only wish to condemn us? We are more powerful. We should be the ones leading the way!"

"But what about Ruby?" Blake said. "You ran away from her when she began splitting the ground in two! Not to mention those rabid fiends skulking around!"

"We didn't go to the asylum for Ruby," Pearl stated. "We came there for you."

Jet couldn't hide his surprise when her stare landed directly on him. "Me? What did you want from me?"

"Because we want the strongest allies at our backs," the Vampir explained and accepted a glass of red liquid from his cohort, Amelia.

Jet tried not to grimace as he realized the cup she gave him was filled with blood, not wine.

"You have the ability to remove one's sense from them completely. Do you not understand how powerful you are?"

Never had he been complimented by anyone other than Blake. He fought tooth and nail for acceptance from a father who never wanted him. He could never make William Calvert proud, no matter what he did. He had received the validation he wanted in mere hours of meeting Jebriel. He didn't need any more convincing to follow the Vampir; he would follow impulsively without reason.

The Vampir suddenly glanced over his shoulder, his nose flaring in and out as he sniffed the air. The room went silent; his sudden change in demeanor had adrenaline coursing through Jet's veins, and that's when he heard it. Sirens screamed down the street as the sounds of those vicious beings screeched on the roads.

Jet took a step back with trepidation.

Jebriel gazed at him curiously. "I can smell your fear, and it's pointless. You have been led to believe you are nothing; therefore, you believe it. You, who holds magic in his veins, fear not only man but the Nephilim and the Shedim? They should be cowering at the sight of you! It is I who was sent to serve you. To protect you and make you see reason."

"You wish for us to stop them?" Jet said, twisting his hand to emphasize his power. The veins in his arm illuminated blue and flowed down to his palm.

"Let's give the citizens of Bel Deaux a reason to choose us over the Elite. Over the Queen!"

Jet failed to hide his grin; it was all he ever wanted. The Vampir understood his deepest desires and demanded that he unleash his power openly and unafraid.

"Now this is more like it," Pearl beamed as she jumped up from her chair. "I was getting rather bored sitting around."

"You gather up the victims and bring them to the Vaults," Jebriel ordered Blake and Augustus. "We'll take care of the fiends."

Jet refused to glance at Blake for approval; he no longer needed the acceptance of anyone.

There was no need to hold back…. not anymore. The electricity stemming from his hands left the Nephilim and the Shedim slain in the streets. He openly revealed his secret without apprehension, distributing magic into the air and saving those running for their lives. Along with Pearl and Jebriel, they were saviors to Trinity Row when the Queen's guard fled in the opposite direction. The amount of destruction left in their wake may have been significant, but it didn't matter when people began to realize they were their salvation.

The Nephilim and the Shedim lurked in the shadows, waiting. It seemed as if there were hundreds of them, scurrying about and their mouths dripped with a black substance. The people they bit didn't stand a chance; their venom was lethal. Yet so were Jet and Pearl.

Jet struck the fiends directly in the chest, overwhelming them instantly. Jebriel tore the fiends apart with his bare hands while Pearl manipulated the air around them. But for every five they destroyed, ten more came.

"Where are they coming from?" he yelled, and there was a brief moment of sheer panic that he thought they would be overwhelmed by the creatures with the face of men.

"Take cover!" Pearl yelled.

The wind picked up around them, and the ground began to shake. Jet staggered toward the nearest building with the Vampir at his back. Pearl conjured a small cyclone; the faster it spun, the more significant it grew. Jet peered around the building, squinting in the dust that flew around them all. Pearl stood in the middle of the road with her arm raised in the air, her hair and dress flowing behind her. The cyclone sucked the Nephilim and the Shedim up into the sky and began tearing apart the derelict buildings surrounding them.

Jet dropped to his knees and covered his head when the construction above began to crumble. The Vampir shielded Jet with his body; every emotion rose to the surface and threatened to explode out of him. It was unbearable, the ground shook beneath them, and the wind threatened to pick them up and throw them into the unknown. The noise was unbearable, promising to hinder him impaired.

And then, it was silent. There was no more wind, no dismantling of buildings, and no more shaking. The Vampir slowly eased off him, and Jet looked up. Pearl had destroyed the entire street; there was simply nothing left.

She turned to face them. "I had no choice."

It was hard to determine Jebriel's mood, but he wasn't paying attention to his sister or the dismantled street. He bared his teeth and darted for something hidden beneath the rubble, pulling a creature from the wreckage and holding it above his head with a one-armed grip.

"I think it's time we show the masses what we're made of."

The Vaults were swarming with people. After Blake agreed that they were to witness what the Vampir had to say, though Jet knew he wasn't entirely convinced it was a wise decision, he prayed he would listen to reason—considering that his sister had just been murdered. He didn't initially grasp how much Blake cared for her. Primarily because Blake never acted as if he cared for her.

Blake had yet to meet his eye, continuing to scowl at those around them. Being confined in a small space with the impoverished made his stomach turn; the number of unwashed bodies penetrated the chamber, and he covered his nose.

The fear in the air was palpable. He wanted to reach out and touch Blake's hand when he noted how he angled himself in the other direction; he could feel the anger radiating off him in droves.

"We can live how we choose under his reign," Jet murmured.

"Your greed blinds you," Blake answered dismissively. "All he wants in return for our loyalty is our souls. It's purely a lie, and I cannot understand how you fail to see it!"

"I would do that for you," Jet said, finally causing Blake to gaze at him. "To be with you uninhibited, without judgment."

"That's what frightens me," he whispered, forcing Jet to think about what he had just said and question his decision.

The crowd grew quiet as Jebriel walked onto the stage, his arms behind his back. His eyes swept over the group in a frighteningly devilish way. "I bet you're wondering why I've called you here tonight. The city has been in disarray these past few weeks, and I can only imagine the terror you must feel." He paused, watching. The creases on his forehead disappeared as his face transformed into something soft. "The rabid creatures that have infested your city as the Dollhouse Slayers stalk the alleyways of Trinity Row. How far Bel Deaux has fallen, and this is all your Queen's doing!" His voice echoed above them all. The room was entirely silent, everyone hanging on the edge of their seats.

"Your Queen allowed the Dollhouse Slayer murderers to walk free because they are her kin. Is this what you want for a leader? To be spat on, starved, and attacked while she throws lavish parties in her castle?"

Again, no one said a word.

"How do you support a monarch who could care less if you lived or died?" A low murmur began to ripple through the crowd. "How do you support a monarch who starves you and laughs at your misfortunes? Do you grow tired and weary by the injustice of trying to survive? Even the Elite steal from your table and force you into poverty and addiction!"

Blake finally gazed at him, but he didn't look over. Jebriel wasn't necessarily handsome, although he had a presence on the stage. Terrifying and captivating altogether.

"You have been deceived and told witchcraft is evil and that anyone who possesses magic should be hanged. And yet, they saved you from death, from being eaten alive, while your Queen hid in her castle!"

The crowd began to boo, causing Jet to repel a shiver. He had the entire group in his hands, and it was clear they would do whatever he asked.

Jebriel raised his hand and made a twirling motion. Jet watched as Amelia pulled a lever, and two men hanging by their ankles were slowly lowered over the ring. Jet gasped as recognition set in. It was Teddy and Edward. This time he met Blake's unwavering stare.

"How many of you have been subjected to mistreatment by Theodore Kensington and Edward Wright?"

The crowd continued to boo and jeer. Jet glanced back at the affluent sons with his heart in his throat. They were gagged and looking wildly around the crowd.

A blood-curdling screech ripped through the room. It was the fiend Jebriel had captured; he was using it as bait to convince the group he was a protector. A savior. They jumped from their seats as they watched him tear through the room. The Nephilim were fast, but Jebriel was faster. He grabbed the creature by its neck and lifted it off the ground. The group of people watching gasped when it gnashed its teeth and tried to tear into Jebriel's neck.

The Vampir slammed his fist into the creature's chest and tore out its heart. The fiend went limp in his grasp, and the crowd screamed. Jebriel tossed the Nephilim onto the ground and held up its black heart. "I can offer you salvation. I can provide you with freedom, with food, and with protection. You will never go hungry again! Take my mark and give all your worries to me; I will never let you down. Take my mark, and I will save you from the Queen and her tyranny!"

The crowd cheered for the Vampir, yet Jet couldn't find the same enthusiasm as he did before. Complete and utter fear tore through every inch of him with the sudden comprehension of what the Vampir demanded for surfaced. How foolish it would be to follow such a fiend into the depths of hell.

He grabbed Blake's hand and pulled him toward the exit before his sister or the Vampir noticed their flight into the night.

LII
Jackson

The bells from the tower chimed loudly; it was a rather somber day for an execution. The sky was covered in blackened clouds, and thunder taunted wildly from a distance; a menacing storm hovered on the horizon. Jackson and Elijah Hadley were to be hanged on this very morning. A most peculiar outcome as they were Queen Elizabeth's kin and very well thought of throughout the community. That, of course, was until the citizens of Bel Deaux learned of their true sadistic and deranged nature. Their crimes were undoubtedly the worst in recent history, and these prolific murderers deserved nothing less than death.

Each brother struggled against their restraints, and it took several officers to pin down the both of them. They were cuffed, beaten with a baton, and dragged out of their cells. Jackson relented after fighting proved useless and began to laugh maniacally. It frightened the officers who had to remove his elongated frame toward the noose; his howls echoed throughout the bastille.

Elijah continued to fight and kick his legs. He begged, but none of the officers cared to hear his plea for his life.

They were carried through separate barriers and finally came face to face with one another. Elijah stopped struggling, and Jackson quit laughing.

"Jack!" Elijah wailed.

Jackson's smile fell, and he began to breathe heavily at the sight of his brother; his eyes widened in fear as he whispered, "Eli."

The officers escorting Elijah tugged him with impatience, and he screamed for his brother.

Constable Merfan walked in from the hanged man's square, smiled broadly for Jackson, and said, "I told you I'd be there to watch you burn."

Jackson spat in his eye when he came within distance.

Merfan punched him in the gut and yelled, "Take him to the noose!"

Jackson heaved as he was dragged out into the courtyard. Dozens of citizens hovered to watch the proper execution of these beasts. The crowd erupted with unrestraint and began not only to hurl insults in their direction but rotting food as well.

"Jackson!" Elijah screamed as he was led up the stairs toward his unfortunate fate.

Someone threw an apple, hitting Jackson in the right temple; he groaned and turned his head to the side. Constable Merfan began to smack people with his baton and yelled, "Back off!"

Jackson was dragged slowly up the stairs, a noose had already been placed around Elijah's neck, and his eyes had doubled in size as he glanced around wildly. When in place, a noose was positioned around Jackson's neck, and a priest began to read their last rights. The crowd chanted for them to swing, and it muffled the priest's words.

Pearl Atwood and Dominic Kane stood in the crowd, watching the effect of their misdeeds play out. Jackson began to laugh once more. The killers were in the crowd hiding in plain sight, and he and his brother would die as innocent men.

Elijah's breathing was erratic, and he wanted to say something to his brother that was comforting in return. The pain wouldn't last long, and he hoped Elijah understood that. He only wished he could see Jade one last time and tell her how much he loved her. Tell her how much she changed his life for the better, even in a short time. He didn't have any regrets in this life, save for not getting enough time with her.

The hangman placed his hand on the lever that controlled the ground beneath him. He couldn't deny his pounding heart nor the fear that had suddenly ensnared his senses. Before the hangman pulled the lever, he locked eyes with Ruby Calvert. Her hood was drawn over her head in disguise, but what was more confusing than seeing her in the crowd was the Vampir standing behind her with a hood pulled over his head, silver eyes glinting in the shadow. Caelum Black was no longer grotesque and decaying; the Vampir was no longer bound.

"I hereby condemn you to death for your crimes against God and country. You are to be hanged by the neck until dead," Merfan stated, and Jackson refused to give him the satisfaction. He continued to stare at Ruby instead, breathing heavily when she raised her hand in the air, illuminating a faint green. "May God have mercy on your souls."

He closed his eyes as the floor dropped from beneath them.

-EPILOGUE-

Nestled deep within the Val Haven wood lay the unfavorable village of Vendekk. A village that once flourished with life and trade was now left to rot in ruins and persistent unattractive clouds that hovered above. Only a fair few dared to venture anywhere near this peculiar village, and those who did, never returned. Whispers of a curse that lay within the baleful trees to the east had reached the entire kingdom. It was said that creatures dwelled within, creatures that could rip the flesh from the bone if you were so bold as to enter it. Divulging on the meat of innocents and sinners alike, none were safe when the sun bid its farewell to the day.

"Were you scratched," an unrelenting voice asked, causing her to stir. "Or were you bitten?"

"I don't know," a familiar voice answered. "I can't remember."

"The girl seems all right," another voice said. This one, if possible, was gruffer than the first. "I can see the claw marks clearly. Your leg, however, doesn't look good. The shape seems distinct for a bite."

"Ah, it's too hard to tell," the first voice interrupted. "Unless the beast knew to cover his tracks, and this was on purpose. Perhaps the fiend is creating himself a pack."

"So, what are you suggesting?" the familiar voice wailed.

"I hope you enjoy raw meat and the moon, laddy!"

"Stop it. You're scaring him," the first voice scolded. "There is only one way to tell if you have been changed."

"How?"

"Wait until the full moon. If you sprout hair and fangs, then you were bitten!"

Her eyes snapped open. She was lying on a small bed in a small room. She sat up fully and looked over her shoulder. The room fell quiet as the occupants of the room stared at her. She didn't recognize the rugged man in the corner or the woman tending her leg, but she did recognize the man at the foot of her bed.

It was Gainsley.

To be continued...

-Dollhouse Slayer Victims-

1st known victim - Helena Wimple (41-Deceased)
2nd victim - Anne Dombrowski (44-Deceased)
3rd victim - Melody Andrews (37-Deceased)
4th victim - Elizabeth DeWitt (29-Deceased)
5th victim – Unknown (Thought to be Roslyn Emerich)

Thiana Grady (42- Possible first Slayer victim)
Isabella Stoatshead (35- Possible slayer victim)

-Copycat Victims-

1st victim - Mary-Anne Stafford (31- Deceased)
2nd victim - Charlotte Dubois (38 - Deceased)

The Fallen

Eliel – Seraphim - Creator of the Nephilim / Shedim Line

Obil – Cherubim - Creator of the Vampir / Succubus Line

Malachai – Cherubim - Creator of the Lycan / Werewolf Line

Elders – Offspring of the sons of God and daughters of man.

Jebriel (Apollyon) – 1st Vampir

Kael (Abaddon) – 1st Lycan

Azrael (Asmodeus) – 1st Nephilim

Perennials – Everlasting. Perpetual. Eternal.

Vampir – A preternatural being who feeds off the blood of the living. Venom – mildly poisonous – survival rate: low. Death by venom or transition into immortality by drinking the blood of a Vampir.

Succubus – Cousin to the Vampir – A Preternatural being who feeds on the blood of the living. Venom – mildly poisonous – survival low. Death by venom or transition into immortality by drinking the blood of the fiend.

Lycan – Derived from the word Lycanthrope: the professed ability or power to change into a wolf at whim. Feeds of the flesh of the living.
Venom – highly contagious – survival rate: cursed with lycanthropy.

Werewolf – Shapeshifters – Cousin to the Lycan- transforms into a wolf under a curse during a full moon. Feeds of the flesh of the living. Venom – highly contagious – survival rate: cursed with lycanthropy.

Nephilim – Demon – Feeds off the blood and flesh of the living. Venom is highly poisonous. Survival rate: Fatal.

Shedim – Demon – Cousin to the Nephilim. No humanity intact. Venom is fatal to every living being.

Seirim – Shapeshifting Demon that can take the appearance of any person or creature (Thought to be extinct)

Sirens (Mermaids) – The daughters of man who mated with the sons of God.

The Cursed Ones – The Perennials who were bound for a millennium.

*Witches differ from the immortal race. While gifted with supernatural abilities, they are as mortal as any human.

-Immortals-

Jebriel (1888-First Vampir- Creator-) - Amelia (1882-Vampir)
Caelum Black (1234-Vampir- Creator) – Dmitri (1108-Vampir) – Kala (1111-Vampir)

Kael (1888-First Lycanthrope- Creator) - Guinevere (1887-Lycanthrope)
Orion Black (1235-Lycan)
Thackery Mueller (1205-Lycan)
Aleksandr Petrov (1004-Werewolf)
Artem Roberts (1010-Werewolf)
Maren Tudor (1008-Werewolf)

- ACKNOWLEDGEMENTS-

Vanessa and Daxton - My babies. My loves. Thank you for the endless amount of love and laughter you fill our home with. You have given me a second chance at life and driven me to follow my dreams. I hope that when the day comes for you to find your place in the world, you follow your dreams and never give up. Thank you for choosing me to be your mama. I love you more than you will ever know.

Mum and Dad - Isn't it crazy how far we've come? Remember that punk teenager who wouldn't listen to anyone? Least of all, you? My opinions have changed quite dramatically since I've had my own children, and I simply cannot thank you enough for everything you have given me. I could never repay you for how much support you give me daily. You help with my babies, with my dogs, and you encourage my dreams endlessly. You do it without complaint, and though I might not have always realized it at the time, you were my number one supporter, and I feel so incredibly blessed to be your daughter.

P.s. Sorry about the sex scene… just skip it, or don't.

Grandma B – Thank you so much for the endless love and support. You have been such a wonderful light in my life, and I will cherish our memories together. The best was when we were at Disneyland, and I had to get off the ride to use the bathroom, and when I got out, I could hear you laughing all throughout the park.

Daniel Maloy - The joy and happiness you give are endless, and I hope to share more of that with you in the future. Thanks for showing me punk music and taking me to my first Rancid concert. It was a super rad memory I will never forget!

Jeff Maloy - Blood of my blood. Thank you for the late-night calls, the ridiculous texts, and the ongoing support with my writing. You read this story in its infancy (when it was absolute and utter garbage), and yet, you still encouraged me to follow my dream. I can never thank you enough!

Amber Smith - We've drifted far apart, but I still think about you often. Thank you for taking care of me when I was lost. I wish you the absolute best in life.

Patrick Maloy - My ride or die. We have been through it, haven't we? And after all these years, we're finally coming into our own. Thank you for being by my side, being my best friend, and pushing me to be a better person. I cannot thank you enough for helping me with this book. You helped me more than you know this last year, and I sure miss those grand slam breakfasts.

Whitney Hendershot - My absolute best friend and sister. I have no idea where I'd be without you. You've taken care of me for many years while sharing Harry Potter and books, some of my fondest moments. Going to Starbucks and Barnes and Noble was an absolute highlight when we lived in the blue house, as well as many others, but that's for another day. Thank you for being a friend, a sister, and a soulmate.

Jeffrey Hendershot - Thank you for making work bearable on days when I didn't feel so great. You are the definition of making the best of a bad situation. I knew the day would be better with you around. You are a fantastic friend, and I cannot thank you enough for your support and laughter.

Crystal Halliday - My soul. It's a great thing to find a friend who understands you completely, and I feel very fortunate to have you in my life. Thank you for being there for me in my hardest moments as well as my best. Thank you for talking me down whenever I'm having a panic attack and encouraging me to fulfill my dreams. You are the best kind of friend and sister.

Cristina Jensen - Thank you for reading this book when I didn't know where I was going with it. You gave me the courage to continue with my writing when my characters were just a shell and supported me without batting an eye. I'm so blessed to have a friend like you. Thank you for everything you do.

Lorrin McGinnis Gehring – You have been an advocate of literally everything I do. You have supported me in all things, no matter how crazy it sounded. Thank you for seeing me as an individual and validating my dream. You are my sister, and I love you so much, and how I wished we lived closer. You and Leilani saved me, and I don't think I'll ever be able to repay you for that. Either of you.

Bob and Becky - Thank you for the inspiration to bring Pikitis and Mahala to life. You are the salt of the earth, and I feel so very fortunate to know you both.

To the countless people who read this book, listened to me go on and on about it, and still persuaded me to finish until the end. You know who you are, and I cannot thank you enough for putting up with me and my characters. Thank you from the bottom of my heart.

Thank you to Ivy from beautiful bookcoversbyivy for creating the most amazing cover. I am so in awe of it. Thank you for taking my vision and bringing it to life. It exceeded my expectations, and I will come to you time and again as well as recommend you to anyone looking for a dope artist. You are so wonderful and patient. I cannot thank you enough!

And lastly (but by no means the least), to you, dear reader. Thank you for taking a chance at this book and supporting my dream. I hope you enjoyed this journey and want to stick around for the long haul. It has been a long process for me. These characters are my heart and soul, and I cannot wait to further their tale. Thank you enough for your support; it means the world to me.

I did a thing and wrote a book... or two. I'm a bit of an odd individual and take delight in the mad and macabre. I tend to avoid human interaction at all costs, preferring to hide in my house where no one can find me. I have a couple of dogs that like to play hide and seek, and I often spend Saturdays finding new ways to make them exceptionally happy. I also have two kids that are pretty rad and I don't know what I did right in this life to deserve them. Occasionally, I'll step out into the world for live bands and food, both are favorable. So are books, and well, family. Friends and running rival the list, and I'm starting to suspect men can be added…but I'm talking about the exceptional ones who make you laugh when you aren't feeling yourself and notice the little things you said in passing. As always, I hope you take a chance on an introvert and step into my world. I created relatable characters with heart and even threw in a joke or two. Although, I failed in a sense, straying far from what's most popular, and it's probably where I missed the mark in this writing gig, but what can I say? I don't want to be another statistic. I want to be the next Stephen King.

Visit me on Instagram: @malloryvrobertson

And on Facebook: Facebook.com/malloryrobertsonauthor

Printed in the USA
CPSIA information can be obtained
at www.ICGtesting.com
LVHW031600280624
784232LV00029B/674/J